To D

Merry Heart

A Novel

John Shivers

9-4-10

CRM BOOKS
Publishing Hope for Today's Society
Inspirational Books~CDs~Children's Books

Copyright © 2009 by John Shivers. All rights reserved.
www.johnshivers.com

Cover artwork by Christine Pace. All rights reserved.

Cover design by Mark Barden. All rights reserved.

CRM BOOKS, P.O. Box 2124, Hendersonville, NC 28793

Visit our Web site at www.ciridmus.com

No part of this book may be reproduced or utilized in any form or by any means, electronic or mechanical, including photocopying, recording, or by any information storage or retrieval system, or transmitted, without prior written permission from the publisher, except by a reviewer who may quote brief passages in a review.

This book is a work of fiction. Names, characters, places, and incidents either are the product of the author's imagination or are used fictitiously. Any resemblance to actual events, locales, or persons, living or dead, is coincidental and beyond the intent of either the author or publisher.

Printed in the United States of America

ISBN: 978- 1-933341-34-7
LCCN: 2009937407

Dedicated to Two Sisters

Ruby Edwards Shivers
September 13, 1918 - September 21, 2008

Born the "runt" in a family of nine children, she lived to be older than any of them, and she was my mother for 32,881 days. I am better for it. You never told me I couldn't do it, Mama. Even when you didn't know how to make it happen, you had faith that I did, and you never wavered in your support.

I love you, always.

Johnnie Edwards Greeson Mitchum
January 22, 1924 - May 13, 2009

She was my "other" mother, as she was to many of my Edwards' cousins. The Jolly Green Giant owes her a deep debt of gratitude, because she taught me to eat English peas served "bird nest style", in a mound of mashed potatoes. I occasionally still eat them that way. She always believed in me, and I never doubted her love. Plus, she and I were named for the same uncle.

I love you, Aunt Johnnie

Books by John Shivers

"Create My Soul Anew" Trilogy

Hear My Cry
Paths of Judgment

"Renew A Right Spirit" Trilogy

Broken Spirit

AUTHOR'S NOTES

How can I even begin to say thanks to the many individuals whose contributions have, in some way, resulted in **Merry Heart** being a reality rather than just an idea in the author's mind?

In short, there is no easy or equitable way. If I name names, I'm going to leave out someone who definitely needs to be included. Yet there are those that I feel I must recognize, because they have done so much.

The first individuals who deserve the biggest round of applause are my readers, who have encouraged and demanded to read the next part of Saralynn Reilly's story. (Harassment is a convoluted form of encouragement, isn't it?)

Then there's Ann Ates, Ann McCallum, Tracy McCoy, and Kathy McGrew. Each of you know what you've done, and I'm grateful. The Reverend Jon Kaufman and his wonderful members at the Iuka United Methodist Church have been so warm and welcoming and helpful, even when it seemed that confusion was determined to reign supreme.

Thanks, also, to Jan Anglin at the Tishomingo County Historical & Genealogical Society, for her encouragement before and after the fact. A special word of thanks must be offered to the members of the august Coffee Club in Iuka, for allowing me to invade their meeting one morning and to participate in their deliberations.

Saralynn Reilly's story began in Boston. It carried her against her will to Simpson County, Mississippi, where she not only found herself, but a faith she never knew she possessed. She found her genealogical roots and a route for the future.

The next step in her journey, both physically and spiritually, takes her to the other end of the state, and the transformation she undergoes is one that only God could have orchestrated. Thank you, Iuka and Tishomingo County for being there for her.

The people in Simpson County have been so supportive of me and this book series, and I would be remiss not to recognize them and especially my friends at Rials Creek United Methodist Church, for they have literally set the basis for the adventure on which Saralynn and I have embarked. Equally, the Iukans in northeast Mississippi have been there for us, with the same wonderful spirit of support, just different faces and different buildings, same God-inspired spirit. I have to offer a word of appreciation here specifically to Mrs. Billie Burke Thomas and her son, Frank, who, between them, are a walking encyclopedia of Iuka, Tishomingo County and the Iuka United Methodist Church. Their contributions will become more evident in the third book, **His Mercy Endureth**, but I had to have their input now, in order to know how the last installment will fall together.

A word of appreciation must go to Jan Timms, Lakemont, Georgia co-innkeeper at the Barn Inn there, and undercover proofreader extraordinaire, who made certain I finished my quotes and that my questions were a question. Ditto for cover artist Christine Pace of Cedar Mountain, North Carolina, who delivered once again just what I wanted. And, as always, much gratitude goes to Mr. and Mrs. Elmer Ritch and Catherine Ritch Guess for prayers and encouragement from day one of my novel writing journey.

There are many others whose inquiries and concerns have made a difference and please know that I am deeply appreciative of the many collective helping hands I've had on this project.

Thanks to Sarah, Lindsay, Grant and Lillie Lewis, and Mike and Janet Shivers, but most especially to my wife, Elizabeth, who, despite a year of injury and pain, has never waivered in her support and encouragement of what I do. I love you.

John Shivers
July, 2009

Renew A Right Spirit Trilogy
Book Two

"A merry heart doeth good like a medicine: but a broken spirit drieth the bones."
Proverbs 17:22

Chapter 1

The trees, lush with their midsummer greenery, hung low like a protective canopy over the narrow, two-lane asphalt strip that stretched ahead, over the hill then sharply down and around the curve. Saralynn Reilly lifted her foot from the accelerator, as much for safety as to slow her passage through a magical area, unlike anything she remembered. At that moment, it was as if she was the only person on earth.

"We almost there?" The voice came from the front passenger seat, from a traveling companion who had been mostly silent during the journey from south-central Mississippi. But Saralynn was accustomed to the tomb-like atmosphere in her car. It had been that way every time they made the trip.

I will admit, that first time, I wondered if I had made a serious mistake. I don't think Emma uttered one single word the entire way, until we pulled up to her mama's door in Fishtrap Hollow.

Since that fateful January day, when she had innocently volunteered to transport a resident from Boswell Center in Simpson County, Mississippi, home to the northeast corner of the state for a funeral, Saralynn and her charge had made the trip on several occasions.

"We've got about another two hours," she finally remembered to answer the voice on the other side of the car. "But isn't it pretty right along here? So cool… it's so peaceful."

"But it ain't home."

Gosh. Emma's an absolute chatterbox today. She rarely speaks when we travel.

"You miss home, don't you, Emma?"

There was no answer, but Saralynn caught sight of a slight up and down movement of the woman's head and realized, with more than a tinge of guilt, that tears were slowly tracking down the wrinkled cheeks.

I don't even know how old she is, but I don't guess you ever get too old to miss home. Especially when you don't have the ability to go there whenever you want… I sure know how that feels.

As she piloted the car steadily northward from the village of Taylor, Saralynn couldn't help but reflect how, in the last few months, her life had taken more unexpected turns than she could have ever imagined.

Then it hit her. *It's been a year today! How could I have forgotten?* She wanted to pull to the side of the road, just to sit and cry, but she knew she didn't dare. Emma was highly excitable. *If I go to pieces, there's no telling how Emma will react.*

"You know, Emma. I'm from a place called Boston. It's a long way from here. We'd have to drive for at least three days to get there. So I don't get to go home as often as I'd like, either."

Emma didn't respond, but Saralynn found that just talking to the silent form inches to her right kept her from flying to pieces. It was an impulse that hadn't haunted her since early last fall, when she'd been dragged against her will to Mississippi. *I can't tell Emma about Marc and Peter, how they were taken from me so suddenly. I can't burden her with my problems with Mama, either.*

The car emerged from beneath the trees while the unmerciful late July sun beat down on them again, quickly raising the temperature in the car a few uncomfortable degrees. Saralynn's hand shot out to lower the air.

"Got to make it cooler in here, before we roast."

Again, there was only silence from the passenger seat. Saralynn couldn't decide if Emma even heard her. The icy blast from the vents reminded her of how frigid her mama had been since last fall, when she had disowned Saralynn, her only child. In a tirade of vicious accusations and cruel barbs, her mother had hopped a plane back to Boston.

She tried numerous times to call her mother, only to have the phone ring and ring. *Mama's got Caller ID. She knew it was me. Emma doesn't answer because her mental impairment makes her react that way. I'm not sure what Mama's problem is.* It had been less than three months earlier, on a pristine day in early May when, to her amazement and delight, her efforts had finally borne fruit. *Mama actually answered.* Saralynn's joy, however, was short-lived. Instead of the reconciliation she expected, her cheery "Hello, Mama, it's so great to hear your voice," had been met with more venom than she could handle.

I hung up on her. Something I never thought I would do. But then, I never thought my own mother would turn rabid simply because she didn't want me to live here. Why can't she understand that in Boston the memories are too excruciating to even describe?

"I'm sure your mama will be glad to see you, Emma. I think she really likes it when you visit."

Emma bobbled her head up and down.

"She's old."

"How old is your mama?"

The other woman unfolded one of her brown spotted hands and began to extend one finger at a time. "Don't rightly know. But she's older than me," she said proudly.

"And how old are you?"

I'm not supposed to ask the clients for any personal information, but gosh knows they volunteer whatever comes to their minds.

"When was Mr. I-zen-hair pres-e-dent?"

"I-zen-hair? Eye-zen-hower?… Eisenhower!"

"You mean President Dwight Eisenhower?"

There was only silence.

Has Emma gone back into her shell? I'd kind of gotten used to her company.

Finally the other voice replied. "Don't rightly know his first name. Just know Mama said I was born the same year Mr. I-zen-hair went to th' White House."

Saralynn had to watch the road in front of the car, because the wilderness was giving way to the hustle and bustle of the north Mississippi college town of Oxford. Still, she searched her brain for remnants of her old American History classes. *President Kennedy was killed in 1963 after he took office in 1961. Which meant the former military general went to the White House in 1953.*

She did some quick math. "That would make you over fifty, Emma."

"If you say so."

Obviously Emma isn't concerned with her age.

The remainder of the trip passed quickly as the young woman behind the wheel guided the car through the turns until finally, the red cupola of the old courthouse just south of the Iuka business district came into view.

"We're almost there. Next stop… Fishtrap Hollow."

"Home," Emma replied. "My real home."

"Don't ever forget home, Emma. There's no place like home."

"My home. My real home."

"You're absolutely right, my friend." She patted the older woman's arm.

Only sometimes home isn't always where we think it is. I should know. For me, home truly is where my heart lives. Only every time my heart gets set, something changes. Since I began coming to Iuka, I don't know where I belong anymore. There's part of me here. Part of me lives in Simpson County. And despite what Mama thinks, there's still a big part of my heart that remembers Boston, with an ache that cuts quicker than a sharp knife.

The car rounded the wide bend in the road as Saralynn heard, "There's home." The pronouncement was quick, full of emotion and assurance. *The only time Emma's voice ever takes on any personality is when she talks about Fishtrap Hollow.*

"Yes it is, Emma."

God, I thought I knew where my home is. But it's not in Boston any longer, although a part of me still claims it. And before I came to Iuka the first time, I was so sure Miss Sallie's house in south Mississippi was where I was supposed to be.

Saralynn pulled the car to a stop in the worn dirt driveway, and before she'd even gotten the gearshift into PARK, Emma opened her door and was climbing out.

"I'm home, Mama. I'm home," she called in a loud and joyous voice, as she lumbered unsteadily across the sparsely sodded yard.

Now that I've uncovered my roots here in Tishomingo County, I've got all kinds of doubts again. Where do I belong? Where is my home? She watched the reunion of hugs and kisses between her friend and a stooped, shriveled up white-haired old woman. The yearning for such a reunion with her own mother caused an ache in her heart that completely closed up her throat.

How much hurt do I have to stand, Lord? How much pain is too much pain? She choked back a sob, fearing that to give it reign would unleash a torrent of emotions she wasn't ready to handle. *How do I know where home is?*

It was a subject she broached reluctantly that evening while talking with Donna Hasty, from Rials Creek United Methodist Church in Simpson County. All the members of the small, rural church had adopted Saralynn early on, taking on the role of her mainstay after her mother's abandonment.

Saralynn had called her friend after she remembered she'd told no one she was returning to Iuka. *I don't want them to feel I've run out on them like Mama did on me.*

"Hey, friend, you sound like you're a thousand miles away tonight," Donna commented. "Is everything OK?"

Saralynn laughed, amazed at how much better she felt. *I didn't really realize I was uptight.* "I'm in Iuka," she told her friend. "It came up sudden like."

"Is it Emma? Something wrong with her?"

"I drove Emma, yes. Something must be wrong, because her mother called Boswell and asked that she be brought home as quickly as possible."

"So?"

Saralynn massaged her right shoulder somewhat awkwardly, while attempting to balance the cell phone against her ear. *My neck and shoulder really ache. I must have been tied in knots driving up here.* "From what I can see so far, nothing's wrong. But I also know Mrs. Jackson doesn't cry wolf."

"Then something must be wrong," Donna counseled. "I'm sure if it's anything major, you'll find out soon enough. So how are you otherwise?"

Saralynn hesitated. *Do I really want to open this door?* "Donna? May I ask you...?" Her words trailed off. *Should I or shouldn't I?*

"Is this something you don't want repeated?"

Saralynn could picture Donna with her face screwed up in its customary expression of concern. *She is one of the sweetest people I've ever known. Always worried about someone else. But she's also trustworthy. She's proven that.*

"It's not a deep dark secret or anything, but I'm not comfortable having it talked."

"If you want to unburden yourself, I'm ready to open my ears and shut my mouth. And if you still need some more time, you just tell me when."

"It's going to have to be tonight if I expect to get any sleep." That said, she began to explain how, since first coming to Iuka and finding her roots, she felt a pull to the area in much the same fashion she'd felt Simpson County calling to her in the months before. "So am I fickle? Two-faced? Wishy-washy?"

"No. Of course not. What would ever make you think that?"

Once started, it was like Saralynn's conscience couldn't stop. "It's just that I have come to love so many of you there. If I were to decide to relocate here, I wouldn't want anyone to think I had used all of you and then, when something better came along, I jumped ship."

"Is Iuka better? Have you found something there that's an improvement over what you have here?"

Saralynn struggled to answer. "I can't say it's any better, but it's at least almost as good as what I have there. Sort of."

Donna snickered. "A most definitive answer if ever I've heard one."

"You're making fun of me."

"No. Please. I truly am not," Donna assured her. "But let me offer a few words that might clarify things for you. Or maybe not. At any rate, there's no charge, so take this for what it's worth."

Where is she going with this? Please… not another tree analogy. The minute the thought left her mind, Saralynn was sorry. *That was very unkind. Thank goodness Donna can't read minds. At least I don't think she can!*

"Saralynn? Have you zoned out on me again?"

Oh, boy, does she know me! "I had, but I'm back. Sorry. Please, do go on."

As she lay on the bed watching the fan blades cutting wobbly circles in the ceiling, Saralynn braced herself for what she might hear. Donna wouldn't be cruel, but she would be honest.

"OK, friend. Here goes. First, you've been through a lot in the last year – and by the way, isn't today the first anniversary of Marc and Peter's deaths?"

She remembered. My own mother didn't even call to see if I was coping with it, but this dear, sweet angel remembered. Someone who didn't even know my guys remembered them... Saralynn gulped, "Yes, it's been a year today." She choked back a sob. "It blows me away that you remembered. And you never met either of them."

"In a manner of speaking, I've met them," Donna said. "Through you, with all your traits, your gentle nature, it's really easy to see both the Reilly men."

"Thank you, Donna. I can't tell you what it means to me. I felt certain I was the only one who knew, and it's been all I could do to keep from just bawling."

"You're welcome. But, as I was saying... You've been through a lot. You've lost your husband and son and, to some extent, your mother as well. That's a load. Naturally you're searching for an anchor. Plus, there's the excitement factor that goes along with discovering family you didn't know you had." She giggled. "At least as long as they're not related to Jesse James or Bonnie and Clyde!"

It was Saralynn's turn to laugh.

"So don't let this yearning for an anchor confuse you. It's normal. Very normal."

"But what if I should decide to move here permanently? What would all my friends there have to say about me?"

"We'd be thrilled that you'd found a place to land, we'd throw you a giant going-away party, and we'd pray for you. Before you left and after." She hesitated a moment. "We'd probably cry a little, too. Not for you, but for us. But in the end, we want what's best for you."

"You mean no one would be mad or insulted?"

"Good grief, no. Why would we? Disappointed? Yes. Angry? No way."

This isn't at all what I expected to hear.

Donna continued, "Let me ask you something."

"OK."

"First, are you truly in love with Iuka, or are you just in love with the idea of being in love with that area and your McIntire roots?"

"Gee, that's a hard one."

"And the second part may not be any easier."

"Go ahead."

"Have you asked God where He wants you to be?"

Saralynn was taken aback. *Why would I need to ask God? I pray to Him to help me do whatever I need to do. Not whether I should do it or not. Isn't that right?*

"No, I haven't asked God. I don't guess I realized I was supposed to."

"You don't have to," Donna advised. "But since God has a plan for each of us, it sometimes makes life a lot easier if we bring Him in on the decision process, instead of when it's time to clean up the mess because we made a wrong turn."

"You've given me a lot to think about," Saralynn assured her friend. "And now, I'd better get off this phone and get ready for bed. I just wanted you to know where I was. Didn't want anyone to worry."

"Pleasant dreams, Saralynn. Call me tomorrow and let's talk some more."

Donna's observations had given her too much to think about, and during the night, she had done exactly that. Her infatuation with the Iuka area had happened quickly and easily, almost without warning, just a few days after the New Year. In that way that life so often slips up on a person's blind side, Saralynn had been cleaning up after her daily art class with clients at Boswell

Regional Center near Magee, Mississippi, when she chanced upon a conversation between two staff members. Their words were mere background buzz until she heard the word "Iuka".

Iuka! That's where Miss Sallie lived before she came to the Sanitorium as a tuberculosis patient. I've wanted to go there ever since I first heard about the place.

In a matter of minutes, before she could even take time to debate the merits of her hasty decision, Saralynn had volunteered to drive a middle-aged client named Emma Jackson home for her father's funeral.

I may have taken unfair advantage of the situation, because I don't know if I could have found the courage to make that trip without a reason.

With only a few minutes to pack, Saralynn quickly found herself on the road with a sobbing, middle-aged woman who spoke not one word during the entire trip. She already knew where she was headed because, soon after she discovered the Iuka connection with her grandmother's family, she'd routed a trip to the far northeastern corner of the state. But she had never been able to find reason enough – or was it the courage? — to strike out for what felt to her like a totally foreign country.

Now she had a reason and, if she got there and discovered she'd made a mistake, no one would ever be the wiser. *Is it wrong of me to exploit the death of Emma's father to disguise my own private agenda?* After seeing the way in which Emma and her old mother clung to each other during those three days, she decided she'd done no harm.

As for her personal agenda, she soon discovered that her family's Tishomingo roots were as fascinating and rewarding as she'd found the Simpson County portion of her background to be.

The main difference was that she didn't have the Rials Creek United Methodist Church family and her new friends in south Mississippi to help her understand her family connections.

Over the course of the next six months, she and Emma had made the trip every four or five weeks, with the blessing and full permission of Mrs. Jackson, who seemed to resurrect and thrive on the presence of her only child. While she had stayed in a motel when she brought Emma for the funeral, from then on mother and daughter had insisted she stay in the Jackson home in Fishtrap Hollow. She had accepted their gracious hospitality.

At night the three would gather in the living room of the old farmhouse with a go-funny list and talk and watch TV. But during the day, Saralynn explored the area, conducted some quiet research, and asked questions when she couldn't discover the answers any other way. *Who would ever have dreamed, Lord, that I'd come all the way to Fishtrap Hollow to discover Miss Sallie's family lived just down the road from where I'm staying?*

The more she learned about her McIntire roots, the more intrigued she became. And with each trip to the rural hamlet that still wore the charm of an old and vintage town of the previous century, the more at home she found herself.

The latest trip home, as she had silently begun to consider the area, had come at the urgent request of Emma's mother, who had called Boswell to ask that her daughter come home at once. It was an emergency but she requested that Emma not be unduly alarmed.

To her, it's just another chance to go home, to see her mother. Oh, Lord, I know just how she feels.

Try as she might, Saralynn couldn't identify any type crisis or emergency that existed, even though she was consumed with curiosity and a deepening sense of dread. But she was too polite to ask. That evening, following one of Mrs. Jackson's simple but tasty country summer suppers, complete with fresh garden produce, the older woman asked Saralynn to take a walk. It was on that stroll through the flowerbeds that were somehow thriving in spite of the stifling summer heat, that the south Mississippi visitor learned the nature of the problem.

Mrs. Jackson's got a burden on her mind.

In a fashion that reminded Saralynn of Emma's particular manner, Mrs. Jackson didn't waste any words or try to sugarcoat her message. "I'm dying. Got maybe three months, the doctor says."

Saralynn saw the old woman's weary face in the orange rays of the setting sun. She felt an immediate empathy for this woman who had sent her only child to a residential care facility, when her own energies were no longer sufficient.

"I'm gonna tell Emma while she's here, but it won't be easy. Lord only knows how she'll take it."

What do I say, God? How do I respond? "I'm so... sorry," she managed to mumble. "How are you with it?"

"How else can I be? Don't have no choice. Sometimes God gives you more than you think you can handle, but somehow you do. He helps you with it."

"So you're resigned to..." she stammered, suddenly uncomfortable about being so blunt, "you're at peace with it?"

"We all got to die sometime," Mrs. Jackson said very matter of factly. "When it's your time, it's your time."

"I don't know if I could be so accepting," Saralynn said.

"Oh, I don't want to go. I'm human enough to be selfish and ask why I can't have some more time."

"That's how I'd feel, too." *I wonder if Peter and Marc were this accepting when they discovered they were dead?* Her emotions were still too raw when it came to the subject of her boys, who were now only containers of ashes on a closet shelf three hundred miles away in Simpson County.

"But I'm more worried about how Emma's going to be with it. And how can I assure her that she'll be taken care of after I'm gone? She's gotten so accustomed to coming home since you came into her life, I'm afraid knowing she's always going to have to stay at Boswell is going to hurt her so bad.

As the older woman spoke, she wrung her hands. "Maybe I made a mistake letting her keep coming back, but after her daddy died, she was all I had. And I knew I wouldn't be here always, I just didn't think it would be this quick." The little country woman looked Saralynn straight in the face. "I didn't do the wrong thing… did I?" she implored.

Lord, how do I answer this woman? My own mother doesn't want to see me and this poor soul wants me to reassure her that she hasn't made problems for Emma, simply because she loves her and wants her close.

Saralynn struggled with her response. "You can't ever make a mistake when you love someone," she reassured the defeated looking woman as she put her arm around her shoulders. "Emma has many friends and staff at Boswell who love her, who will be there for her. I know I certainly will be." She didn't feel like the answer was adequate, but it was all she could manage at that point.

"I've always felt so guilty because I couldn't take care of her here at home, because I had to send her off. Now I'm gonna die and she'll have to lose me all over again."

The two women continued walking until long after the

lightning bugs began their nightly light show. Later, as Saralynn lay in bed, in the room she had possessively come to think of as her room, her heart ached. And despite her best efforts, the tears that had lurked just behind her eyes all day finally burst loose and flowed freely, until her pillow was damp and salty.

The problem is... I don't know if I'm crying for Mrs. Jackson and Emma, or for Peter and Marc? Or me?

True to her word, after the breakfast dishes were finished the next morning and the mid-day meal was underway, Mrs. Jackson asked Saralynn to join her on the porch where Emma sat in a high-back rocker with a hand-woven rush seat, rocking gently in rhythm with the music that played on the radio just inside the window. She appeared to have no troubles or worries.

Is she going to be able to understand all this?

The older woman pulled up a nearby rocker. "Emma? Honey? I need to talk to you a minute and I want you to listen carefully to what I have to say."

Emma's face glowed. "I always listen careful, Mama. That's what Miss Ann always tells us," she said proudly. "Don't I, Saralynn?"

"Yes, you do. You're very good about listening."

Saralynn watched as tears welled up in the faded blue eyes of her hostess, and she felt her own emotions churn with empathy. *It was hard enough to hear that Peter and Marc would never be coming home again. But I believe it would have been harder for me to tell them that I wasn't going to be there any longer.*

If Emma noticed her mother's tears, she said nothing, but continued to rock. Only the look of expectancy on her face hinted that she understood something was about to happen.

"Emma, honey. Mama's got to tell you something and

you've got to promise me you won't get upset."

Emma said nothing. Only her body language betrayed her uncertainty, as she kneaded her hands in silence.

"I'm gonna be leaving you real soon, Emma."

"You going to She-cargo to see Aunt Charlsie?"

A look of pain crossed the old woman's face. "Not this time, Emma. Not this time." She reached up and touched each side of Emma's wrinkled face, her work-worn hands cradling her child's head so gently. "No, honey, I'm not going to see Aunt Charlsie. But I am going to see your daddy."

Emma stopped rocking. Her perpetually happy face took on a suspicious, guarded expression. "But Mama. Daddy... Daddy..." she struggled with the words, "he's in heaven with Jesus."

"And I'm going to be with him and Jesus real soon, honey. Probably before Christmas, even."

Emma jerked her head from her mother's grasp and her face took on a look of pain and confusion. "Daddy's dead. I came home. Remember? Saralynn brought me. Didn't you?" She gave Saralynn a look of panic... "Mama! You can't go be with daddy!"

Saralynn felt her heart squeeze with grief. For the old woman who had such a burden. For the younger woman who would have trouble understanding what was about to befall her. And for herself. *The old pain is back, Lord. That old choking pain is about to tear my heart out.*

Mrs. Jackson reached out for her daughter's face again with resolution in her touch. Yet Saralynn marveled at the tenderness. And at the inner-strength the older woman displayed during what had to be a very painful time for her.

"Listen to me, Emma. You have to pay close attention to

what I've got to tell you."

"But Mama… but Mama… you… can't… go… be… with… Daddy… and… Jesus… unless… you… die." She had spit the words out one at a time, as if each one consumed all of her energy. "You… can't… die… Mama. I… love… you."

"And I love you, too, Emma. You're so very precious to me. And I wouldn't leave you if I had any choice. But the doctor says I'm sick, Emma."

Emma's face brightened. "I was sick last winter and the doctor gave me some medicine." She looked at her mother, her face alight with assurance that she had resolved the problem. "He can give you some medicine, too."

Saralynn noticed that Mrs. Jackson raised her head a bit higher, as if she were jacking up her reserve, preparing for a battle she knew she must win. "I wish the doctor could give me some medicine, Sugar. But it's my heart. It's worn out and there's no medicine that can make it better."

Tears began to course down Emma's face, and Saralynn could see her withdrawing from the situation. Her rocking chair began to move back and forth, and the harder the expression on her face became, the faster the chair moved.

Lord, what do I do? How can I help these people who have come to mean so much to me? And who needs me worse? Emma or her mother?

Mrs. Jackson rose slowly from her rocker with what Saralynn saw was difficulty and defeat. "She took it about like I figured she would. I've seen her like this before. She'll just have to let all this sink in before I can do anything else." She sniffed the air. "Do I smell my beans burning?" She shuffled from the porch into the house, and Saralynn could hear the rattle of pot lids coming from the direction of the kitchen.

Emma, meanwhile, continued rocking at a pace Saralynn was certain would soon wear grooves in the porch floor. On her face she maintained a stubborn, wooden expression that sent the clear message she didn't wish to be bothered.

And I won't bother her, Lord. Until You tell me I should.

Emma refused to abandon her armchair journey into acceptance and did not join her mother and her friend for the noon meal. Saralynn tried to make conversation, but it was clear from Mrs. Jackson's responses that she, too, wanted time alone with herself. She even declined Saralynn's usual help with the dishes, and her guest wandered back to her bedroom, uncertain how best to help the situation.

As she lay on her bed, attempting to keep her eyes trained on the pages of the book she'd begun the evening before, Saralynn found that her mind's eye was the more dominant one. Instead, her memory replayed the events of the past year at dizzying speed.

I couldn't ever have imagined over a year ago that I would confront all that I have in the past twelve months. Peter and Marc being killed in that terrible accident back in Boston. Mama insisting that I come with her to Mississippi to settle Miss Sallie's estate. Learning that Mama had lied about so many parts of the past, and then her abandonment when she realized that I would no longer blindly do her bidding.

It had only been after she found Miss Sallie's diaries that Saralynn had learned, through her grandmother's own words, how her mother had deceived her for so many years. *I never dreamed Mama could have been so mercenary, capable of extorting money from my father's family to divorce him and take me far away.*

A sob escaped her lips. *She told me my father was dead. Dead!*

Knowing how painful Marc and Peter's deaths had been for her, Saralynn found it impossible to fathom how her mother could have so easily created the death of her husband and lived with that lie for a lifetime. *Mama is so hard-hearted. Nothing like Mrs. Jackson.*

Suddenly Saralynn wanted nothing more than to withdraw, to curl up in a knot, and forget that the world existed. *I don't want to think about Mama… or Peter and Marc… or even about Emma or Mrs. Jackson right now.* She turned over and buried her face in the pillow.

A nearby knocking coaxed Saralynn from the slumber that had consumed her. *I must have fallen asleep. What's that noise?* She raised up on one elbow.

"Saralynn, honey." There was the knock again. *It's Mrs. Jackson.* "Saralynn? May I come in?"

Saralynn swung her legs over the side of the big wrought-iron bed and limped her sleep-deadened body over to the door. "Yes, Mrs. Jackson. Please come in."

Her hostess took a close look at the younger woman. "Oh, dear. You were asleep and I disturbed you. I'm sorry, honey." She patted Saralynn's arm.

"I was just waking up. Honest," she reassured her hostess. *It's not totally the truth, but I needed to be up and doing, if the evening light is any indication.* "So don't give it a second thought. Besides, don't we need to be working on dinn… supper?"

"There's time enough for that," Mrs. Jackson said. "I wanted to apologize for earlier."

"Apologize?"

"I pushed you away and that wasn't fair to you." She leaned

over and kissed Saralynn's cheek. "You've become like another daughter to me, and we've put you in an awkward position. Can you ever forgive us?"

"But there's nothing to forgive, I assure you."

Mrs. Jackson hugged her in a comfortable and familiar way. "You really are one of us now, you know."

"I've certainly come to feel that way, thanks to you." *I really have discovered that home is where the heart is. Thank you, Lord, for sending Mrs. Jackson into my life. Only now I have to adjust to the idea she's going to leave me, also.*

Chapter 2

Despite her best efforts, once back in Magee, Saralynn couldn't put the events of the previous week in Iuka behind her. Emma had cried and clung to her mother when it was time to leave. It wasn't until Mrs. Jackson promised Emma she would still be there when Saralynn brought her back for the next visit, that the woman could be convinced to get into the car.

The trip south had been a silent one and, despite noticing the absence of sound more than she normally did, Saralynn hadn't tried to engage Emma in conversation. *I know exactly how poor Emma feels. Only instead of reassuring me that she would be there for me, my own mama has disowned me.*

She had called her friend, Katie Brooks, even before she left the parking lot at Boswell after dropping Emma by the group home where she lived. "Oh, Katie. You're never going to believe what the emergency was in Iuka." She paused to catch her breath,

"Mrs. Jackson is dying and wanted to tell Emma in person." *I can't believe I didn't call Katie from Iuka! I guess I was just so caught up in what was happening.*

"Poor Emma. How is she handling it?"

As she maneuvered the winding drive leading out of the campus, Saralynn replied, "You know how she is. Emma didn't want to understand at first. Now I think she does, but she doesn't know how to cope with what's to come."

"I'll pass the word along to Charlie," Katie promised. "He may be my husband, but he also can give a heads up to Emma's counselor, so she'll know what's going on."

"Thanks. I think that's a great idea."

"So how long does Mrs. Jackson have left?"

I feel so uncomfortable talking about people dying when Katie and Charlie live with the knowledge that precious little Paul is slowly slipping away. But they seem OK with it. "If the doctor is correct, she'll be gone before Christmas."

"That quickly, huh?"

"'Fraid so." Tears ran unbidden down her cheeks and for once, Saralynn didn't try to stop the waterworks.

"You're crying, aren't you?"

"Is it that obvious?"

"It is, my friend. But don't be ashamed."

"I'm not. But I am wondering what it must be like for Mrs. Jackson, waking up alone in that house everyday, knowing that she has one day less than she had. How does she face that? How can she deal with it?"

Saralynn's car was approaching the drive to the home she leased from Walter Kennedy, who was also little Paul's grandfather. Paul's parents, Mr. Walter's son and Katie's sister, had been killed in a vacation accident. That's when Katie and Charlie Brooks had taken the boy into their home. Although he had already been declared terminally ill, Saralynn realized that her friends didn't mark another day off the calendar after they put the four year-old to bed each night.

The emotions that coursed through her body every time she negotiated the curving driveway through the stand of pine trees and caught the first glimpse of the beautiful New Orleans style home, was always a cherished moment for her. This had once been a loving home and was now safe haven for her from all of her problems. Yet she never hesitated at the doorway to the nursery that had once been Paul's kingdom, without grieving for the little boy whose life was literally slipping away. Once it had bothered her, but even she had to admit that death was no longer the only thing she saw whenever she encountered the precocious toddler.

Now she was taking a new worry into the spacious home where she lived and operated her fabric arts business. Indeed, her crowded and troubled mind was already straying into what issues she would confront once she was unpacked. *Before I do anything else, I've got to check to be sure that last shipment to the gallery in Atlanta was delivered. That could be a great new market for me.*

"Did you hear what I said?"

The voice from her cell phone caused Saralynn to remember that she'd been in conversation with her friend. "I'm sorry, Katie. I was pulling into the drive at home and you know how that first sight of this house always affects me."

"I knew you'd zoned out."

"Guilty." *Thank goodness my friends understand me... and accept me anyway!*

"I said, you can't live life concentrating on how many days

you have left. You live it to ensure that the days that have passed have been lived to the max."

"In other words you're telling me that Mrs. Jackson isn't sitting there watching the sands run out?"

"You got it. Remember, none of us are guaranteed any specific number of days. That's why we ought to live each day as if it were our last."

"You sound like you don't worry about dying. I'm not all that anxious to go."

"Oh, I don't sit around waiting to die. But I know that sooner or later, it will happen."

"Aren't you just a little bit afraid?"

"Afraid of what?"

The entire time she'd been talking, Saralynn had been removing her luggage from the trunk of her car and setting it inside the back door. Now, as she headed to her studio on the other side of the garage, she stopped in her tracks. "You know… afraid… afraid of…" she stammered. "Afraid of dying. Aren't you afraid it will hurt? I mean we don't know what will happen when we die. Do we?"

"None of us know how we will die," Katie advised. "But I know where I'll go when I die, so how I get there really doesn't matter, since I can't do anything about it anyway."

"You… you… YOU KNOW where you'll go! How?"

"All of us who know Jesus as our Savior know we'll go straight to Him, so what might happen in the blink of an eye in between isn't a concern."

"Know Jesus. What do you mean by that? I know that Jesus is God's son. Is that what you mean?"

There was a silence on the other end of the line and

Saralynn could visualize her friend searching. "Knowing that He's God's son is only part of what I'm talking about. Until He's also living in your heart as your Lord and Savior, you're only part of the way there."

Saralynn struggled to understand what her friend was saying as she juggled the phone and the key ring and attempted to unlock her studio door. "So how would I know if He's my Lord and Savior? Why does it matter?"

Katie was talking, but Saralynn had been distracted again; this time by the light blinking on her business answering machine. She was only half listening as her friend explained how believing that Jesus had died for her sins would allow Him to live in her heart. She glanced at the Caller ID screen and saw that three of the messages were from the new Atlanta gallery that was handling her work. *I've got to call them; it's almost five o'clock there.*

"Hey, Katie. Don't mean to cut you off, but I've got to make a call to Atlanta before the gallery closes and… she consulted the clock across the room… that's only ten minutes from now. Let's talk about this later. OK?"

Without really waiting for an answer, or even caring about her friend's parting words, Saralynn switched off her cell phone and grabbed the office land line, not even taking time to listen to the accumulated messages on her machine. *I hope nothing's wrong with that shipment.*

"Archer Gallery of Fine Art," a male voice on the other end answered.

"Good afternoon. This is Saralynn Reilly in Magee, Mississippi. May I please speak with Christina Jacobs?"

"Hello, Ms. Reilly. This is Robert Maddox. We haven't met, but I'm very impressed with the pieces you shipped to us last week.

Everyone has been blown away with the detail you're able to incorporate."

The shipment was delivered. So why have they been calling me? Then she remembered her manners. "Thank you, Mr. Maddox. I appreciate those encouraging words."

"Please, it's Robert. And before you ask, Christina is out for the afternoon. Is there some way I can help you?"

Saralynn laughed, feeling somewhat chagrined. "I may have jumped the gun," she confessed. "I returned from a trip just a few minutes ago and saw that three calls had been logged from Archer Gallery, and I didn't even take time to listen to the messages. I wanted to call before you closed." She hesitated. "I was afraid there might be a problem."

"There's no problem as far as I know," Ms. Reilly. "May I tell Christina you called?"

"Why don't you do that and tell her if she needs to talk with me, to call me on my cell phone? That way I know we won't miss each other." The voice on the other end agreed and she gave him her number.

As soon as she cleared the line, Saralynn punched the message retrieval button on her answering machine. *Something I should have done in the first place, before I made a fool out of myself.*

Of the eleven new incoming messages, seven were supplier solicitation calls. Expecting the next voice to be one of the Atlanta calls, Saralynn was startled instead to hear the definite Boston accent of her mother's best friend, Elsie. "Call me, Saralynn, the voice instructed. We need to talk." Elsie had left her number and then, as an apparent afterthought, had added, "Don't panic. But do call as soon as you can."

Before she could even begin to digest that message, she

heard Christina's Georgia accent wishing her a good morning. "Just wanted to let you know the pieces arrived and we're all thrilled with them. We'll be talking."

The next message asked that Saralynn call her back. And the final message sent tingles up her spine. "Saralynn," her Atlanta representative's voice whispered with excitement, "You've got to call me as soon as possible. I've got a client who is very interested in commissioning several pieces for a project he's building. Call me. Please!" she implored.

The room, large and spacious, accented with bolts of colorful fabric and the natural light which entered through the large bank of southern-oriented windows, was usually her sanctuary. But at that moment, it was anything but a quiet and peaceful place – at least as far as her mind was concerned. The young woman massaged her temples, and her face assumed an expression of both confusion and despair. She had arrived home, anxious about Emma, only to be met with two highly conflicting sets of circumstances. *On the one hand, I'm thrilled that Christina loves my work and is already marketing me. But Elsie wouldn't have called unless something was terribly wrong. And I guess I might as well find out about that problem right now. I just hope she's not calling to rake me over the coals.* Saralynn knew from long experience that Elsie was very blunt, and could sometimes be extremely cruel when making her opinions known. *She and Mama always got along fine, but I think I've always been a little bit afraid of her.*

Saralynn punched in the number she knew from memory, and only two short rings later, was rewarded with a distinctly Bostonian brogue that was anything but warm and fuzzy.

"I called you two days ago and you're just now returning my call!"

Same old Elsie. I'm sorry, Elsie, but I was on a trip and just got in less than thirty minutes ago." Rather than give her mother's friend time to get up a full load of steam, she continued, "So tell me what's so urgent. Is something wrong with Mama?"

"You mean besides the fact that her only child abandoned her?"

Saralynn pulled her resolve a little closer around herself, and braced for the worst. "There's two sides to that abandonment story, Elsie, and if that's all you called about, I'm afraid you're wasting your time."

As she listened to the angry breathing on the other end of the phone, Saralynn's creative side was taking mental inventory of the fabrics she had stacked on the end of one of her work tables, and from that selection, she was creating in her mind's eye a massive stained glass window depicting anger and frustration and a little despair.

"That's not why I called, although you don't know how many times over these past few months I've wanted to straighten you out. I've swatted your bottom before, you know."

Yes, you have. Never hesitated to discipline someone else's child. Like you, who has never had any children, or even a husband, would know how to raise a child. I can see now why she and Mama always got along. Elsie truly is Mama's only friend. It was disheartening for Saralynn to acknowledge the fact that her mother was so isolated. *And I was the same way in Boston. Mama never let me make friends, either. Not real friends. I've been here less than a year and have more friends than I can count.*

"Are you listening to me, Saralynn?" Elsie's tone was demanding and angry.

I was doing it again! "I'm listening, but please repeat what you just said. These cell phones drop out words some times."

"I said…" Elsie's voice became hard and louder, "you've got to come see about your mama. Something's wrong with her."

In my opinion Mama's got several things wrong. Could this be a trick she and Elsie have devised to get me back to Boston? "Of course I'll come if there's a need. Can you be more specific Elsie? Exactly what's wrong with her?"

"She's losing her mind."

"Oh, come now, Elsie. You're many things, but you aren't a psychiatrist. What do you mean she's losing her mind?"

Saralynn thought she heard a soft sob from the other end of the phone. Then Elsie continued.

"I don't know my own friend any more. She doesn't act like herself and she can't remember anything. Then there are those headaches she been having."

"Headaches? Mama's never had headaches." *She always claimed headaches were a sign of weakness.*

"She's been having them for about two months now, every day. I finally got her to see a doctor, but she won't tell me what he said. ME! Her best friend for more than thirty years. She's always told me everything."

I'll bet she didn't tell you how she took her husband's family for a huge chunk of change and how she lied to her daughter! I know I should feel sorry, but I don't. The truth is the truth.

"She won't tell you anything? How bad are the headaches?"

"When I ask her what the doctor thinks, she just says 'I don't want to talk about it.' But she's in pain. And over the counter medicine doesn't give her any relief. I do know the doctor gave her a prescription for pain medication, but she refuses to have it filled. Says she doesn't want to take drugs."

I have to ask this. "So what do you want me to do?"

"Come home, of course. Maybe Alicia will tell you what she won't tell me. But you've got to do something. Her whole personality has changed. And not for the better, either," Elsie sniffed.

"I'd be glad to come, but I'm not sure what I can do. Mama's not even speaking to me about general stuff. What makes you think she'll suddenly confide in me about this?"

Saralynn's brain was already thinking about Boston, but her heart was aching at the thought of having to leave again, even for a short trip back. *While I miss my studio when Emma and I go to Iuka, I don't feel like I'm being punished. So why does the thought of Boston make me feel like I'm being disciplined?*

"Because she's scared, Saralynn."

"Scared?"

"You heard me. Alicia Bankston is scared, and that's a behavior I've never known in her for as long as she and I have been friends."

That's been a long time. Mama and Elsie met each other when Mama moved into her first apartment in Boston. In fact, it was Elsie that took her to the hospital when she had me.

"Let me think about this. If I come, it's got to accomplish something and right now, I'm not sure how to make that happen. Mama won't even take my calls, and the one time she did, the hatred in her voice made me hang up on her."

"Your mama has always been a hard person, Saralynn. If I didn't love her like a sister, it would be difficult to be friends. But trust me on this, something's wrong. Something's different. And Alicia is scared. She needs you, whether she wants to admit it or not."

I'm going to Boston. That's a given. It's the how I've got to figure out. "Let me get unpacked and re-organized and I'll call you tomorrow. We'll figure out something."

"Oh, thank you, Saralynn. That's such a load off my mind."

After she hung up, the young woman found herself unable to concentrate on any one thing. Instead, her mind wandered as aimlessly as she did through the studio, until finally she admitted defeat and turned out the lights and locked the door. *Tomorrow is another day.*

Later that night, after she fixed herself a frozen chicken pot pie and a salad, and had thrown a load of dirty clothes into the washer, Saralynn remembered she hadn't called her friend Donna after the two talked earlier in the week. Now she knew what Mrs. Jackson's emergency was. What she didn't know about was her own mother's problem.

"Hey, friend, I'm home." Saralynn tried to sound cheerful when the phone was answered at the Hasty residence. "So what's new on this end?"

"You don't sound so good, for starters. What's wrong? Did you find out why Mrs. Jackson wanted Emma home so quickly?"

Good old perceptive Donna. She doesn't miss much.

"It was bad news. Mrs. Jackson only has a few weeks, maybe ten or twelve at most, to live. That's what she wanted to tell Emma."

"Poor Emma. How did she take it?"

She didn't take it well at all. Now I'm wondering how I would react in that situation. "At first she refused to believe what her mother was telling her. Now I think she's accepted it, just doesn't know how to deal with the prospect that her mother is going to die." *I don't know how to deal with it either.*

"We'll have to add her to the prayer list at church. Emma and her mother both. I'll get an e-mail out before I go to bed tonight."

Do I or don't I? "Well," Saralynn said, hesitation obvious in her voice, "you might want to add another name to that e-mail." She went on to relate the news she'd received from Boston, and added, "I've got to go. There's no question about it. But what do I do when I get there? If Mama won't even talk to me on the phone, she's not going to let me in her house."

"Gosh, I'm sorry about Alicia. I'll certainly include her in this e-mail. And you, too."

"I just wish I knew what to do."

"Do you have your Bible close?"

The only one I have is Miss Sallie's. Maybe I need one of my own? But she was too embarrassed to ask, so instead, she simply responded that she did and found her grandmother's well-worn, thick Bible.

"Look in the book of Philippians, the fourth chapter and the third verse."

It took her a couple of minutes because she knew nothing about the different books in the Bible, but finally she located the verse Donna had indicated. "I can do all things through Christ who strengthens me," she read.

"Do you know what that means?"

"I'm not sure. You know I'm not really up on all this religion stuff. How can just reading a few lines out of the Bible show me how to handle things in Boston?"

"It's not just in Boston. It's anywhere. Anywhere you are, there's direction to be found by reading God's word."

Saralynn fingered the fragile pages well worn and lined

with notes and comments in the margins. *Miss Sallie must have believed what Donna says, because it's evident she read this book from cover to cover. Many times.*

"What it means, Saralynn, is that God is stronger than we are. He is there for us, especially when we're overwhelmed or uncertain of where or how to go. But He doesn't intrude Himself on us. He's put it out there, but we have to want it; we have to seek it for ourselves."

"I'm really weary, Donna. And I don't mean to cut you short. But I'm going to go now and try to get some rest. Tomorrow is another day. I'll deal with all this then."

"Good-night, Saralynn. We all love you, and we're praying for you. And remember, God loves you, too."

The young woman slowly put down the phone, confused and weary. *It's bad enough that I have to worry about everyone else, but now I have to wonder if I'm doing this God thing right. It seems to be so easy for everyone else. It just doesn't come that way to me.*

She readied for the night and climbed in to the big king size bed she'd brought from Boston, the one she'd shared in happier times with Peter. Nowadays, she was sharing it with a good book. She retrieved *Dare to Die*, the latest who-dunit by Carolyn Hart, from the nightstand and flipped it open to the page she had marked. *This is a book I understand.*

The next thing she knew, sunlight was invading the spacious bedroom, the lights were still on, and she was tangled in the covers. As she rolled over, trying to get a handle on where she was, she felt something hard beneath her. *My book. I must have fallen asleep reading.*

Not only was she unable to remember anything she'd read the night before, but even before she was awake good, the images of Emma and her mother, the gallery in Atlanta, and the call about her own mother flooded her consciousness.

"Then it wasn't a dream," she said aloud, as she staggered toward the bathroom. *Reality calls, and I'm going to answer. In a few minutes.*

Chapter 3

True to her word, following a hasty dash through the shower, and a cup of tea, which she carried to the studio, Saralynn was on deck and working. She didn't intend to wait another minute to find out why Christina at Archer Gallery was so insistent, so the first call of the morning was to Atlanta. Christina was in and was overjoyed to share that a condo developer planning a very unique and exclusive thirty-unit complex, wanted to incorporate one of Saralynn's original designs into each unit.

"He fell in love with the farmer and the little calf the moment he saw it," the gallery owner gushed. "This could be big time for you, Saralynn." Then she sobered a bit. "But he is going to be tough on price. I'll be e-mailing you his specs and the architect's drawings later today. Figure what you'll have to have and how long it will take you to produce these, and give me some numbers as soon as you can"

Saralynn thanked her for the encouragement and cleared

the line. The next call she made was to Boswell. *I've got to check in on Emma.* A conversation with the housemother revealed that her friend was rather depressed and cried occasionally, but that she was talking freely about her mother's impending death and how she would always be living at Boswell.

The third call, one she hadn't planned to make, was to Fishtrap Hollow. "Good morning, Mrs. Jackson, this is Saralynn."

"Why honey, it's good to hear your voice." She hesitated. "Nothing's wrong is there? Is Emma alright?"

"That's why I called. I just talked with her housemother." Saralynn shared the news she'd gotten from Boswell, and added, "I'd say Emma is handling things about as well as can be expected."

"It does relieve my heart to hear that. I was worried about her when you all left here yesterday."

"So how are you?" Saralynn asked.

"To be honest with you, I'm feeling pretty peaked." *She pronounced the word as peak-ed. I guess it means tired?*

"Is there anything I can do for you?"

"Sugar, you've already done too much. But I must admit, it does make me feel better to know that when I go, I can go peaceful, not worried about Emma. You are an answer to prayer, you know."

This isn't the first time I've heard this, but I still don't know the correct way to respond. In the end she finally said, "I haven't done anything at all, but you're kind to say so." *Gosh, that answer sounds so stilted and snobbish. Almost like something Mama would have said as she looked down her nose at someone!*

"Oh, my dear. You've done more than you will ever know. And I love you for it."

The words sneaked out before Saralynn could catch them.

"And I love you, too. You and Emma both."

After making certain there was nothing more she could do for the woman who was facing death, she ended the call and paced the area around her desk for a few minutes, almost as if she were unable to find a direction. *Why is it that I can feel genuine affection and sympathy for a woman I've only known for six months, and I can't find the same degree of concern for my own mother? Could it be because Mrs. Jackson is sincere and I'm beginning to see just how manipulative and insincere Mama is? And if she's worse now than she's ever been, I'm not certain I'm up to the task.*

She screwed up her courage, grabbed the land line phone and punched in Elsie's number. *I just hope this isn't some kind of trick. At this point, I wouldn't put anything past Mama – including holding me hostage, if she ever got me back in town again.*

"I'm glad you called, but why did you wait until almost lunch? I've been sitting here wringing my hands, waiting."

"It's not almost lunch for me, remember? I'm an hour behind you. And why are you wringing your hands? Has something happened since we talked yesterday?"

"I'm worried that you're not going to do what's right."

Saralynn was stunned. *It never occurred to me that I wouldn't do "what's right", as Elsie puts it.* "So how can I be certain this isn't a rouse to get me back to Boston?"

"Huh?" Silence filled the distance. "You're accusing me of trying to pull a fast one on you?" The last few words were pronounced with a significant amount of huffing and puffing, and Saralynn could visualize the woman's anger.

"I'm not accusing you of anything. But knowing my mother as I've come to understand her, it's something she would consider."

"Why you ungrateful little snit!"

"Trust me, Elsie. I'm far from ungrateful. And, I'm willing to give Mama the benefit of the doubt and, as you put it, 'do the right thing.' So talk to me about particulars. Who is her doctor?" She doubled up her fist and struck the top of the desk, then added, "Tell me everything you know, and don't leave anything out."

Thirty minutes later, when they finally ended the call, Saralynn's head was reeling. She had promised to return to Boston as soon as possible, in an effort to see what she could do. In return, Elsie had committed to getting Saralynn into her mother's condo, even if she had to be deceptive about it.

Thankful that the art classes she taught at Boswell were on hiatus, Saralynn busied herself straightening the studio and following up on several marketing contacts she'd made earlier in the month. In the back of her mind loomed the worry that was Boston.

I used to think it was neat having been born in such a historical setting, but now I understand the place of my birth was all part of Mama's deal with the Bankstons. They didn't want their grandchild born inside Mississippi, which fit in beautifully with Mama's yearning to escape. They paid the freight and Mama got her one-way ticket out. And everybody was a winner except me and Miss Sallie.

The next few days were a blur. At church on Wednesday night, Saralynn brought her friends up to date on Alicia and Emma and Mrs. Jackson. "All of us need your prayers, because the next few weeks are going to bring many challenges, I'm afraid."

Walter Kennedy was the first to speak. "Of course we'll be praying. And for you, too. Emma is going to lean on you, of that we're certain. As for Alicia, only time will tell there. Dealing with her won't be easy, and if something physical has happened to make her more difficult to manage, you've got your work cut out."

"Those are my thoughts, too," she admitted. "I'm not looking forward to what lies ahead with Mama."

"But you'll stand up to it, because that's what you have to do," Dave Hasty added. "God will be with you, and we'll be here, prepared to do whatever He directs."

How can he be so sure? "You mean God is going to tell you what to do to help me? How can He do that?"

"The same way He told us to invite you to church and to our house for chili almost a year ago."

She looked closely at her friend.

"And before you ask, no, He didn't say it out loud or even write it on the wall for us to see. God speaks to the heart and that's the ear you must listen with."

At lunch with Katie Brooks later in the week, she asked her friend about Dave's belief that God spoke to the heart, rather than the ear. To her surprise, Katie not only agreed with her friends at Rials Creek, but she went on to explain that when you've made God a part of your life by believing in His Son Jesus, it's not hard for your heart to hear His wisdom and guidance.

"But I don't understand how you can hear with your heart."

"It's like this. Do you remember telling me that after you checked on Emma the other morning, you called her mother, even though that call wasn't on your task list for the day?"

Saralynn agreed.

"You were listening with your heart right then. That wasn't you alone who decided Mrs. Jackson might like to hear a good word about her daughter, whom she obviously loves very much. God told your heart to call, your heart listened, and you were in tune enough with your heart to follow through."

Saralynn looked at her, dumbfounded.

"I'll bet you thought that idea came strictly from you?" Katie laughed.

I'm not sure I'm comfortable with the idea of someone being inside me, pulling strings, like a puppet. Not even God!

Saralynn and Elsie continued to talk daily, and Saralynn learned that her mother had a return visit to the doctor in two weeks. Also, after doing some investigative work, Elsie had determined that the doctor in question was a neurologist.

"I'm going to wait until after she keeps that appointment, then I'll fly up and together, we'll try to get her to tell us what's happening."

Elsie agreed, and Saralynn encouraged her mother's friend to stay in touch. "If anything should change, don't hesitate to call me immediately. I will drop what I'm doing and come."

Saralynn began to schedule her work around at least a week in Boston and was making preparations for the trip when, as so often happens, life got in the way! It was an early morning phone call that jerked her from a sound sleep. Her eyes were so bleary she couldn't focus on the Caller ID and literally answered the call blind.

"Is this Ms. Reilly?" an unfamiliar male voice on the other end of the phone inquired.

"Yes, I'm Saralynn Reilly," she mumbled, trying to clear the cobwebs from her brain.

"This is Dr. Howerton, Dr. George Howerton, in Iuka, Mississippi. At the word Iuka, Saralynn's antenna went up. "I'm sorry to have to call you so early, but do you know a Mrs. Homerline Jackson?

Homerline? Is that Emma's mother's name? I don't guess I ever heard it called. "I'm not sure about the Homerline part, but I do know a Mrs. Jackson there. She lives at Fishtrap Hollow."

"Then we're talking about the same Mrs. Jackson," the doctor agreed. "She's very ill; I believe she said you knew she was dying?"

"Yes, but she said three months. It's barely been two weeks since I was there."

"Unfortunately," the doctor explained, "three months was the very outside edge. Mrs. Jackson's condition has deteriorated rapidly in the past few hours, and I've just put her to bed. She has a nurse with her."

"Is this the... the end?" Saralynn could hardly bring herself to voice the words.

The doctor didn't hesitate. "I'm afraid it is. She doesn't want to be moved to a hospital, and has asked that no heroic measures be taken. I would say, based on what we're seeing now, twenty-four hours at most. And that's being very generous."

"Then I need to get Emma home as quickly as possible." Even as she was saying the words, Saralynn was mentally adjusting her schedule.

"That's why I'm calling," the doctor advised. "Who do I need to speak with at Boswell to arrange for Emma's release? And how long will it take you get here?"

Saralynn did some quick calculations. A look at the clock told her it wasn't yet six o'clock. "I can be ready to pick Emma up in an hour, give or take a few minutes. So we should be there by lunch time."

"There's no time to waste," the doctor advised. "I'm afraid Mrs. Jackson's heart is weakening by the minute."

Saralynn gave him the Boswell contact information and headed for the shower. Obviously this was going to be a rough trip and for the first time, in a long time, she dreaded the drive north.

It was a few minutes past seven o'clock when she pulled into the parking space at Emma's group home, where she found her friend waiting on the porch, suitcase in hand. Saralynn and the doctor had agreed it might be kinder to Emma to wait until she was in Iuka to let her know the true extent of her mother's condition.

"Hey, Saralynn!" Emma greeted her chauffeur enthusiastically and Saralynn immediately felt guilty that they were deceiving the woman. "Why we going home?"

"God, forgive me." Now I sound like my friends at church. "I heard your mama was lonesome for you, and I just decided we'd go."

Emma grinned as she settled her bulk into the front passenger seat of Saralynn's Honda and allowed her seatbelt to be buckled around her.

"We'll see you when you get back," her housemother, Miss Ann, told the older woman as she patted her on the shoulder. Saralynn and the housemother exchanged glances over Emma's head, and each reflected the sorrow that was showing on the other's face.

Saralynn concentrated on driving, on trying to make every mile count, thankful for once that Emma was a silent passenger. Very little was said at all, until, near noon, the two ladies caught the first glimpse of their destination.

"That's the old courthouse," Emma announced.

Her driver crossed the tracks on South Fulton Street and dead-ended on Eastport, where she made a sharp right. Just a couple of minutes out, she hung a left, and then, a mile or so down the road, another right turn and then a left put them in Fishtrap Hollow.

It wasn't until they rounded the curve and Emma spotted several cars in front of the house, that a look of suspicion crossed her otherwise placid face. "Why so many people at Mama's house? It looks like when daddy died and you brought me home. Remember?"

Saralynn cringed inwardly, but struggled to maintain her composure. "They've probably heard your mama was sick and have come to see her." She could tell Emma hadn't bought the story, but before her friend could raise further questions, Saralynn pulled the car into the driveway, and Emma was out of her door in record speed.

"Mama. Mama! You alright, aren't you. It's me, Emma. I'm here."

Saralynn saw that Emma was met by a man she assumed was Dr. Howerton, who took her gently by the arm. *Oh, please Lord, let her still be alive. I drove as fast as I could.*

Emma disappeared inside the house and Saralynn was right on her heels. There were several people sitting about the living room, and a nurse was coming and going from inside Mrs. Jackson's bedroom. *Maybe we're in time?*

"NO, Mama! No… no…please, NO!"

The screams were clearly Emma's, and they were coming from the bedroom. Almost immediately the nurse Saralynn had seen moments earlier was in the doorway, beckoning frantically.

The young woman complied and was immediately ushered to the bedside, where Emma stood, tears streaming down her face, quietly stomping in place, a behavior Saralynn understood was commonplace when she was frustrated.

The woman in the bed was almost unrecognizable. *Her heart isn't working enough to even clear out all her fluids.* She was shocked to hear Mrs. Jackson's voice come out of the swollen body. "Saralynn… please… come closer," she pleaded in a voice so soft, Saralynn had to strain to hear.

She bent to the bedside and put her face in the patient's line of vision.

"Thank you… for bringing her." The words were but a mere whisper.

"You're so welcome." Saralynn bit her lower lip and fought back tears. "Is there anything else I can do for you?"

"Just take care of Emma," was the reply. Mrs. Jackson's left hand sought Saralynn's, and when they connected, the older woman squeezed. "I've got everything fixed." With that, she closed her eyes and the hand in Saralynn's went limp.

Oh, my, gosh! I was holding her hand and she just died. Is this what death is like?

The doctor and nurse began attending to the deceased, and Emma, who suddenly realized what had just happened, began to wail like a small, heartbroken child. Before it was over, the doctor had assisted Emma to her room, where he gave her a shot to calm her, then he and Saralynn helped the now motherless woman to stretch out on the bed.

"I'll be right here, Emma," Saralynn reassured her friend. "Right outside the door. If you need me, you call for me. OK?"

Emma nodded, and from her actions, it was obvious the medication was already taking effect.

Saralynn and the doctor slipped quietly from the room, where they were met by a young man carrying a leather business case. "I'm Jonathan Walthall," he said by way of introduction. "I'm an attorney and I assume you would be Saralynn Reilly?"

How does he know who I am? I don't know him. Although Saralynn had met a number of people during her visits to the county, she knew she had never met this man.

"Yes, I'm Saralynn. Do we know each other?"

"Not formally," the lawyer acknowledged. "But from the way Mrs. Jackson described you, I'd have known you anywhere."

Saralynn wasn't sure how to respond and was even more uncertain why Mrs. Jackson would have been describing her to an attorney.

Sensing her confusion, the lawyer continued. "I was Mrs. Jackson's attorney during her lifetime. She consulted me after her husband died, and again after receiving her recent medical prognosis."

He should be a lawyer, he talks just like one!

"You'll be happy to know," he continued, "that all the arrangements are made. Everything is handled so your job will be easy."

"My job? You mean I've got to plan the funeral?" *I didn't even have a service for either of my guys.*

"Oh, no ma'am, the service is already planned, Mrs. Jackson prepaid her funeral, and the funeral home is en-route now to collect the body."

He talks so detached. Almost like he were on the outside looking in. "Then what, exactly, is my easy job going to be?"

"Surely Mrs. Jackson talked to you."

"About what?"

"About your job, as executor of her estate and Emma's guardian."

"Excuse me?"

"Uh oh." The lawyer grimaced. "She didn't talk to you, did she?"

"At the risk of appearing rude, I don't have the slightest idea what you're babbling about."

The attorney motioned her into the dining room, where she'd enjoyed so many of Mrs. Jackson's mouth-watering meals. She took a seat and he pulled out a chair for himself across the corner of the table.

"When Mrs. Jackson learned that she had a very short time to live, her primary concern was Emma. Boswell can take care of her, physically, for the remainder of her life, but by law she must have a guardian. Her mother made three separate but equally important provisions in her will, in order to make things as easy for Emma as possible."

"And all of this involves me?"

"Yes, Ma'am, it does." The lawyer continued, "Mrs. Jackson made her funeral arrangements, paid for the funeral, and planned her service. The mortician already has the clothes she will wear, so there's nothing for you to do there."

"Go on."

"The second thing was Emma's guardianship, and it was you that she named to oversee her daughter's welfare for the remainder of her life.'

"I see." *Although I really don't.* "So what do I have to do?"

"Practically, just more of what you've been doing for Emma, although legally, Boswell and doctors and hospitals will look to you for medical permission when necessary. And you'll handle the finances, but Mrs. Jackson fixed it so you won't have to make annual reports to the court."

What have I gotten myself into?

"And last, the attorney said, "is the matter of this property. Mrs. Jackson left it to you, with the stipulation that as long as you feel Emma is physically and emotionally able to make the trip, that you will bring her here for visits two or three times a year."

It felt like Twilight Zone time. "I own this house? Mrs. Jackson left it to me?"

"That's right. Plus, she left a trust fund which should be more than adequate to pay the utilities, the taxes and insurance, and cover modest upkeep. She knew you'd have to hire someone to mow the grass, and paint and shingles have to be replaced eventually."

I own this house? And Emma is my responsibility!

Saralynn rose slowly from her chair, feeling at that moment as if she were hundreds of years old. "You'll have to excuse me, Mr. Walthall, but I'm going to have to take a walk. Or something. I've simply been hit with too much, too quickly and I need some time to bounce back."

"Of course, Ms. Reilly. I understand completely." He thrust a small cream-colored square of cardboard in her direction. "Here's my business card, and my cell phone number is written on the back. Call me if you have any questions over the next few days. That's why I'm here."

Saralynn thanked him, then sought the front door and freedom.

"Oh, and by the way, Ms. Reilly…" his face wore an anxious expression, "we will need to sit down and talk before you leave, before Emma goes back to Boswell."

"Yes, sir. Of course."

The shell-shocked heiress spent much of the afternoon simply walking the yard, remembering past visits, and trying to comprehend that it all now belonged to her. It was the sight of Emma stumbling down the steps that brought her back to reality.

"Saralynn? Saralynn! Mama's dead and I don't know what to do. I need you."

Chapter 4

It is so good to be back home. Saralynn rolled over in bed and squinted at the clock. It had gotten knocked out of position, like everything else in her life over the past few days, and without getting up, it was impossible to see the time.

Oh, well, I might as well get up. Return to reality is going to be rough, so the sooner I get up, the easier it will be.

As she worked shampoo into her strawberry blond curls and followed with the mandatory conditioner, the young artist reflected on all that had happened.

It was still difficult to believe, but Mrs. Jackson was gone. Saralynn and Emma had buried her beside Mr. Jackson in the little church cemetery, in accordance with her wishes. Emma, who had been an emotional basket case the entire time, had clung exclusively to Saralynn, spurning all attempts by her relatives to comfort her or to provide for her. For Saralynn, having been in Emma's position less than a year before, dealing with grief the magnitude of Emma's was unsettling at best. *Was I this bad?*

Following the service, the two women met back at the house with the attorney who explained to Emma that Saralynn would be her guardian. For the older woman, no mere legal document could more completely guarantee the relationship she had already established. When it was explained to Emma that her mother's house now belonged to Saralynn, Emma was equally nonplussed. For her, everything was life as usual. In the end, Emma continued to look to Saralynn in much the same fashion as had always been the case.

I lost a toddler but gained another child who is older than me. And more dependent than Marc. I certainly didn't bargain on all of this when I first agreed to transport Emma home.

It wasn't that Saralynn felt put upon, but that she doubted she was fit for the task. She had said as much to Katie Brooks when they talked for the last time before the two women returned to south Mississippi.

"You're a business woman, you know. So handling Emma's finances should be no problem. And you've got a heart as big as Texas, so dealing with her emotionally should come naturally. Another thing in your favor is your…"

"Soft spot in my head that lets me get involved with people. Is that what you were going to say?"

"It was not and you know it. I was going to comment on your own recent experience with grief, which should make it easier for you to understand Emma's recovery from her mother's death."

"Looks like to me it's going to make it harder, because I'll forever be reminded of my guys as well."

"I think you'll be surprised. At any rate, there are plenty of us here at Boswell, not to mention all your church family at

Rials Creek, who are ready and able to help you. Don't be ashamed to ask."

As she toweled off and began to dry her hair, Saralynn recalled the mood swings from grief to euphoria that Emma exhibited during the five-hour drive back from Iuka the day before. They had hugged and said their goodbyes on the porch of her group home long after the other residents of her cottage had gone to bed. The lateness of the hour, Saralynn recalled with a grin, hadn't stopped Emma from announcing her return to one and all, complete with the news that her mother had died and now Saralynn was going to be her mother.

Suddenly the word "mother" had taken on a totally different distinction.

Noting that it was then a decent hour at which to place a phone call, she dialed the Boswell number and was soon speaking with Emma's housemother. Her ward, as the lawyer had referred to Emma, was up and doing her morning chores and was her normal self. The housemother promised to call if there were any problems.

I've got to call Elsie and check in on Mama. But after breakfast. I don't care if it will be almost lunch time there. When she called Elsie after she arrived in Iuka, to let her know her whereabouts, the woman in Boston wasn't impressed that Saralynn couldn't drop everything and fly north to see about her own mother, but that she could get all involved with someone to whom she owed nothing. *I knew Elsie would never understand, so I didn't even waste time or breath trying to explain. In truth, I'm not sure I understand it myself!*

It was after eleven o'clock in Boston before Saralynn got a break and could place the call. An e-mail from Christina Jacobs in Atlanta, with enthusiastic endorsement of the various designs she had submitted to the condo builder, had derailed her momentarily.

"I can't believe that out of thirty different designs, you didn't duplicate anything. Mr. Chambers was very impressed."

Saralynn was equally impressed with the amount of the check Christina said would be mailed to her that day, as the first one-third of the total job, less Archer Gallery's commission, of course. *I can finally breathe in this business, with this commission under me. I've got Iuka to thank.* Saralynn had taken one of her smaller pieces to show Mrs. Jackson. A relative who had dropped by had a close friend who worked in an Atlanta, Georgia art gallery. A few days later, Saralynn received a call from Christina Jacobs, who had visited Saralynn's new web site, then placed a phone call.

I wouldn't believe it if I hadn't lived it.

Finally, however, her desk was fairly clear, and she placed the call to Boston. As the phone rang, and rang, her emotions ran the scale from excitement to dread. *Where was Elsie? Surely she wasn't pulling an Alicia and deliberately not answering her phone.*

When she was convinced no one was there, a voice suddenly whispered. "Call you back. Can't talk."

Saralynn regarded her cordless phone with an expression not unlike one would give an errant child who had misbehaved and then proudly proclaimed his misdeeds to the world. *If she can't talk, she can't talk. At least she answered.* While she waited for the promised return call, Saralynn busied herself inventorying her fabric and supplies. Creating the thirty individual pieces would keep her busy. Fortunately, the developer still had several months of work ahead and would not need them until everything else was finished.

She had explained the concept to Katie Brooks when she called to tell her about the commission. *After all, this was her sister's studio, and had she not been killed, I would probably never have had the inspiration, or the courage, to undertake such a challenge.*

"Each of the thirty condos in this old rehabbed industrial building will have a niche in the foyer wall, where my designs will hang, and the unit's color scheme will draw its inspiration from the colors I use in each piece. Since he expects the owners in the complex to become friends, and be in and out of each other's homes, he doesn't want any two pieces to be identical."

"Whew! That would have been enough to stop me dead in the water right there," Katie vowed, "not that I've got the talent to get the commission in the first place."

"I have to admit, at first I was overwhelmed, too. But once I realized that I needed to consider each one as a stained glass window, composed of various geometric shapes, it was really quite easy to design thirty totally different concepts of the same thing."

"Yeah. Right. If you say so."

Saralynn had laughed. "Come on, quit giving me a hard time."

"I'm not. Really. I'm in awe that you could find definition in all of that. I'd still be struggling with the first piece and sweating, wondering how in the heck I was going to find twenty-nine other ideas."

The ringing of her business line dragged her back to reality and she noted by the Caller ID that it was Elsie. She looked at the clock as she punched the talk button. *It's been almost an hour. So much for not calling until lunch time!*

"Thank goodness your mother had to go to the bathroom!"

That's really not the report I was calling for, but thank you for that update, Elsie. "So where are you? Why can't you talk?"

"We're in the mall and your mother is buying everything in sight. She's like a crazy woman."

My mother, Alicia, the original tightwad who lives on a fixed income is buying everything in sight? "When you say everything, can you be more specific?"

"I can't talk but a minute, and if I hang up on you, I'll call you back. I don't want Alicia to know we're talking."

Good old Elsie makes it sound so clandestine. "Like I said, what all is she buying?"

"You name it… clothes, linens, knick-knacks. About the only thing she didn't buy was a sofa we found that would have cost her retail."

"Does Mama need a new sofa?"

"Of course not. She's got a condo filled with new furniture. You ought to know, she bought everything through you."

That she did, and argued with me over every penny, when I already wasn't making anything off the deal. A broken water line in the wall next to Alicia's Boston condo several months earlier had forced a complete renovation and almost all new furniture. Saralynn was certain that the last thing her mother needed was another sofa.

"So does she give any explanation for her actions? Her spend-thrift ways? Because that's definitely not Mama."

"All she will tell me is that you don't live forever, and that she might die some day. I'm telling you, Saralynn, your mother has undergone some intense mood changes over the past few months. She's not the mother you… uh, oh. Gotta go. Call you later."

Saralynn was again left holding the dead phone, not a whole lot more in the know than she had been. Instead of stewing over what she didn't understand and couldn't change anyway, she got out her calendar. Somehow, some way, in between trips to Boston and a return trip to Iuka, she had to begin working on the

Atlanta commission.

After struggling with her planning calendar without much success, she grabbed the phone and dialed Donna Hasty. When her friend answered, Saralynn didn't even mess around with niceties, but announced that she was taking the two of them to lunch and would pick Donna up in forty-five minutes. "We're going to Zip's."

Zip's in Magee was a dining landmark in Simpson County, famous for its good southern home cooking, a brand of cuisine Saralynn had learned to love since her first exposure. *There's nothing like good food to cure whatever ails you.*

Soon the two ladies were digging into plates that had been served by their favorite server, Kay Austin, and Saralynn was picking her friend's brain over how to deal with Alicia. "From the way Elsie describes her, I'd say she's definitely undergone some personality changes. Whether they're for better or worse where I'm involved, remains to be seen."

"I think you've got reason for concern," Donna agreed. "Those headaches don't bode well for what the problem might be, and the fact that your mother's doctor is sending her to a neurologist troubles me."

"Then you think it might be a brain tumor?"

Donna speared a bite of broccoli casserole. "Ummm, this is good! Could be, but now remember… not all tumors are malignant. Even a benign tumor could put pressure on the brain and cause the headaches."

"That does give me some comfort." She attacked the sweet potatoes on her plate and reported their excellence. "If not a brain tumor, then what?"

Donna chewed her chicken and Saralynn could see her

mind working as well. "Could be Alzheimer's, or just plain dementia, although your mother is fairly young for both of those. Could be hormones. And it might even be that she's had a change of heart and is too embarrassed to call you and make amends."

"You don't really believe the last one, do you?"

Donna took another bite of chicken and a swig of tea. "How do they make this tea taste so good? No, I don't really believe that the leopard has changed her spots."

"Then what's your gut take on this?"

"I think you've got enough cause for concern. When is the appointment with the neurologist?" Donna forked up a generous clump of mashed potatoes dripping with gravy. "Ummm this is so good. Thank you for insisting that we do this."

Saralynn was thumbing through her calendar pages. "She sees the doctor a week from today, as a matter of fact."

"Hmmmm." Another fork-full of casserole was chased with a bite from the corn muffin on her plate. "If it were me, I'd want to be there to see the doctor. That's how you'll get the complete story."

"I agree." Saralynn put down her fork, oblivious to the food left on her plate. "I should be there for the appointment, but Mama would never allow it. I don't expect to even be welcome in her home. Forget going with her to the doctor's visit. Mama's a very private person, and she's been this way as long as I can remember."

"But if you don't try, you'll never know."

"True enough." She speared another bite of beans. "But how do I do it?"

"Would your mother's friend be willing to cut some corners, so to speak, or is she so loyal that she would refuse?"

"Once I'd have said she wouldn't, but now she says she'll help. Whatever has happened to Mama has spooked Elsie. That much I'm sure."

"Then here's what I'd do." Donna waved her arm in the air. "Kay? Can we get more tea, please?" She turned her attention back to Saralynn. "I'd fly in two or three days before the appointment, but don't alert your mother. Alicia will open her door to Elsie without question. Right?"

"As far as I know."

The conversation ceased while the petite black-haired server poured more tea. "Ever' thing else okay?" she asked.

"Great, Kay. Just great. Thanks!"

The server flashed her trademark grin and left them to their conversation.

"Here's what I'd do," she said again. "I'd go up ahead of time and use Elsie to get into your mother's condo. Between the two of you, perhaps you can make her see reason."

"It might work." Saralynn let go a big sigh. "With Mama you just never know."

"I don't think you have a thing to lose, and it just might help." She reached across and took Saralynn's hand in hers.

This is just how Mama would have done it!

"I'll tell you something else. I'm just brassy enough to march myself into that doctor's office and inform them that my mother is sick and won't let me help her."

Saralynn grinned. "They arrest people in Boston for stunts like that."

"Then I guess I'd be seeing the inside of the Boston jail, because I wouldn't go down without a fight."

While they enjoyed their dessert of fresh peach cobbler,

another southern delicacy Saralynn had learned to eat, they talked about church and upcoming events there. "You know, right after I met you, you talked about how much you missed church when you didn't get to attend."

"I did?"

"You did, and now I understand exactly what you meant. These past few weeks have been so hectic, what with me out of town so much. I really feel like something happened and I missed it."

"And we missed you," her friend assured her. "You'll be back Sunday, won't you?"

"Those are my plans. Even if I do decide to go on to Boston ahead of time, I won't leave until Monday or Tuesday."

"So you've decided to go?"

"I wouldn't say that just yet. But I have decided to talk with Elsie again and see how far out on the limb she's willing to go. Besides, I'll need to see when I can get a seat on a Delta jet heading north."

Just as Donna was about to get out of the car a few minutes later, she turned to Saralynn. "Would you mind if we had a word of prayer about all of this?"

"I don't mind, but when Mr. Walter prayed before we talked to Mama about selling Miss Sallie's house, it didn't work."

Donna fixed her friend with a steely gaze and said, "It may not have worked at the time. But God does everything on His timetable. It may still work, but on His schedule, not yours and Mr. Walter's."

"I hadn't thought of it like that."

"Then let's pray. You never go wrong with prayer. Trust me."

The two joined hands.

Dear Lord, Saralynn has been through so much, and now she's faced with the possible illness of her mother. It doesn't make it any easier that her mother has chosen to abandon her—physically and emotionally. All of this is taking a toll on Saralynn, whose only concern is her mother's welfare. While her mother has in effect disowned her, Saralynn is about to fly home to try and help in any way that she can. She goes with no agenda, no scheme, just concern for her mother. Given past experiences, this visit doesn't promise to be an easy one. In fact, even getting into her mother's home may take some slight deception. You've told us that we can do all things through You. We're claiming that promise now, Lord, for Saralynn and ask that You would walk with her, strengthen her and yes, Lord, even protect her from her mother's verbal and possibly physical barbs. Only You know whether it's in Your will for a reconciliation between this daughter and her mother. We have faith in whatever You have designed for this situation, Thy will be done. In Jesus' Holy Name we pray. Amen.

Saralynn couldn't stop the tears that trickled down her cheeks. "Thank... thank you," she snuffled, as she grabbed for a tissue. "Thank you so much."

Conversations with Elsie later that day brought the woman's promise to help Saralynn gain entry to Alicia's home. "I never thought I'd see the day I'd be a party to something like this," she explained, "but I'm telling you: something is bad wrong with your mama. If it gets her the help she needs, then I'll do it."

Once she had Elsie's commitment, Saralynn booked a plane reservation for the following Monday morning. Elsie had already agreed to meet her at the airport, and Saralynn conveyed her expected three-forty arrival time by e-mail. She also reserved a hotel room. *I'll let Elsie help me with Mama, but I'm not staying at her house, and I have grave doubts that I'll be welcome at Mama's. A hotel is the best plan. And I'll probably have to rent a car, but I'll wait until I get there and learn the lay of the land.*

The rest of the week passed before Saralynn's eyes in record speed. At church on Sunday, she shared with her friends the challenges she had before her, both with her mother and with Emma. As she expected, her church family rallied round as they had always done.

"You need any help when you get to Boston, you call me. Hear?" Walter Kennedy had stopped her between Sunday School and worship. "Anything. I mean it."

She hugged his neck and planted a kiss on his cheek. "I love you so much. If Miss Virginia hadn't already snagged you, I'd be after you!"

He laughed.

They both knew she wasn't serious. *But it feels so good to be this open and free with people you care about.*

Others in the congregation made similar offers, all of which Saralynn took to heart.

It was after church on Sunday evening when Mr. Walter approached her again. "I've got a piece of news you might find interesting. It's also something you should know before you see Alicia, since her venom seems to be directed specifically at you.

"You've got my curiosity aroused."

He led her to a pew near the back of the church, away

from the crowd. "The deal just fell through on Miss Sallie's house."

"I didn't know there had been a deal." *In truth, there's been so much going on the past few weeks, I hadn't even thought about the house. Does that mean it's not my dream house any longer? Especially since I have a house in north Mississippi now?*

"The realtor sign had an 'Under Contract' banner across it about a month ago." He grinned. "I'll admit, I ride by every so often, just out of nosiness."

"This is the Jackson Realtor's sign?"

"One in the same."

I'll never get over being embarrassed at the way Mama took the listing away from Mr. Walter and reported him to the state board. Thank goodness they saw her complaint for exactly what it was. She listed it with a hot-shot agent from Jackson, who threatened to have Mr. Walter arrested for trespass if he so much as walked on the property.

"… anyway, when I drove by today, I noticed that banner was missing."

"So what happened? I haven't been there since the day you picked me up and took me to your house to stay."

Mr. Walter slapped his knee. "I'd like to take pleasure in what happened, but because I believe it directly relates to why you're headed to Boston tomorrow, I can't."

"I don't understand."

"The change of signs indicates there was a purchase in progress and for whatever reason, it fell through. Now the house is back on the market. The question is, 'why?'"

"I'm with you so far."

"I called the agent and told him up front that I saw the property was back on the market, that I had a client who might be interested." He looked at her. "I assume you're still interested."

Saralynn had to chuckle. *Trust Mr. Walter to split hairs and still stay ethical.*

"I'm still interested," she told him, and then she shared about the house she now owned in Iuka.

"You do get around, don't you? Anyway, the Jackson agent was so angry at Alicia, he spilled the entire story. Seems he had the place sold to a young professional couple from Jackson, who wanted the prestige of driving into the capital city each day from their country estate."

Saralynn snickered. "You're serious?"

"That's what the man said, and that's how he said it. What's more, they had a near-perfect credit score and they had adequate resources to buy and restore the house. In other words, a real estate agent's dream client."

Saralynn glanced at her watch. *I've got to get home and finish packing. But this story is too good to miss.*

She hadn't been discrete enough.

"I know it's late, but you need to hear this. I'll make it short. Everything was set, although Alicia refused to come back to Jackson for the closing. In the end, the couple and their lender agreed that it could be done by long distance and overnight mail, so that she could sign all the papers right there in Boston."

"Is that so out of the ordinary?"

"It's done, but usually it's a case when the seller is old or institutionalized. You know," he spread out his hands, "extenuating circumstances."

"So what happened?"

"The closing was set for Monday of last week. The buyers would meet at their lender's office, sign all the necessary papers. Their check would be held in escrow, while the papers went to

Boston for Alicia to sign and put back in overnight mail. By Wednesday it should have been a done deal, and then her check would be overnighted to her."

"Sounds like a plan."

"That's what everyone thought. Then on Friday a week ago, the agent gets a call from your mother. She claims she's decided she doesn't trust him, the buyers, or their lender. She demands that they all fly to Boston to meet in her lawyer's office, and that they should bring the check with them."

"Sounds like the Mama I remember."

"It sounded familiar to me, too. But you have to remember, these other folks don't know Alicia as well as we do. When the agent told her she was crazy, that her buyers weren't about to submit to that, she went ballistic. That's when she told him she wasn't signing any papers unless she was paid up front."

"Mama can really pull some stunts." *I'm learning more about my parent than I ever wanted to know.*

"When the agent told her that no bank was going to cut her a check until and unless her name was already on the dotted line, she informed him that if their bank didn't trust her, she certainly didn't trust their bank."

"Oh, Mr. Walter."

"Naturally the buyers balked. And then they walked." He snickered at his own poem. "The agent is entitled to collect a commission from Alicia, because he had buyers ready, willing and able to perform."

"Is he going to sue her?"

"He would be within his rights, but remember, he hasn't had the experience with her that we have. She sang him her 'I'm just a poor widow on a fixed-income' song, and he bought it."

"Wonder when he'll figure out he's been had?"

"Who knows? At any rate, he agreed to put the property back on the market and she agreed to try and find a way to come for the closing next time."

"Like I believe that."

"That makes two of us. But I didn't want you to head out of town tomorrow without knowing this. I have horrors of Alicia somehow blaming me, or worse yet, you, for something neither of us knew anything about until it was all a done deal."

"Thanks for the heads-up. I'll go forewarned and forearmed." She patted his arm. "I can't believe the agent even talked to you, given the history, if you will."

"Under any other circumstances, he probably wouldn't have. But I imagine he already had his commission spent, and Alicia jerked the rug out from under him big time."

"Mama makes me so angry."

"You aren't alone in that club. This guy is so desperate to sell, he would have talked to anybody when I called today. Because he knew that Alicia and I had problems in the past, I guess he felt comfortable spilling his gut to me."

"I wouldn't be surprised if he didn't have a little better understanding of how she abused you, before she went to him."

"You're probably right. But at any rate, go on to Boston and do what you can do. But go knowing that Alicia is either up to her old tricks again, or she's truly ill. Either way, it doesn't bode well for you. Which is why you'll go with all our prayers."

For the second time that day, she kissed his cheek.

If only she could have known what awaited her in Boston, Mr. Walter's tale would have paled by comparison.

Chapter 5

The flight to Boston's Logan International Airport was uneventful. Getting to the airport in Jackson had been an ordeal, however. After having to return home to retrieve a packet of papers she had forgotten, Saralynn ran into a second delay when she arrived at Boswell to tell Emma she was going out of town.

Emma immediately thought I was going back to Iuka, and became so upset when I wouldn't take her with me. It had required both Saralynn and the housemother to assure the woman that Saralynn was going elsewhere, and to get her ward calm enough that she could leave without feeling guilty. *I didn't dare tell her I was going to see about my mother. That would have unleashed another torrent.*

In the end, she was one of the last passengers to get through the security screening and board the plane. *Another couple of minutes and I wouldn't have made it!*

As she promised, Elsie met Saralynn's plane, and as they drove back into the city, her mother's friend brought her up to date. "Did you know anything about the sale falling through on your grandmother's house?"

Startled to have been met with that from Elsie, Saralynn was immediately wary. "I knew it was on the market," she replied. *I didn't lie… I just didn't tell everything I knew.*

"It was supposed to have closed last Monday, but something Alicia did threw a monkey wrench in things." The friend passed her hand across her brow, as if in exhaustion. "Ever since, she's been on a tirade like you wouldn't believe. What's more, she won't tell me what happened. All she'll say is, the bank was trying to cheat her."

"Gee, that's too bad." *As usual, Mama was twisting facts to fit the picture she had designed. Without sounding crass, this is the old Mama. How am I supposed to tell if she's sick?*

Elsie dropped her at her hotel. Saralynn had found it interesting when she told her volunteer chauffeur that she had taken a room, there were no protests to the contrary, no insistence that Saralynn stay with her. *Just about like I figured.*

The women agreed that it would be better to wait until Tuesday morning to put their plan into action. Saralynn checked in, and extracted Elsie's promise to call for her at nine-thirty the next morning. Once in her hotel room, Saralynn unpacked, grabbed a quick shower to revive herself, and headed out. The doorman, resplendent in his burgundy and gold and gray, hailed a taxi for her.

Once in and seated, she handed the driver a list of addresses. *The first place I want to go is my house. I want to get a look at it from the outside, to be sure it's being kept up. Then we'll go by Mama's condo. I'm curious to see if her van is in its parking place and if Elsie's car is there.* In the back of her mind still remained the niggling doubt that all of this was a set-up and that she was walking into a trap. *Then I just want to visit some of the old haunts. I'm curious.*

Saralynn surveyed the crowded room at The Butcher Shop, once a favorite of theirs when Peter was alive and they had been a couple. She didn't know if it was because she was dining alone, or if the restaurant was now a closed part of her past. But something was different. While the food was excellent, as she had known it would be, the atmosphere put a definite damper on an expensive meal.

The servers are so aloof, almost like they're doing you a favor to even wait on you. Nothing like Kay Austin at Zip's. There's no warmth, no genuineness.

It had been the same story, earlier, when she asked the taxi driver pull to the curb in front of the house where she and her guys had enjoyed such a good life. It wasn't that the façade was unkempt, or that it wasn't still a beautiful home. But it was a frozen beauty, as if there was no warmth, no legitimacy behind the elegant façade. *This house was one of my first major projects, and now it leaves me cold. If the work I did for all my clients was this artificial, I did all of us a favor by getting out of the business!*

At Revere Hills Pointe, where Alicia's condo was located, Saralynn could glimpse both the vehicles she sought in their respective parking stalls. By shading her eyes against the sun, she could see onto the balcony outside her mother's living room. But it was as if no one was home.

In the end, she ate only a portion of her meal, paid the check, left an acceptable tip and departed the restaurant. It was, she knew, the last time she would ever go there. *It's a shame I couldn't leave that server a real tip; like defrost and live. Really live.*

Back in her room, she got ready for the night, and began turning out the lights. Just as she was about to climb into bed, she hesitated, then crossed the room to her luggage. She dug into an inner compartment and brought out Miss Sallie's Bible. *I don't know why I felt it was necessary to bring this.*

Saralynn plumped her pillows into a back rest and settled into the bed and, almost hesitantly, opened the ancient, bulging Bible. *How are you supposed to read this? I mean, there must be instructions.* She had thumbed through the Bible enough in the past, in a detached sort of way, to know that there were many books and within each book, were chapters and then verses. But the story begun in one book didn't continue into the next book. *And the language! Who can understand the language? I'm fairly educated, but this all reads like Greek to me.*

She envied all of her friends at Rials Creek who could flip open their Bibles to any place they wanted and understand the meaning of what they read. *But I can't be like them, because I've never been involved in church until just recently. This must be God's way of rewarding them.*

She flipped from one part of the Bible to another, reading first one passage and then another. Only instead of finding peace and comfort, as she had been promised by others, she found only more torment and confusion. *See, God? I knew You weren't real for me.*

After more than half an hour of reading and getting frustrated, she closed the old Bible - the same one that had been her grandmother's rock - and laid it aside. "I sure wish I knew how Miss Sallie found the peace she did, because I could use some beforpe morning," she said to the room at large. "God, why aren't You there for me?"

Then she slept, although upon closer inspection in the morning's new light, it wasn't a very restful slumber, because the entire night had been consumed with both strange and troubling dreams.

She would later classify that sleep as a nightmare, but nothing compared to the one to come.

Before leaving her room, Saralynn stated loudly, "God, everybody at Rials Creek seems to have a conversation with You before they undertake anything dangerous or challenging. So I'm going to do the same thing. You know what I'm about to do, and I need Your help."

She ended the prayer the way she'd heard others, when they said, "in Jesus' name. Amen." *I never have understood why that's so important.*

True to her promise, Elsie was in the lobby when Saralynn got off the elevator. The two had breakfast together in the hotel coffee shop, where Saralynn learned that her mother had been up most of the night with an excruciating headache.

"She says it's the worst one she's had," Elsie supplied. "Even the medicine the doctor prescribed didn't help."

Instantly suspicious, Saralynn asked, "I thought you said Mama refused to have it filled."

"She did, until day before yesterday. Then the pain got so bad, she sent me to get it."

"All of this doesn't sound good, Elsie."

"You're telling me."

"So what's our plan of action?"

"Actually, it just got easier for us," her friend explained. "When I left this morning, Alicia gave me her key. She said she felt so bad, she might not be able to get up to let me in."

"You're saying we won't have to strong-arm our way?"

Elsie dug in the pocket of the slacks she wore and brandished the key. "Not this time, we won't."

It was a short ride from the hotel to her mother's high-rise condo. Elsie opened the door and called out, "Alicia? Alicia? Where are you?"

The response was faint, and indicated that its owner was not well. "I'm in my bedroom. I don't feel right."

Elsie closed the door and indicated for Saralynn to follow. "I'm coming back, Alicia."

As they walked toward the master bedroom, which Saralynn knew was on the back side of the unit, she marveled at the decorating job her mother had done on the condo earlier in the year. *As I've often said, Mama was the one who should have been the decorator. She has more inherent artistic skills than I had after I graduated from design school.*

But the journey to her mother's room wasn't long enough to fully appreciate the artistry that was apparent in every room. Almost before she was ready, the two ladies stood outside Alicia's door. At that moment, Saralynn wasn't sure if she wanted to enter or not. *What happens in the next few seconds could determine both mine and Mama's future.*

Elsie stepped inside first and walked to the side of the bed. "Alicia, are you any better?"

Saralynn could see a lump under the covers. She recoiled

with shock when a voice she didn't even recognize replied from beneath that mound of linen, "I've never hurt so bad in my life. I don't know if I can live until I see the doctor on Thursday." The voice sounded old, like that of an elderly woman; someone much older than Alicia's fifty-six years.

"I know you're hurting. Did you take any more of your medicine?"

"Can't," the voice replied. "Can't have another one until noon. That's what the label says."

Mama has never had any use for medicine, so for her to be taking it and counting the hours until the next dose, it must be bad.

Elsie patted her shoulder. "I've brought you something that should make your head better."

Alicia struggled to raise up on one elbow. "What could you possibly have that would make any difference?" The voice was thin and whiny…and weak. Extremely weak. Then she saw Saraynn, and as their eyes met from about twelve feet apart, the younger woman saw pure hostility replace the pain in her mother's eyes.

"Get her out of here," Alicia screamed. "Get her out of here NOW!"

"But Mama," Saralynn protested. "You're sick and…"

To the amazement and alarm of both Saralynn and Elsie, Alicia Bankston rose up in her bed, to where she was standing on her knees. "Get that ungrateful brat out of my house right now. She's no longer my daughter and I won't have her here taking pity on me. NOW GET OUT!"

Elsie tried to reason with her, but only succeeded in making Alicia more agitated.

"Get her out of here! And you… I thought you were my

friend!"

"But Alicia, I am your friend. And you're sick. Saralynn needs to be here to help you."

Those were exactly the wrong words to have spoken, Saralynn decided later.

Her mother screamed a stream of obscenities and, when the other two women decided things couldn't get any more dicey, Alicia grabbed the bedside lamp and heaved it across the room.

"Get out of my house NOW. Both of you. Because I'm calling the police!"

Saralynn had seen her mother in rages before, but nothing in the past had prepared her for this spectacle. *It's almost as if her headache is gone; she's nothing like the suffering patient she was only a minute ago, before she discovered me.*

While both Elsie and Saralynn stood with their mouths hanging open, Alicia bent to grab the phone and dialed Nine-One-One. "I'm calling them," she crowed. "Then both of you will go to jail."

Saralynn stood with her mouth hanging at half-mast, in an absolute state of shock.

Alicia was still screaming when Elsie grabbed the phone from her hand and punched the off button. Her reward was to be beaten about the neck and shoulders by Alicia Bankston in a display of violence more graphic than any Saralynn had ever witnessed. *And I've seen her pull some pretty big stunts.*

Saralynn found her senses and went to Elsie's aid. Between the two of them, they were able to subdue Alicia and begin to coax her back into bed.

Then the doorbell rang.

"You get it," Elsie ordered. "I don't want to leave you here alone with her."

As she left the room, headed to the foyer, she heard Elsie say, "Now Alicia Bankston. You listen to me…"

She opened the door to discover two uniformed police officers on the other side. Both men tipped their hats, while the taller of the two said, "There was an interrupted Nine-One-One call from here and we're required by law to investigate."

"Yes sir," Saralynn answered honestly, "that was my mother who placed the call. But she was angry. She didn't really mean to do it."

"May we see her?" the other officer asked. "We'll need to hear that from her."

"Well, certainly. Sure. Only you have to understand that she is terribly ill, and in a great deal of pain with headaches that won't go away. She's not herself."

"Be that as it may," the first officer said, "we'll have to talk with her before we can leave."

Saralynn led them back to her mother's bedroom, not quite understanding the feeling of disaster that dogged her steps.

The officers presented themselves in the room and inquired of Elsie, "Are you the party that placed the Nine-One-One call?"

Before Elsie could answer, Alicia shot up from under the covers where she had taken retreat. "I'm the one who made the call. She pointed at Elsie. "And she's the one who took the phone away from me and hung up."

The shorter officer looked at Elsie. "Is that the way it was?"

"Yes, but you don't…"

The other officer interrupted her and addressed his remarks to Alicia. "What was the nature of your call, Ma'am?"

Alicia, who had burrowed back under the covers, rose up

again to point her finger at both Saralynn and Elsie. "This woman," she charged, pointing at Elsie, "betrayed my trust and caused me to fear for my life." Then she turned full force on Saralynn. "This woman used to be my daughter, but she lied to me, stole from me, and has attempted to manipulate legal matters so as to cost me thousands of dollars." Alicia's voice was reaching full crescendo. "I've told her never to call my phone or darken my door again, and this… this Judas…" she pointed at Elsie, "took advantage of my confidence and brought her into my home."

"But Mama…"

"Please be quiet, Miss, and let the woman speak." The first officer's command was anything but polite.

"I'm very sick, officer. I'll be seeing a specialist on Thursday, and I'm braced for the worst. I have horrible headaches that won't go away." With that said, she collapsed again on the bed. Both officers rushed immediately to her aid.

Mama should have been an actress!

"Don't worry about me, please. But get this woman out of my house. I suspect that she and my former best friend are in partnership to rob a poor, dying woman of the last possessions she has on this earth."

The older of the officers turned from the bed, while the other officer continued to tend to Alicia. "You… and you," he barked, indicating first Saralynn and then Elsie. "OUT!"

"But officer," Saralynn protested. "She's lying and she's ill. I've flown all the way from Mississippi to try and get help for her."

The officer took each one by an arm and propelled them toward the door. "I would advise you ladies to get away from this condo right now and to never come back."

As they were leaving the room, two steps ahead of the officer, all three heard Alicia's voice commanding, "The older one has my door key. Get it from her. And I wouldn't be surprised if my former daughter didn't have a copy made for herself. I'd suggest you strip-search her."

Strip-search me! Mama, you have topped yourself this time.

Saralynn was so weak with rage that by the time they reached the foyer, she collapsed on a decorative bench next to the doorway. If she hadn't been so fried, she might have been tempted to commend Alicia on her furniture selection. But that was not to be.

"You got that key?" the officer demanded of Elsie.

"Of course I do. Mrs. Bankston is ill and has to have assistance. She gave it to me."

"I'll need the key," he said coldly, as he held out his hand, palm up.

"But how am I supposed to bring her food and check in on her if I can't get in?"

"Doesn't look to me like the woman wants your help. At least that's what I heard."

With poor graces Elsie produced the key, which the officer tested in the lock and, once he was convinced it worked, dropped it in his pocket.

"I'll be giving this back to its owner."

He then opened the door to the hallway. "Remember, Mrs. Bankston wants both of you gone. That's on record."

This is absolutely insane. "But officer," Saralynn protested, "my mother is very ill – we're afraid it may be a brain tumor. I've come all the way from Mississippi to try and help her."

"The lady doesn't want your help," he growled. "Don't

they grow brains and ears down in Mississippi?"

That does it! "You haven't heard the last of this, Officer, uh…" She looked closely at his name tag, "Officer Brannigan. I'm calling my attorney."

"OUT!" he barked. "And as for that attorney, you call him! 'Cause if you're caught back at this condo, you're gonna need a lawyer!"

Unable to convince him otherwise, Saralynn and Elsie moved out into the hall and were rewarded with the sound of Alicia's door being slammed in their faces.

Elsie leaned wearily up against the wall. "Well, I never… What are we going to do now? This is insane."

Saralynn was digging in her purse for her cell phone. "I wasn't kidding when I said I was calling an attorney." She located the number for the law firm she'd used for a number of years for various matters and hit TALK.

As the number began to ring, the door to Alicia's condo opened, and both policemen prepared to leave. When they saw the two ladies still standing in the hall, the officer who'd escorted them out demanded, "You two ladies were ordered off the premises. Are we going to have to arrest you to get you to leave?"

"But Officer," Elsie protested, "I live in this building."

"Maybe so, but you don't live by this door. Go to your condo and stay there! And you…" he confronted Saralynn who, at that moment, heard her call being answered. She turned to give herself some privacy.

"This is Saralynn Reilly. I really need to speak to Mr. McCollough immediately. This is an emergency."

"Mr. McCollough is with a client, may I have…"

The young woman suddenly felt a brutal hand grabbing

her shoulder and she was spun around so hard, the cell phone flew from her hand, hit the wall nearby, and ricocheted, then hit the carpeted floor and slid.

"You don't ignore a direct order from an officer of the law," the older policeman screamed in her face. "In fact, you've flaunted everything we've told you."

"But Officer," Saralynn protested at the same time that she tried to squeeze free of his painful grip on her left forearm. "I was calling my attorney and I simply turned away to give myself some privacy."

"You want privacy? We've got a cell with your name on it where you can have all the privacy you want!"

"You're not arresting me?"

"Officer, Ms. Reilly wasn't doing anything wrong. She's my guest in this building," Elsie pleaded. "You can't arrest her."

"You," the officer pointed directly at Elsie's face, "have been warned and ordered to go back to your condo. You can obey that order… NOW… or you can accompany this woman down to the lock-up. Take your choice."

Elsie gasped, but said nothing as the color drained out of her face.

Then Saralynn found her hands being bound behind her with a plastic tie, as she was forced up the hallway, toward the exit.

"Elsie," she shouted, "get my phone. Get my phone and hit redial. Tell my attorney I need him."

Elsie's in such a state of shock I don't know if she'll even hear me, let alone do what I asked. Oh, Mama… has it truly reached the place that you'll do whatever you can to hurt me?

Then the tears came, but she wasn't sure if they were from anger or fear.

Chapter 6

*I*n her hotel room that night Saralynn showered for the third time since her attorney brought her back almost at dark. It was like she couldn't manage to wash away the filth and stench of the holding cell, where she'd stayed for what seemed like days. *In truth it was only about five hours, but it was something that didn't seem like it would ever end.*

As she scrubbed her body, already tender from two previous attacks by soap and scruffy, the young woman mentally pinched herself. *If I didn't know better, I'd think I'd been dreaming. Unfortunately, that's not the case.*

"Don't go near your mother," Lawrence McCollough advised just before he left her room. "You and I both know she's out of control, but unfortunately, at this point she has the law on her side."

Lawrence said I could be re-arrested if I even enter Mama's building, because she's getting a protective order against me. She's even accused me of stalking her.

"Mama has always been a control freak," she told the lawyer. "But now it appears that she's also ill. Gravely ill. That's why I came here, to see what I could do to help."

The attorney shrugged his shoulders as he grabbed his case and prepared to leave. "She doesn't want your help; she doesn't even want you around. She's made that very plain to the authorities. You're just lucky I was able to get you out on bail."

"But Lawrence," she wailed, "I didn't do anything!"

"Not according to Alicia. The story she tells is that you killed a money-making real estate deal in Mississippi, because you knew if you could stall it long enough, you could ultimately inherit that property yourself."

"That's insane! Mama killed that deal herself, and I know the agent who put it all together. He'll confirm what I'm telling you."

The lawyer smiled, although somewhat sadly, Saralynn thought. "It's not me you have to convince. I'm on your side. But you keep that guy's name handy, because if we can't get Alicia to see reason and drop the stalking charges, I may have to get a deposition from him in order to cast at least a shadow of doubt on her story."

I never in a million years dreamed that Mama would carry a vendetta this far. My attorney says the only way I can get control would be to petition the court to have her declared incompetent. Like I see that happening.

"Don't worry," she reassured him, as she closed the door, "I won't go anywhere near Mama. You can depend on that."

Thank goodness I still own my house here. That's the only way Lawrence was able to arrange bail so quickly. Otherwise, I would probably have spent this night in jail. The mere thought of being locked in that rancid pig-sty overnight repulsed her. *I wouldn't have slept a wink, not that I'm sure I will anyway.*

Before going to bed, Saralynn put in calls to Walter Kennedy and Donna Hasty. *I need to let someone in Magee know where I am and what's going on.*

"Oh, my gosh. You're kidding, right?"

"I'm afraid not, Mr. Walter." Saralynn had called to make sure he could give her the Jackson real estate agent's name. "I was arrested for stalking, for refusing to obey an officer, and the judge hinted that he might consider other charges as well."

"I never dreamed it would come to this, but yes, I will be glad to provide that agent's name if you need it."

Saralynn had a sudden, troubling thought. "Mr. Walter? What if the agent is so fearful of Mama he refuses to back-up what he told you."

"Let's cross that bridge when we come to it. It will cost some money, and take a little time, but your attorney can subpoena the agent's records and we can get the name of the couple who were buying the place. I doubt they would feel any loyalty to Alicia."

Her call to Donna was more of a gut-spilling, to which Donna listened and said little, allowing Saralynn a chance to vent. Once she sensed the tirade had run its course, she intervened. "Listen, friend. You've been through the mill. No doubt about that. But you know, at the end of the day, none of those charges your mama has made are true. You can hold your head high, look yourself directly in the mirror, and close your eyes tonight and sleep with a clear conscience."

"But it's so unreal. I know Mama goes to extremes, but even this is way out there for her."

"True. True enough. But you also don't know what effect

her health may be playing in this."

"Are you defending her?"

"No... no, of course not. I'm just saying that it's not logical to expect rational behavior from an irrational person. For your own protection, you need to remember this and distance yourself from her as much as possible."

Mama's made sure I'll be far away. She's getting a restraining order against her own child!

"In fact," Donna continued, "if I were you, I'd be on the first flight back tomorrow. If you're here, she won't have a basis to bring any other charges."

Donna's probably right. But if I turn tail and run, I've traveled all this way for nothing except a criminal record.

"I hear what you're saying, but I can't return until after Mama sees the doctor on Thursday. I've got to know what they tell her."

Saralynn recalled the conversation she had earlier in the afternoon, when her attorney came to post bond. Elsie was with him, brandishing Saralynn's cell phone. "Thought you might need this."

What's Elsie doing here? I've been so wrapped up in my own problems, I haven't even thought about her.

"Mama didn't have you arrested, too?"

"No," the friend replied, "but you aren't going to believe what she did do."

The two women were standing in the hallway outside the booking area, near where the lawyer was signing the last of the bond papers. "She's dropped all her charges against me and I'm back to being her best friend again."

"You're what?"

Elsie held up her right hand. "On my oath, she called me not more than half an hour after the officers left with you, to ask if I would come over and help her get to the bathroom. Said she was dizzy and was afraid she might collapse."

"You didn't fall for that, I hope."

"Nope. I'm not that stupid. I told her I couldn't come because I was under threat of arrest if I even stood by her door." Elsie paused and wiped her forehead.

"And…?"

"Alicia said that was crazy, that she didn't mean to have me arrested. Just you. Said she knew you'd manipulated me to get inside the condo, but that she forgave me."

"And you were gullible enough to swallow that?"

Elsie grinned. "Not without permission from the police. I told Alicia if she needed me, she'd have to make sure I didn't get arrested."

"She did that?"

Elsie's grin grew. "Sure did. Called Nine-One-One again."

Mama is really over the edge.

Saralynn leaned against the grimy wall, but was too fried to even care. "And that did it?"

"Not immediately. Nine-One-One dispatched officers. Would you believe, she told them she was being held prisoner in her bed?"

"So cut to the chase, Elsie. How did you get back into Mama's condo?"

"This is a new one for Alicia. When they got there, they had to break in the door. Then your mama told them that I was holding her prisoner in bed, because I refused to come and help her get to the bathroom!"

"She didn't?"

Elsie looked at Saralynn with a cocked eye. "'Fraid so. That's when one of the officers came to my door – now remember, this is the first I knew about Alicia calling for help again. When he told me what was going on, I brought him up to speed right quick on all that had gone down."

"And…?"

"Bottom line: I'm back in Alicia's good graces. At least until I mess up again." She grinned.

Lucky you! I wouldn't sleep a wink if I were in your shoes. "You didn't do anything wrong the first time. Neither did I, for that matter." Sarallynn slapped at her arm, where a black streak of grime had somehow attached itself to her. "And now, I've spent the time and money to come here. What do I have to show for it? A criminal record and I'll never know what the doctor tells Mama on…"

Elsie interrupted, "That's what I'm trying to tell you." She grinned again. "Alicia has informed me that I have to take her to the doctor Thursday."

Mama is waffling from one extreme to the other. Then it hit her. "So… so you'll be able to tell me what happens!"

"With any luck, I will."

The next forty-eight hours crawled by, as Saralynn fought to keep busy, to keep occupied. She had brought business financials with her, which helped to pass the time, but at the end of the day, she questioned if she had done them correctly. And she began brainstorming ideas for a marketing campaign centered around her Atlanta commissions. *I've got to get back home and get going on those projects. Can't afford to drop the ball on this.*

In between she made so many calls back to Mississippi, she began to fear she was becoming a nuisance. If all that wasn't enough, when her cell phone rang just minutes before Alicia's appointment time with the neurologist, displaying an unfamiliar number, she answered without even hesitating.

Something's wrong. Is it about Mama?

"Ms. Reilly?" a man's voice inquired.

"Yes, this is Saralynn Reilly." *Who is this?*

"Good afternoon, this is Jonathan Walthall in Iuka, Mississippi. Mrs. Homerline Jackson's attorney. Have I caught you at a bad time?"

The six-six-two area code should have told me this call wasn't about Mama. "Not a problem, Mr. Walthall. How can I help you?"

The lawyer went on to explain that some additional legal work would need to be done before everything connected to Emma's mother's estate was closed out. "I wondered when you were planning to be back in the area?"

When am I supposed to get any work done? "I really hadn't planned on any specific time. When do I need to be there?"

She heard him clearing his throat on the other end. "It would be good if you could be here next Monday or Tuesday. Is that a possibility?"

So quick? I don't even know when I'm going to leave here. Saralynn had purchased a round-trip ticket, but left the return open. "That depends, Mr. Walthall. I'm in Boston right now, where my mother is seeing a specialist this afternoon. The outcome of that visit will determine how much longer I'll be here."

There's that throat clearing again. It must be a telephone habit of his.

"I'm terribly sorry to hear about your mother. Why didn't you tell me you were at the doctor's? We could have talked later today or tomorrow."

But I'm not at the doctor's office with Mama, although it would be reasonable for him to assume that I was. And there's no easy way to explain why I'm not.

"It isn't a problem, I promise." She hesitated, trying to mentally juggle her work schedule, Mama's possible needs and a trip to Iuka and came up totally confused. *If only there were two of me. And on top of everything else, I'm going to have to plan to be back here in Boston to be in court at some point.*

Before she could agonize further, the attorney interrupted her thoughts. "Why don't you call me back tomorrow, after you know more about your mother's situation."

Relieved, at least temporarily, Saralynn agreed. A look at the clock confirmed that, if the doctor was on schedule, Mama was with him right then. Thus began some of the longest minutes of Saralynn's life, as she tried to imagine what was happening just a few miles away at an appointment where she wasn't welcome. *This is as bad as it was in jail, only I'm not having to sit in all that nastiness.*

After an hour, one in which Saralynn counted every minute as it passed, she was a basket case. When two hours had passed without word from Elsie, Saralynn was unable to stay seated and had begun to imagine the worst. *Has something happened between Mama and Elsie? Is the doctor running late? This late? What…?!*

Finally, after two hours, when it was approaching four-thirty, Saralynn could stand the suspense no longer and dialed Elsie's cell number. *It went to voice mail. She's not answering her phone.*

Why doesn't she call?

It was almost five-thirty, three hours after Alicia's appointment, when Saralynn's anguish was rewarded with Elsie's cell number displayed on her phone. "What has you taken so long? I've been frantic."

"Because I couldn't get free of your mother long enough to call, that's why," Elsie's tired and frustrated voice replied. "She wouldn't let me so much as get out of her sight."

I'll bet this is the first time Elsie has ever had to deal with Mama like this. "So what's the verdict?"

Elsie replied, weariness resonating in her voice, "She needs some pretty invasive tests done. But the doctor was very clear that these are more than just ordinary stress or tension headaches."

I'm not surprised at any of this. "So when are the tests?"

"That's what we don't know. His office will be scheduling them and then call Alicia with the dates and times. But for sure it won't be until sometime next week at the earliest, although this doctor says the sooner the better."

"Now I'm in real limbo… Don't know what to do. I've got commission work waiting at home that has to get done, and I've got some business in north Mississippi that I need to deal with." *I'm not going to tell Elsie about Emma and the property I've inherited. She might accidentally let it slip to Mama and I don't need to give her any more ammunition.*

"I think your best bet is to go back home." Elsie released a long and audible sigh that Saralynn interpreted as frustration. "I tried my best to talk to your mama today, but where you're concerned, her mind's made up. She doesn't want anything to do with you, and for certain, she doesn't want you anywhere near her."

Mama's serious about this. "Tell me, Elsie. What did I do to deserve this?"

"I was about to ask you the same question, because it's one your mama will not discuss under any circumstances. Not even today, even after the doctor told us he strongly suspects a brain tumor, she still won't budge."

"You know Mama's always been stubborn."

"But I've never seen her this determined to have things her way. So tell me, Saralynn, just what did happen between the two of you?"

Do I tell her the truth? I have no reason to be ashamed. Yet I feel very unfaithful sharing the details. "I'm not going to give you the nitty-gritty, but once we got to Mississippi last fall, I learned that everything is not exactly the way Mama always told us. Without meaning to, I caught her in some serious lies, and she's uncomfortable because I know the truth."

"Whew! Knowing Alicia as I do, that wasn't an easy pill for her to swallow." She was quiet for a moment. "But it would explain the response I got when I suggested she should make amends with you. After all, you're her only kin, and she may need you by the time all of this plays out."

"I'm almost afraid to ask, but what was her reply?"

"She said everybody connected to Mississippi had always mistreated her and now you were one of them."

Poor Mama. Always the martyr. Only this time she may be mistreating herself. "I'm sorry she feels that way Elsie. You can believe me or not, but things in Mississippi were… well, let's just say, different from the way we've always been led to believe. And I know what I'm talking about."

Saralynn played with the knick-knacks on the sofa table; stacking and re-stacking the geometric blocks, as if somehow, she could make sense of all that was happening and somehow fix it. However, the more she listened to Elsie, and the more she re-arranged the cubes, she became convinced Mama was the only one who could fix the situation. She herself was incapable of even creating something from the simple miniature blocks.

"Earth to Saralynn. Earth to Saralynn…"

"Huh? Oh, sorry Elsie. I was just trying to find some sort of solution that would allow Mama to save face, but the sad fact is, she's already been caught. As the old saying goes, it would be easier to put the toothpaste back in the tube."

There was a quick intake of breath that echoed across the distance. "You're not washing your hands of Alicia, are you?"

"I'll be there for her, regardless, if she'll ever let me. But that doesn't look very likely at this point. And I'm not going to sit still and let her have me arrested again."

"So you're going back to Mississippi?"

Elsie makes "back to Mississippi" sound so suspect. "If you mean I'm going home, the answer is 'yes.' I'm going back to Mississippi where I live now. That's where home is and that's where I belong."

The two talked for a few more minutes, before Saralynn ended the conversation to call and book her return to Jackson.

Back in her bed in Magee the next evening, Saralynn reflected on all that had happened over the previous thirty hours. Elsie had picked her up the next morning and the two had breakfast, where the older woman promised to stay as close to Alicia as she was allowed, and to keep Saralynn posted.

Chapter 7

Saturday was spent washing clothes and repacking for Iuka, working in the studio on the first of the thirty commissions, and visiting with Emma at Boswell. *I feel guilty not telling her I'm going to Iuka. But right now, I think I need to fly this one solo and give Emma some more time to adjust to her mother being gone.*

Sunday at church, it was like all the good for the entire week had been saved up and was being enjoyed at one time. One after another, friends and even good acquaintances had to hug her neck, ask about Alicia, and to tell her they had missed her.

And I've missed them, as well. I didn't realize how much until just now.

During the morning worship, Saralynn sat with Donna Hasty, in the same pew where she sat the first time she ever visited Rials Creek United Methodist Church. *I don't want to call it "my" pew, but it does feel like home! And I like the feeling. But I still feel like the* rest of these people have something I don't.

The pastor, before he began his talk for the morning, which Saralynn had learned months before was called a sermon, read a verse from his Bible that he said came from Proverbs, chapter three, the fifth verse. Saralynn had begun using one of the pew Bibles, and she read along with him, *"Trust in the Lord with all thine heart; and lean not unto thine own understanding."*

Following this, the choir sang a song that was obviously selected to accompany that verse, because it was about learning to lean on God. There was one line in the song that stayed with Saralynn well into the next several days. *"All that He asks is a child-like faith…" I can well remember how easily Marc believed whatever he was told.*

Once church was over, Donna insisted that Saralynn have lunch with them, and she eagerly accepted. Back home, full and content after second helpings of marinated pork tenderloin, sweet potato casserole, English peas and Waldorf salad, she continued packing and loading the car, planning for an early morning departure.

At church for the evening service, it was like a family reunion all over again. *Family reunion. I'd never thought about it like that, but these people are my family; at this point the only family I have.*

As she inserted the key into the vintage front door of the house in Fishtrap Hollow, Saralynn was once again overwhelmed with the knowledge that this house now belonged to her. *Of course I know Mrs. Jackson left it to me, as safekeeping for Emma. So it's not really my house. Never mind whose name is on the deed!*

Merry Heart

The drive up had been long and lonesome. *Emma never talks a lot, but I guess I got more accustomed to having someone with me than I realized.* Saralynn unloaded and settled in her customary room, then walked through the house to ensure that everything was in order. *Got to make a grocery list and go to the store.* As she looked through cabinets and drawers to determine what she might need, Saralynn was struck again with the reality that the house she stood in, and every possession in it, belonged to her. *I'm still not sure how I feel about all of this.*

Driving back into Iuka just before dusk, she noticed farther up Eastport Street, ahead of her, a brick building with a soaring steeple. *That's a church, but I never noticed it before. Maybe because I always had Emma with me.* As she got closer, she could see the lights were on inside the church, and the illuminated stained glass windows glowed warm and inviting.

She read the sign out front. *Iuka United Methodist Church.* Then, as she stopped at the four-way intersection, she realized that the church on the opposite corner was the First Baptist Church. *What's the difference between a Methodist church and a Baptist church? If they all worship the same God, why do they* have *different names?* She made a mental note to ask Mr. Walter.

Once in the supermarket, Saralynn was kept busy learning the layout of a different store and finding the items on her list. That night, following a microwaved frozen lasagna, toasted garlic bread, and a green salad, she elected instead of watching TV, to go on to bed with a good book. Before crawling in, however, she laid out her clothes for the next day then, after checking the locks one last time, allowed the weariness of the day to claim her.

As she snuggled to find her comfortable spot under the covers, the image of the brightly-lit stained glass windows of the

Iuka United Methodist Church revisited her. And for reasons she could not fathom, save for the cosmetic aesthetics of the building, she realized that the church was drawing her.

Brrr!

When she awoke very early the next morning, the first thing Saralynn noticed was a chill in the room. *Gosh it's a little nippy. I keep forgetting I'm not in south Mississippi any longer.* She knew, having ventured out to explore the area on an earlier trip, that she was only about ten miles south of the Tennessee state line. *The climate is different here.* The first thing she did after bravely crawling out from beneath the warm covers was to close the windows she had opened the previous evening.

After she fixed herself a couple of slices of buttered toast and a bowl of cereal, it was off to the shower, then to Jon Walthall's law office downtown in Iuka.

I thought everything was already settled, but I guess not. The issue caused her to think about her grandmother's estate and what, if anything, Alicia had done on that matter. *I don't see how she could have closed out the estate without selling the house, but then I'm not a lawyer..*

It was a quick drive into town. The attorney's office was in one of the old historic buildings within sight of the railroad tracks running parallel to Front Street, across from Jay Bird Park. The temperature was warming rapidly, the sun was shining, and there wasn't a cloud in the morning's blue sky.

It would be a great day to be anywhere, except cooped up in an attorney's office. I hope this won't take all day.

While she was dressing, Saralynn had been struck with the realization that all of her previous research into her McIntire roots had been conducted around respect for Mrs. Jackson and Emma, and their schedules and needs. *For the first time, I don't have anyone to consider or report to. I can come and go as I please.*

She had made up her mind right then, even if it meant staying a few extra days, while she was in Tishomingo County she was going to track down every piece of McIntire genealogical information, every tidbit she could.

"Ms. Reilly, it's good to see you again." Jon Walthall came out to greet her once the secretary announced her arrival. He shook her hand and directed her into his private office. "I've got everything ready, and I think we can make short order of it."

Saralynn accepted his invitation and seated herself where he indicated, in one of the chairs at the small, round conference table at the far end of the long office. She was amused to find an abundance of college-related memorabilia from both the University of Mississippi, better known as Ole Miss, and Mississippi State University. *Ian Scarborough in Magee calls State "Moo Miss", and says he's proud to have graduated from the cow college.*

She couldn't help but comment. "You have a beautiful office, Mr. Walthall." Then she grinned. "You'll have to forgive me, I was an interior designer too long, I guess. Once it gets in your blood, it never leaves."

"Thank you, I'll be sure to tell my wife, because she's the one who decorated it."

"Your wife's a designer?"

"Not professionally. She just has a knack for putting colors and shapes together."

"I was the designer, but my mother was born with more

design ability than I acquired in school." *Speaking of Mama, I'm going to need to call Elsie when I leave here.* "But there is one thing that puzzles me, if you won't think me too forward."

The attorney looked expectantly, and not without some degree of curiosity. "Go ahead."

"I've haven't been a Mississippian for quite a year yet, but I've been here long enough to understand that you don't pay tribute to Ole Miss and Mississippi State in the same breath. So why…?"

"So why is this office riding the fence?" he interrupted. "Remember my wife, the designer? She's a diehard State alumnus. Every member of her family for the past four generations has graduated in Starkville." It was his turn to grin. "Me, on the other hand, I went to Ole Miss like every good Mississippi lawyer worth his shingle."

It was Saralynn's turn to grin. "So let me guess… your wife wouldn't agree to decorate your office with your Ole Miss ties if she didn't get equal billing?"

Jon Walthall's face colored and he ducked his head. "That's about how it shakes out."

"Again, my compliments to your wife. She's equally as adept at negotiation as she is at design. I'd like to meet her sometime."

The attorney had retrieved a folder of papers from his desk and now settled in a chair at Saralynn's left. "It's more like intimidation, at least where I'm concerned. And if you're serious, she's meeting me here at eleven forty-five to have lunch. We'd be glad to have you join us."

"Surely you don't want me tagging along."

"On the contrary, I think Maryanne would love to meet you."

Why not? "If you're really sure she won't mind, I'll gladly accept." Then she thought for a moment. "I do have a couple of short errands to run, but maybe I'll have time to do that and meet you back here at about the right time."

"Great! As soon as we finish, you can be on your way. I'll call and give her the news."

There were a number of documents that required Saralynn's signature, and several procedures pertaining to Emma's guardianship that the two covered over the next half hour. Then Saralynn was ready to leave.

"We could have done this over the phone, or even by mail," the attorney explained as he walked her to the door. "But I just thought if we could both sit down at the same table, it would make you feel better to be able to ask questions and understand how the laws apply."

"And I do; feel better, that is." She consulted her watch. "If I'm back here by eleven-thirty, that gives me almost an hour and a half. That ought to be enough time."

"See you then."

Saralynn's first stop was the Tishomingo County Historical Museum and Genealogical Society. Jon Walthall had pointed out the large red and white, two-story structure as they stood on the sidewalk outside this office. "It used to be the county courthouse," he explained.

For Saralynn, discovering it was so close meant even more time for the task at hand. It had been a comment someone made at Mrs. Jackson's funeral that inspired her to see if the archives housed there might yield more complete information than she could gather piecemeal, on her own.

Once inside the restored structure that still retained much of its architectural integrity, Saralynn found a helpful volunteer named Kathy Lucas. "That's Kathy with a 'K'," the woman told her. "Just how can we help you this morning?"

Saralynn explained that she was researching her family's roots in the area. "My grandmother's maiden name was McIntire," she explained. "I'm not even sure what her parents' names were. All I know is they were from Fishtrap Hollow."

"What are you trying to find?" Kathy with a "K" asked. "We can go several different directions with this."

What am I trying to find? Exactly? I don't guess I've ever defined for myself what I want. "I'm greedy," she said with a laugh. "I want it all." Then she sobered. "I know so little about my grandmother's family, until anything I learn will be new and certainly more than I had."

The volunteer had grabbed a note pad and was scribbling as Saralynn talked. "Let me ask you some questions."

The woman's smile immediately put her at ease, and it was with a breath of relief that Saralynn said, "Of course. You do this everyday." *Normally I don't go anywhere as ill-prepared as I am today.*

"Your grandmother's full name was what?"

I don't know what her other name was, or even if Sallie was her first name or middle name. In her mind's eye she tried to picture Miss Sallie's headstone at Rials Creek Cemetery, but couldn't. "Her name was Sallie – that was spelled 'ie', not 'y'. And I don't know if she had another name besides Sallie." Saralynn halted, uncertain of how best to proceed.

"When was she born?" the volunteer prompted.

I can't remember. "Again, I'm not sure," she said, apologetically. "I know that she was sixteen when she was taken from here to the TB sanatorium in south Mississippi in about 1943. So that would have made her born in, what... about 1927?"

"And her last name was McIntire? Spelled with a capital 'I', not an 'E'?"

"That much I know," she said, happy to finally be able to answer some of the questions.

"This may not seem like a lot," Mrs. Lucas explained, "but in genealogy, it's the little facts that can open all the doors. Now..." she looked at her list. "Her parents. Do you know their names?"

I've never even thought about Miss Sallie's parents, other than to condemn them for not loving her enough after they sent her to the hospital. She searched her scanty memories of conversations and what she'd read in the diaries. Then, without warning, it came to her. In one of the newspaper clippings Miss Sallie had kept from her hometown newspaper, was the mention of her parents. But what was it? Their names were right on the tip of her tongue.

Kathy Lucas attempted to come to the rescue. "It's OK if you don't know. It's just that the more we know now, the faster we can come up with what you're lacking."

"But I should know this. It's this close," she indicated with two fingers about half an inch apart, "it's this close to the end of my tongue."

"Don't worry, we can find..."

"J.W. McIntire!" she squealed. "J.W. and... and... Nona..., no... Naomi. That's it! J.W. and Naomi McIntire." She felt very pleased with herself. "But now don't ask me what J.W. stood for, because I don't have the first clue."

Mrs. Lucas laughed. "Maybe you will after we finish. Let's see," she said, looking at her notes again. "I assume you'd like to know where they're buried, who their families were... oh, I nearly forgot... do you know if Sallie was an only child?"

I don't know? I came here to learn things and the main thing I'm learning is that I didn't know nearly as much as I though I did! "You know, I don't. I just never heard it mentioned." *Of course, if Mama had anything to say about it, I wouldn't know what little I do.* She immediately felt a pang of guilt. *I promised myself I'd call Elsie as soon as I got out of Mr. Walthall's office, but when he pointed out that I was just across the tracks from the museum, I totally forgot.*

"That's one I can't answer, but now you've got me wondering."

"And I suppose," Kathy said with a wide smile on her face that Saralynn suspected was a permanent feature, "if there are still any family members living here, you'd like to know that as well?"

"Oh... but..., yes... of course." She stuttered and stammered over her words. *What a dunderhead I am! Of course there might be later generations of Miss Sallie's family still living right here in Tishomingo County. I wonder how they would feel about discovering a new cousin?*

As she contemplated the possibility of still more family she didn't know, her eyes traveled around the room, to the photographs of days past, and of the often stern, austere individuals who had populated those brown-tinted pictures. *Could some of these people be my ancestors and me not even know it?*

Then the thought hit. "I know it's a long shot, Mrs. Lucas" she pleaded, "but if you have any photos in the files of any of my family, I'd love to find those as well."

"Please, just call me Kathy. And as for photos, we do have a collection. But we'll take it a step at a time. Let's find who your family is, and then, perhaps, we can scare up some photos to help bring them to life."

Saralynn left, after telling her new friend that she would

be in town for the remainder of the week, and would check back before leaving. *I also told her that I didn't necessarily expect results before I left.*

After consulting her watch and seeing that she still had about twenty minutes, Saralynn headed for the post office where she purchased stamps and dropped a couple of letters in the mail. *Tonight I've got to chain myself to the table and not quit until I have this PR mailing ready to go.* In an effort to be as conservative with time as possible, she had brought paperwork and marketing campaigns with her, in the hope she could get at least some of her work out of the way.

Then it was back to downtown to meet Jon and Maryanne Walthall for lunch. *I wonder what she's like? He's so outgoing, it would be hard to imagine him married to a wallflower.* She chuckled. *I'll be very surprised if that's the case. That was no wallflower that got equal billing for her college in decorating his office. Nope... I want to meet this woman.*

As she pulled into a parking space near the law office, she saw a titan-haired woman of average build entering the firm's front door. *Could that be her?* Saralynn made her way up the sidewalk and into the foyer, where she greeted the receptionist. "I'm Saralynn Reilly. I'm supposed to meet Mr. and ..."

"Jon and me for lunch."

Saralynn turned around, in the direction of the voice, to find the red-haired woman she'd seen earlier, beaming at her.

"I'm so glad Jon suggested that you join us. To be honest, I've been wanting to meet this person Mrs. Jackson couldn't say enough good things about." Her smile wrapped from ear to ear but, as Saralynn noted, there wasn't anything contrived or insincere about it.

I'd give most anything to know what Mrs. Jackson told people. It's hard enough to live up to your reputation when you know what it is. This is like trying to hit an invisible target.

"Believe me," she told the attorney's wife, "I'd like to meet that person as well. I'm afraid Mrs. Jackson may have stretched the truth a little."

"My husband doesn't think so."

Obviously I've been the topic of conversation.

"Your husband is too kind."

"He has his good points," his wife said and chuckled. "Say, why don't we sit over here where we can talk and get acquainted while we wait on Jon? If he says eleven-forty-five, he really means about twelve-fifteen."

This woman has no illusions that her husband is perfect. But I like her. I'd have said the same thing about Peter.

The two sat and visited, until Saralynn remembered she still hadn't called Elsie. *I'd like to think that no news is good news, but I'd better not take the chance.* "Will you excuse me just a minute," she asked her new acquaintance, who had insisted that she be called MA, "Mother is having some health issues and I promised I'd call this morning to see how things were going."

"Of course," the redhead agreed. "Take your time. This isn't court week, so Jon isn't pressed at lunch time." She laughed and it sounded like bone china. "We've waited on him, he can wait on us."

Saralynn excused herself and went out to her car, where she called Elsie's cell. Three rings later, she was rewarded with the sound of the older woman's voice. "I'm glad to hear from you. I wondered if you'd forgotten us."

"Far from it, Elsie. It's just that I've been so covered with everything that stacked up while I was away."

"Looks like your mother would be at the top of your list regardless."

Don't try to run a guilt trip. It won't work. Or, as I heard Dave Hasty tell somebody the other day, "That dog don't hunt". Saralynn was secretly delighted that she'd managed to remember the southern expression and had found an occasion to use it. "Mama is at the top of my list, which is why I came home to try and get some work done, just in case I'm needed later, and Mama can be convinced to let me help her. So how are things?"

"No worse, but definitely no better. I'll take her tomorrow for some kind of sophisticated MRI the doctor thinks will tell us what step is next. As for Alicia, she's still from one extreme to the other with her actions."

"Like what, for example?"

"Yesterday, after lunch, she threw me out, screaming that I was spying for you and planning to kill her."

"She said that!?"

"So I left. An hour later, she called me and wanted to know why I'd left her, didn't I care about her any more?"

If I didn't know what a control freak Mama is, I'd be very worried. I don't know if we're dealing with someone who is seriously ill, or is she being deceptive and playing all of this to her advantage? "I don't know what to tell you, Elsie. I'm sorry she's jerking you around, but there's not much I can do at this point." *Oh, Mama, if only you could understand the damage you do and the people you hurt when you act like this. We don't know if you're crying wolf or not.*

"You have the MRI tomorrow, but when do you see the doctor?

"He said he would call after he got the results and had a

chance to review them."

Just then she spotted Jon and Maryanne...er, MA leaving the law office. "Elsie, I've got to go. I've got a business lunch and the rest of my party is here." *I don't want to sound like I'm insincere or using her.* "Hang in there with Mama as long as you can, and please call me tomorrow, after the MRI." *I can make the promise, but can I keep it?* "If I'm truly needed, I will come immediately. I just don't want to be arrested again."

Elsie agreed that Saralynn should stay away for the present, and promised to call. Saralynn waved at her lunch partners, who walked over to her car. "Why don't you both hop in with me and I'll drive. Provided you give me directions, that is!" *I don't even know where we're going.*

Jon Walthall was the first to speak. "Not necessary. We're going to walk. The exercise will do us good."

We're walking? But I've got on heels. Oh, my aching feet.

MA snickered. "Don't let him fool you, Saralynn. We're going right down the street to Café Memories." She pointed to a building a few doors away. "You'll love the food... and the atmosphere."

And Saralynn did. "This place would be worth the price just to come in and look at all the history on the walls," she told her companions. "Add in the good food, and you for sure can't beat it."

The three enjoyed a long, leisurely lunch of fresh, French onion soup, deli sandwiches and tea. Over dessert, MA asked, "So how long will you be here this trip?"

I've been acting like I'm a lady of leisure, but I do have other responsibilities. Emma, for one. "I'll leave no later than next Monday. Early. I'm trying to touch base with Emma, at least every other day – although that obviously won't happen this week – and I have a business to run."

"A business? What do you do?"

Saralynn explained about her fabric arts business and, before she realized it, the two women were talking decorating. "I'd love to see some of your work. I might find some clients for you in this part of the state."

"I'll be glad to share some of my PR with you. As a matter of fact, I brought the contents of a mailing with me to work on while I'm here. I can drop the brochure by to you tomorrow."

"Or…," Jon Walthall said, looking at his wife…

"Are you thinking the same thing I am?"

"Saralynn, don't let us put you on the spot, but we'd love to have you join us for supper at our church tomorrow night."

"Gee… that's awfully nice of you, but I don't know…" Her voice trailed off. *I don't even know what church they attend.*

"It's very informal," MA assured her. "We gather in the Fellowship Hall to eat a prepared meal, then we have a time of devotion afterwards." She hesitated. "Please say you'll come. We'll even pick you up and take you back home."

Saralynn couldn't see how to decline without being rude, so she said, "I'd love to come, but you probably will have to chauffeur me, because I only know a few main roads around here."

"We'll be glad to drive you, but you'd have no problem finding our church," Jon advised. "It's Iuka First United Methodist on Eastport Street, about two blocks from here." He pointed toward the northwest corner of the building where they still sat around the lunch table.

"Is that the brick church with the beautiful stained glass windows?"

"One and the same. Why?"

"I came by there last night, when the lights were on, and the windows were lit and were so inviting. It really made me want to stop and go in."

"Then that settles it," MA vowed, "you have to be our guest. And we'll still pick you up, and I can get the information on your business at the same time."

As they were about to leave, Saralynn was struck with an idea. Cautiously, she asked, "Jon, do you have time on your calendar either this afternoon or tomorrow, to see me in a professional capacity? And I expect to pay you."

"Well, sure. I'm pretty wide open this afternoon. But everything is settled on Mrs. Jackson's business. And she's already paid my bill."

The three were walking back up Fulton Street from the café. "No, no. This is something else, personal to me, and I need some legal advice. If you won't let me pay you, I'll take my business to another attorney!"

The lawyer laughed. "You drive a hard bargain, Saralynn. I'm available right now, and the sooner I can begin earning my fee, the better I'll like it."

Jon and his wife hugged, then MA and Saralynn hugged, before MA slid into her car and the other two continued inside to the private office where Saralynn had begun her day.

Once they were settled, Jon Walthall with a yellow legal pad in his lap, and pen in hand, said, "OK. So what's this all about? You truly do seem troubled, if the expression on your face is any indication."

"The matter I need to discuss with you is extremely serious, but as I go over the facts in my mind, I wouldn't blame you if you thought I'd gone 'round the bend."

Jon laughed, then quickly sobered. "The last thing I'd do would be to doubt your sanity. So whatever it is, lay it on me and let's see what we can do to relieve your anxiety."

"OK. Here goes. And when I'm finished, don't say I didn't warn you." Saralynn began at the very beginning, of her earliest years in Boston and the manner in which her mother had raised her, including the slant she had placed on family matters. When she reached the part where Peter and Marc were killed, the attorney interrupted.

"Oh, gosh, Saralynn. That had to have been rough. And now, a year later, we've put you through the wringer again with Emma and Mrs. Jackson."

"That's OK, Jon. I'm a lot stronger today than I was a year ago." She continued her story of how she initially came to Mississippi, the discovery of Miss Sallie's diaries and the revelation of her mother's lies and fabrication that led to the estrangement. She concluded with the events of the last few days, including her arrest and pending case for stalking."

"Whew!" Jon Walthall was shaking his head. "That reads like a made-for-TV movie script. And you're right, if I didn't know you, I would question your grasp on reality."

"I told you."

"That is some more story. So what do you need from me?"

"I have an attorney in Boston, but I'm truly not comfortable telling him all that I've just told you." She laughed. "Which makes no sense, because I've known him for fifteen years and I haven't even known you for fifteen weeks. But for some reason, I'm comfortable laying all this dirty linen out before you."

"I take that as a high compliment." His face beamed.

"Thank you. Now what is it you need to know, exactly?"

Saralynn hesitated. *This is silly. I've opened the door, I have to go through. Tell this man what you need!* "What are my rights? Or do I have any rights? I don't have a good feeling about how all this is going to shake out, and despite what she has done, I want to be there for her, to help her. But I cannot walk in there again with no defense against another arrest." She spread her hands, palms up, in an expression of defeat. "Is there anything I can do?"

"Your own mother actually charged you with stalking and had you arrested?"

"That's about the size of it."

"That's cold. To say the least." The attorney rose and began to pace the room. "I'm not ignoring you, it's just that I think best on my feet." He grinned. "Comes in real handy in the courtroom."

Saralynn matched his grin. "I can only imagine."

He walked the length of the room several times in silence. Then he turned, faced her, and began to speak. "First of all, I'm not familiar with Massachusetts' laws, so anything I say would be subject to me checking those laws to be certain I was advising you correctly."

"I understand."

"We're going to look at this as if it were a matter confined to Mississippi. Then if you want me to, I can do some research and see if things would be any different there."

"That's what I want." Saralynn had risen from her seat. "You'll have to pardon me, but sometimes I listen better while I walk."

Jon swung his arm in invitation. "Make yourself at home. My office is your office." Then he continued. "I think we're safe in assuming that your mother isn't going to listen to reason. At least not until and unless something gets her attention big time."

"I would agree. So what gets her attention?"

"Before we talk about that, let's talk about her current mental state, which is also possibly connected to her physical condition, if I'm hearing you correctly."

Saralynn stopped pacing and turned to face the attorney. "Mama has always been a control freak. It literally was her way or the highway. It's only now that I realize she and I didn't have problems earlier because I simply didn't fight her. Now that I have, she's freaking out, and I've seen truly bizarre behavior out of her for the past year." She paused, seeking her words. "Behavior... behavior that I would never have believed possible. Now it's even worse."

"Here's what I think you should do. If, indeed, your mother truly is ill with a brain tumor, her behavior may become even more irrational than it is now. Should that occur, as her closest blood relative, you might find yourself having to petition the court for her guardianship, or whatever they call it. If you already have a court action against your mother and, if as a part of that action, you can get sworn depositions from two or three of the people who've been on the receiving end of this behavior, it would give you a much better basis to ask the court for control of all her business and her welfare."

Saralynn's face displayed her astonishment. "You're saying I should sue my own mother?"

"'Fraid so."

"But for what?"

"Slander. She accused you of stalking her and stealing from her in front of witnesses. False arrest. Abuse of the judicial system by filing a frivolous lawsuit. By using the judicial system to assist her in doing a hatchet job on you." He looked at her with no trace of a smile on his face. "Face it, Saralynn, you're the underdog in this situation, and the only way you can hope to even level the playing field is to play the same game she's playing."

"But it sounds so cruel, so callus."

"Doesn't it? But it's also the game your mother has been playing. When you put two teams on the field, and one plays baseball and the other plays football, you're never going to have a winner. That's where you are right now."

"There's no other way?"

"Sure. You can do nothing and let the game play out as it will. But I can tell you that unless you get some court-ordered protection for yourself, you're never going to be able to care for her – unless she's unconscious and unresponsive, and then there are other laws that come into play." He walked over and placed his hand on her shoulder. "It's tough, I know. But by filing this lawsuit, you force her to have to respond. When... if... she does, you're compelling her to come into court and bring proof of the charges she has brought against you. If you allege that her behavior toward you, and others, is the result of conditions relating to her physical well-being, then she has to counter those charges as well and show that she does not have a tumor... or dementia... or Alzheimer's... or whatever."

"And when she does come to court and either can't substantiate those charges, or worse yet, for her, better for me, she exhibits some of the same behaviors she has shown for the past few weeks, the judge is going to recognize that she is not a rational person."

"Now you're getting the picture."

"I rather there were some other way, but I don't know what it is. So how do I go forward from here?" She looked at him and smiled, but the expression didn't make it to her lips. "I really wish you could represent me."

"Well, I can't. But there are several things I can do."

"Such as?"

"For starters, I'm going to make some calls to Boston, both to inquire about Massachusetts law in particular and, to try and find an attorney who would be right for you and for your mother. After all, Saralynn, remember… at the end of the day, you're not an ungrateful child out to rob her mother. You're a daughter who is truly concerned for her mother's situation, and is seeking a safe way to provide for her welfare."

Saralynn turned to face him. "We're not looking for someone who will go for the jugular, but we do want someone who is hard-nosed and determined."

"Exactly. And, I would suggest that you get everything ready to file this suit, but hold off until after she gets the results of the MRI. It sounds like this doctor is pretty convinced there's a tumor there. The questions are, first of all, is it malignant? Or is it benign? In either event, if it is pressing on her brain, is it responsible for the behavioral changes and mood swings? And last, but equally important, can it be removed and give her an enhanced quality of life?"

"Gosh, I hadn't let my thinking go that far, but it all makes sense. And as you say, I'm not trying to rob my mother, despite her protests to the contrary."

"You've got the picture, Saralynn. Shall I proceed?"

"Take it and run with it." She grinned at him as she pulled her checkbook from her purse. "Now, how much do I owe you?

I'm sure you'll need a retainer, as well as today's consultation charge."

The attorney rubbed his chin with his fingers, grabbed his legal pad and made some scratches, then announced, "Let's just put today's charge on a tab, I promise I won't stiff you."

"That I can live with, but how much do you need for the retainer?"

"Come here and hold out both hands."

Confused, but trying to cooperate, Saralynn did as he asked. When both hands were out in front of her, he took each of her hands in his, and said, "Would you bow your head with me for a word of prayer?

Without waiting for an answer, he began, *Lord, we would ask Your blessing on this young woman who has seen more than her share of grief in the past year, and is now faced with the unenviable task of trying to care for an ill mother who is determined not to be cared for. Please guide our actions and our thoughts in this matter, so that always our focus in on Alicia Bankston's welfare, not our own grievances or greed. Lord, to sue one's parent is a hard action but is one that we believe is necessary under these particular circumstances. Hold us close, Lord. Walk with us, and let the words of our mouths and the meditations of our hearts be acceptable in Your sight. In the holy name of Your Son, Jesus. Amen.*

Saralynn realized that tears were again trickling down her cheeks, and speech was difficult to come by. *Can I never hear a prayer without crying?* Finally, she was able to find her voice, and although it was shaky, she said, "I don't think I've ever paid an attorney in quite this manner."

"You've never had to sue your mother before, either.

Chapter 8

Saralynn returned to Fishtrap Hollow burdened with the news she had received and the steps she had approved. *Mama, if only you could understand how your stubborness pushes people into actions they would never have considered otherwise.*

Still, the knowledge that she had agreed to sue her own mother rested uneasily. In the end, she placed a call to Walter Kennedy in Magee. *I've got to bounce this off someone, and I trust Mr. Walter to tell me if I've done the right thing. It's not too late to call a halt.*

"I can understand why you're feeling hesitant," he told her after she brought him up to speed. "It is a rather drastic step." He hesitated. "That said; however, I believe this lawyer fellow is right on target. You've got to protect yourself, and I don't mean just from arrest. Alicia may well become incapable of managing her own affairs."

"That's what Jon Walthall said. And I'm certain that both

of you are on target. It just feels so strange, so ungrateful to sue my own mother."

"I'm very sure it does. It's not the way things are normally done.p"

A second call to Katie Brooks elicited a similar response. "Under no circumstances, except in dire need, would you take such a step. You know that, so stop beating up on Saralynn. You're playing the hand that was dealt you."

I guess she's right. To a large extent, I am beating up on me. But I'm also questioning if there was something that I could have done way back that would make a difference now. And I can't think of one single thing, except…to have knuckled under to Mama."

"So how is Emma? *Don't want to forget to ask before I end this call.*

"Emma is doing fine. She's a lot more resilient than anyone realizes."

"I just feel so funny being here in her house, and she doesn't even know. It doesn't seem right."

"It may not seem right, but it's the way Mrs. Jackson wanted it. Just think of it as you protecting it so that Emma can enjoy it when she's had enough time to accept all that's happened."

"I guess you're right. It's just that I walk through the house thinking I'm going to find Mrs. Jackson cooking or cleaning. And I can't walk across the front porch without seeing Emma in one of the big rockers."

"That's all very natural, Saralynn. After all, this is your first trip back since Mrs. Jackson's funeral. Give yourself time."

"Part of what hurts is that this reminds me so much of what it was like in my house after Peter and Marc died."

"That's all very normal, too."

"I wish it felt normal to me. Between Mrs. Jackson not being here and actively planning to file what amounts to a frivolous lawsuit against my own mother, I'm not sure I know me any more."

"You're Saralynn Reilly. And you're not a bad guy, so don't try to give yourself the stripes for it."

Saralynn was still unconvinced. "I guess."

"Listen, Paul is waking up from his nap and I need to grab him before he has a chance to get into mischief. Just wait 'til you get home and I bring you up to date on some of his "accomplishments" so far."

"You go see to him, and give him a kiss from his Aunt Saralynn."

As the connection was breaking, she called out, "And thanks for taking time to deal with a basket case." Only she didn't know if Katie heard her or not.

Still seeking reassurance, she dialed Donna Hasty's number, praying silently that her friend would answer. After five rings, when she was about to admit defeat, a harried voice on the other end announced, "Hold on, Saralynn. Right back..."

Evidently I called at a bad time. She consulted her watch. Two-seventeen. *The kids shouldn't be home from school yet. I hope nothing's wrong.*

After what seemed forever, and Saralynn was beginning to really worry, there was the reassuring voice. "Hey," Donna called out, "I'm sorry. But I was up to my knees in water. Well, almost."

Initially too shocked to respond, Saralynn finally found her voice again. "Knee-deep in water? What happened?" Then, realizing that perhaps she was contributing to the problem, she announced, "Let me hang up and you call me back when you get things straight."

"No, no," Donna protested. "It's all under control now. That's why I had to keep you waiting."

"Whatever happened? You've got to tell me."

Donna laughed. "I promise it isn't going to be nearly as exciting as you're making it out to be."

It was Saralynn's turn to laugh. "So tell me and I'll be the judge."

Five minutes later, the two ladies were still laughing about Donna's efforts to combat a new washing machine that had been connected incorrectly.

"Water was going everywhere," Donna explained. "I didn't think I would ever be able to get to the faucets to turn off the water, because I kept slipping and losing my footing." She laughed again. "That water was pouring out like a geyser."

The mental image of Donna fighting the water made Saralynn think of the extensive damage the broken pipe did in Alicia's condo. "Please tell me you were able to get it shut off before it did any damage to your house."

"That's why I was working so hard and couldn't talk."

After a few more comments about the damage that runaway water can do, Donna asked, "So why'd you call? Not that it isn't good to hear from you."

Saralynn hit the high spots regarding Jon Walthall's suggestions. "I just can't help feeling that I'm over-stepping here. After all, she is my mama."

Donna was quiet for a minute, before she asked, "Have you thought about calling Mr. Walter? He's awfully good at things like this."

"I already did."

"Well, what was his take?"

Saralynn groaned. "He felt like it was pretty drastic but that probably it was the only way to resolve all the problems we have here."

"So let me get this straight…"

Saralynn could see her friend's grin on the other end of the conversation. "Mr. Walter gives you the green light and then you call me?"

The grin was still there, but Saralynn hadn't caught it. "I just needed reassurance."

"Well, honey. You got it. If Mr. Walter thinks it's the thing to do, far be it from me to disagree."

"Gee, you're no help."

"Seriously, Saralynn. I would trust Walter Kennedy with my life, because he's a lot smarter than I am. I can understand why you feel as torn as you do, but if Mr. Walter thinks it's the right course of action, I'd be right there with him."

"I guess you're right."

"Has he ever steered you wrong? Or placed his own agenda over your welfare?"

Saralynn had to think back at how he had rescued her when Mama basically threw her out of Miss Sallie's house. About how he had seen to it that she was able to rent a beautiful executive home, complete with a studio for her business, at a fraction of the market value. And how he was always available when she needed his shoulder or his judgment.

"No, he's never steered me wrong. So I guess that answers that." The two continued to talk, until Donna said "Whoops! Here come the kids. Gotta go."

With no one else left to call, Saralynn spent the remainder

of the afternoon and early evening wandering around the house. "I feel lost, so much at loose ends. What is happening to me?"

With the darkening shadows of evening, the brightness of her mood didn't improve, but her stomach did tell her it had been a while since lunch. Almost out of duty, she made her way to the kitchen where she put together a sandwich and a bowl of soup and made herself a large cup of hot tea.

This is a long way from what Mrs. Jackson would have prepared, but I'm not Mrs. Jackson and there's no joy in cooking for one person.

She cleaned the kitchen and moved back into the little sitting room where the three of them had always enjoyed TV, board games and just visiting and talking. *It's obvious that I'm not going to lose this blue funk tonight, so I might as well try and be productive. After all, I do have a business to run and a living to make. Especially now that I'm about to incur the expense of a lawsuit.*

Jon Walthall had explained that suit would have to be brought in Massachusetts, and all court hearings would be held there. That meant plane tickets, hotel rooms and meals and, of equal importance, time away from work. Something she could ill afford at this juncture. *But it can't be helped.*

In an effort to lift the mood, she turned on the old TV in the corner, more for the company of the noise than for any true entertainment value. *I've lived by myself for well over a year. I don't know why it's particularly bothersome tonight.*

Saralynn cranked the lights to maximum strength, left the TV at a *reasonable* volume, and began working on the direct mail public relations campaign she'd put together. Professionally printed brochures, using her Atlanta commission as the cornerstone, would be mailed to professional design, construction and architectural organizations.

Mailing two thousand of these isn't cheap. Why the postage alone is running almost a thousand dollars. I only hope it will pay off.

She finished attaching address labels to the envelopes and was attaching postage, when the room suddenly went dark. *Power's off, I'll bet. Mrs. Jackson warned me about that. She said it's bad to go out on beautiful, sunshiny day when the sky's cornflower blue and there isn't a cloud in the sky. So who knows why it went off tonight?*

Saralynn elected to keep her seat for a few minutes, in hopes service would soon be restored. After more than fifteen minutes, when the lights hadn't returned, she knew she'd best call it a day and try to get to bed.

It's after ten o'clock. If only I had a flashlight or a candle, although the prospect of stumbling around in an unfamiliar house in the dark with a lighted candle doesn't excite me.

Then she remembered Mrs. Jackson's words from an earlier visit. "I keep a flashlight by my bed in case the power goes down." *I've not even been in her bedroom since the day she died, but I'm about to try and find my way there now.*

After what seemed like an eternity and more than a few bruising kicks of furniture and doorways, Saralynn found the bedroom and felt her way along the wall toward the bed. *If she kept it by the bed, it would almost have to be on the table beside the bed or in a drawer next to the bed.*

"Ouch...!" she yelled, as the toes on her right foot met the bedpost just as her body fell across the mattress. Saralynn wanted to grab her aching foot and give it some attention, but she was too afraid she'd hurt herself again in the process. *OK. I've found the bed, and my toes will always remember the moment. Now to get myself oriented and find the flashlight.*

She had determined she was at the foot of the bed, on the

opposite side from where Mrs. Jackson's lamp was located. *It makes sense the flashlight would be somewhere near the lamp.* Saralynn had only been in the room twice that she could remember; nevertheless, she struggled to recall the layout. She inched her way around the bed, gripping the mattress hand over hand, until she literally bumped into the edge of a small chest.

That'll be a nice bruise on my hip tomorrow morning, I'm sure. Still, she couldn't contain her excitement that she had managed to locate the night stand. She felt around with her hands, all over the top. She handled many things that she couldn't identify without sight, but nothing that screamed "flashlight".

The chest, she remembered, had either two or three drawers, and she began to fumble for a handle. *It makes sense she'd keep a flashlight close at hand. I'll start with the top drawer.*

She managed to inch open the wide drawer, being careful not to pull it too far and dump the contents. *No telling what else she has in here that I can't see.* After feeling from front to back on one side of the drawer, Saralynn felt her way across to the other side and began a similar search.

Nothing!

Fast losing hope, and wondering if she could find her way back to her own bed in the dark, the troubled young woman pushed the top drawer back and felt for the handle to the second one. *Found it!* Again, exercising caution, she pulled out that drawer, which felt heavier and deeper. Her hand began a systematic search, much like the one she had conducted in the drawer above. She reached the back of the drawer without finding the light she needed. She was about half way back on the other side, when her hand bumped into a cool, round cylinder. *It feels like it could be a flashlight.*

She began to examine the long object and was rewarded

with a bulbous head at one end.

Let there be light! Oh, Lord, please let the batteries work. With a momentary hesitation, a reluctance to know whether it worked or not, Saralynn found the switch and whispered a split-second prayer. *Please let this work!* Her reward was a dim but steady glow.

Batteries are weak. Wonder if any more are in this drawer? Thanks to the light, she was able to dig around in the drawer where she found an open pack of batteries with two remaining. *Thank you, Lord.*

As she was about to close the drawer, the sight of a wrinkled envelope with the letters SARA written in shaky, block letters caught her eye. Without thinking, she moved the book that was on top of the envelope to discover the word. SARALYNN. *It has MY name on it. Why?* She snatched the envelope from its resting place, along with the two batteries and, without bothering to close the drawer, scooted back to her bedroom by the rapidly fading glow of the flashlight.

New batteries gave the flashlight renewed life and for the first time since the power went down, Saralynn felt safe again. *It's almost cozy, although I'd hate to have to go around with a light in my hand all the time.*

So curious was she about the envelope bearing her name, Saralynn didn't even take time to change for sleep before she plopped down in the middle of the bed, holding the light with one hand, and awkwardly pulled open the flap. Inside was a folded piece of paper in the same shaky script as the name on the outside. *It's a letter. To me.* Saralynn's eyes quickly fell to the bottom of the sheet, where Homerline Jackson's signature greeted her. *Mrs. Jackson wrote this to me.*

Dear Saralynn,

    By the time you read this, I'm sure I'll be gone. Please forgive me for not talking to you before I fixed all my business to make you Emma's guardian. I thought I'd have more time than I'm gonna have and I'm an old woman. I couldn't take a chance you'd turn me down.

    You see, not everybody would be willing to take on Emma, and as her mama, I have to make certain that someone who will love her and understand her will be looking after her. There ain't nobody I trust with that job more than you. You have a good heart and a good head, and Emma loves you. That's important to me.

    I can't help that I'm dyin. Like I tole you, I don't want to. Not yet. But God has taken that out of my hands and He knows what's best. But as a mama, I have to be sure my little girl is looked after. I can die peaceful knowing that you'll always be there. I've fixed everthing so that it won't cost you nothing. All I ask is that you bring Emma back home whenever you think it is best. And after Emma is gone, you do what you want to with the place. I don't care if you sell it for a million dollars. You earned it.

    You been like a daughter to me and I love you. I hope I've made it where you'll get some payback but it will be down the road a ways, I imagine. Thank you for making an old woman's last days easier.

    Through tear-filled eyes, Saralynn read the signature: Homerline Emma Jackson.

    Evidently she planned to leave this for me, but she must have been stricken and put to bed before she had the chance. Oh, Mrs. Jackson, you don't know how it makes me feel to know I'm about to sue my own mother, because she doesn't care about me. Yet you used some of the last of your time and strength to make certain that Emma was provided for.

    She sat for the longest on the bed, cross-legged, turning

the letter over and over in her hands. Finally, the peace she had sought from others all day, found her. *Mrs. Jackson has demonstrated how a mother is supposed to provide for and protect her child. Jon Walthall is right. For my protection, and yours, we have to go forward. Mama, you could take a lesson from Homerline Jackson. Of course you'd probably find her too backward, and refuse to listen. Just like you've been doing for more than fifty years.*

When she crawled under the covers a few minutes later, it was to dream of court battles and acrimonious confrontations with Alicia that she couldn't win.

Chapter 9

Saralynn awoke the next morning to find lights on all over the house. Power had been restored during the night, but her sleep had been so deep and troubling, she hadn't noticed. With the new day – one filled with possibilities and uncertainties — also came a resolve that uncomfortable issues had to be met head on.

As long as my motives are to protect Mama and to help her, rather than taking from her and enriching myself, then however cruel the means may sound, it doesn't make it wrong or me a bad person.

She spent the day finishing the work on her marketing campaign and began working on posting to her accounting system – all things on which she'd gotten behind.

Occasionally she'd pick up the letter from Mrs. Jackson and re-read it. With each new investigation of the document, she found her respect for the old country woman growing tremendously. *She should win a "mother of the year" award.* It's clearly evident that she loved Emma unconditionally. *I wish I could say the* same for my mama. But I don't take it personally. Obviously this "need" she has to control began long before I ever entered the picture.

As she thought back over the events of the past year, she realized that the people Alicia most disliked were those who exhibited the same traits as Mrs. Jackson and Miss Sallie… they cared about others to the exclusion of themselves. *Virginia Kennedy says she believes Mama never felt good enough to be one of them. The more I look at how things have played out, I have to agree.*

Try as she might, however, Saralynn couldn't understand how Alicia could have developed such a severe inferiority complex; one so deep that it drove her to severely self-destructive acts.

As the day wore on into afternoon, and Saralynn began to contemplate visiting a new church, she found the butterflies that had dogged her stomach before she worshipped at Rials Creek the first time returning. *I didn't let them have their way then and I won't this time, either. Although I am a little nervous. I wish I knew why.*

MA had called earlier in the day to say they would be there at five-fifteen. "Remember, dress casually. Nothing fancy is required." In accordance with those instructions, she had selected a pair of khaki slacks, a multi-colored pull-over sweater in tones of rust and peach and hunter green and gray. *I hope this is casual enough. I still marvel that everyone doesn't dress up for every occasion at church. But it sure doesn't seem to mess with their abilities to worship God or to receive His blessings.*

That night, when she was alone again in the house at Fishtrap Hollow, Saralynn realized that for the first time in days, she didn't feel wound so tightly. *It's a lot like it was after I visited at*

Rials Creek the first time; I feel more relaxed and less like I'm all alone. But this is a totally different group of people and it's over 300 miles back to Simpson County. So how can I get the same feeling in a different place?

As she allowed sleep to claim her that evening, it was with the unspoken agreement that she was once again a changed person... a change that happened at church, whether she completely understood it or not.

When the family-style supper in the fellowship hall had concluded, the pastor led the group in a short devotional, followed by a time of prayer for various members of the church and the community. *Even people who don't go to this church. Evidently this praying for your neighbor thing isn't just something they do at Rials Creek.*

"We need to remember Saralynn, too," MA volunteered at one point, and she patted her friend on the shoulder. "Not only is she caring for Emma Jackson now, but her own mother back in Boston is sick. I know I'd need some extra starch if I had all that facing me."

Saralynn felt her face coloring. *I wish MA hadn't done that!* Yet at the same time, it felt good to know that others cared and were willing to pray for her.

They were leaving the church by a side door, when Saralynn caught sight of the lighted stained glass sanctuary windows. "Those are so beautiful. Lit up like that, they really make you want to come inside to see what's so special."

"So do you want to go inside?" her attorney asked.

Saralynn stammered. "Uh... uh... right now?"

"Sure thing," MA answered, as she grabbed Saralynn's arm and began to drag her around to the front door. "Now's as good a time as any."

Once inside, Saralynn was even more mesmerized.

"Look here," Jon encouraged. "See the brass plates beneath each window? They tell who gave each window and who is being honored."

Saralynn heard his voice, and glanced in Jon's direction, but it was the window behind the pulpit that had caught her eye. *The choir at Rials Creek sits behind the pulpit so I guess that's the choir area in this church as well.* This window was one she hadn't been able to see from outside, and was a beautiful depiction of a man in scarlet and white robes holding a lamb, with other sheep clustered around him.

The scene had such an impact that Saralynn felt her breath taken away. It was almost like someone was tugging on her heart. "Jon?" she whispered. "Jon! What's that window? Why is it different from the other windows?"

It was MA who answered first. "That's the Good Shepherd window."

Saralynn was confused. "But what does a shepherd have to do with God?"

"Let's go down and look at it, and I'll try to explain."

Saralynn felt so ignorant about church and God, but one more time, instead of being aggravated about it, someone was only too happy to explain. *I must not be a very good person if I have to ask questions like this.*

The three had reached the back of the choir loft, MA had called it, and were standing in front of the window in question. "What do you see in this picture?"

"I see Jesus – at least I guess it's Jesus; this man looks like other pictures I've been told were him. And I see a group of sheep standing around. Plus He's holding that little one in His arms."

"Do the sheep look like they're frightened, like they fear

Jesus?"

Saralynn continued to study the many colorful and intricately shaped pieces of glass before finally responding. "None of the sheep look like they're scared, and certainly none of them look like they're mistreated or starved." She stopped, uncertain of how to continue. "They look like they're well cared for," she blurted, finally.

MA pointed to the small lamb cradled in the shepherd's arms – in Jesus' arms. "You see, here is a baby lamb, not too old, and also in the flock around Jesus are some lambs that are obviously older." She lowered the tone of her voice ever so slightly. "But in every instance, young or old, Jesus is taking care of them."

"So that's why it's called "The Good Shepherd" window?"

Jon chimed in, "Actually, Saralynn," he said, smiling at her as a parent might smile to a child, "the term Good Shepherd refers to how Jesus cares for those who believe in Him, who have made Him first in their lives, and who call Him Saviour."

"Have you ever heard a hymn called *Without Him I Could Do Nothing*? MA asked.

I'm about to really show my ignorance again. "I'm sorry I haven't heard that one." She hesitated, then plunged ahead. "You see, I haven't been going to church but about a year, and there's still a lot that I don't know."

Saralynn could see the shocked but unspoken exchange that passed between husband and wife, but was at a total loss about how to respond. In the end, she kept silent. *Better to be thought a fool than to open my mouth and be proven one!*

"How is it that you've only been in church a year?" MA blurted out. Her face turned a deep shade of crimson. "Oh, I'm so sorry, Saralynn, that just popped out." Her face was a study in confusion. "Please forgive me. I didn't mean to pry."

These two people have done nothing but befriend me and now I've made them very uncomfortable.

"Don't worry. You're not the first one who has asked and I'm certain you won't be the last." She smiled, trying to put her friends at ease, and to indicate that she wasn't insulted. "The short version is that my mother has no use for religion, so I wasn't raised that way. It wasn't until after I moved to Mississippi last year that I first began to attend church."

"Well you're in church now," Jon replied, and in a manner Saralynn knew was meant to move them past the awkward moment.

But it was MA who picked up the conversation. "The hymn title I asked you about, the words of that song, I think, illustrate the story of the Good Shepherd better than any way I know."

She began to sing without accompanyment, in a beautiful voice that awed Saralynn, but that also spoke to her heart unlike anything ever had before. "Without Him, I could do nothing, without Him I'd surely fail, Without Him I would be drifting, like a ship… without a sail."

Saralynn felt tears come into her eyes and without thinking, dabbed at them with her hands. *What has come over me?* "You have such a beautiful voice. I'm impressed."

"But you're still confused, right?" Jon asked. "The expression on your face says you still don't understand."

"Well, yeah. More or less," Saralynn stumbled over the words, once again hating to acknowledge just how little she knew about all this business of religion.

"Let's sit down and I'll try to explain." He motioned for both the ladies to take one of the choir chairs. "I think that God chose sheep and the Good Shepherd analogy because it fits so perfectly."

I still don't understand but I'm not about to confess that!

Jon continued, "You see, sheep are very helpless creatures, almost ignorant of how to fend for themselves. They don't have common sense or street smarts, as we'd call it today. If a sheep gets on its back, for example, it often will not be able to right itself. A good sheepherder is constantly watching his flock for those who get into trouble, so that he can help them. That's how Jesus is with us."

"And unfortunately," MA explained with a laugh, "human beings can often be even more ignorant and helpless than those sheep. Which is why it's so wonderful to always have Jesus there to help us."

There's a lot about religion that I didn't know, but this sheep and the shepherd story makes me wonder. Maybe Mama was right about church people?

"So God sent His Son to be a sheep herder?"

Jon rose from where he had been sitting and placed his hand on Saralynn's shoulder. "Not in the literal sense of the word. But you need to understand that in Jesus' day, sheepherding was a common occupation, one that everyone understood. It's still so very appropriate today."

"That's right," MA volunteered. "We humans, with all our faults, are still as needy as those sheep and we still need Jesus' influence in our lives even today… two centuries later."

How do I respond? They're both so sincere.

"This is a story I've never heard before. But I thank you for telling me about this beautiful window. It certainly is the focal point of the sanctuary." Saralynn laughed. "There I go wearing my decorator hat again."

The remainder of the evening Saralynn felt there was an undercurrent of misunderstanding, but she couldn't decide if it truly existed, or if it was a figment of her guilty imagination. *I can't help it because Mama didn't believe in religion. I haven't always been in church like they have. I don't know all this stuff.*

It was a great relief when the Walthall Mercedes pulled into the drive at Fishtrap Hollow and she was able to bid her hosts goodnight. They parted with promises to get together again, soon. "I hope I'll have some word for you from Boston before Friday afternoon," Jon promised before he backed out of the drive. "I've already put in some phone calls."

As she closed up for the night and adjourned to her bedroom to read, Saralynn couldn't forget the evening's conversation about the Good Shepherd. Instead, she kept hearing the echo of MA's voice: "Human beings can often be even more ignorant and helpless than those sheep."

Is it possible she's right? Could I be one of those ignorant people and not even realize it?

Even though she knew it was late, she realized she wouldn't sleep that night unless she was able to get past this stumbling block her friends had thrown into her path. She calculated whether it was too late to make a call. *I know they didn't do this deliberately, or to embarrass me, but I won't rest tonight unless I can talk to someone. And I know just who it needs to be.*

The phone on the other end was answered on the fourth ring, long enough for Saralynn to question the wisdom of bothering her friend at that hour of the night. "Katie. It's Saralynn. I hope I'm not messing with Paul's bed time."

"Hey, friend. I was wondering if you'd forgotten all about

us down here. Hang on a second, OK?"

Saralynn could hear the sound of objects being moved around in the background and then Katie Brooks was back on the line. "Not to worry. Paul's been down for almost half an hour. This is a good time."

"How is our Paul, by the way?"

There was hesitation, then her friend's voice came across the miles as strong and optimistic as ever. "He's weakening a little. You can tell it if you look back over the long haul. But it's nothing more than the doctors told us to expect."

Having lost Marc when he wasn't much older than Paul, I don't know how Katie can live with that precious little boy every day and watch him slowly drift away. I don't think I could hold up under the load.

"Well give him a big hug for me and tell him I'll see him soon. One day early next week, probably."

As she spoke, she looked around the small room and contemplated how differently it looked from just a few hours earlier, before she had gone to church and had heard the improbable story about the Good Shepherd. *It's uncomfortable, but suddenly I don't feel as much at home here as I did this afternoon. But how can what happened tonight make such a difference?*

"I'll sure do that," Katie's voice promised. "But something tells me you didn't call just to tell Paul hello. In fact... you sound troubled. Is everything alright? It's not your mother, is it?"

How do I explain this? I don't even understand it myself enough to talk about it. But I can't back out now? Katie would never buy it.

"No, it's not Mama. Not this time."

"But you are troubled." It was stated, not as a question, but a given.

"Can't fool you, can I?"

"You said it, I didn't. But evidently I was right. So spill it, my friend."

Saralynn stalled. "It's kind of... kind of awkward. I don't quite know how to say it."

"Hey, this is just you and me."

"OK." She giggled nervously. "But you have to promise me you won't think I've gone off the deep end."

"You haven't gone off the deep end, but I'm not so sure you won't be collecting Social Security before you get around to getting whatever it is off your chest."

She's right. I am stalling. And that's not fair to either of us.

"I heard a story at church tonight and I want to know if they were pulling my leg."

"You went to church tonight! That's great; you must be making friends there. Where did you go?"

Saralynn filled her in on the particulars, then asked, "Have you ever heard of the Good Shepherd?"

The response, immediate and certain, wasn't what Saralynn expected to hear. "Sure. Jesus is the Good Shepherd. At least I assume this is the Good Shepherd you're asking about."

I thought maybe this was just something in this church, because Rials Creek doesn't have a window like that. Could Jon and MA have been sincere?

"I guess that's the one I mean." She went on to relate the story her friends had shared earlier, and concluded by saying, "I wasn't sure if they were serious or not. But I guess they were."

Katie was quiet for a few seconds and Saralynn worried that her ignorance of most things religious had spoiled their friendship. *After all, there's no way I can ever know all that Katie and Donna and Bess know. They've been in church all their lives.*

"And how did you feel about the story of the Good Shepherd?"

"Can I be honest?" Saralynn caught her breath. The words had popped out even before she'd had time to think about a response.

"I wouldn't accept anything else."

Saralynn began to explain how unsettled she had been after her friends explained the meaning of the beautiful window. "I've heard about cults and all, and I didn't know if they were serious about worshipping a God that appears as a shepherd. That seems so... so... unholy... or something."

"You mean like Jesus isn't good enough for you if he's a shepherd standing in the midst of a flock of sheep, instead of sitting on a designer throne wearing ermine and jewels and a large gold crown?"

"You make me sound like a snob."

"Not intentionally, I assure you. And besides, I know you aren't a snob."

I'm not doing a very good job of this. Perhaps I should just drop it for the moment.

"Well," she offered lamely, "the main thing I wanted to know was if Jon and MA were pulling my leg. I wasn't sure what I'd gotten myself into. So what's happening in Simpson County. I really am missing everyone there."

"Good try, but don't change the subject. This is really bothering you or you wouldn't have called. So let's see if we can't erase some of that doubt that's going to keep you awake tonight."

Katie knows me too well.

"It is troubling me, but I guess the biggest problem I had is that God and Jesus seem so much greater than life. And to see

Jesus as a common sheepherder was almost like He had lost some of His... His... I don't know... His... holiness, I guess."

Saralynn could see the wheels turning in her friend's head on the other end of the phone connection. Finally, Katie spoke again."

"You have to understand, Saralynn, that when Jesus first began his ministry, the people he ministered among were ordinary people. The role of a shepherd was one they understood. They also knew that a shepherd worth the title would risk his own life to save one of his sheep. This was a metaphor that those people could understand and even identify with."

"So it doesn't degrade Jesus to be called a shepherd?"

"Not at all!" came the reassurance. "Just like it doesn't degrade us to be thought of as sheep."

"Well, I never..."

"But it goes deeper than just the sheep and the shepherd metaphor, Saralynn. Do you know why Jesus is so loving toward us... his sheep... even two thousand years later?"

I keep getting myself in deeper and deeper in this religion stuff. When will I ever learn to keep my mouth shut?

Instead of voicing the vow of silence she had just made, Saralynn answered, "MA and Jon said something about how sheep are basically dumb animals and that the shepherd has to constantly watch after them and save them..." she hesitated, unsure of how to proceed. "I guess, to save them from themselves?" *I know that sounded like a question. That's because that's what it was.*

"You're on the right track. You just haven't gotten deep enough into the subject to really understand."

It felt pretty deep to me! "Then I'm all ears. Please explain it, because my mind is so messed up right now, I know I won't close my eyes tonight."

Again, Saralynn could sense a hesitation on the part of her friend. Then, when she thought perhaps the connection had been broken, she heard, "To begin with, you'll do better to listen with your heart than with your ears, and you'll see more with your eyes closed than if you're looking to understand things rationally."

"Huh?"

"Just listen." Katie continued to talk, explaining how God had sent Jesus as His Son, to be crucified on a cross and die, so that everyone who believed in Him might be saved from their sins and have eternal life.

I knew that Jesus was God's Son, but I never understood all of this.

"So you see, Saralynn, when Jesus is portrayed as the Good Shepherd, that's exactly what He is to us. We are the sheep who can't find our own way without help, and Jesus is our guide. All we have to do is believe in Him, follow Him, and He will lead us in the path that is best for us. That's why so many of us mess up when we try to go our own way, instead of listening to the guidance of our shepherd. In this case, the Good Shepherd, also known as Jesus Christ."

Saralynn was speechless.

"But Katie… how… how can you believe something like that? How can one person dying do all that? Do you mean that if I believe in Jesus that I won't die? *Miss Sallie believed in Jesus and she died.*

"Everyone has to die. The victory in Jesus comes after you die, when you're assured that if Jesus lived in your heart while you were alive, you'll live with Jesus after you're dead."

"That sounds so… so final, almost cruel."

"What sounds cruel? Death?"

"Well, yeah. Why wouldn't God want everyone to live forever?"

I mean, death takes you away from everything you love. Or it steals those who love you! I didn't want to lose Marc and Peter.

"There are just some things we don't know this side of Heaven and won't. We just have to have faith that the God we love knows what's best for us, and we'll get the answers to all those questions once we're with Him."

So how do I know if I'll be with Him?

By this point Saralynn was regretting she'd ever opened the conversation. Yet, at the same time, there was an urgency spurring her on, despite her mounting discomfort. "Katie? I don't know if I'd go to Heaven or not. I don't think I know how."

"This is why I told you, listen with your heart and see with your eyes closed."

But that doesn't make any sense. My heart doesn't have ears and how can anyone see if their eyes are shut?

Her friend was speaking again, and Saralynn pulled herself back from the mental check-out that was about to happen. "Say that again, Katie. Please?"

"I asked if you knew what faith was."

"Well, I think I do." *At least I hope Donna's definition of faith is the same as Katie's.* "Faith is believing that God will do what He has promised to do."

"That's right. So I have to ask you, do you believe if God says He will take us to Heaven if we believe that Jesus is His Son, and that Jesus died to save us from our sins, that He will keep that promise?"

"Well, yeah, I guess." *That didn't sound very positive.* "Yes, I believe that now. I don't think I would have a year or so ago."

"What happened in the past doesn't matter. It's what you believe now that's important. Do you believe that Jesus died for every single person on this earth? Those who were alive when he died, and for future generations?"

Saralynn hesitated again. *This is getting deeper.* "I guess I do. I want to. But I just don't see how that could be, how one man could save millions of people simply because He died."

"That's because you're trying to listen with your ears and see with your eyes open."

"But practically, it just doesn't make sense." Saralynn felt like she was on shaky ground. "At least to me it doesn't," she offered defensively.

"And it won't, until you can listen with your heart… until you can see with your eyes closed. This is the real reality, and mortal eyes alone can't see it."

"I want to," Saralynn cried, and was astounded at the angst she heard in her own voice. "But I'm not sure I know how."

"Let me share something with you," her friend offered. "Two things, in fact."

"Whatever. I just know that I don't understand."

"First, there is no doubt in my mind that God is working in your heart right now. He wants you to believe in Him and trust Him. If He weren't at work, you would never have been bothered enough by the story of the Good Shepherd to call me."

Saralynn said nothing.

"The second thing is, I'd like to pray with you, right now, over the phone."

Church people here pray like my friends at home. Whenever and wherever!

"God says He will hear us wherever we are when we come to Him, and I know without a doubt that He will hear us tonight. *Dear Lord and Heavenly Father, You've heard the doubts and concerns of Your child Saralynn. You know her heart even better than she does herself. I pray now, Father, that in the days ahead, You will show her how her heart's ear is closest to Your mouth, and how closed eyes can see beyond the reality of this world into the reality that is the eternal life You have promised. We know with all surety that You are dealing in Saralynn's heart and life right now. Have Your own way, Lord. Have Your own way. In the precious name of Your Son, Jesus, we pray. Amen.*

"Amen," Saralynn echoed. *I still don't think I'll sleep tonight. And what exactly did Katie mean by "Have Your own way, Lord"— like I don't get any say-so in what happens? I'm not sure I'm comfortable with that.*

Still frazzled from the way her search for information had ended, Saralynn said, "Thanks, Katie. It was good to talk to you."

"But you're still confused and questioning."

Can't fool Katie. "I'm afraid you're right," she confessed. "I didn't get the answers I was looking for."

Saralynn heard her friend clear her throat, before she said, "Is that because you truly didn't get any answers, or the answers you got didn't match what you wanted to hear?"

By this point, Saralynn could feel beads of sweat popping out on her body – a sure sign of panic. "I don't know, Katie. I just don't know."

"I love you, my friend. But I think you do know. You just don't want to admit it. This is probably hitting below the belt, but I'd say you have at least a touch of your mother in you. Think about it."

I'm nothing like Mama. Am I?

"I'm sorry if I spoke out of turn."

Saralynn couldn't decide if her feelings were hurt, and she was too tired to care about anything except losing Katie's friendship. "Don't worry about it. I'll call you tomorrow. Right now, all I want to do is crash. Suddenly I'm very tired."

Did I just hear a little sigh of relief?

"OK. We'll talk later. Sleep well."

Saralynn closed her phone and made quick work of getting ready for bed. Despite her fears that she would not sleep, her eyes were closing by the time her head hit the pillow.

The last conscious thought she had that night was the phrase from Katie's prayer, "Have Your own way, Lord," which kept repeating in her mind until she could remember no more.

Chapter 10

It was mid-morning on Thursday before Saralynn remembered the events of the previous night and actually questioned if all those memories might have been a dream. The illusion was quickly destroyed, however, when a call from Jon Walthall, about the suit against Alicia, removed all doubt she might have had.

"MA and I were glad to have you as our guest last night. I hope you enjoyed yourself."

I did enjoy myself. I'll have to admit it was a lot like Rials Creek, the same family feeling.

"Thank you for inviting me," she replied. "Maybe we can do that again sometime." *Isn't that the polite thing to say?*

"We were hoping you'd say that," the lawyer crowed. "You'll have to come Sunday and be our guest at Sunday School and stay for church."

I've done it again. I've gotten real comfortable at Rials Creek, but I don't know about a new church. What if it's not the same?

"And we won't take 'no' for an answer, either."

"All right," she conceded, realizing that protest was futile. "I'll be happy to join you, but you don't have to come get me. I'll drive myself in." *That way if I need to make an escape, I've got my own wheels.*

"Great. See you about 9:15 Sunday morning. We'll meet you out front."

"I'll be there," she replied with slightly more enthusiasm than she felt.

"Oh," Jon interrupted, "you told me but I forgot. When are you headed back south?"

"Monday. Early, Monday. And depending on what's happening in Boston, I may have to go home, wash clothes and re-pack my suitcase."

"Can you delay leaving long enough to come by my office at nine o'clock? Shouldn't take but about 30 minutes, but we need to have a conference call with the attorney in Boston who's going to be working with us."

He makes it sound so cut and dried. So arranged, but yet so normal; nothing out of the ordinary. "Sure, I can make that work. I'll just be loaded and plan to head out of town when I leave your office. It won't delay me that much."

"And plan to go out to eat after church Sunday," the attorney said as they ended the call.

Everyone in the south must go out to eat after church. It's almost like eating is a part of religion.

The rest of the day and into Friday, Saralynn spent working on her personal business. In between accounting and figuring quotes for jobs she'd been asked to bid, she had a home inspector go over the Jackson house on Friday morning, just as a precaution.

Not being here all the time, there's too much chance for problems. I want to know if we have any issues that need correcting before disaster happens. After all, who would have thought an icemaker line rupturing in Mama's neighbor's kitchen could do so much damage?

It was with great relief that Saralynn wrote the check to pay for the inspection, and learned that the house was fundamentally sound.

"You're going to need a new roof in another five to seven years, but that's nothing to worry about now," the inspector, a pencil-thin man wearing blue coveralls reported. "Looks like the outside has recently been painted, and I don't see any signs of rotting woodwork. Inside, the plumbing and the electrical look great, and the central system looks fairly new. The only things I see are strictly cosmetic and they aren't significant."

"This surely is a relief," she confessed to the white-haired gentleman. "I could just visualize walking in late one afternoon and finding everything under water… or worse," she said with a self-conscious laugh. *Perhaps I ought not tell him that I'm not going to be here all the time? Can he be trusted?*

"Yeah," he said, "I heard in town that Miss Homerline had left you the house and Emma. Guess since Emma's down south, you'll be spending most of your time there close to her?"

That's one way to put it.

"Tell you what," he continued. "What you ought to do when you leave here every time is to turn the water heater off in the breaker box and then turn the water off at the meter outside."

"I don't even know where the water meter is."

"Then I better be showing you." He picked up his fold-over notebook and motioned for Saralynn to follow. The journey took them to the side yard, to a hole in the ground covered with an iron disc. The inspector made a dash to his truck and came back with a tool that looked like a long-stemmed "T".

He removed the disk to reveal a piece of machinery with a dial, kind of like a clock face, Saralynn decided. Behind the dial, on the side closest to the house, was an elongated bar.

"This is the cut-off," he explained, pointing to the bar, as he placed the slotted end of the tool and gave it a quarter turn clockwise. "I've just turned off your water," he explained. "See how the bar is perpendicular to the pipe? When it's in this position, no water is going into your house." Then he repeated the action in reverse. "And when the bar is parallel, in this position, water is flowing. It's easy. Here… you try it."

Saralynn did as he directed and, while she felt extremely clumsy, she discovered that he was exactly right. It was easy. *A quarter-turn this way… a quarter-turn that way.*

"I've learned something new," she admitted. "Now where do I get one of these tools?"

The inspector scratched his head. "I would've thought Miss Homerline had one, but I didn't see it in all the plundering I've done today. Then his face lit up. "Here," he said. "Tell you what. I've got several. This one's your housewarming gift. That way I know you've got one."

"But Mr. Andrews," she protested, "at least let me pay you for it. I'll just run get my checkbook."

"Tell you what, Ms. Reilly, let's trade it out."

"Trade it out?" *What have I got to trade?* She immediately wondered if she was in danger. *But he doesn't strike me as that kind of man. After all, Jon Walthall recommended him.*

If the older gentleman realized that his proposition made Saralynn uncomfortable, he didn't let on. "I know you visited our church this past Wednesday."

"Your church? You means the Methodist Church in Iuka?"

"One and the same."

"But I don't remember seeing you there." Saralynn was searching her memory for some recollection of him. *Maybe it's the blue coveralls. He wouldn't have worn them to church, I don't imagine.*

"That's 'cause I wasn't there," he explained. "The wife, Geneva's her name, she had a doctor's appointment in Tupelo and we ran late getting home."

"Oh." *So if he wasn't there, how'd he know I was?*

"But folks in small towns talk, you know." His face took on stricken expression. "I don't mean in a bad way."

"But folks have been talking about me being there?"

The man wiped the back of his hand across his forehead. "I hope I haven't spoken out of turn. It's just when you live in a small town, you don't get a whole lot of visitors. Those you do get become a topic for conversation."

I think I liked Boston better where no one knew my business or where I was. I think. "And what is the conversation about me?"

He wiped his brow again. "Nothing bad, Ms. Reilly. I promise you. Everbody's real thankful that Emma didn't have to be made a ward of the court; that you could look after her. And… and, everbody says you seem so nice." He flashed a weak attempt at a grin her way. "Which I'd have to agree with, Ma'am."

I think he's sincere. "So what am I going to trade you for this… this…" she pointed at the tool that was still attached to the control bar on the water meter. "This tool you say I need?"

"I handled that badly, didn't I?"

Saralynn said nothing.

"All I want is for you to say you'll come back and visit with us on Sunday. We'd love to have you."

He wants to charge me a trip to church for this tool?

"I'll be singing in the choir, but my wife, you remember, Geneva's her name, will be glad to meet you and sit with you and everything."

Well, I never…

"Look, Mr. Andrews…"

"Just call me George," he interrupted. "You're one of us now."

"I really appreciate your invitation Mr. An…" At the pained expression on his face, she amended what she was about to say, "George, I really do. But I've already promised Jon and MA Walthall that I'll be their guest."

The gentleman's face fell.

"So I guess I'll just have to pay you for this tool." *He looks so crestfallen.*

"No Ma'am, you won't," he protested. "You just wait 'til I see Lawyer Jon and jump him for poaching my prospect!"

Saralynn wasn't sure if he was truly angry or just making a big joke. After a moment, when he flashed a large, toothy smile, she decided this was more of the southern brand of humor she still found difficult to understand. *When folks in the north say they're angry, they're usually angry.*

"Nope," he vowed. "I'll not take a dime for that tool. It's a house-warming present. But me and the wife, you remember,

Geneva's her name, why we'll be waitin' to see you come Sunday."

"When I get through with Jon Walthall," he mumbled on his way to his truck. "Me and Geneva wanted her to be our guest."

They're fighting over me here just like they did in Simpson County. I'll never truly understand the south. But I have to confess, I kind of like it.

Saralynn returned to the house to finish up the last of her work. *Thank goodness for laptop computers and fax machines, but I sure wouldn't want to have to haul my office everywhere I went.* She began tidying up her work area and packing things away. In the back of her mind was the trip she had planned to the genealogical museum that afternoon. *I wonder if Kathy Lucas has been able to find out anything about Miss Sallie's family. And do I still have relatives living here?* Then, out of the blue, a most staggering thought crossed her mind. *Why I could have already been dealing with my relatives and neither of us knew it. Mr. Andrews... I mean, George... or maybe his wife, Geneva, could be my kin.*

"My grandmother was a what?"

"She was a twin."

Saralynn sat down in a chair near where she was standing. *I sure wasn't expecting that.*

"Sallie McIntire had a twin sister who was still-born at birth," the smiling Mrs. Lucas said. "Fortunately, they named her before they buried her. That allowed us to have a listing for her in this cemetery index.

Miss Sallie was a twin. Wonder why she never mentioned it in any of her diary entries? Or1 at least none of the ones I've read. Maybe I need to be looking at them again.

Saralynn finally found her wits. "Did she have any other siblings? Younger or older? A brother, perhaps?"

The museum worker consulted her notes. "There's no indication that J.W. and Naomi McIntire ever had any children besides Sallie and Pansy."

Pansy. Her name was Pansy. How quaint, and beautiful, too!

"I also discovered something else that I think will probably surprise you."

Is it possible to know more than you should? Nope! I came here seeking information. I should be thankful she's found something.

"You might as well tell me," Saralynn encouraged. "I'm too nervous to stand the strain. Then a troubling thought hit her. "This isn't something I'm going to regret, is it?"

Kathy Lucas smiled her disarming smile again. "I don't think you'll regret it at all." She hesitated, while her wide grin further piqued Saralynn's curiosity. "Would you be surprised to learn that you're distantly kin to Homeline Jackson?"

"Whaaaaa…?" Saralynn felt the breath leave her. *This is too much to absorb in such a short time.*

"According to the records, Miss Sallie's mother was Naomi Cochran before she married J.W. McIntire. Naomi had a brother, Homer Cochran, who married Caroline Studdard. They had a daughter whom they named…"

"Homeline…!" Saralynn interrupted. "You're right. I remember seeing it listed on Mrs. Jackson's death certificate. Her maiden name was Cochran. So that would have made her my… my…"

"Great-aunt," Kathy supplied.

Saralynn's head was spinning, but not in a bad way. Still, she had other questions, if only she could remember them. "Uh… uh, other family? Do I have any other relatives here now, some who are alive?"

Kathy pulled out the chair across from Saralynn and sat down. "Well, there is Emma, you know. This means you and she are cousins."

Emma and I are cousins! How will I ever explain that to her?

Kathy continued, "Although I doubt that will mean anything to her either way. From what I'm hearing, Emma has already made you a part of her family. She could care less how you're connected."

Small town again. News travels really fast. "I suspect you're right there. So is there anyone else?"

A frown registered momentarily on the woman's face, but it was quickly replaced by her usual grin. "If you had some type of a family reunion in mind," she said with sadness evident in her voice, "I'm afraid you're going to be disappointed."

"No one is left."

"No one you'd want to claim."

She found a black sheep? "No one I'd want to claim?"

Saralynn could tell the woman was hesitant to share this bit of news, but she also knew that she couldn't leave without knowing everything there was. *Good, bad and catastrophic.*

"First," Kathy explained, "both the McIntire line and the Cochran line have died out in Tishomingo County. Homeline did have one brother, a few years older than her, named Jefferson, and he's still living. At least as far as we know."

"You mean he doesn't live here?"

Kathy smiled a sad face. "Hasn't lived here in years and

won't ever, at least not 'til they bring him back to be buried. Or, I guess they will."

Saralynn sensed there was a deep story lurking right under her very nose and she was determined to get the details. "Whatever it is, Kathy, I have to know. You have to tell me."

"OK. You asked for it. But I promise you, it's not pretty."

If only you knew about all there is in my life already that isn't pretty. Like all this mess with Mama, for example.

"Jeff Cochran was trouble to his parents from the moment he learned to walk and talk. It was almost like he was incapable of minding or doing what he was told. And whenever they would discipline him, he would rage at them." She frowned. "You know this was in a day and time when children didn't disobey. At least not more than once."

"Anyway," her new friend continued, "as Jeff got older, he lied, he stole, from his parents and from others. And it didn't matter what his mama and daddy did for him, it was never enough, never good enough. It looked like there was no end to what meaness he would do. 'Bout broke his mama's heart."

Saralynn couldn't stand the suspense. Even a fly buzzing near her ear didn't distract her. "You said he would be brought back to be buried. So where is he now?"

"Parchman." She spit the word out devoid of emotion or explanation.

"I beg your pardon?"

"The state penitentiary. Parchman. Up in the Delta in the northwest corner of the state."

"My relative… my great-uncle, is in prison? For what?"

"Murder. He killed his mother."

The fly was droning around Saralynn's ear again, and she

swatted absently as she fixed her friend with a stare, unable to believe what she had just heard. "He killed his mother?"

"It was a sad, sad situation. But nobody was really surprised."

"I don't understand."

Kathy began to doodle with her pen on the bottom of the pad where she had written the details she was sharing. "He was going to come to no good. The whole county knew it. When he was about seventeen years old, he left these parts. I'm not sure where he went. There were several different stories. What's important is he tried to get his daddy to give him his share of a future inheritance so he could leave and never come back. He swore if he ever got out of Mississippi we'd never see him again."

Where have I heard those words before?

"He stayed gone for about twenty years. I think he kept in touch with Homerline, but even then she'd go several years between contacts. Then Homer Cochran died and Homerline convinced her mama they should delay the funeral and try to find Jeff and get him home."

"And did they?"

"It was more than a week before Homerline tracked him down, and she begged him to come."

"You could tell it made all the difference to Caroline to have him here, and ever body thought maybe a reconciliation was gonna happen."

Saralynn's head was reeling. She could feel sweat breaking out on her body and she physically hurt. *I don't know if I want to know this or not.*

"Things were fine for a few days. Then Jeff demanded that Caroline give him the money his daddy denied him all those years before. Said if she didn't, he was going to leave and she'd never see him again. Said he wouldn't even come back for her funeral. But she refused."

Saralynn felt faint. "Did she have a good reason?"

Kathy doodled harder. "A really good reason. She didn't have it to give."

"She really didn't have it?"

"Nope. Homer didn't have a very good head for business and he lost more than he made, especially in those last years. Between bad judgment and poor health, he and Caroline lost just about everything they had."

"That is so sad."

"What Jeff didn't know was that Homerline and her husband were supporting her parents. In fact, they had bought the Cochran home place and moved in to help take care of them. Homer and Caroline didn't even own a house to call their own any longer. Let alone have any money for Caroline to give Jeff."

"But because Jeff had been gone, he didn't know that."

"Precisely."

"So what happened; I'm almost afraid to ask?"

"There was a big blow-up when Caroline told Jeff she couldn't give him any money. He interpreted couldn't as wouldn't, and his hair-trigger temper surfaced big time. From what Homerline told the sheriff when it was all over, Jeff was totally out of control. She and her mama and Emma were there alone with him. Mr. Jackson was here in town at his store."

"This just gets sadder by the minute."

"Oh, it was more than sad. Tragic. So many lives were affected."

"More than just Caroline being killed?"

"Much more. That's what people don't understand when they do wrong; the circle of hurt just gets bigger and bigger. But folks don't see that."

"But this is what sent Jeff to prison?"

"It was a wonder he didn't get the chair. The judge sentenced him to life without parole."

"So how old is he now?"

"Let's see. Homerline was 74 so that would make Jeff about 78."

It's hard to imagine an inmate in prison being 78 years old. Try as she might, she couldn't visualize what it might be like to be an imprisoned senior citizen.

"So tell me the rest…"

"Caroline tried to explain, but Jeff wouldn't give her a chance. All he could hear was that he wasn't getting any money. Homerline tried to reason with him, and that's when he accused her and her husband of stealing Homer and Caroline blind."

"I can sort of imagine how ugly that scene must have been."

"But it gets uglier. Jeff started to leave, but Caroline latched onto him to try and stop him. He slung her to the floor like a rag doll. Homerline said she heard her mama's neck when it broke, and where her head hit the wall, there was blood everywhere."

"Ohhhh…"

Kathy plucked a handkerchief from her pocket and dabbed at her eyes. "I'm telling you, the whole community was in a state of shock. When Jeff saw what he'd done, he cut and run. Folks didn't lock their cars in those days, so Homerline's truck was sitting in the side yard with the keys in it. He jumped in and took off." She banged her fist on the table. "Too much of a bully and a coward to stay behind and see to his mama or take responsibility for his actions."

"So he went to prison for murder?"

"That and aggravated assault on Emma."

"Emma?"

"Yeah, Emma wasn't born like she is now. Jeff did that, too."

Saralynn's head was spinning with grief and confusion. *I just always assumed that Emma's condition was probably a birth defect.*

Kathy continued. "Emma would have been about nine or maybe ten. She was out playing in the pasture and when she saw the truck coming down the road, she ran out to meet it. Jeff was in such a rage, when he saw her, he aimed the truck straight for her and ran her down."

"How awful!"

"About that time the ambulance Homerline had called for her mama arrived on the scene and began to doctor on Emma instead. They had to take her to Tupelo and she almost died on the way. She was in a coma for several weeks, and when she woke up, the accident had affected her mind. She never was the same."

"Poor Mrs. Jackson. She lost her daddy, her mother, her daughter was injured for life, and in truth, she lost her brother, too. Although I'd have to question if she ever really had him."

"That's what others said, too. But Homerline never gave up on him. Even after all these years, she still sent money to the prison so he could buy cigarettes and toiletry items. She even left money to bury him when the time comes. But he never spoke to her again after he stormed out of the house that day, even though she was there in the courtroom every day of his trial."

"How did she do it? How did she cope with all that and not be totally warped for life?"

"If you knew Homerline, you knew that it was her faith that got her through. Just like it was her faith that let her release Emma to go down south when Homerline got where she couldn't care for her at home."

Lord, what have You shown me this afternoon? I am in a state of shock, to put it mildly.

Saralynn became conscious of the sounds around her and realized that the sun was low in the afternoon sky and that people were securing the museum for the day. "Oh, Kathy, I'm so sorry. I hope I haven't kept you too long this afternoon."

Kathy smoothed back her hair and rose from her chair. "Not to worry. I knew this was going to hit you hard. I just never dreamed when you came in the other day that I was going to find a connection between you and Homerline."

Saralynn thanked her again, and made a mental note once back home to send the museum a nice donation. As they were walking across the old courthouse lobby, to the double front doors, something Kathy had said echoed across her brain again: *They had bought the Cochran home place...*

"Kathy?" She hesitated, not certain if she wanted confirmation of what she already suspected. "Where was the Cochran home place?"

Her new friend eyed her suspiciously, almost as if she couldn't take Saralynn's question seriously. "You know exactly where it is. It's your house in Fishtrap Hollow."

Caroline Cochran was killed in my house... in Homeline's house. And Emma was injured in the road near the house. How could she bear to continue to live there? I cut a trail from my house in Boston because I didn't have what it took to live inside those same four walls where Peter and Marc had been. But Mrs. Jackson spent the rest of her life there and even died there. She had something I don't.

Saralynn bade her new acquaintance good-bye, and drove slowly back to Fishtrap Hollow, her mind in confused turmoil, with the setting sun dropping lower in her rearview mirror with every mile she made.

I didn't even think to ask Kathy if Pansy is buried where Mr. and Mrs. Jackson are. I'll have to call her back.

Chapter 11

The alarm sounding on her cell phone dragged Saralynn out of a satisfying and restful sleep. *Wha... why... why is the alarm ringing?* Then she remembered. It was Sunday morning. *I'm supposed to meet MA and Jon for Sunday School.* She glanced at the clock on the dresser across from the bed. *Seven-thirty. I've really gotten lazy. Got to get back on a more scheduled routine soon, or I'm going to be ruined for everyday life.*

She rolled out of bed and stumbled to the kitchen for a bowl of cereal and toast. *Cheese toast, I think. After all, it is Sunday.* A cup of hot spiced tea completed her breakfast menu. As she ate, Saralynn realized she had less than twenty-four hours before she'd be back on the road to Magee. As she thought back to the events of the past week, it was amazing, all that had happened and all that she had learned.

These are the type things I'd love to be able to share with Mama.

Unfortunately, even if she weren't sick, even if she hadn't disowned me, I still wouldn't be able to tell her all that I've discovered.

A phone call to Elsie on Saturday had revealed things were about the same, but afterward, Saralynn was struck with the sad comparison between her mother and her great Uncle Jeff Cochran. For some unknown reason, they both hated Mississippi and their circumstances. And in the end, it has cost both of them dearly. *I'm not sure it was worth it. I wonder if Jeff would do things differently if he had the chance?*

At the appointed time she was nosing her Honda into a parking space across from the church and, true to their word, MA and Jon were standing nearby. As she exited the car and locked the door, MA called out. "Good morning, friend. We're so glad you came." She crossed the pavement to join Saralynn and snaked her arm around her friend's waist. "Let's go this way; our class meets in this building over here. We're running out of room in the main building."

The three entered what had obviously once been a commercial building which now housed the church offices, Jon explained, and some of those rooms did double duty as adult classroom space.

Sunday School was a low-key, friendly hour. Saralynn was momentarily hesitant about meeting so many new faces, but soon found herself at ease. *Sunday School here is a lot like it is at Rials Creek. Just different faces and different surroundings.* Somehow the similarities gave her comfort and a degree of confidence.

Too soon, however, the class ended and everyone trooped across the street to the main church building, to the sanctuary with the beautiful stained glass windows. In particular, the Good Shepherd window. As she entered the building, a woman standing in the foyer reached out and touched Saralynn's arm.

"Ms. Reilly?"

She was momentarily startled. "Yes? I'm Saralynn Reilly."

"I'm Geneva Andrews, George, your home inspector's wife."

I had totally forgotten about them!

"Oh, Mrs. Andrews. Your husband told me you'd be watching for me." She shook the woman's hand. "It's so nice to meet you."

Jon Walthall, who had stopped to speak to someone outside, walked up about that time. "Have you two met?"

"Yes, we have…" both ladies replied in unison, as if on cue. Then both halted and laughed.

"No introductions necessary, then" Jon replied. "Would you like to sit with us, Geneva? I know George is in the choir."

That's how Saralynn found herself seated in the comfortable sanctuary between MA and Geneva Andrews. Jon sat on the other side of MA, and the few minutes before the service began were filled with different ones stopping to introduce themselves to Saralynn, and to welcome her to their church.

Then the organ music began and the sanctuary quickly became quiet. *Reverent is the word for it.*

Saralynn was relieved to discover that the service progressed in a manner similar to what she had become accustomed, allowing her to feel very much at home. As she studied her bulletin, she noted that there was a guest vocalist scheduled to perform a medley of prayer hymns just prior to the sermon. *I wonder just what prayer hymns are?*

Before she knew it, more than half an hour had passed and the pastor, a young man with a very friendly face and short, dark hair, began to speak. "We're delighted today to have with us Catherine Scarborough, Eleanor Austin's sister. Catherine is somewhat of a professional musician in Georgia, where she and her husband, Grant, make their home. They're visiting with Eleanor and Richard this weekend, and she has graciously consented to share her God-given musical talent with us this morning." He smiled over at the petite, dark-haired woman who had stepped into the chancel as he spoke. "Welcome to our church, Catherine."

The pastor resumed his seat as the guest stepped to the pulpit, where she arranged her music, then looked at the congregation and smiled. "I know the bulletin says I'm going to sing a medley of prayer hymns. Unfortunately, there's been a slight change in plans." She laughed. "Yesterday morning at Eleanor's, I was practicing, when the tape deck ate my background music."

A murmur of sympathy rose from the congregation.

She laughed again and Saralynn found her smile infectious. "I called the choir director, who told me not to worry, he had the same tape and that we could practice this morning."

The congregation hung on her every word expectantly.

"However, that tape was also destroyed earlier this morning by the tape deck here; so I have to conclude that, for whatever reason, God doesn't want me to sing those hymns."

That's a funny way for her to phrase it. How could she come to that conclusion?

"Instead," she continued, "I'm going to sing one of the old, favorite hymns of the church, "The Old Rugged Cross.""

I don't think I've ever heard that one.

The first notes of the piano sounded and Saralynn joined the congregation in anxious anticipation, waiting for the solo that was to follow. She wasn't disappointed as the first words began to pour from the little woman at the pulpit. *Oh, she has such a beautiful voice. The pastor wasn't kidding when he said she was a professional.*

Saralynn was mesmerized and listened intently to the words the soloist sang: "In the old rugged cross, stained with blood so divine, a wondrous beauty I see; for 'twas on that old cross Jesus suffered and died, to pardon and sanctify me." Then slowly, as the musician continued to sing about sharing "Glory with Jesus," Saralynn realized something was happening. Something she could neither explain nor understand.

She felt more than a little panicky. Yet at the same time, she had no desire to run for safety. *I don't think I've ever felt more exposed and vulnerable and yet totally safe at the same time. What's happening?*

"Are you alright?" MA whispered. "You're trembling."

Can everyone see that something's wrong? I've never been so embarrassed, but I don't know what this is!

"I'm fine," she replied softly, if not totally honestly. "The music is so beautiful I guess it's giving me chills."

Her friend seemed to buy the explanation, but Saralynn herself was far from convinced. Truth be told, she was totally unnerved. *I've never experienced anything like that before, and I've heard a lot of beautiful music.*

The musician finished and the pastor stepped back into the pulpit. After offering complimentary remarks, he launched into his sermon. It was a delivery that might have been stellar, but Saralynn heard none of what he had to say. Instead, she sat, her body tensed, willing the minutes to pass so that she might get up and exit the pew without calling undue attention to herself.

Just when it seemed the service would never end, the minister pronounced the benediction, the acolytes led the procession to the back of the church, and the congregation began to stand. If Saralynn thought she would be able to make a hasty retreat, she was wrong. In fact, it took almost ten minutes as one member after another stopped to speak, or came up behind her and tapped her on the shoulder.

"Well, I never," she finally said to MA when there was a momentary lull. "I don't think I've ever been this welcome anywhere. Where's Jon?"

Her friend laughed. "We're a pretty friendly bunch here. Which is exactly where Jon is… outside pressing the flesh." On the other side, Geneva Andrews who had been snagging those who didn't automatically stop, echoed MA's comments.

"We're like one big family." She smiled at Saralynn and patted her arm. "We really are glad to have you with us, my dear. My husband was totally taken with you."

As they were about to finally exit the pew row and leave the sanctuary, Mrs. Andrews, who was leading the way out into the aisle, stopped so suddenly Saralynn and MA crashed into her.

"And speaking of my husband, here he comes now. We'll wait because he'll certainly want to greet you properly."

Saralynn and MA just looked at each other and grinned a "if you can't beat 'em, join 'em" expression.

"Well, well, I see you two met," George Andrews said by way of greeting when he reached the ladies. "Ms. Reilly, I'm so glad you came." He waded past his wife and enveloped Saralynn in a gentle bear hug. "We're big huggers around here," he explained as he pulled away.

"I can see that," Saralynn mumbled. *I just want to get out of here.*

MA, evidently sensing Saralynn's discomfort, suggested,

"Let's move on outside where we've got more room."

Once outside the church, Saralynn realized that she felt less claustrophobic than she had only a few minutes earlier. But before she could revel in her newfound freedom, MA grabbed her arm. "You didn't get to meet the pastor Wednesday night, so let me introduce you."

Before she knew what was happening, Saralynn found herself speaking with the man she had seen only at a distance, and answering his questions about how she liked Iuka, how fortunate Emma Jackson was that she had come into her life, and extracting the promise that she would consider the Iuka congregation her church home whenever she was in town.

All I want to do is get to my car and go back to Fishtrap Hollow. I don't know what happened here this morning.

"Come on, Saralynn, remember we're going out to eat." The voice belonged to Jon Walthall and reminded her, painfully so, that she had promised to join them for lunch. *Something tells me I won't have much luck ducking out at this late date.*

Instead, Saralynn allowed herself to be guided to the Walthall Mercedes, where she settled herself in the back seat. *I'm just along for the ride.*

Conversation in the car revolved around the service, comments about various members and prayer concerns that had been voiced, and plans for the church's anniversary celebration scheduled several months away.

Over a Sunday lunch that looked to Saralynn more like an elaborate holiday meal, talk turned to plans for the week ahead. "Don't forget you're coming by my office in the morning before you leave town," Jon reminded her. "And don't be late," he warned her, wagging his finger. "I have an appointment at 9:30 that I can't break."

"I'll be prompt, I promise."

MA in turn shook her finger at her husband. "Don't let him frighten you, Saralynn. His appointment that's so important is the regular daily meeting of the coffee club in the back room at the Cozy Corner Gift Shoppe."

"I beg your pardon?" *Did I hear her correctly?*

"Now, MA. You're going to give Saralynn the wrong idea."

"Hush, Jon."

"One of you is joking, right?"

"MA's just trying…"

"MA's just trying to set the record straight," the lawyer's wife interrupted. She turned to look at Saralynn at the same time that she said to her husband, "Now you just be quiet."

I feel like I'm the butt of some joke I don't understand.

"A group of the town's stellar, self-anointed male leaders meet Monday through Friday in the stock room at The Cozy Corner for coffee and who knows what in the way of conversation."

"They meet in the stock room?"

"There's a story behind that…" Jon interjected.

"I told you to pipe down." MA laughed. "Jon's right. There is a story, and once you and I can meet out front for coffee while they're in session in the back room, I'll give you the whole tale. The accurate account!"

"Is it a secret society or something?"

Jon opened his mouth to speak, but seeing the warning on his wife's face, shut his mouth without ever uttering a word.

"To hear them tell it, the town, and probably the whole world, would collapse without their input on the issues. Personally I think it's just a chance for guys who can pull away from their jobs without getting fired to do so."

"Now, MA. You're not being fair," her husband protested. "It's no different from that hen klatch you and your friends call those Bunco games every other week."

"There certainly is a difference. If we have conflicts, we don't go. I do believe you guys would walk by a burning building and leave it in flames before you'd miss the Coffee Club."

"Now that's hitting below…"

By this point, Saralynn was unable to contain her laughter. "You two," she interrupted. "I don't think I've missed my husband, Peter so much as I have in the last few minutes listening to you." *Peter and I used to go on at each other in exactly the same way that Jon and MA have been mixing it up. It really makes me lonesome for a soul-mate.*

"So you have a husband?" It was MA who posed the question. "I wondered why someone as nice as you wasn't married."

"Uh, MA… don't…" Jon interjected.

I've shown my hand again. So I might as well give her the condensed version.

"I was married," she explained quietly. "My husband, Peter, and our son, Marc, were killed in an accident a little over a year ago."

She saw that MA had tears in her eyes, and in a husky voice Jon said, finally, "I'm sorry, Saralynn. I forgot to tell MA. I don't usually share…"

She flashed them both the smile she had finally been able to find within herself to put others at ease over this subject. "I'm glad to be able to tell you about them both."

"How have you managed?" MA asked. "I can't imagine what I'd do if I lost Jon."

"You'd do the same thing I did. You'd get by because you don't have much choice. But I don't mean to imply that it's as simple as that."

Over the next few minutes Saralynn shared with her friends the story of her loss, and in the end, she whipped out the photos of both her guys she still carried in her wallet.

"They were great looking men. Both of them," MA said as she handed the pictures back. "I know you must miss them."

"There's not a day that goes by, regardless of what I'm doing, that I don't think about both of them. It still hurts, just not as bad as it once did. She traced the circle of condensation left on the table by her tea glass. "They say time heals all wounds. I'm not sure it heals the wounds, as much as it scabs them over. Every day is a little easier."

The ride back to Saralynn's car, was low key and relaxed. *I feel very comfortable with these people. I just wish I felt secure enough to confide how the service this morning affected me. Especially that song, "The Old Rugged Cross". I can't decide whether to feel frightened or... or what.*

Saralynn declined their invitation to return for the evening service, saying she had to pack and make preparations to leave early the next morning. "After all," she told Jon as she was getting out of the car, "I certainly don't want it on my conscience as I head south tomorrow that I kept you from the Coffee Club."

"Touche'," he said, as the three parted company amidst much laughter.

Saralynn headed her Honda east, her mind already at work on all that she had to do to be packed that night. *I don't want to be rushed tomorrow morning. And I've got several things to do to ready the house, since it's probably going to get really cold here before I get back.*

While they were standing outside the church earlier that day, George Andrews had shoved a folded piece of paper into her hand. "This is a list of things you need to do to winterize your house before you leave tomorrow." Saralynn had thanked him and placed the paper into her purse without even looking at it. *That was nice of him to do that. He and his wife are both nice, just a little intense at times. I can't imagine being with the both of them long term. But then I've become somewhat of a hermit these last few months. Maybe I've forgotten what life is really like.*

She recalled the banter, the easy give and take of her lunch hosts and realized that indeed she was missing out on a lot. *But what can I do about it?*

Once back at the house, Saralynn set about washing dirty clothes, cleaning the house, gathering her business files and getting ready to load the car. *It's soon going to be fall weather here and between Mama and the Atlanta commission, I simply don't know when I'll be back.* Plus, Saralynn was reluctant to bring Emma home too soon, not knowing how she would react to the house without her mother. *I don't know if I'm prepared to deal with her emotions. So maybe I'm chicken.*

She was already loaded, except for her overnight case and toiletries, and was ready to settle into bed, when she remembered that she'd promised to call Katie Brooks and hadn't done so. *I told her I'd call her on Thursday, and I totally forgot.*

Hoping it wasn't too late, she snatched her cell phone from the bedside table and hit the speed dial code for her friend's home. Two rings later she was rewarded with the sound of a voice that she realized anew was special.

"Saralynn! I was so hoping you'd call tonight."

"Oh, Katie. Can you ever forgive me? I promised to call

you last Thursday, but I got involved in work and somehow," she explained rather lamely, "the days just got away from me."

"I was afraid I'd offended you, and I'm sorry if I did."

"You didn't, don't worry."

"You know I love you enough to never want to hurt your feelings."

"I know you…"

"But I also love you enough," her friend interrupted, "to tell you the truth as I see it. And that's what I did."

"Not to worry," Saralynn assured her. *I need to tell her what happened at church this morning. Don't I?*

"Is something else bothering you? I assumed when I hadn't heard that you'd call after you got in tomorrow."

Saralynn hesitated. "There is something I want to talk to you about when I get home, but if I don't tell somebody tonight, I feel like I'm going to explode."

"Now you've really gotten my curiosity aroused."

Saralynn recounted the episode in church and her reaction to the song the soloist sang. "Why would I have done that, Katie?"

There was silence on the other end, and then Saralynn was certain she heard sounds of quiet sobbing. "Katie! Are you crying? Is something wrong?"

"On the contrary, my friend who is more like a sister, something is very right."

"Then you are crying?"

"Yes, but they're tears of joy."

"OK. Now you've lost me."

"Oh, Saralynn, don't you see? God is speaking to your heart. There's nothing more basic to salvation than the ownership of our place on that cross where Jesus suffered such a horrible death. Whether you realized it or not, you were listening with your heart this morning… your heart that is truly aching for you to give it to Jesus."

But I don't understand how to do that. It's not that I'm against doing it. I just don't know how.

"I think I see what you're saying," she assured her friend. "But I'm still very confused about how you give your heart to a man who is dead. Whether He's God's son or not."

"Listen, Saralynn. Just trust me on this. All you have to do is acknowledge to God, and yourself, that you believe that Jesus is His son, that He died on the cross for everyone who is willing to trust Him, and that you're ready to do that."

"It sounds so simple. Too simple. How can I know that I'm good enough for God? You forget I wasn't raised in the church; I don't have the background all my friends do."

"Salvation is a simple matter," Katie went on to explain, "because in truth, none of us is 'good enough for God', as you put it. We're all sinners, even those of us who have been in church since we were babies."

"Then if we're sinners, how can we go to God?"

"That's what is so beautiful. It doesn't matter how old we are, how rich or poor we are, whether we're guilty of gray sins or dark, dark black ones, God promises to meet us wherever we are, and make us His. All we have to do is ask. But He won't force us. He'll nudge us and show us, but He won't force us. Because He wants us to come to Him willingly."

"So you're saying that even though I've only been in church a year, I can be assured of the same future in heaven that you expect?"

"The very same one, only mine will be just a little bit better than yours, because I'll have someone who has come to be like the sister I lost there with me."

Saralynn was so choked up, she couldn't speak. So when Katie asked her to allow her to pray, a mumbled "uh, huh," was all she could manage.

Oh Wonderful God and Father, we give You thanks and all the glory tonight for the emotions that Saralynn experienced this morning. We know for the first time that she was truly hearing with her heart, and that what she heard through that singer's words, was Your voice, Your invitation to her, to join You in Heaven some day. Continue to work on her heart and her mind, Father. And give those of us closest to her the wisdom to know how to help her find her way to You. In Jesus' name, the only pathway to You, we ask. Amen.

"Thanks, Katie," was all Saralynn could utter, she was so fearful of totally losing composure. "I'll talk to you when I get in tomorrow."

"Good night," her friend replied. "Drive safely. I love you."

"I love you, too."

She turned off the light, but it was a long time before her mind extinguished itself. And then it was to dream of crosses and heaven and, yes, even Peter and Marc.

Chapter 12

As Saralynn guided the Honda south on Monday morning, her mind was on everything except what awaited her back in Magee. True to his word, Jon Walthall had made quick dispatch of the tele-conference with the Boston attorney.

I don't have a clue if we did everything we needed to do. Should it really have taken only thirty minutes, or was MA serious that Jon wouldn't let anything mess with his Coffee Club meeting? Since I trust him, I'm going to assume we dotted all the i's and crossed all the t's.

Those i's and t's included a detailed conversation with attorney Quincy Adams – absolutely no relation to the former presidents, he had assured them both – which ended with his promise to begin drafting the suit that day, pending results of Alicia's upcoming doctor's appointment and service of the papers.

I still can't believe it's come to this, but knowing what I do about Mama, I've got to protect myself. Thank goodness Mr. Adams agreed to represent me on the stalking and theft charges as well.

Saralynn willed herself to think about something else. Anything else. *Otherwise I'll be stark raving mad by the time I hit south Mississippi, if I haven't been so distracted that I have a wreck before I get there!*

It feels so good to be back in familiar surroundings. Saralynn had arrived home at mid-afternoon, and hadn't stopped since her feet hit the ground. *I had to unpack the car, check out the house, make a grocery list, and head back to town to the store. Thank goodness I picked up fast food for dinner… I don't think I would have made it if I had tried to cook.*

Once the wrappers from her meal were trashed, Saralynn headed for the studio. She spent the remainder of the evening listening to phone messages, making a to-do list for the next day, and getting her tools and supplies organized. She wanted to be ready to go right to work on another of the commissioned designs the next morning.

It gave me goose bumps to hear the message from Christina that they're bringing me to Atlanta when the pieces go up in the condos. She said they might even host a gallery showing for me then as well.

Finally, at eleven o'clock when she could neither physically nor mentally do one more task, she dragged herself across the garage and into the house. Once upstairs in her bedroom, she stood in the shower until the water ran cold, then pulled on a gown and collapsed on the bed.

Merry Heart

The ringing phone slowly penetrated her sleep-induced stupor, and Saralynn finally got awake enough to realize that she was being summoned. *But which phone? I don't know which phone to answer.* She grabbed for the landline on the night stand. "Helwo," she answered, her voice still thick with sleep.

"Uh... uh, I'm trying to reach Saralynn Reilly."

"Thisss ish she," she replied, trying to peel her dry tongue off the roof of her mouth.

"Saralynn! Is that you? My gosh, what's wrong?"

It's Katie! Then realization hit. *Oh my gosh, I promised I'd call her when I got in last night and I totally forgot.* "It's me," she responded, thankful that she could finally speak clearly. *Now if only I could get the fog to leave my brain alone!*

"Are you sick? Do you need me?" Saralynn could hear the concern in her friend's voice.

"No, not ill. Just exhausted." She watched the sun making shadows on the bedroom carpet as the clouds moved and obscured and repositioned themselves. *From the angle of that light, I'd say I've overslept. It's got to be at least nine o'clock.*

"Did something go wrong that made you get in late last night? I was getting worried when I didn't hear from you by the time Paul went to sleep."

Saralynn laughed. "Actually, I got here just before three o'clock yesterday. But re-entry was rough. Not to mention that I had phone messages and work tasks piled up past the wazoo."

"Surely you didn't come in and try to tackle all of that?"

She laughed again, except she felt no humor in the expression. "Oh, surely I did. And got so involved that before I could find a stopping place, it was eleven o'clock and I did good to crawl up to my bed."

"Then I woke you up."

A glance at the clock showed her that her estimate was slightly off. The large numerals read 9:29. "Yes, you did, and thank you. No telling when I might have awakened. I didn't even have enough sense last night to set the alarm."

As she spoke, Saralynn pulled herself upright and stumbled toward the master bathroom, where she paused long enough to stare at a face in the mirror she didn't recognize. It was enough to cause her to move on to the shower, where she reached in and hit the mixing valve, purposely pushing it to maximum hot.

"Listen, friend. Let me get a shower and get awake and I promise, I'll call you back." *I've got to call Elsie, too.*

"Good enough. Get your shower. But call me back because I was worried."

It feels so good to know that someone worries about me. "I know you are," she replied. "And I love you for it."

When the first spray of water struck her back, Saralynn screamed, jumped, and grabbed for the lever to add a little more cold to the mix. *Not much use being wide awake if you're too scalded to enjoy it!*

Even though she knew she had tasks awaiting, the young woman luxuriated in the cascading waters as long as she dared and, only when she felt the coolness beginning to conquer the hot, did she reluctantly push the valve into the off position and grab for her towel.

I wouldn't trade a good, hot morning shower for any amount of money. It's what get's me going.

She dressed, ran a brush through her tangled hair and

headed to the kitchen. As she took the steps two at a time, her to-do list was running through her head and she was mentally prioritizing the chores that awaited her that day – starting with returning Katie's call.

She brewed a cup of tea, a mainstay of her morning routine and grabbed the land line, dialed Katie's number and activated the hands-free function.

"Hey. That was quick," her friend responded after answering on the second ring. "You didn't have to break your neck."

"I wanted to be sure I didn't forget. Besides, you're going to have to share me with my breakfast preparations. I've got you on speaker so I can work while we talk."

Katie had no objections and asked, "In general is everything going according to plan? How's your mother?"

Saralynn detailed the conversation with the Boston attorney, and recounted all the backed up tasks that had confronted her upon her return. "I really thought the work I took with me would keep me ahead of the game. WRONG!"

"So did you under-estimate, or did more than you anticipated crop up?"

Saralynn scratched her head for a moment. "Probably a combination of the two, if I'm honest. I shouldn't have stayed as long as I did in Iuka, but I have to tell you what I learned." *I haven't shared this with anyone, not even MA and Jon.*

"This sounds good."

"You'll never believe it, but I got a line on Miss Sallie's ancestors while I was there. And guess what? My grandmother had a twin sister that was still-born. Her name was Pansy."

"That sounds so beautifully old-fashioned and little girlish too."

"That's what I thought. And guess what else? You'll never believe this one!"

"I'm afraid to guess."

"Emma and I are distant kin. Can you get ready for that?" *And I've got to go check on Emma today. I forgot to put that on my list.*

"You're kidding?"

Saralynn offered the condensed trip back up the family tree. "I don't know whether to tell Emma or not."

"Hmmm…" was all Katie said. Then, after a moment, "You know, I don't think I would. Emma already considers you family, so the details aren't going to make any difference and would probably confuse her."

"I guess you're right." Saralynn served up the French toast she'd assembled while the two talked. "My breakfast is ready, so let me go while it's hot. I'll call you back later tonight. After Paul goes down, probably, because I've got a hectic day ahead."

She was already forking into the food on her plate when Katie said, "And when you call tonight, we're going to talk some more about you asking Jesus to come into your heart."

I'd forgotten all about that topic. Evidently Katie hasn't. "Yeah," she agreed half-heartedly, "we can talk about it then."

Breakfast finished, Saralynn quickly cleaned the kitchen and washed her few dishes. Then it was out to the studio, where a full day of work awaited. First on her list of tasks was to begin cutting the fabric pieces that would form three of the commissioned pieces. *It just makes better sense to do all my cutting at one time for several pieces. Then I can clear the cutting table and begin to assemble. Sort of a mini-assembly line.*

She worked steadily until shortly after noon, when the French toast wore off. She knew from experience her production would suffer if she didn't stop and get something to eat. *I know... I'll drive over to Boswell and check on Emma and get something to eat there... at LeGrand Café there on the grounds.*

Her visit with Emma lasted longer than she'd planned, but the older woman was so excited to see her, Saralynn couldn't bear to pull away. Her ward had a thousand questions that Saralynn patiently answered, constantly aware she couldn't disclose she had actually been in Iuka. *Emma wouldn't understand, but I feel so guilty skating around the truth.*

"Oops," she said finally making it a point to look at her watch. "We've really been visiting a long time, Emma. "It's after two o'clock. I've got to get back home. Being gone all this time has put me far behind with my work."

Still, it took another few minutes to disengage herself from Emma's neck hugs and get back behind the wheel of her car. As she started the engine, her stomach growled as if in answer to the sound of the motor. *I missed lunch, too. The LeGrand has already stopped serving, so I guess it's fast food take-out again.*

A detour through a convenient drive-in burger outlet served to satisfy her hunger pangs, if not her desire for some good food, as she drove on home. *I should have taken the extra few minutes and driven down to get a Zip's burger. Now that's a real hamburger.* Just the thought of the house specialty burger at Zip's Restaurant caused her mouth to water, while it made the franchised burger taste more like cardboard on a bun.

Back at her studio she placed several phone calls to check the status of proposals she'd made, and to respond to queries from a team of decorators in Oregon who had heard about her art second-hand. The last call she made that afternoon was to Boston, to Elsie.

I don't want to make this call, but I can't decide if it's because I might learn bad news, or because I'm just so weary of dealing with all Mama's self-inflicted problems. Except, of course, the tumor we suspect in her head.

Elsie answered on the ninth ring and Saralynn had been ready to punch the OFF button on her phone when she heard what sounded like the line being answered on the other end. "Elsie? Is that you?"

"Oh, hi, Saralynn." Her words were thick, and were followed by an obvious sigh and a yawn.

I never knew Elsie to sleep during the day. "Did I wake you? Is everything OK?"

Another yawn. "Your mother is about to drive me up the wall. This is the first time I've closed my eyes in more than twenty-four hours."

"What's Mama done now? She's not worse is she?"

Elsie yawned again. This time she said, "I'm sorry. I don't mean to keep yawning in your ear."

"Don't worry about it. I'm sorry I woke you. So what's the deal?"

"I was going to call you when I woke up, anyway. So it's just as well you called me." Another yawn. "We've got to go back to see the doctor tomorrow. His nurse said they were working us in. And it must be a work-in, because they made it for four-fifteen."

That special MRI must have shown something the doctor doesn't like. "You weren't expecting to go back so quickly, were you?"

"Well, your mama wasn't. All I can say is, after she got the call yesterday afternoon, she's been like a crazy person. I couldn't get her to lie down or even sit. All she does is walk the floor and cry about how badly her head hurts and how scared she is."

Mama's scared and admits it? Something's definitely not right here.

"I finally got her down for a nap about a half hour ago, but I think it was more exhaustion than me convincing her."

"And since she was asleep, you decided to make the most of it?"

"That's about the size of it."

Saralynn glanced around the studio, at the three commissioned pieces in mid-production and all the bolts of fabric she'd bought to fulfill the entire order. A look at the large wall calendar with a color picture of playful Cavalier King Charles Spaniel puppies reminded her that the days were ticking down.

And I've still got twenty-five more to go after I finish these. But I have to ask this. "Do you need me to come? I'll get a plane out of here early tomorrow if you say the word." She was already pulling up the air line web site. "I can get there in time to go to the doctor with you."

"I don't think she'll let you," was Elsie's snap response. "I've tried floating your name a couple of times in conversation and almost walked away with my head in my hands both times."

Mama. If only you could understand how difficult you make it for all of us. "I just hate for you to have to shoulder all this alone."

Saralynn got up to check the fax that had sounded while she and Elsie were talking. Seeing that it was only a bulk-distribution specials flier from a supplier, she wadded the piece of paper and aimed a free-throw shot toward the large waste basket by the cutting table. It missed.

"For right now, stay where you are until we see the doctor tomorrow. After that, depending on what he says, you may have to come whether Alicia wants to see you or not." There was another sigh. "I'm just not as young as I used to be."

"Alright, Elsie. We'll do it this way for now. But I may well come this week regardless of what the doctor says. Just let me know as soon as you can."

I'm going to have to put in some late hours again tonight if I even entertain the thought of going to Boston. This commission is too valuable to mess it up.

Even as she tackled her work with renewed vigor, Saralynn was aware that the next twenty-four hours were going to be both the longest and shortest for her. *Because I'm waiting for an answer that perhaps I don't even want, time will really drag. But when it comes to knocking down my to-do list, something tells me I won't even make a good dent between now and tomorrow.* For the first time in a long time, she felt really stressed. *I'm beginning to feel like I did back in Boston, when decorating commissions snowballed on me. Only that was then and this is now.*

Determined that if she threw herself into her work, time would pass faster, Saralynn stayed in the studio until almost midnight, before she fell into her bed and slept a sleep that was tormented with strange but unexplainable dreams. The next morning she continued to drive herself at the same punishing pace. Still, she was unable to keep her eyes from straying to the oversized clock on the wall and her mind from mentally adjusting the time zone difference and calculating how long it would be before Elsie could possibly call.

I may not know anything until late tonight, until she's able to get free of Mama long enough to call me. The thought that she might have to wait even longer for information was maddening.

The only break she had taken the previous evening was the promised call to Katie who, when she heard the situation, agreed that was not the time for serious discussion and that Saralynn needed to get back to work. "Just promise to keep me posted," she said, as they were hanging up.

At lunch Saralynn fixed herself two peanut butter sandwiches and kept working. *At least I'm making some headway that I can see, but I wouldn't want to attempt production under this much stress every day.*

The sun was even with the bottom of the studio windows when the land line phone rang. Since she'd told Elsie to call on the cell number, Saralynn was caught off guard when she looked at the Caller ID and saw a Massachusetts' area code followed by an unfamiliar number.

"Ms. Reilly?" the man's voice inquired. "Ms. Saralynn Reilly?"

"Yes, that's right… I'm… I'm Saralynn Reilly," she stammered. "Who is this?" she blurted.

"I'm sorry, Ms. Reilly. This is Chance Lawson in Boston, I'm a paralegal working with Mr. Quincy Adams."

It's the lawyer's office!

"I believe you've retained Mr. Adams to file suit against a Ms. Alicia Bankston?"

"Yes, that's right." *What does he want? And why hasn't Elsie called?*

"Mr. Adams wanted me to relay the message that we have the papers ready to file, we're just waiting your go-ahead. Do you have any idea when that might come?"

Sounds like an ambulance chaser! "As my attorney here in Mississippi and I both explained to Mr. Adams, we're not doing anything until after my mother sees a doctor. As a matter of fact, I'm waiting now for a call to learn how that appointment went and what the doctor had to say."

"Then we can expect a call from you tomorrow with the authorization to proceed." The words were spoken as a foregone conclusion, not a question.

Saralynn tried to mask her irritation. "You may expect a call from me as soon as I decide. I don't know when that will be."

"I'll relay the message to Mr. Adams. He would really like to move forward." He pronounced the word "fahh-wad" and for the first time ever, Saralynn found no interest in the trademark Boston accent that had charmed her hearing for so long.

She glanced at the clock when she hung up and decided it was too late to put in a call to Jon Walthall. *He's going to have to put a lid on that lawyer. I'm not going to have these papers filed until I know how today came out. I'll call him first thing in the morning.*

While the temptation to knock off work was almost overwhelming, Saralynn pushed on, determined to make every minute count, and to stay busy so she wouldn't be counting those minutes. It was already dark, and she hadn't eaten, when her cell phone rang and she was finally rewarded with the familiar sight of Elsie's number.

"I thought you'd never call!" she proclaimed as she answered the phone. "I've about gone crazy waiting."

"I'm sorry," an exhausted and defeated voice replied. "I did the best I could."

Saralynn didn't want to appear unfriendly or unsympathetic to her friend's burden. *After all, she is standing in for me when it's certainly not her place.* But she also didn't think she could stay calm much longer.

Fortunately Elsie was too tired to take offense at the unintended but obvious curtness of Saralynn's tone. "The news is bad and good and bad, and before you accuse me of riding the fence, I'm telling you just like the doctor told us."

Saralynn immediately regretted her impatience. "First of all, before you explain all of that, WHERE is Mama?"

"That's what I'm trying to tell you. She's in the hospital, and not very willingly, either, I might add."

The hospital! "What happened?"

"The bad news is that it is a rather large tumor as brain tumors go."

Saralynn felt her legs go weak and she had to lean against the cabinet in the kitchen where she had been making another sandwich. *We knew this was a very real possibility, but still, hearing it officially makes it a whole lot more scary.*"

"Because of its location and particular characteristics – again, I'm quoting the doctor – the chances are ninety-nine percent that it's benign."

Oh, thank you, Lord! "Then that is good news. So why's Mama in the hospital?"

She went about the kitchen replacing items in the large refrigerator and wiping down the counter. Her sandwich lay on a napkin, on the end of the island with only one bite missing. For the moment it was forgotten.

"That's the other part of the bad news," Elsie continued. "Benign or not, the doctor says it has to come out, because it shows no signs of slowing its growth."

Saralynn went cold all over. *Brain surgery? Mama?* "Oh...

Elsie," was the only response she could muster. Suddenly all the starch deserted her and she sank down to the Travertine tile floor and braced herself against the island, momentarily unable to speak.

I know I should be saying something, asking something, or at least thanking Elsie for all she's done. But it's like my vocal cords are paralyzed. And my brain isn't far behind.

"Saralynn!" Elsie's voice demanded. "Did you hang up on me?"

"Oh... no... no, Elsie. Of course not." Her head was spinning and Saralynn wondered seriously if she were about to faint. "I'm just trying to take it all in." *And not doing a very good job, either.*

"You're going to have to come, Saralynn. Whether Alicia wants you here or not, you've got to be here. You're her closest living relative."

Saralynn reached up to the edge of the granite countertop and pulled herself into a standing position. *Yes, I've got to be there and that won't happen by me sitting here in the floor, although right now even that is more of a task than I feel capable of handling.* "I'll get the first flight out that I can tomorrow. When are they planning to do surgery?"

"The doctor would like to do it tomorrow, but when he found out I wasn't blood kin, he didn't want to do anything until you got here."

"Did he tell Mama that?"

"Uh-huh."

"It didn't fly, did it?"

"I think between this doctor's hard-headedness and your mama being scared, she may have just met her match this time." She hesitated, then with just the tiniest bit of mirth in her voice, continued, "But, no, 'it didn't fly', as you put it."

I'm going to be there and Mama's just going to have to accept it.

"But the doctor told her he was calling you. That's the other thing I needed to tell you. Expect a call from him sometime tonight. But I wanted you to hear it from me first."

"Thank you, Elsie. I don't know what I would have done without you." *And I don't!*

"Alicia has been my friend, really more like my sister, for longer than I can count." Elsie's voice was quiet, and Saralynn thought she detected a sob. "I'd do anything for her, but I'm so glad you're coming home. I'm exhausted and my heart is hurting as well."

Poor Elsie. "You think the doctor will call tonight?"

"He said he would."

"Then let me hang up and get on-line and buy a ticket and start pulling clothes together. I'll be waiting to hear from him."

Saralynn had barely finished booking a reservation when the land line phone rang. "Hello?"

The voice on the other end was definitely male, certainly from one of Boston's first families, if the brogue and diction were any indication, and was one of the coldest Saralynn had ever heard.

"This is Dr. Dudley Martin in Boston calling for Saralynn Reilly. Put her on, please. I don't have much time."

He doesn't care about niceties. I guess I've been in the south too long. "This is she."

"Ms. Reilly, I believe Mrs. Alicia Bankston is your mother." *It wasn't phrased as a question.*

"Yes sir, she is. What can you tell me about her? Elsie told me you'd be calling."

"Did your friend explain the nature of the problem?"

The nature of the problem is she has a brain tumor. Can we get more specific here?

"I understand she has a benign brain tumor that you feel must come out."

"It's not that I feel it," he snapped. "I know it. From many years of experience, I know that this tumor will only continue to grow, even if it is benign."

"I understand." *This guy isn't going to budge an inch, so I best play his game.*

"The tumor has doubled in size in the past two weeks. I have no reason to believe it will voluntarily cease to multiply."

"So what happens if we don't remove the tumor?" *I'm going to play devil's advocate here.* "Are you convinced this is absolutely necessary?"

"Ms. Reilly! I'll have you know that I have a tremendous amount of money invested in my medical degree, and in my practice. Surely you don't doubt me!"

Touchy… touchy.

"No. Dr. Martin, I don't doubt you and I'm sorry if I gave that impression."

"You know your mother is a difficult woman."

Saralynn was caught off-guard by this shift in conversation. Nevertheless, she had to chuckle. *Evidently Mama turned on the charm.* "Why do you say that, Dr. Martin?"

"She wants to argue about everything I say. I do so hope you aren't just like her."

Saralynn chuckled. "I hope not, either, Dr. Martin."

'Hummph!"

"So give me the details, please."

"This tumor is growing rapidly. We have it on scan, and your mother's description of her symptoms – the headache that worsens instead of improving – support this premise. If we don't get it out, it will continue to grow until the pressure inside her head causes permanent damage."

"Permanent damages... such as?"

"Good grief, young lady. Think about it. It could crack her skull. Press on a nerve and cause her to go blind or be paralyzed or totally change personality."

He is touchy, touchy.

"I understand. So when will you do the surgery? And how much risk does it carry?"

As she talked, Saralynn was walking about the bedroom, pulling open drawers and retrieving clothing items which she carried to the spacious king size bed, where an open piece of her custom luggage was waiting.

"As with any surgery," the doctor explained, "there's always some degree of risk. Without the surgery, she will die. That's a given in my opinion." He hesitated. "The only question in my mind is when and how much will she suffer in the process?"

Talk about painting a bleak picture. "Did you explain all this to my mother?"

"I did."

There was more unsaid there than said. "I assume she didn't agree?"

"Oh... it was much more than disagreement. She knows more about medicine than I do. At least that's what she informed me."

Saralynn dug in the dryer for clean underwear which she carried to the bed to be packed. A glance in the dresser mirror as she passed caused her to almost drop the clothes in the floor. *I look like I've seen a ghost.*

"So let's cut to the chase. What has my mother agreed to do? And when?"

The first response from the other end was a long and exasperated sounding sigh. "As I said, Ms. Reilly, your mother is a difficult woman."

I know. Tell me something I don't know!

"At first she fought me," he admitted. "But I was even more direct with her than I have been with you."

Whew! I almost feel sorry for Mama.

"In the end, she agreed to have the surgery and we have it scheduled for late tomorrow afternoon. I don't even want to wait until Monday if we can help it."

"That quickly?"

"I'm afraid so. But I also informed your mother that I would not put her under anesthesia unless her next of kin was at the hospital."

I'll bet that conversation was rich.

"At first she claimed she had no blood relatives, but thankfully, your friend who was with her, contradicted her and told me about you."

I'm sure Elsie will pay dearly for turning traitor. That's probably why she didn't mention it when we talked. "So what was the final outcome?"

"First," he said, "I must ask you. Will you come?"

"I've already booked a flight and I'll get into Boston around two o'clock tomorrow," she assured the physician.

"Thank goodness," he replied, showing the first hint of humanity. "Even though it's almost a guarantee this tumor is benign, it's still going to be a risky surgery. I'm just not comfortable doing it without a family member in the waiting area."

Do I air my dirty laundry or not? Finally she said, "You know that my mother has disowned me and even had me arrested for supposedly stalking her and stealing from her?"

"Yes," he said, "your friend filled in the blanks for me while they were getting your mother into bed. I'm sorry you're having to put yourself on the firing line again and I wouldn't insist if I didn't think it was necessary."

"I agree that I have to be there." She hesitated. *Should I?* "I have to ask, does my mother know that you're calling me?"

"Oh, she knows alright. I was very straight with her." His voice was emphatic. "I also told her that she would not use me or this hospital to pursue a personal vendetta and should she attempt to legally entrap you for coming, I am prepared to swear under oath that I asked you to come in my official capacity as a licensed physician."

Bless you. Mama may not be civil, but at least I won't have to worry about being set up. Besides, maybe she will be too groggy after surgery to do much damage, at least for a few days.

"Thank you, Dr. Martin. I would have come regardless, but it does ease my mind that I don't have to worry about being arrested again."

She and the doctor concluded their conversation with his promise that Alicia wouldn't be sedated until Saralynn arrived and had a chance to speak with her, if she was willing.

After she ended the conversation, Saralynn wandered about her bedroom, unable to tackle the task at hand. Only the sound of her cell phone ringing provided any structure and guidance, and she grabbed to answer it, thankful for any distraction.

"Did you forget to call me?" Katie's voice came across the distance from the Boswell Campus.

I did forget. "I'm sorry Katie, right now I'm in a real stupor. I've just gotten off the phone with Mama's doctor."

"Her doctor? Saralynn, what has happened?"

"She's having surgery tomorrow afternoon for a benign brain tumor." *I can't believe I said that so calmly.*

"Oh, Saralynn. I'm so sorry."

"I am, too. I was hoping it wouldn't come to this. But I'm leaving Jackson at six-forty tomorrow morning." She choked back a sob. "The doctor promised he wouldn't start before I had a chance to see her."

"Saralynn, you're crying. I'm on my way over to spend the night with you."

"No. No. No. It's not necessary. And, yes, I am crying. It's the first time I've given way to tears." She stuffed her fist in her mouth to stifle another sob that threatened to overwhelm her. "Mama could die, Katie. My Mama could die."

"Please let me come over."

"No, I'm alright. I've just got to get my arms around this situation and I'll be OK." She choked back another sob. "But there is something you could do for me."

"Name it."

"I need to let my friends here know, but I've got to get to bed and try to get a few hours sleep."

"Say no more. Let's hang up so I can start calling. And I'll ask some to make other calls, so we can get the word out before it's too late tonight."

"Thanks, Katie. I love you."

"And I love you, Saralynn. Can we have a quick prayer before I hang up?"

Saralynn choked back yet another sob and her friend took

silence as consent.

Loving Lord, our hearts hurt tonight. For Alicia who is facing serious surgery tomorrow. For Saralynn who will travel to be with her at this critical time. For Alicia's hardened heart that has made it difficult for Saralynn to maintain a relationship with her mother. Be with Saralynn as she travels tomorrow and give her safe passage. We know that You are all powerful and if anyone can speak to Alicia's heart and bring her to an understanding of how much her daughter loves her, we know that You can do that. We thank You that when we need You, You're always there for us. In the name of Your Son Jesus who ministered to Lazarus even after he was dead and restored him to life. Amen.

Saralynn was so choked up she couldn't even echo Katie's benediction and instead, just ended the conversation by closing her phone. It promised to be a short long night.

Chapter 13

The Friday morning flight from Jackson to Atlanta, where Saralynn would change planes for Boston, was only forty-seven minutes. *It feels more like forty-seven years.* She constantly checked her watch and repeatedly calculated the flying time for the last leg, reassuring herself that she would make it in time.

She had told Elsie she would take a cab to the hospital, feeling that Alicia might want her friend close as the time for surgery neared. *And as upset as Elsie is, I didn't want her driving out to the airport. Better I grab a cab.*

Saralynn had called Elsie's cell phone as soon as she landed, but had gotten the voice mail function instead. *I would have thought she was expecting my call. Oh, well, perhaps there's a problem with the signal in that area of the hospital. Maybe they made her turn it off.*

The afternoon traffic in the city was already heavy, but the cabbie maneuvered his way easily through the congestion from

Boston's Logan International to the historic South End where Boston Medical Center was located on Massachusetts Avenue.

If Mama has to have surgery, I'm glad her doctor is here. This is one of the best hospitals in the state.

Much faster than Saralynn could believe, the taxi soon turned the corner and deposited her right outside the main entrance. Once inside, she spotted the elevators that Elsie had promised were just off the lobby. "Come to the fourth floor. When the elevator doors open, go to the left just past the nurses' station and take a right. Your mother is in room 479, four doors down on the right."

Following those directions, Saralynn quickly felt herself being whisked upward. When the elevator opened, a group was waiting to get on, but they stepped back to allow her to exit. "That woman just died so suddenly," she heard one of the women say. "So sad."

Sounds like they've had a death on the floor. I hope Mama doesn't hear about it. That's the last thing she needs right now. Saralynn realized that the pace of her steps was increasing the closer she came to the corner at the nursing station. However, she wasn't prepared for the sight that met her eyes when she turned that corner and glimpsed Elsie being comforted by one of several people bunched in the hallway. She took a deep breath and subconsciously began counting doorways on the right.

Oh my God! They're standing outside Mama's door!

Her mind told her to run, but her feet and legs felt like concrete, firmly anchored in place and, despite orders to the contrary, they weren't moving.

"Elsie," she screeched, as much out of frustration as fear, her voice resounding with the irritation of chalk scraping across a blackboard.

At the sound the short, plump woman in the royal blue pant suit jerked her head around and, when she caught sight of Saralynn, broke into fresh tears at the same time that she broke loose from the stranger's embrace. She began to hobble toward Saralynn, crying, "Oh, you poor thing. I'm so sorry. I'm so sorry."

Without warning, Saralynn found herself again standing in the doorway of her Boston home, with a uniformed policeman on the stoop telling her that Peter and Marc were dead. Only this time, instead of a policeman, it was Elsie. But the message was the same, and the emotional impact was even more devastating.

No! No! No! Not Mama, Lord. Please not Mama. Please!

Elsie reached her where she stood rooted to the floor and, with tears streaming down her cheeks, delivered the news Saralynn already instinctively understood. Alicia was dead. It had all happened suddenly, her friend explained. So suddenly that no one knew quite what to make of it all.

Saralynn grabbed the older woman and refused to turn lose, even though she could tell that her actions had frightened her friend who was already badly spooked. "I've got to see her!" she screamed. "I don't want her moved until I can see her!"

Elsie was making every effort to both calm and comfort Saralynn, when a distinguished looking older gentleman in a lab coat and wearing rimless bifocals approached them.

"Ms. Reilly?" he inquired.

Saralynn recognized his voice immediately. She had spoken at length with him just the previous evening. *Although his voice didn't sound like he had snow white hair.* "What happened, Dr. Martin? she begged. "You promised me you wouldn't begin until I got here."

"But sugar, he didn't," Elsie interjected. "We were waiting on you when suddenly Alicia screamed, cried that her head felt like it was splitting, and those were the last words she ever said."

"Let's go down here where we can have some privacy," the doctor urged. "I'll be glad to answer all your questions, but here and now isn't the place."

"I want to see my Mama," Saralynn insisted.

"And you will. I've given orders that she isn't to be moved until you've had a chance for some time with her."

With poor graces, but too emotionally paralyzed to resist, Saralynn allowed the doctor and Elsie to guide her into a small room with a couch and two chairs, just a few doors down from Alicia's room. *The sign on the door said FAMILY-PRIVATE. This must be where they deliver this kind of news.* The space, she noticed, had been expertly decorated, down to the smallest accessory. Unfortunately the decorator in her was unable to appreciate the talent the room reflected. Instead, she was numb.

"What happened?" she asked again, once they were all seated. "It's not supposed to be like this," she cried. "Mama was supposed to have the surgery and be OK. She didn't even get to surgery?"

Elsie grasped her right hand so tightly the circulation was leaving, but Saralynn chose to ignore the sensations. All she could do was look at the doctor with a mixture of fear and anger and confusion.

"Without an autopsy, I can't tell you conclusively. But I know what I think."

Both ladies looked at the doctor expectantly.

"Your mother's tumor was growing by the hour. We knew that, which is why I didn't want to postpone surgery until the first of next week." He rubbed the palm of his hand across the side of his face in a gesture of frustration. "I believe the tumor, without warning, pressed on a crucial motor area of her brain, cutting off circulation. What resulted was a massive stroke."

"But people recover from strokes," Saralynn protested.

"Usually, yes. But there are those massive strokes that don't give you a second chance and that's what we had here."

"You're certain?" Saralynn stared him eyeball to eyeball.

"In my considered opinion, this is what happened. The symptoms are all indicative of such. But as I said, only an autopsy can tell us for certain."

"Even then it won't bring my mother back."

The doctor placed his hand on hers as he said to Saralynn. "No, Ms. Reilly, it won't. If I could reverse this, I would already have done so."

Autopsy. I don't know how Mama would have felt about such. I don't even know how I feel. I'm too numb.

She lifted her eyes to again make contact with the doctor. "Does there have to be an autopsy?"

"Not if you're satisfied with my diagnosed cause of death."

She regarded him silently for what seemed to her to be several minutes, though in truth it was only a few seconds. "If this were your mother, would you be satisfied?"

He said nothing at first, then, with strong conviction, "Yes. I can stand by what I believe."

"Then I don't want it done. But I do want to see my mother, and I want to see her right now."

"And so you shall." Dr. Martin led them back down the hall which was now, thankfully, clear from the rubber-neckers that had been standing at every doorway. At the door to room 479, he stood aside and allowed Saralynn and Elsie to enter. "I'll be right outside if you need me. Take as long as you want."

The room was quiet and still and it took Saralynn several seconds to comprehend that the small mound beneath the sheet in the middle of the bed was actually Alicia.

"Oh, Elsie. I can't believe this. Surely it's a nightmare and I'm going to wake up just any time." Her face brightened, "I know. I've fallen asleep on the plane and I just have to wake up and Mama will still be here and we'll be getting ready for her to leave for surgery."

The older woman patted her hand. "I wish I could agree with you, sugar. But hard as it is to accept, this is the way it is." Tears were again tracking their way down her chubby, wrinkled cheeks.

Elsie looks so old. If I don't look at Mama, maybe it won't be so. Maybe she's in another room somewhere. In the end, however, Saralynn knew that what was, was, and loathe to waste even another second, she approached the bed and took hold of her mother's right hand. *It's still got some warmth in it!*

Alicia lay on her back, her eyes closed, and there was still just a trace of color in her face. "Look at her, Elsie. Even in death she's still one of the most beautiful people I know."

"She was a pretty one, alright. Always was. Even when she was carrying you, she never lost her looks."

Alicia had, Saralynn noticed, a perplexed expression on her face. *Almost like things happened so suddenly even she had been caught unawares.*

"I can't believe this, Elsie. I got here as fast as I could." She buried her face in her hands as the impact of what she had just said settled on her shoulders. "I killed her, Elsie. I should have told Dr. Martin to operate this morning. " Sobs racked her body and Elsie had to shove a chair under her to keep her from hitting the floor. "I killed her, Elsie. Why did I have to be here? She wasn't going to see me anyway."

"Now you listen to me right now," the older woman lectured. "You just stop talking that way, because you didn't kill her. The tumor killed her. Dr. Martin said so."

"But he also said that the tumor was growing by the hour. I should have let him go ahead. But I was selfish enough to want to see her, to hope to make peace, and I made him promise not to do anything until I got here."

Elsie took Saralynn's chin in the palm of her hand, and turned her head so the two could look directly at each other. "I'm going to tell you something and when I finish, I don't ever want to hear you say another word about how you killed your mama."

"There's nothing you can say that will make any difference."

"I think maybe there is."

Saralynn, looking expectantly at her friend, didn't respond.

"Alicia wouldn't even admit it to herself, let alone me, but she was waiting for you to get here. She wanted to see you as bad as you wanted to see her."

"You're just saying that to make me feel better."

"On this, I promise I'm not. I know in my heart that Alicia was holding out for you. I think she wanted to make things right with you before she went to surgery."

Oh, I want to believe that. I really do. "How can you be so sure?"

"I spent the night on that narrow little bench over there, less than three feet away from Alicia. I know that twice during the night, I heard her crying, but when I asked what was wrong, she pretended I was hearing things."

She pulled that same thing on me in the motel room that night so long ago when we were on our way to Magee that first time.

"But she was crying; you can mark my words. Then, this morning, she looked to be sleeping and I didn't want to disturb her." The woman paused. "But I stubbed my toe on the leg of that dresser over there, and Alicia cried out. She called out for you, 'Saralynn! Is that you? Darling, did you finally get here?'."

"That doesn't prove anything conclusively." *But Mama did always call me "darling";, but then Elsie knows that.*

"But there's more. For the rest of the day, I was able to drop your name in conversation. You know, 'Gosh this room is drab looking. They need to get Saralynn in here to make it pop.' Alicia agreed."

Could she really have had a change of heart? Did Katie's prayer make a difference, or did Mama sense she wasn't going to make it?

"Before, just the sound of your name sent her into orbit. But today, for whatever reason, Alicia was OK that you were coming."

"I want to believe that, Elsie. I really do. For more reasons than one.

"Then you believe it, sugar, because I do." She took Saralynn by the hand and led her back to the bed. "You need to be saying your good-byes now. Because life goes on and there's been a death. Things have to happen, you know."

Saralynn buried her head in her hands, as much out of confusion as grief. "Mama's dead and I don't have any idea what her wishes would have been. I don't even know where to begin. Mama did all this for Peter and Marc."

Chapter 14

"I can't go to Mama's condo right now. Not tonight. Tomorrow. OK?"

Saralynn and Elsie were standing in the main lobby at Boston Medical Center, unable to make even the most basic decisions. "I know I'll have to go there. But I can't handle it now."

In the two hours that had elapsed since her arrival, Saralynn had said her good-byes to her mama and had signed for release of the body to the same mortuary Alicia had chosen for Peter and Marc. *Beyond that, and cleaning out the hospital room, nothing else has been done. Maybe once I'm outside these walls I can think again.*

"Well, if you won't go to your Mama's and you won't come home with me, we've got to get you a hotel room," Elsie insisted. "You've got to be tired. You left Mississippi in the middle of the night, and it's past five o'clock right now."

Unable to resist or come up with a better plan, she allowed

the short, dumpy woman who'd been like her mother's sister, to pilot her across the street to the parking deck. There they rode the elevator to Elsie's car.

"I'm going to take you to the same hotel where you stayed before," her friend suggested. "Let's just hope they have a vacancy."

"Whatever." *I feel like I'm a million years old. Nothing about me, nothing about this whole thing feels real.*

The hotel did indeed have a room and the desk clerk even remembered Saralynn. *At least he said he did. I suspect the computer told him I'd been there before.* Saralynn understood good public relations, and that everyone is egotistical enough to believe they have been personally remembered.

Once in her room, she sat down on the bench at the end of the bed and stared into space. Elsie hadn't wanted to leave her, but Saralynn had insisted. "I'll order room service," she countered, when Elsie made plans to return to pick her up for dinner. And she hadn't wanted Elsie to check in and stay with her, either.

"I'm not trying to be cruel Elsie. I just have to have some time alone. Time to digest all that's happened and to make some phone calls. Then I want to sleep. If I can. And tomorrow, I promise, whatever has to be done, we'll do it all tomorrow."

I can't bring Mama back and she's going to be just as dead in the morning as she is right now. So I'm going to take care of me.

"I'll be alright. I promise," she again assured her friend who stood, wringing her hands, with tears running down her cheeks. "You're going to be alright, too. I promise." It had suddenly occurred to her that Elsie might need her as well. *After all, she was there when Mama died, and she has carried a heavy load these past few weeks.*

She hugged the woman. "Let me grab my key and I'll take

the elevator down with you."

"I just don't see how it happened," Elsie moaned and shook her head from side to side. "One minute she was fine. We were waiting on you. The next minute she was screaming and clutching her head, and almost immediately she lost consciousness."

"I'm sorry you had to go through that, Elsie. But I'm so thankful that somebody Mama loved was with her."

As they walked arm in arm across the lobby, Saralynn could see through the large front glass foyer that dark was fast approaching. "It's getting late, Elsie. You be careful, and call me when you get there, so I'll know you made it."

Saralynn had already turned and was making her way across the lobby, when a thought hit her. She whirled on her heel and raced back out the door, calling her friend's name once she was outside the hotel. "Elsie… Elsie!"

Up ahead, just disappearing into the adjacent parking deck, the little woman in blue stopped and turned. When she saw Saralynn running towards her, she headed back to meet her.

"I'm sorry," she told her friend, as she gasped for breath. *I'm out of shape.* "But something just occurred to me. Do you know if Mama had a will? And do you know where it is?"

"Why are you worried about a will? You're her only heir. You'll get everything. *Maybe I will and maybe I won't. This is Mama we're talking about.* "I'm not worried about that," she explained. "I just thought, knowing Mama, if she had a will, she might have funeral instructions stuck in with it."

She spread her hands wide in front of her in a display of confusion. "I just don't know where to begin."

Elsie used her right hand to rub her left forearm, a trait Saralynn had witnessed many times before, whenever the woman was upset. "If she had a will, she never told me anything about it."

Saralynn's bubble burst and her hopes ran out in all directions. "OK," she said at last, defeat evident in her voice and manner, "it was just a thought."

She stood and watched as Elsie unlocked her car and, as her friend was driving out of the parking garage, Saralynn turned to make her way back upstairs to her room.

I'm all alone in this world. My Mama is dead. How do I go on?

She didn't have any idea how much time had passed, but when she finally came back to reality to find herself sitting on the floor, in the darkened room, with the lights of downtown Boston twinkling like a gigantic Christmas tree, Saralynn knew she had to get a grip. *Somehow, I've got to hold myself together; I can't let this do what losing Peter and Marc did. After all, Mama's not here to save me.*

Saralynn didn't want to question a good thing, and while she had an aching in her heart different from any hurt she had ever endured, she didn't feel like she was about to fly into a million pieces the way she had before. *Does this mean I didn't love Mama;, that I didn't care about her?*

After she had pulled herself up from the floor and turned on some lights, Saralynn knew she had some phone calls to make. Yet the thought of spending the evening on the phone was something she found totally unappealing. Just as she was pondering how to handle things, her cell phone rang. *Elsie!* She punched the TALK button. "You made it home OK."

"I'm here," she heard a tired voice on the other end reply. "I don't think I'm going to be much good to anybody, but I'm here."

"Get something to eat and go to bed, Elsie. That's what I'm going to do." She felt a moment's guilt that she hadn't agreed for the two of them to grab a bite before they parted company. "Tomorrow's going to be a hard day, and I'm going to need you more than you know."

That's no joke. I'm suddenly realizing that I know very little about my mother's business or finances. I don't even know if her water bill has been paid. Elsie is my only hope.

"I'll be here for you, sugar," Elsie replied. "I just don't know how much good I'll be."

"We'll worry about that tomorrow. OK?"

The two agreed that Elsie would be at the hotel at nine-thirty the next morning to provide transportation and they said good night.

Saralynn picked up the room phone and pushed the specified code for room service to order a chef's salad. *I doubt I'll eat very much, because I'm simply not hungry. For sure I don't want anything heavy.*

Once she had her meal ordered, she reached for the cell phone to make one more call, her last call of the evening. She had finally hit upon a plan and she knew exactly whose voice she wanted to hear, whose voice she felt could soothe her most. She wasted no time placing the call.

"Mr. Walter," she said, "it's Saralynn. I really need to talk to you."

"Well, hey, honey. We weren't expecting to hear from you tonight, but we were hoping that someone would get a progress update tomorrow. Katie called us, you know."

This is so hard to say, but I have to get the words out. As she would reflect later, her delivery probably left much to be desired, but in the end, all she could handle was to blurt out the news.

"Mama's dead, Mr. Walter."

"Dead?"

"Yes, sir. She died just before I got here."

"Oh, Saralynn," his honeyed tones consoled, "I am so terribly sorry. So sorry."

I needed to hear his voice. There's so much comfort in it. I felt like I was in a foreign country at the hospital this afternoon.

She could hear him relaying the news to Miss Virginia. "What do you need? What can we do for you?"

Before Saralynn could answer, a woman's voice interrupted. "Saralynn, sugar, it's Virginia. Excuse me for butting in, but I just had to speak to you, to tell you how badly Walter and I are hurting for you right now."

"We are that," Walter affirmed.

They're on extension phones.

"You know, dear, with no offense to your Mama, we love you like you were our own daughter. And we're here for you. Just tell us what we can do."

I knew it wasn't a mistake to call them. "Tonight I need you to spread the word. You're the one I've called and I just don't feel like spending the night on the phone."

"Of course you don't," Miss Virginia agreed. "We'll be glad to make those calls, but surely there's something else you need."

I've never asked for prayer before and I don't know if God will even hear one since I haven't exactly been in contact on a regular basis. "I need you to pray for me, because tomorrow I've got to try and make some sense of all of this and make arrangements, and I don't have the first clue how to begin."

"Didn't Alicia leave any instructions?"

"Not that I know of, Mr. Walter. But that's one of the

searches I've got to make first thing tomorrow. The mortuary is waiting."

"You know we'll be praying. In fact, I think we should have a talk with God right now. That is, if you don't mind, Saralynn."

"Please, Mr. Walter. I'd appreciate it."

Oh, Lord, what a sad time it is when we must give up someone we love. Saralynn has experienced that this day, when You took Alicia home to you. Saralynn's body is weary and her heart is heavy, Lord. We pray for restful sleep for her, that she would awaken armed, both physically and emotionally, for the day ahead tomorrow, and for the wisdom and strength to make all the necessary decisions and arrangements. Remind her consistently, Lord, of Your presence and of the presence, albeit from afar, of friends and family who love her dearly. We commend to Your safe-keeping the spirit of your child, Alicia, until we shall see her again, as You have promised. In the name of Jesus whom You once mourned, we pray. Amen.

Saralynn was sobbing quietly. "Thank you, Mr. Walter. I love you both so much," she finally managed to say through tears.

"And all your many friends here love you, too. Never doubt that, Saralynn. You have family here."

"I know and that's one thing that's sustaining me now."

"Sugar, you need to get to bed and try to get some rest. Have you eaten?"

Saralynn chuckled to herself. Ever the Southern hostess, Miss Virginia firmly believed that when someone died, the survivors ate. She had lived in Magee long enough to understand that concept. "Yes, Ma'am. I ordered a salad from room service, just before I called you. It should be here soon."

"Well you be sure you eat it all. You really need more than

that, but I guess it's better than nothing. Now you eat it, you hear?"

"Yes Ma'am." *It feels so good to be mothered.*

"Saralynn?"

"Yes, Mr. Walter?"

"If you don't feel like answering just say so, but we are concerned to know what happened. Did we misunderstand Katie, because we thought Alicia's prognosis was good?"

"I'm still not totally sure how all this came about. I got to the hospital about five minutes after she died. The doctor says he suspects from the way she acted, the tumor caused her to suffer a massive stroke and it was all over very quickly."

"It must have been so traumatic on you to walk into it not knowing," Miss Virginia offered.

"Oh, it was," Saralynn agreed. "I just couldn't believe it, and I'm still not sure that I do now."

"That's a normal reaction, sugar. Don't beat yourself up," the lady advised.

"No, you just eat and get some rest tonight and let tomorrow take care of itself tomorrow."

"I will."

"And you call us back if you need us, even if it's the middle of the night. You hear?"

"Yes, sir. I hear." *Do I dare ask? I don't think I'll sleep a wink if I don't.* "Mr. Walter? I have a question."

"Let's hear it."

"Well, it's kind of awkward, but I really need to know." She gulped with nervousness. "In your prayer, you asked God to take care of Mama. Do you really think she went to heaven?"

"What do you think?"

"I want to hope she did, but her heart was pretty hard. As

we all know."

"In truth, we'll never be certain until we reach heaven ourselves, but I want to believe Alicia is there right now, celebrating with Miss Sallie and Tony, and her daddy, and I'll tell you why."

He sounds so convinced.

"My God is a loving God and He wants all His children with Him. There isn't a one of us who hasn't strayed, hasn't sinned, and hasn't disappointed God at some point in our lives. Some of us more than others. But you and I can only see the outward person. God sees the inner person, who is often hiding a hurting and vulnerable heart behind a rock-hard façade of venom and hatred."

I never thought about it like that.

"Only God knows what was truly in Alicia's heart. And He is a loving God."

"Thank you, Mr. Walter. That helped me a lot right now."

"But since you brought it up, Saralynn, may I ask you something?"

"Well, sure, Miss Virginia."

"You're concerned if Alicia went to heaven. Don't you want to be certain you can be with her again some day?"

There's that salvation issue again. I know they care and that they're concerned. But I'm too weary, too hurt to deal with that tonight.

As if she was reading Saralynn's mind, Miss Virginia continued, "But now isn't the time to talk about this. You need to grieve and get some rest and get ready for tomorrow."

"Thanks to the both of…" A knock at the door interrupted her words. "There's room service. Let me go and I'll call you back tomorrow."

"Good night, Saralynn. We'll start calling all your friends immediately."

The ringing of the bedside phone intruded into Saralynn's slumber at about the same time a shaft of morning sunlight penetrated the draperies. Struggling to raise up in bed, she grabbed the phone, only to be met with a canned "Good Morning. It's 7:30!"

Did I ask for a wake-up call?

She struggled to get awake, wondering through her sleep-sodden stupor what adventures awaited. Then reality struck, and she collapsed back into the bed. *I'm not at home. I'm in Boston and Mama's dead.*

When she knew she couldn't deny the truth any longer, Saralynn crawled out of bed and headed resolutely for the shower. The water was running and she was just about to step beneath the flow when her cell phone rang.

Shoot!

She raced back into the room, grabbed the phone, and saw Katie Brooks' Caller ID.

"Hi, Katie," she greeted her friend. "May I call you back? I was just stepping into the shower."

"Sure. Of course you can. I just wanted to let you know I care."

"I know that and I care about you, too. I'll call you back in just a few minutes."

As she stood beneath the pulsing waters and felt the sleep wash down her body, she reflected on the day to come and what she would encounter. *I might as well get ready for calls from Simpson County. They're going to be ringing my phone. But I don't care. It's nice to be loved.* The thought of Magee reminded her that she needed to touch base with her friends in Iuka as well. *And Mr. Adams, the attorney. I've got to call him!*

Before she had time to look up his number, her cell phone rang again and it was Elsie announcing her arrival in the lobby. Saralynn invited her up while she finished dressing and the two women went down in the elevator together, to get breakfast in the hotel coffee shop.

After they had given their orders, Saralynn placed a call to Jon Walthall's office in Iuka. "This is Saralynn Reilly," she informed the secretary who answered, "I really need to speak with Jon. Is he available?"

"Good morning, Ms. Reilly. It's good to talk to you again." *Always those Southern manners.* "Mr. Walthall is expecting a client momentarily, but let me tell him you're calling. Just a moment please."

While she waited, Saralynn watched steaming plates of breakfast food leaving the kitchen. *I'm actually hungry this morning.*

"Good Morning, Saralynn." Jon Walthall's voice boomed through her phone, making him sound as if he were right beside her. "To what do I owe the pleasure?" His voice lowered to a conspiratorial level. "And where are you, if you're free to tell all?"

"It's so good to hear your voice, Jon."

"Something's wrong, isn't it? I can tell."

"I'm afraid you're right. I'm in Boston."

"Problems with your mother, huh?"

A young woman in a black and green outfit was serving their breakfast… an omelet for Elsie, while Saralynn had opted for Belgian waffles and fruit.

"Yes, there are problems with Mama, but not the way you

mean. Oh, Jon..." she choked, "Mama's dead. Yesterday afternoon. They think it was a stroke caused by the tumor."

"Are you all right? What do you need? MA and I will be there before the day is out."

"No... No, Jon. There's no need for that. But I do appreciate your offer." She hesitated while she speared a plump, red strawberry and popped it into her mouth. *I'm starving... I can't wait any longer.* "I just wanted you and MA to know, but besides that, we need to call Mr. Adams and cancel all that business and find out what we owe him." *I don't want Elsie to know I was about to sue Mama.*

"Obviously there's no need to move forward now," Jon agreed. "But what about settling your mother's estate? Are you going to need him for that?"

She forked a bite of syrup-laden waffle topped with a bit of whipped cream into her mouth and struggled to chew before she said, "I don't have a clue what I'm facing there, but I have a long-time attorney here who can work with me. He just doesn't handle...", she hesitated, "you know," she finished lamely.

"I see," the Iuka lawyer said. "Then let me let you go and I'll call Mr. Adams this morning and have him send us a bill."

"Thanks, Jon. I've got a full day and I appreciate you taking that chore off me."

"Hey, you bet. Any time." His voice softened. "And Saralynn, I'm sorry you had to lose your mother like this. Please let us know if there's any way we can help."

"I will, Jon. Give MA my love. We'll talk in a day or so."

"Keep in touch," he said. "Bye."

"Who was that?" Elsie asked as soon as she laid down the phone.

"An attorney friend in Iuka. He and I were working together on a little project."

"And now that your mother is dead you don't need to do it any more?"

How do I answer her? "Let's just say since I'm going to be tied up with Mama's business, I don't have time to pursue this other."

Can we say I know how to lie? She could tell that Elsie didn't totally buy her explanation, but the other woman didn't ask further questions. *And I hope she never does.*

Before she was even half finished with her breakfast, the phone rang again and she was aghast to see Katie Brooks on the Caller ID. *Oh, shoot. Once again I forgot to return her call!*

She punched the TALK key. "I'm sorry, I did forget," she confessed. "Can you ever forgive me?"

"I'm not calling to chastise you, Saralynn. I know you've got a load on your shoulders."

Man is she ever right on that.

"Still, I seem to make a habit of forgetting you and that's the last thing I would ever want to do."

"So are you alright? Do you need me to do anything?"

Saralynn used the last bite of waffle to clean up the syrup and whipped cream left on her plate. Once in her mouth, she savored the taste. "I'm still in shock, I think. But I'm sure it's going to hit me soon. I'm just hoping I can get all the details resolved before that happens."

"So is there going to be a funeral service? A memorial? What are you going to do?"

Saralynn could see Elsie across the table taking in every word being said. She was fairly certain her companion could even hear much of what Katie was saying. *But there's no way to get rid of her.*

"All that's still up in the air right now. I'm about to go over to Mama's condo to see if I can find any instructions before I make those decisions. I'll let you know."

"OK. Then I'll hang up because I know you're busy. Just wanted you to know that we care."

Of that I have no doubt.

"I'll call you before bedtime. And I promise. This time I will!" The two shared a laugh and Saralynn flipped her phone shut.

"Another lawyer?"

"No, no. Of course not. Just a good friend from Magee wanting to be sure I was OK."

"Alicia used to talk about how everyone in Mississippi meddled in everyone else's business. I see what she meant."

Mama may be dead, but the propaganda she spread is alive and well, I fear.

"It's not like that at all, Elsie. In fact, I wish you could meet some of my friends. I think you'd be very surprised."

"Maybe. I just know what Alicia always told me." She rose stiffly from her chair. "I've been sitting too long. Old joints, don't you know? You about ready to go?"

Saralynn knew it was a chore she couldn't delay any longer. "Yes, I'm ready to go to Mama's house and get that behind me."

On the way there, as Elsie drove, Saralynn picked her brain about places Alicia might have placed final instructions.

"Either in her desk in the office, or somewhere in her bedroom would be the two places I'd think," her friend advised. "If it's not there, I don't think you're going to find anything."

Saralynn massaged her temples, already feeling the stress of the day. "Did she ever say anything to you about her wishes?"

"I don't mean to sound tacky," Elsie replied. "But this is your mother we're talking about, and the Alicia I know… I mean, knew…" Her face reflected the pain her verbal slip had inflicted. "The Alicia I knew didn't think too much about dying if you ask me."

Tacky or not, it's true. Even I know that. I don't remember Mama ever going to a single funeral. I can't believe she never encountered death. And she was the main reason I didn't have anything for Marc and Peter. She discouraged me.

As they approached Alicia's front door, Elsie shoved a key into Saralynn's hand. "This belongs to you, now, you know. The workmen used the same lock when they replaced the door that the police broke in."

"Now Elsie. You know as well as I do that Mama wasn't real happy with me these last few months. I wouldn't be surprised to find out she left everything to a total stranger."

It feels like a sacrilege… going into Mama's house when she's not here. But I don't have any choice. She fitted the key into the lock and gave it a turn, then depressed the thumb-latch and the door swung open.

Once inside, Saralynn caught a lingering scent of the perfume that Alicia had worn for years. *I still expect to see her walk out from the back to see who's here.*

"Let's start in the office," Saralynn suggested.

For the next few minutes the two women worked silently as they opened drawers and doors and pawed through file folders and accumulated stacks of papers.

"Nothing," Saralynn finally declared. "We have handled

every piece of paper in here and there's nothing that would hint to either a will or her final wishes."

"You're going to have to decide something pretty soon," Elsie advised. "The mortuary is waiting."

"I know. I know." Saralynn brushed back a stray curly wisp that was tickling her forehead. "I'll tell them something by lunch time."

The trill of her cell phone deep in the bottom of her purse sounded, and she ran to dig for it, not taking time to even check Caller ID. "Hello?"

"Saralynn? Is this Saralynn?"

Donna Hasty! I might have guessed.

The two talked for a couple of minutes while Saralynn assured her friend that she was bearing up. Then Saralynn begged off, saying that she was trying to make arrangements, and promised to call her back that evening. Just as soon as she ended that call, the phone rang again. This time it was Brother Tommy, the pastor from Rials Creek. And before she could finish that conversation, her call-waiting beeped... Reverend Kirk, the pastor of the Iuka United Methodist Church.

"I'm glad you like all that," was all Elsie said when the phone finally was returned to the front pocket in Saralynn's slacks. "It would drive me up the wall."

"It wouldn't if you knew these people, Elsie. They're... they're... genuine, and I hate to tell you, but you don't find a lot of that in Boston."

"Could be because we don't want it in Boston."

At Elsie's suggestion the pair moved to the master bedroom.

"You know," Saralynn mentioned, as they stood in the

doorway, "this truly is a beautiful room. I really didn't get to appreciate it the last time I was here."

"Your mother had an eye for design, that's for sure."

"I always told her she should have been the professional, not me." She motioned around the room. "You take that side, I'll work over here."

They had been at it for over half an hour when Elsie called, "Saralynn?" She said it so softly, until she had to say it a second time to be heard. "I think this may be what you're looking for."

Saralynn dropped the stack of magazines she had been sifting through and raced around the bed. Elsie stood by the open armoire, where a drawer had been pulled out. In her hand was a business size envelope, which she eagerly handed over.

Could it be?

The envelope carried the inscription "To be opened in the event of my death". *It's definitely Mama's handwriting. What's more, the envelope looks like it's been around for some time.* Her hands shook. "It's fairly old."

I don't know if I can do this.

"You need to open it, Saralynn. The mortuary is waiting, and still this may not give us any idea of what Alicia wanted."

She flipped the envelope over and slipped her nail under the glued flap. *Oh, well. Here goes nothing.* She could feel an uneven thickness as she fumbled for the contents, which she brought out with trembling fingers. There were several sheets of paper, folded. As she moved to open the packet to the first page, a photograph mounted on a thick piece of pasteboard dropped out and fell to the floor. *So that's what's was making the bulge.*

Elsie bent to retrieve the object. She picked it up, looked at it and straightened. "It's an old photograph of some woman."

Saralynn took the photo and her mouth slowly sagged open. *It can't be. Can it? But it is!* "Elsie. This is Miss Sallie!"

"Who's 'Miss Sallie'?"

Suddenly she felt weak and Saralynn allowed herself to drop to a seat on the edge of the bed. "Miss Sallie. That's what I call Mama's mother, since I never really knew her as a grandmother."

"I never saw that picture. Alicia never talked about her mother, except to criticize her." She motioned at Saralynn, "Open the papers. See what you've got."

As she thumbed through the sheets, she counted five pieces of paper. "It's a letter to me," she reported. She continued to flip pages, until the top of one caught her eye. "Last Will and Testament, Elsie. It says 'Last Will and Testament'. There is a will."

"Read it. What does it say?"

"I'm not worried about the will right now. I want to see what she says in this letter. Why would she have written to me? Obviously from the discoloration of the paper, it was done a number of years ago."

Saralynn found the first page and there, at the top of the paper was a date. "Elsie she wrote this when I was only five years old. She's held on to this for almost thirty years." She began to read aloud.

Dear Saralynn,

This letter is not meant to be seen by you or anyone until such time as I am dead, which I hope will be many, many years away. I will safeguard it until that time, because there are things in this letter that you need to know, but I am not prepared to talk about. Now or ever. It pains me tremendously to even put this in black and white, but I can't die and leave you wondering about so many things. Please forgive me because I couldn't tell you before now. But I couldn't.

The enclosed picture is of my mother, Sallie McIntire Watson. It's the only picture of her I have, and I stole it from her cedar chest the night before I left Mississippi to come to Boston. I had to have something of her to be able to remember. I couldn't find one of my father, Ralph. I also had a brother, Tony, who was killed in service when he was still just a teenager. I know you always wanted to know about your family, but I couldn't tell you.

Saralynn's voice was coming in gulps. "I've seen another picture of Miss Sallie that must be a different pose of this one. It was made when she was about the same age I am right now."

There's something else you need to know. Your father didn't die and he and I were only married for a few weeks. His parents were very wealthy, very well-connected planters in the Delta, and his mother let me know the first time we ever met that I wasn't nearly good enough for her son. I wasn't pregnant when we got married – she swore I was – but I did get pregnant with you within just a couple of weeks after we married. I know they always believed I got pregnant to trap Marshall. That was your dad's name. Marshall Bankston.

Marshall was tall and broad-shouldered and was such a good looking man, but the tuberculosis had really sapped him, as that disease does. That's how I met him. He was a patient at the Sanatorium and when he was well and released, we ran off and got married. His parents felt like I took advantage of a sick and vulnerable man, and maybe I did. A little. But Marshall loved me and I loved him. I don't know if he was just weak because he'd been sick for so long, or if he was just incapable of standing up to his family. At any rate, his father walked into our room one morning and in front of your father, ordered me off the plantation permanently. He knew I was pregnant, so he knew he was banishing his grandchild as well. Marshall knew I was pregnant, too, but he just sat there, looking at the floor, and when I asked him if he wanted me to go, he wouldn't even look at me. He never answered.

One of the farm hands drove me into town in an old pick-up truck and paid for a one-way bus ticket to Jackson, connecting to Magee and I came back home to my mother. She and I never had seen eye to eye. I was always embarrassed by how poor we were and how she and my daddy would ask me to do without, and then they'd give their money to the church or to someone they thought was more needy than we were. Of course she didn't understand why I had come back, and I didn't try to explain.

A few days later a lawyer showed up at Mama's front door asking for me. When we sat down, he told me he was representing Mr. Bankston, your grandfather. Said the old man was prepared to pay any reasonable amount to get me to divorce Marshall and if I would agree to leave the state with you and never return, they would give me an additional sum of money. Of course they weren't offering much, but I made up my mind. They'd stolen my husband from me, because they thought I was poor white trash. (Maybe that's because that's how I felt, too, but I can't do anything about that now.) Only Marshall was stuck, because we were legally married. I was sure his mama had some high society Ole Miss debutant picked out for him. But as long as we were married, whether we ever lived together again or not, or whether the Bankstons ever laid eyes on me or not, old Mrs. Bankston couldn't get the blue-blood daughter-in-law she wanted.

So I decided to make them pay and pay dearly. They'd stolen my husband, but they had plenty of money and I didn't. I'm sure this sounds so mercenary, and perhaps I was, but I named my price, and I refused to budge. I had the upper hand and they knew it. I told them what I had to have to give Marshall the divorce, and then I told them what it would cost to get me to leave Mississippi. That lawyer about choked, but he agreed to pay it and in just a few days time I had more money than I had ever imagined in my purse and a new car sitting in the yard.

I had been searching for a place to live outside Mississippi and I read a book in the Magee Library about Boston and I said, "That's my new home." My mama couldn't understand why I wanted to come here and I didn't think I could tell her. I didn't want to leave her, but she refused to come with me. And I couldn't stay, because I'd taken the Bankstons' money. In the end, we had a big fight and I left. I don't know if I'll ever go back, even for a visit. And I don't know if I'll ever see my mother again. There have been so many times I've wanted to throw everything I had in the car and go back. I wanted her to hug me and tell me it was going to be OK. And at the same time, I was angry with her. I felt like it was her fault the Bankstons thought we weren't good enough to be part of their family.

But I want you to have this picture of your grandmother. If she's still alive when you find this, she lives outside Magee, Mississippi and I wish you'd contact her. You'll really like her. I've come to see what a good mother she was, only I never had the chance to tell her that. I didn't realize it until after I came here and was totally on my own. It's not nearly as glamorous as it looks on the surface. When I was pregnant with you, there were so many times I wanted her close, to hold me and tell me I wouldn't be pregnant forever. If I hadn't had Elsie who sort of adopted me, I don't know what I would have done.

Saralynn looked at Elsie and smiled through the tears that had been flowing for sometime. "You became her mother. Thank you." Then she went back to reading.

I'm going to make a final request here, but if by some chance you don't find this letter until after other arrangements have been made, don't feel like you've failed me. It's me that's failed you – so many times. And *don't try to undo what's already been done.*

If possible, I'd like to be taken back to Mississippi to be buried. Boston has been a wonderful place to live, but I've felt like I was in exile all the time I've been here. I had taken the money and I couldn't go back. And my pride wouldn't let me confide in my mother the truth about everything. All I knew to do was to maintain my distance. I couldn't even communicate with her because I knew if I did, I'd weaken and want so badly to return. I just wasn't strong enough to have her in my life and maintain my distance too. If I can go back home to be buried, I'd like to be in the Rials Creek Cemetery where the rest of the Watsons are buried.

Surely the Bankstons won't begrudge me the right to be buried there. What they don't know, I'm sure, is that only about a year ago, your father contacted me. He'd hired private detectives to find me. Just as I suspected, he'd remarried almost immediately to a girl his mother selected. He said he didn't love her and that he was miserable. He wanted to divorce her and re-marry me, but I told him I wasn't a home-wrecker and to go on back to the Delta. He'd had his chance and he wouldn't stand up for me and you when he had the chance. You'll never know how much that hurt, because I did love Marshall Bankston with everything I had. And he's the only man I ever loved. I wasn't interested in another man after him. But I knew it would never work.

The tears continued to flow, but Saralynn wasn't certain if they were because of the letter she was reading or if the reality of Alicia's death had finally hit home. "I wish she had included a picture of my daddy. I've always wanted to know what he looked like."

Saralynn stopped and bit her lower lip. "She wants to go home to Mississippi, Elsie. I never would have dreamed it."

"Neither would I, the way she talked."

One other thing, Saralynn. You are the best daughter any mother could ever have and I am so proud of you. I just hope I can do right by you, but my track record isn't real good in the relationships department. I've taken the money Mr. Bankston paid me and I've invested it. I hope never to have to touch it, so that it will be there for you some day. The other demand that I made of Mr. Bankston's lawyer was for a trust account that would let me live on the interest, so that I never had to work and could be a full-time mother. I hope you don't think that I am a gold-digger, but they had more money than they could ever hope to spend. I felt like I was entitled, so I stood my ground.

You're probably wondering why I wrote this letter. You're at the age where you're asking lots of questions and the answers aren't ones I want to talk about. Maybe all your questions are giving me a guilty conscience, so I'm putting all this down on paper, in the hopes that I can find some peace, and in the hope that some day, you'll know the truth and be willing to forgive me.

I love you. Don't ever forget that.

Mama

Saralynn dropped the last page and collapsed into a mass of sobs, huddled on the foot of the bed. *Mama did love me. She did love me!* "Oh, Elsie," she wailed. "This answers so many questions. Mama did love me."

She could feel Elsie's hand patting her on the shoulder. "Well of course your mother loved you."

"But there were so many times she didn't act like it. Especially lately."

"Alicia Bankston loved you. Period. But as for all that other information she gave you. She never one time hinted about any of that to me, and I've known her since she arrived here about four months pregnant."

"She moved into an apartment in the same complex where you lived."

"Not in the beginning," Elsie corrected. "The first place she had was a real dump, but I think she was so fearful her money was going to run out, until she spent as little as she could."

"I never knew that."

"That's how it was. She and I met at a coffee shop and struck up a conversation over the course of several weeks. Finally she confided in me that she was pregnant. Not that it wasn't already obvious."

"So when did you both begin living in the same place, because I don't ever remember you not being our neighbor."

Elsie sat down heavily on the other side of the mattress. "It was about two months before you were born. Believe you me, that place where Alicia was living wasn't fit to bring a baby home to. When a vacancy came in my building, I got the manager to work with me and we convinced your mother to move." She waved her hands in the air. "And we've lived in the same complex ever since, even though we all moved a couple of times."

"You were always a constant in my life. After reading Mama's letter, I can see why. You were her substitute mother."

The other woman buried her head in her hands, and sobs began to escape. "And I'm feeling very lost right now. I don't know how I'm going to get through each day without your mother." She sighed. "I always thought it would be her arranging my funeral."

"Speaking of which," Saralynn said, wiping her eyes with the edge of the bed coverlet, "we've got to get to the mortuary and make those arrangements."

"I'm sure they're waiting. Are you going to honor Alicia's wishes?"

Chapter 15

It took less than an hour, Saralynn realized as she and Elsie exited the mortuary, to make the final arrangements that would, in effect, sum up her mother's entire life. Her cell phone had rung twice while they were meeting with the mortician, but she had glanced at Caller ID, then sent the calls to voice mail. Little to her surprise, both calls were from Mississippi, and she had made a silent promise to return them as soon as the details were finalized. *I've made the mortician wait too long. He's going to have my front and center attention.*

"So you're going to take her back to Mississippi." Elsie said as they drove away. "I'm glad, although I hate having to say good-bye to her here."

I thought about that when we were making the plans.

"But you won't be here because you're flying back to Jackson with me. First thing tomorrow morning."

"But I can't afford something like that. Besides… where would I stay? No. I'll just have to make my farewell here." A tear sneaked down her cheek. "It's alright."

"Elsie, this is one arrangement I'm making that isn't open for discussion. You're going back as my guest, and you'll stay with me as long as you're down there."

"Saralynn! I can't let you spend that kind of money on me."

"Sorry. My mind's made up. It's the least I can do for all you've gone through the past few weeks to help me. So we better get you home to get packed."

The two stopped to grab a sandwich for lunch en-route, and Saralynn returned the call to the Kennedys and to the Rials Creek pastor. To both she gave the same information, that she would be arriving back in Jackson mid-afternoon the next day. Alicia's body was being flown back on the same plane, and that service arrangements there would be finalized after they arrived.

"Brother Tommy," she said to the pastor, "you didn't know my Mama, but I would appreciate it if you could handle her service."

"Why you know I will," was his quick reply. "Have you given any thought to what you want?"

"I have, but I need to think about it a little more. I'll call you before we leave Boston in the morning and give you my plans." *Also, it gives me a few more hours to make a decision that only occurred to me while we were dealing with Mama's arrangements.*

"You know," Saralynn remarked to Elsie as the two returned to the condo complex, "we never looked at Mama's will, we got so wrapped up reading that letter."

Both looked at each other and, without exchanging a word,

headed down the hallway to Alicia's door. Once in the bedroom, they found the entire packet of papers where it had landed on the floor. Saralynn gingerly refolded the letter and stuck the photo back inside. Only then did she turn her attention to the other two pages.

"This is dated almost fifteen years ago, which would have been about the time I finished college." She held up the envelope and studied the back flap. And this envelope hasn't been opened and re-sealed, so when she had this will written, she must have combined it and the letter into this one envelope."

"What does it say?"

"Looks pretty standard. I'm the executor. Says she wants all her bills paid, all her property sold, and I get whatever is left. Hmmmm. I wouldn't have thought about this."

Elsie was sorting through jewelry in Alicia's dresser-top safe. "About what?"

"She does make three other bequests. Oh…! Oh, Elsie. I can't believe this."

"She didn't leave money to a bunch of cats or something, did she?"

"No. No. Nothing like that." She clutched the document to her chest. "This makes me so happy."

She pulled the papers in front of her again and began to read aloud. *I direct my Executor to fund three specific bequests out of the monies remaining after all my debts and final expenses are paid, should there be adequate funds available. The first is for $50,000.00, which goes to my mother, Sallie McIntire Watson, of Magee, Mississippi, should I predecease her. Should she predecease me, I direct that this sum of $50,000.00 shall be returned to the assets of my estate. Secondly, I bequeath the sum of $50,000.00 to the Rials Creek United Methodist Church* *in Simpson County, Mississippi, with the expressed wish that they use the funds in any manner they deem appropriate, as long as it is done in the memory of my parents, Ralph and Sallie Watson. Third, to my very best friend and substitute mother, Elsie Reid, I leave the sum of $50,000.00 and all my love and appreciation.*

"You're making that up," Elsie screeched. "You know Alicia didn't leave me any such amount of money. What about you? I'm not taking anything if she didn't leave you something, too."

"But I told you, Elsie. I get what's left. Listen to the rest of the clause." *The balance of my estate shall pass to my daughter, my only child, Saralynn Bankston.*

"So you see, Mama did leave you some money and you most certainly are going to take it."

"Well I never dreamed anything like that."

Saralynn was folding the will to put it back with the letter, when a thought struck her. "You know. I don't know how to go about handling all this. I think I'd better put in a call to my lawyer here. He'll know what to do."

After a few minutes delay while she argued with a receptionist, Saralynn was finally speaking to Lawrence McCollugh himself. When she explained the situation, he replied. "Sounds like it's fairly cut and dried. However it's been a number of years since that will was drawn. You don't think she might have changed it at some point since?"

I hadn't thought about that. She was so in love with Peter when I married him, she might have changed it then, or when Marc came along. "Gosh," she said, "I don't know. I don't know where else to look, either."

"One other question. Where did your mother do her banking? Is it possible she had a safety deposit box? Did she have any life insurance policies? Have you found those?"

Here I thought everything was settled and instead of answers, I'm getting more questions.

"You've thrown me a curve ball."

"Let me make this suggestion. The law requires due diligence on your part to locate the most current will. However, most courts recognize if you've searched her residence, her automobile – some people carry important documents in their trunk; go figure! – and have determined that she had nothing in a safe deposit box, then you've exercised due diligence."

"Did we have to go through all of this with Peter's estate?"

"We did. You just don't remember it. Your mother handled much of it because, as I remember, you were pretty out of it."

That's putting it mildly! "So what's your suggestion?"

"Can you get the will you have in my hands before you leave tomorrow?"

"I'll run it by this afternoon, if that helps." Saralynn saw that Elsie was rummaging through the clothes in Alicia's closet. "Just a second, Lawrence... Elsie, we need to select something for her to wear on the trip down, and then I know what I want her to wear to be buried... "I'm sorry, Lawrence. We're trying to multi-task here and it's rather hectic right now."

"I understand. Which is why I want to try and take some of that load off your shoulders. At least in the short term."

"Which means what?"

"While you're gone, if you can find where Alicia banked, I can use that will as authorization to learn if there are any safety deposit boxes. My guess is, from what I know of your mother, I'm not going to find one. But that's just my opinion, and opinions are like noses.

"If there isn't a safe deposit box, then I think we can conclude that you have definitely exercised due diligence. And, since you're an only child and don't have siblings to consider, I don't think we'll have any problems."

"What if there is a safety deposit box and another will in it? What then?"

"Then the latest will stands."

"OK," she told him. "I'll bring this by this afternoon."

"Just leave it with my secretary," he told her. "I'll be in touch."

"You have my cell number?"

"Right here. And Saralynn… I am sorry about your mother. I know she was a hard woman to deal with at times, but I always had a feeling there was more background than any of us knew."

You can sure say that again. Maybe someday I'll share with him, but not today. Not now. "Thanks Lawrence. We'll be leaving for Magee tomorrow morning. I'll be back in touch as soon as we get everything dealt with there."

"Safe travels. And take care."

Saralynn and Elsie busied themselves finding the clothing items that Saralynn wanted, along with some jewelry. As they were pulling out contents of the miniature multi-drawer chest, it was Saralynn who discovered a small, extremely wrinkled brown envelope in the very back of one of the drawers. There was a lump in a bottom corner. "What's this?"

"Whatever it is, it's old, and it's been around a long time."

Saralynn opened the end flap and upended the envelope into the palm of her hand. *A diamond ring! A beautiful solitaire. Probably two… maybe even three carats.*

"Oh… it's a ring."

"There's something else sticking in there, see that white edge." Elsie was pointing at the envelope where Saralynn had dropped it on the dresser. "See."

She pulled out a small slip of paper that had obviously been folded and refolded several times. "Oh... listen to this. *'My engagement ring. Marshall bought it for me before we went to the justice of the peace to get married. The Bankstons didn't ask for it back and I didn't offer it.'*

"Mama's engagement ring. It's beautiful, Elsie. Look at that setting. It must have set my father back quite a sum."

"Your mother said his family had more money than they could spend. Sounds like she knew what she was talking about."

Saralynn massaged her neck with the back of her hand. "You know what, Elsie? I don't think Lawrence McCollough is going to find a safety deposit box anywhere. We've found two items already in this room that should have been under lock and key." She held the ring up to catch the afternoon sun streaming through the bedroom window. "If Mama didn't put this in a safe deposit box, she didn't have one."

"My guess is you're right. Alicia was suspicious of anyone knowing what she had." She nodded her head. "Makes sense."

"And I'm making an executive decision here. I'm taking this ring with me. If it turns out in the end that it belongs to someone else, I'll hand it over. But for now, it stays close to me. There's no telling what it's worth."

"And that reminds me, I need to find where Mama banked. The desk in her office would be the logical place."

It took only a few minutes to determine that Alicia had one checking account at Boston Thrift and that she had certificates of deposit and stocks managed by one of the city's oldest investment firms.

"Mama picked the best when it came to placing all that Bankston money. This should make it fairly easy for the attorney." She thought a moment. "Investment banks don't have safe deposit boxes. Do they?"

After stowing the clothing items in a disposable bag and double-checking that everything in the condo was secure, Saralynn reluctantly pulled the door shut, checked that it was latched, and inserted her key into the deadbolt. "Don't want anyone getting in here while we're gone."

She and Elsie drove the clothing to the mortuary, dropped the will at the attorney's office and, seeing that it was rapidly approaching the dinner hour, made the decision to go somewhere to eat where they could be seated and enjoy being served.

In between all their stops, Saralynn had called the airlines to schedule her return and purchase a ticket for Elsie, and had fielded several calls from friends in Simpson County. The pastor of the Iuka United Methodist Church also called. *That was a total surprise, but I still appreciated the courtesy. I think this is what I like so much about the south.*

One of the calls had been from Walter Kennedy who informed her that he and Miss Virginia had been involved in medical appointments all day and were just getting back. "We're ready to grab a flight north tomorrow to help you," he informed her. "Not necessary," she assured him. "I'll be back in Jackson late tomorrow afternoon."

"You mean you've already had a funeral and everything?" His voice clearly showed disbelief.

"No, sir," she told him, "I'm bringing Mama home to bury her at Rials Creek."

"You're what?"

"Trust me. Those were her wishes."

"Well, I never. Alicia didn't want to be here when she was alive. I can't believe she wanted to be buried here."

"That's just one of many revelations I've had in a short period of time. I've got a lot to tell you and Miss Virginia. But it'll have to wait 'til I get back."

"Then take care and travel safely. We'll see you tomorrow."

One other call she had made was to Dr. Martin. *I don't feel like I thanked him adequately yesterday, I was in such a state of shock. Thank goodness he gave me his private line, in case I needed him..* When he came on the phone, Saralynn introduced herself and said, "I know you're busy, but I just wanted to take time, before I leave in the morning, to say 'thank you' for your kindness and compassion yesterday."

"Ms. Reilly, you don't know how much I regret the way things turned out. I would do anything if I could reverse it." He added, "I was going to contact you, but I felt it would be best to wait a few days."

Why would he have been calling me? His manner is surely much less abrupt and severe than it was on the phone a few nights ago.

"I understand this wasn't in the plan. Truly I do. But why were you going to call me?"

"If I may be honest, I wanted to apologize to you. But I also wanted to share what I've learned," he said, "I've been going over her scans, double-checking myself. I've even had two colleagues whose judgment I trust explicitly, to look at them. I didn't tell them anything about the patient, I just asked them to tell me what they saw."

Where is he going with this?

"Both doctors, independently of each other, said the same thing. And after studying the scans again, I must admit, I agree."

"Agree with what, Dr. Martin? You understand, I'm not blaming you?"

"Maybe you aren't, but anytime a doctor loses a patient, there's always an internal audit, if you will."

"So what did you discover?"

"My colleagues believe that your mother's tumor may have been there for years. Perhaps since birth, even. And something... it could have been as simple as a hormone shift... something brought that tumor to life, and when it began growing, it made up for lost time."

"That can happen?"

"It's rare, but it can happen, and it does. Let me ask you something. Had you been able to tell any change in your mother's behavior, say over the past six months?"

Well, yes and no. How do I explain this? "Mama had been exhibiting very irrational behavior," she explained. "But you have to understand that Mama was always a difficult person, so while I can say in hindsight that she was more difficult than usual, it still didn't give me cause for concern."

"Those behavioral changes are consistent with the location of the tumor. Unfortunately, her actions weren't drastically different from the norm." He paused, and emitted a long sigh. "Perhaps if they had been, we might have caught this earlier."

Poor Mama. Again, she was her own worst enemy.

Saralynn and the doctor chatted for another minute, while she explained she was leaving the next morning, taking her mother back to Mississippi for burial. "Thank you, again, Dr. Martin. It wasn't your fault."

After they had eaten, Elsie dropped her by the hotel. Their plane was scheduled to leave Boston at nine-ten, and they decided they would need to be at the airport by seven-thirty.

"Tell you what," Elsie suggested. "Let's get to the airport and get through security. Then we can find something for breakfast while we wait."

"Sounds like a plan."

"Then I'll pick you up at six-thirty, so we'll have plenty of time."

As she was getting out of the car, Elsie leaned over and placed her hand on Saralynn's arm. "Sugar, are you all right?"

"I'm fine, Elsie. Why?"

"Well, I don't mean to be ugly, but you aren't crying and taking on like I would if it was my mother. I'm just worried about you."

Oh, Elsie. If only you knew how I've struggled today to keep from going to pieces. My heart has never hurt this bad.

"I'm dealing with it, Elsie. That's all I can tell you. I can't let myself get like I was after the guys were killed. But I'm grieving. Believe me, I'm grieving."

"I wasn't being unkind. I'm just worried about you."

She flashed the other woman a smile. "Thanks, Elsie. It's nice to have someone worry about me."

Upstairs, she showered, repacked her luggage, talked for a few minutes with Katie Brooks, scheduled a five-forty-five wake-up call, and collapsed in the comfortable bed that had been calling her name for some time.

As sleep quickly overtook reality, the last thought she had was that Miss Sallie and her mama were reunited.

Merry Heart

Well, Mama. Now your mother can hold you and tell you everything's OK. Then she cried until the pillow was soggy and she had to toss it away and get one from the other side of the bed. *I wish my mama could hold me.*

Chapter 16

As the plane lost altitude over the Ross Barnett Reservoir northeast of Jackson, Saralynn found that she couldn't wait to step back onto Mississippi soil. *It doesn't seem possible I could feel this way about a place I've only known a little over a year.*

"We'll soon be there," she said to Elsie, who had listened to her i-pod and napped most of the way, coming fully awake only when it was time to change planes in Atlanta. "I can't wait to get to Magee so you can meet my friends."

"How are we getting there? Didn't you say it was about forty-five minutes from here?"

"My car is in long-term parking. We'll follow the hearse back. I don't want to leave until they're ready."

It had taken some doing, but the mortuary had been able to get Alicia's body on the same flight, for which Saralynn was grateful. *I didn't want to have to leave her behind.* As she sat on the plane, waiting for take-off, Saralynn glimpsed the luggage cart bringing Alicia's casket to the aircraft, and had watched it, zipped in a big vinyl bag, disappear into the belly of the plane. *Like it was in a big suit bag.*

Saralynn had spoken with the Rials Creek pastor before they left that morning, and had given him the details of the low-key service she wanted. "Gracious, but low-key," she told him. And she shared with him the other decision that she had solidified that morning, while standing in the hot shower. *It's the right thing to do.*

Marc's and Peter's ashes were be interred with Alicia. *I had wondered what to do with them, but now I know.* She shared her decision with Elsie while they ate a high-priced breakfast at Logan International that morning, and her friend had agreed.

"I never did understand why your mother pushed to have them cremated," she shared.

"You know, I was so out of it, until I don't even remember that being discussed, although I'm sure it was." *Why did I never question this before?* "Maybe Mama misunderstood and thought that's what I wanted."

They deplaned and made their way to the baggage area where they were soon able to claim their luggage. Saralynn asked a security officer where a casket would be picked up by the mortuary, and was directed to an area away from the main carousels.

"Ms. Reilly?" The question originated from a young man who looked to be in his mid to late twenties, with a full head of red hair. *He would really stand out in a crowd.*

"Yes, I'm Saralynn Reilly. Do we know each other?"

He grinned. "No, ma'am. Not yet anyway. I'm Andy Warren, from the funeral home in Simpson County."

"Oh, you're here to receive Mama's casket."

"Yes, ma'am." There was that grin again. "Please accept my sympathies. Mr. Walter Kennedy says you're special to him, and that I'm supposed to take very good care of you."

"You… you know Mr. Walter?"

The young man shuffled his feet. "Mr. Walter and Miss Virginia. They're like my other parents. I used to date their youngest daughter."

I keep forgetting that they had other children, besides their son, Paul's daddy.

"You said "used to."

"Yes Ma'am. We ended up going our separate ways, and she's married to someone else, and so am I." A troubled look flashed across his face. "Not that we're enemies or anything. It was all friendly. And the best part was, I still got to keep her parents. Miss Virginia even gave Gail, that's my wife, a bridal shower before we got married."

Only in the south.

Elsie tugged on Saralynn's elbow. "Does everybody in the south talk that much?"

"'Fraid so, Elsie. But you'll come to love it, like I have."

"Maybe I won't be here that long and I won't… " she halted. "Hey, there's Alicia's casket."

Saralynn turned to look at the same time the mortuary employee saw the casket, and he became all business, she noted. In short order, it was loaded into the black hearse, and the young man slid behind the wheel. Saralynn, who was standing beside the vehicle, asked him to please wait outside the terminal while she got her car from long-term and drove to meet him. "I want to follow you back."

His answer puzzled her. "Oh, that's the plan. We're going to have quite a nice procession."

A nice procession? "Whatever do you mean? There'll just be our two vehicles."

"No, ma'am," he said and grinned again. "I think you'll find some friends waiting when you get to the parking lot."

Friends! "Friends?"

"They wanted to give you some privacy while we loaded the casket, but you've got a bunch of friends waiting outside."

"Elsie! Did you hear that?"

"Uh-huh. I'm not sure I understand it. But I heard it. Did you know that boy has a terrible accent?"

"Come on; let's go!" She grabbed her luggage, indicated that Elsie should do likewise, and the two headed for the doors. Outside, standing in a group on the sidewalk were more than three dozen people, Saralynn quickly estimated.

I didn't realize I knew this many people?

One of the first familiar faces she glimpsed was Miss Virginia. Then she saw the pastor from Rials Creek and his wife, Bess and Doug were there, and even Kay Austin from Zip's.

Saralynn bit her lower lip to try and hold back the tears.

About that time Katie Brooks spotted her and called out, "Saralynn. Saralynn!"

The two began to run toward each other, and others in the group that had been involved in individual conversations, ceased talking and turned their faces and their attention to the scene unfolding. Saralynn reached Katie, and felt her friend's arms wrap around her.

"We're here for you. We're here for you. You're home now."

The tears that had been lurking behind her eyes ever since she watched the casket being loaded in Boston suddenly broke their tethers and, unable to control herself, Saralynn collapsed into Katie's arms, crying harder even than she remembered crying for Peter and Marc.

"It's OK. It's OK. Just cry it out," her friend encouraged. "It's OK."

"I've… I've done so… so good… so far. I didn't want... to do this." Taking the handkerchief Mr. Walter offered, Saralynn wiped the tears from her face, and tried to make herself look presentable.

I can just imagine what I look like. Thank goodness there isn't a mirror close!

"You all shouldn't have done this," she protested to the group that surrounded her. All the while she was seeing more people that she knew from various places in the community. *People I would never have dreamed would take the time to do something like this. Or am I dreaming?*

"Listen," she said, gesturing for their attention. "I cannot tell you what it means to see you all here this afternoon." She laughed. "As you can tell, it blew me away."

Her friends joined her in the laughter.

"But we all need to be getting back home. I'm going to go get my car and meet the hearse over there." She pointed in the direction of the somber, black vehicle. "Then we can go."

"Not quite," Mr. Walter interrupted. "Your drivers license is no good here this afternoon."

"What do you mean?"

He held out his hand. "Your keys, please?"

"Well, sure. Thanks for offering to get the car for me." She dropped the key fob in his outstretched hand. "Here, you'll need some money." She fumbled in her purse.

"Your money's no good, either." He grinned. Then he put his arm around her shoulder and pulled her close to him. "God tells us to minister to our brothers and sisters in their times of need, and that's what we're doing. You and your friend, Elsie" he smiled at the older woman who, Saralynn thought, looked uncomfortably out of place, "will ride back in our car. Virginia's promised to hold her speed down, and I think you'll be safe."

"But my car…"

"I'll drive your car back and we'll all get back to town in short order."

In a matter of minutes, everyone was loaded, and the procession made its way out the airport drive, through the roundabout at the entrance, and up the hill to the ramp onto Interstate 20. A few minutes later the procession merged onto Highway 49 south and Saralynn knew they were almost home.

You're almost home, too, Mama.

Virginia Kennedy kept up a running conversation the entire trip and, true to her husband's word, stayed slow enough that she didn't pass the hearse. Saralynn knew there was a big joke of long-standing about Miss Virginia's heavy-footed driving habits.

Elsie looks like she is miserable. "Are you OK?" she asked. "You're not saying much."

"I'm tired," she mumbled. "I think I'll see if I can nap some more."

You napped all the way from Boston. I hope it wasn't a mistake insisting that she come with me. Oh, well, I'm tired, too. We've both had several hard days.

"So what are the details, Saralynn? I haven't had time to

talk to Brother Tommy."

Saralynn explained that there would be a time of visitation at the church the following afternoon from noon until two o'clock. Then there would be a short service in the church and burial in the church cemetery.

"You know, don't you, that Walter and I are both heartbroken over all of this. We had so hoped that you and Alicia could reconcile."

"I think we have, Miss Virginia. I think we have."

"But dear, didn't I understand Walter to say she died before you got there?"

I want more than anything to share with them what I've learned. But now is not the time and certainly not the place.

"Nevertheless, I'm at peace. And I can't wait to tell you all about it. At your house with a cup of your good hot chocolate in my hand, curled up on your couch, where no one can bother me."

"I'm sure you are exhausted."

"That, Miss Virginia, is an understatement."

Before she was ready, the procession exited the four-lane heading into the parking lot at Tutor Funeral Home, the mortuary service that several of her friends had recommended. As they pulled under the portico, the front door opened, and a big, burly man stepped out and opened the back door of the Kennedy's red Lincoln Town Car. He reached for Saralynn's hand.

"Ms. Reilly. I'm Terry Tutor. Please accept my deepest sympathies and let me also thank you for selecting our firm. We're here to help you in any way we can. All you have to do is ask."

Saralynn looked into his eyes and saw devilment, but she also saw sincerity. "It's good to meet you, Mr. Tutor. And it's I who should thank you."

He grinned through his beard. "Then let's just say we have a mutual admiration society and let it go at that. And by the way, the name is Terry."

I like this guy. "Then I'm Saralynn."

Alicia's casket was transferred into the funeral home, as Saralynn had learned mortuaries were called in the rural south, and she and Elsie went into the office to finalize all the details. In a matter of minutes, they were ready to leave.

"We'll have your mother ready by nine o'clock in the morning," the funeral director told her. "If you'd like to come in for some private time at any point, we'll just close the parlor doors and you can stay as long as you like." He consulted the notes he held in his hand. "It's about a twenty minute drive to Rials Creek," he estimated, "so we need to be underway at eleven-thirty, in order to be ready for visitation there as soon as the Sunday morning worship service ends at noon."

Tomorrow is Sunday, isn't it? I've lost track of my days. Now I know why the pastor suggested we do visitation at the church starting right after the morning service.

Saralynn thanked him again and was walking back to the Kennedy Lincoln, when a thought hit her. She turned around and called, "Mr... er, Terry. One other thing, please?"

He came toward her. "You name it."

"I know it's a little out of the way, but I'd like to take Mama back by the home place on the way to the church. Can we do that?"

"No problem. We might want to pull out of here at..." he looked at his watch. "Eleven-twenty, so that we have plenty of time."

Once settled in the car, Saralynn asked Virginia where they

had to go next.

"We're going to your house," she replied. "And I need to warn you now. There's a world of food there already, and I know there's going to be more."

"Food?" Elsie asked.

Before Saralynn could respond, Virginia said, "You're in the south, Miss Reid. When someone dies, we feel morally obligated to fry chicken and make potato salad and pound cakes."

"People have already done too much, Miss Virginia," Saralynn protested. "How can I ever repay all of this?"

"By frying chicken or making a pound cake when another of us finds ourselves in a similar situation. You should know by now that we don't keep score."

Yep. I was only in Boston three days, but already I'd forgotten what it's like to have friends in the south.

"Do you always meet bereaved people at the airport en-masse? Elsie asked suddenly. "I don't think I've ever seen anything like that."

Saralynn couldn't decide if her friend was being inquisitive or critical. *I hope Elsie isn't going to offend Miss Virginia.*

The driver laughed. "To be honest, Miss Reid, we haven't had that many occasions to do something like that."

Except when you had to meet the plane bringing both your son and daughter-in-law's bodies. Elsie, please tread cautiously. These people are my friends.

To Saralynn's surprise, it was Miss Virginia herself who broached the subject. "There was one other time that sticks in my mind." She hesitated for a second, and Saralynn wondered if she would continue.

"Our son and his wife, who was like another daughter,

were killed in an accident outside the country a little over two years ago. I cannot tell you what it felt like to drive up to that airport and watch those two caskets being off-loaded."

Saralynn thought she detected a soft sob.

"That's when I looked around and saw more people than I could count. All of whom had stopped what they were doing, to come and stand with us during one of the darkest, most painful moments in our entire life. They couldn't bring our children back, but they could remind us that we weren't alone, and that when tragedy strikes, God sends His angels." She turned her head, slightly, and flashed Elsie a friendly smile. "Usually in the form of regular human beings who often never know they're an answer to prayer."

Saralynn couldn't determine from Elsie's expression how she had received that piece of news, and was relieved when, finally, her friend replied, "I'm so sorry to hear about your children. I'm sure that was very difficult."

"It was," Miss Virginia agreed. "But having people who loved us there to support us made all the difference. Which is why," and she exhibited another of her beautiful, toothy smiles, "we're all going to be here for Saralynn. You see... we've come to love this young woman very much."

Elsie was quiet for the remainder of the trip and it wasn't until the car pulled into the garage that anyone spoke.

"This is your house?" Elsie asked, the surprise evident by her tone. "I'm impressed."

Saralynn was quick to set the record straight. "This is the house I'm leasing. I don't own it."

Once inside, she was quick to see that Miss Virginia hadn't exaggerated. There was food sitting on every available flat surface in the kitchen. When she opened the spacious refrigerator, there wasn't room to accommodate even one more container. *And this is a big refrigerator!*

"Well, I never," Elsie commented. "Who's supposed to eat all this food?"

"We are. You and me," Saralynn said mischievously. "You take the right side of the kitchen and I'll take the left. Whoever eats her way to the sink first wins."

"I think you've been up too long. You're getting silly."

"Bed will feel good," Saralynn agreed. "Speaking of which, let me show you upstairs to your room. Then we'll fix our plates and call it quits."

Virginia Kennedy had only stayed long enough to be certain that Saralynn and her guest were comfortable and had no immediate needs. "I'm going to go, because I know the both of you need some rest. No one will be by here tonight; I put the word out that this place was off limits." She grinned. "But I make no guarantees about tomorrow."

Saralynn accepted the warm and loving embrace that had come to be so precious to her, and bade the chauffeur goodnight. "Tell Mr. Walter I'll vouch for your good driving tonight."

"What did she mean about tomorrow?" Elsie asked as Saralynn led the way upstairs.

"After the service, many of those who attend will probably come back here for a late bite to eat."

"Oh, dear. I hope I have the right clothes."

"What you're wearing to the service will be fine. And if you're more comfortable changing into something else once we're back here. That's fine, too," she reassured her. "You'll see, it'll be very casual."

To her surprise the next morning, Saralynn realized that she had gone to sleep easily, and slept until the alarm roused her. *I must have really been zonked.*

She left the bed, went downstairs and started coffee for her guest and water for her tea, then went back upstairs to check on Elsie, who was in the next bedroom. Her knock was answered with a soft "Yes?"

"It's me. Just checking to see if you were awake. I've got your coffee on."

"I'll be right down."

She doesn't sound like herself.

When the two women met in the kitchen, Saralynn noticed that Elsie appeared even more exhausted than she had the night before. "Did you not rest well?" she inquired.

Elsie shook her head. "Every time I closed my eyes, I remembered that today I'd have to say good-bye to Alicia for the last time, and I simply couldn't get my mind to shut up."

I've had a few nights like that in the past year or so! "I'm sorry this is so hard on you. Certainly none of us ever thought things would turn out like this."

After a quick breakfast, the two returned upstairs to dress for the day. "When we leave," Saralynn explained to Elsie, "we'll be going to the funeral home, then to the church, and it will probably be mid-afternoon before we're back here."

Saralynn showered and dressed in a soft teal and peach suit, with a black scarf incorporated under the collar. *This scarf is my only concession to tradition.* Then, before she left the room for the final time, Saralynn reached onto a shelf in the spacious master closet and retrieved two boxes, one considerably smaller than the other.

Well, guys. You're going on a short trip today. But it will be OK. You'll see. It feels so strange that I'm home but I'm not going to church.

Once at the funeral home, she surrendered the boxes she had transported so carefully to one of the staff. "We're going to inter these in the same grave with Mama."

"Yes Ma'am," he answered. "I'm aware of what's supposed to happen. We'll take care of everything."

Then Saralynn and Elsie entered the parlor where Alicia lay in her casket. One of the staff closed the doors behind them. "I'm going to put the "No Admittance" sign in place until you're ready," he told them. "Take your time."

Saralynn gasped when she reached the side of the casket. "Oh, Elsie. She's really gone. Mama is really dead."

The older woman encircled Saralynn's shoulders with her arm, and hugged her tightly. "It's just so hard to believe."

They spent several minutes at the casket, talking about old memories, laughing about the time Alicia mistakenly added liquid smoke instead of vanilla to a chocolate pie she was making, and speculating about a number of "what if's"… such as, what if Alicia's tumor could have been found earlier.

"Well, Elsie. Whether it could or couldn't, it wasn't. And there's nothing we can do to change things. Come on, we need to get this parlor open. I'm sure there's someone out there who's come to pay their respects."

Sure enough, when they re-entered the hallway, there were several people that Saralynn knew from town, and a couple of people from church, patiently waiting. It was a short period of neck hugging and whispered comments, until finally that group had gone.

"Southern people really get into funerals, don't they?" Elsie asked when they were alone. "I've never seen anything like it."

I've got to answer her very carefully. "It's not that they 'get into funerals' as you say, as much as it is genuine compassion. The same crowd would be on hand if it was a wedding or a Fourth of July picnic. That's one of the things I've come to appreciate about people here. They are my friends. In good times and in bad."

"You have friends in Boston."

"I thought I did," Saralynn responded sadly. "But I've come to realize that at best, the majority of them were just good acquaintances. Here I have real friends."

Before she was ready, it was time to leave for the church. The Kennedys had arrived earlier and informed Saralynn that she and Elsie would be riding in their car. In a matter of minutes, the short procession was assembled and the white hearse pulled out. The route wound by Miss Sallie's house which, Saralynn noticed, was looking very overgrown and neglected. Then they arrived at the church to find the parking lot still full, and members standing in small groups, talking. *They're waiting.* The funeral home staff made short work of unloading the casket and getting it set up at the altar rail at the front.

Almost immediately people began to enter the church, pausing to sign the guest register. Then they sought out Saralynn, went to the casket, then many took a seat in the sanctuary.

Just before two o'clock the funeral director approached Saralynn. "It's time to close the casket. Do you want another minute with your mother?"

"Please. Just time enough to say good-bye." She reached down for Elsie's hand. "Let's go see Mama one last time."

The other woman began to sob. "I don't think I can. I can't bear to give her up."

"Then you sit here and I'll be right back." As she stood by the casket and looked down at Alicia, Saralynn was amazed at how young she looked. *Like Elsie said. "Too young to be dead".* She patted her mother's hand, and brushed back a wisp of hair that had broken free. *I love you, Mama. And I have to believe that you went to heaven, because that's where I'm planning to see you again.*

With those words, Saralynn understood what she was committing. *And as soon as I can talk with my friends, I'm going to take care of that.*

The service was short. The pastor's remarks were, Saralynn realized, remarkable, considering the man had never met her mother. But they were just right and created within her heart a warmth she hoped would never go away. And the music, presented by three of the Rials Creek choir members, added just the right touch. *It's fitting that Mama has come back home, and that's what their music said.* Then it was time to adjourn to the cemetery for the final part of the service.

The group was far larger than would fit under the tent that sheltered the grave. Three familiar faces that she never dreamed she would see that day were Jon and MA Walthall who had driven down from Iuka, and Christina Jacobs from the Atlanta art gallery that represented her work. *I never dreamed so many people would come. I just didn't.*

When she looked up and saw her Iuka friends waiting patiently back in the line, Saralynn felt her legs go weak. *They drove all the way down here.* "What are you doing here?" she asked when finally she got a chance to speak to them.

"We came to pay our respects to our friend's mother… and our friend," MA explained.

When the gallery owner stepped in front of her, Saralynn

was momentarily taken aback. She had only met the woman on one occasion and hers was the last face she expected that day. "Christina!" she exclaimed when she realized the identity of the sharply dressed woman standing in front of her. "Oh, Christina. You shouldn't have come. It's too long a trip." *Besides, how did you find out? I didn't call you. Did I?*

"I wouldn't have not come," her guest assured her. "When I called your home yesterday trying to catch up with you and the woman who answered told me what had happened, I knew I had to come."

Yep. Small town at its best. My phone rang and they answered it. I love this place.

"It all happened so suddenly, Christina. In fact, she died just before I got to the hospital."

She made sure that she invited the Walthall's and Christina to the house following the service. "I'll be hurt if you don't come," she assured them all.

The pastor stood at the head of the casket and offered the Twenty-third Psalm and then made a few concluding remarks. "In addition to Alicia Bankston, we're also laying to rest with her today the remains of Peter Reilly and his son, Marc, Saralynn's husband and son who went home over a year ago." He offered a benediction and the service concluded.

As she and Elsie came in through the kitchen, she noted a number of familiar faces from her Rials Creek family who were already at work getting the food ready to serve. Saralynn changed out of her funeral clothes and into a comfortable pair of slacks and a blouse, and almost before she was ready, the doors opened and, in short order, the house was filled with people talking and laughing and enjoying more food than Saralynn thought could ever be eaten. *I know we'll be throwing food out.*

Then she was caught up in the emotions of love as one person after another had to hug her, whisper an encouraging word in her ear, always concluding with "Now if there's anything we can do, you know all you have to do is call." *It may be a stock statement, but the difference is, these people really mean it. Even Elsie hasn't been able to reprise her wallflower role. People are making her talk to them and visit. She needs that.*

Doug and Bess Martin were one of the first to greet her. Dave and Donna Hasty were close on their heels. And she wasn't surprised to see Katie and Charlie, who had Katie's mother and her Aunt Toots in tow. Ian and Angus Scarborough waited while others spoke with her, then they made their way over.

"I've got something I found in Boston I want to show you. When Mama jilted you, it wasn't about you at all."

A tear came into the older man's eye. "I loved your mama, but I couldn't make her love me." He pulled out a handkerchief and wiped his face. "I can't believe we buried her this afternoon. It just don't seem possible."

"Give me a few days, I'll share with you what I've learned." Then she began to circulate through the rooms again, trying to make certain that she spoke with everyone.

Slowly, at first, one at a time, then in groups of two and three, friends began to offer their good-byes and repeated condolences and leave.

There is church tonight, and I'm sure most of the Rials Creek group will be there. But I don't think I will be. Suddenly I am really wiped.

Several women were cleaning and Virginia Kennedy was tying a garbage bag when Saralynn crossed the kitchen from seeing yet another guest to the door. "Honey, you've got to be exhausted. Why don't you go sit down for a few minutes and put your feet up?"

Saralynn smiled at the woman she had come to regard as a substitute mother. *One of several I've been fortunate to have.* "I haven't noticed you sitting down any this afternoon."

"But I haven't had the load on me that you've had either. Now go. Shoo." She made a fanning motion with her hands. "You've got a perfectly comfortable looking recliner in there. Go sit in it."

"Yes Ma'am," she conceded. "Or should I call you, 'General Kennedy'?"

"Go on with you," Virginia shushed. "I'll come join you in a minute. How about that?"

"Deal." Then a thought hit her. "Have you seen Elsie?"

"Upstairs," Virginia said, as she motioned toward the ceiling with her thumb that was still tying the bag shut. "She said she was going to go lay down for a while."

I guess she's OK then.

Once she had her feet elevated in the recliner, Saralynn suddenly became aware of how tired she truly was. *I believe I could close my eyes and go right to sleep.*

"You still want a visitor, or would you rather I let you alone so you can take a nap?"

Gosh, am I that obvious? "No Ma'am, you sit right down here and visit. There's nothing I want more right now than your company. I can sleep tonight." Then she remembered, "Aren't you missing church?"

Her friend settled into the chair near where Saralynn rested. "It is good to get off my feet a minute." She pulled one foot up and rubbed the top of it. "I'll get there. I may be a little late, but I'll get there. Don't you worry about me. Just let me rest a minute and I'll be good to go."

"Well you deserve to rest. I don't know what I would have done without you. But Miss Virginia. I cannot get over how people turned out for the funeral and brought all this food." She waved her hands in a gesture of confusion. "Very few of those people knew Mama and I've only lived here a little over a year."

"The answer is simple, Saralynn. You've made many more friends here than you even realize. What's more, you're genuine. A lot of outsiders would have come in here and insisted that we change to fit their requirements. You didn't. You've made yourself one of us, without any pretense on your part."

Saralynn thought about what she said and, because she felt she would burst if she had to bottle it in any longer, posed the question that had haunted her ever since the moment she learned of Alicia's death.

"May I ask you something? And will you be honest with me?"

"If I know the answer, I'll tell you. And if I don't, I won't make up anything or lie to you."

"I'm afraid I'm being disrespectful to Mama. I've cried several times since the afternoon she died. And when they closed the casket today for the final time, I thought my heart was going to break. But I'm not all to pieces like I was with Peter and Marc."

"Do you want to be the way you were then?"

"Absolutely not! I hope to never be that way again. But I

feel like I'm slighting Mama."

Miss Virginia studied her hands for a few seconds before she spoke. "I promised to tell you the truth about what I thought. So here goes. I think when your husband and son died, you had no anchor, no rock to hold on to. And by your own admission several times, you've decided you had few true friends in Boston. Alicia was the only one there for you. And you had no spiritual anchor."

I hadn't looked at it like that.

"Since then," her friend continued, "you've made some true friends. You've learned to lean on God when things get too heavy, and you've come to realize that you're not all alone in the world."

Once again, the tears that had threatened to overflow at several points throughout the day finally broke through. But instead of the hysterical crying jags that had characterized her recovery process from Peter and Marc, these sobs were soft, and comforting, and Saralynn wasn't frightened of herself.

Chapter 17

The next week passed with lightning speed, although there were moments when Saralynn felt like she was slogging through deep, heavy mud that threatened to pull her down into itself. The terrifying prospect that she might not be able to pull herself out of the mire kept her plugging ahead.

Her out of town guests from Iuka and Atlanta had stayed over at a motel in Magee, and visited with Saralynn the next day, before heading their respective ways. Saralynn was proud to give them, and Elsie, a tour of her studio. She held her breath as Christina Jacobs examined the finished commission pieces and proclaimed them "...absolutely exquisite, Saralynn. Mr. Chambers is going to be overjoyed." She continued to wander about the studio, looking at other work samples. "You know," she told the Walthalls, who had hit it off immediately with the gallery owner, "I think I may have stumbled upon an artist who is going to make me a tremendous amount of money."

"And it won't hurt her any, either," Jon Walthall joked, and everyone laughed.

"I'm sorry the purpose of this trip had to be for your mother's funeral," MA told her before they left, "but now that I've seen your work firsthand, I know I can get you some commissions."

After they'd gone, Elsie and Saralynn were still in the studio, when her Boston friend suddenly stated, without preamble, "Your mother was wrong."

"I beg your pardon?"

"Alicia. She was dead wrong about you."

"I'm afraid you've lost me."

"She had a fit when you sold your design business, but she was wrong and you were right. She was the one better suited to that type work." She picked up a partially-constructed piece. "This... this right here. This is you. It's sheer genius and a lot of talent besides." She hugged the younger woman. "You heard what those two ladies said. You've got no way to go but up. I'm so proud of you."

Later that evening, after they'd gotten Elsie repacked for her trip back to Boston the next morning, the two women drove to the Rials Creek Cemetery to spend a few minutes. It was as if they both knew when the plane took off for Boston the next day, a totally new chapter in each of their lives was beginning. They were loathe to abandon the old chapter without one more goodbye.

Saralynn cried as Elsie walked down the concourse, knowing that her friend was returning to a lonely existence. *Mama didn't mix and mingle. She and Elsie were almost co-hermits. Now Mama's gone and Elsie has no friends, no support group. And at her age – she's got to be at least sixty-two or sixty three – she's not apt to be out there recruiting new friends.* She vowed she would call the lady at least once a week, and would make it a point to invite her to fly back down periodically. *But I'll bet she won't. I don't think she was exactly taken with Southern hospitality. But I sure am glad that I live here.*

Back in home territory, she swung by Boswell on impulse, anxious to see Emma. *I'm not going to tell her that Mama died. I'm afraid it might upset her since it hasn't been that long since her own mother's death.*

As she expected, Emma was overjoyed to see her, and despite her intentions of staying only fifteen or twenty minutes, it was more than an hour and a half later that she finally pointed the car in the direction of the entrance. *Bless Emma's heart. You just can't get away from her.*

One of the things that Emma asked was when she and Saralynn were going back to Iuka. Only she asked when they were going back to Fishtrap Hollow. *She makes it sound like Iuka is the suburb, not the main town. But maybe to Emma, that's how it is.*

"It will be a few weeks, at least. I've got a lot of work to do in my studio before I can leave again." *I feel guilty making it sound like I haven't already been gone a great deal, but Emma simply wouldn't understand.*

As she drove toward home, she remembered that before she could go back to Iuka, she had to go back to Boston to deal with Alicia's estate. *This gets more complicated by the day. I think I'd better put in a call to Lawrence McCollugh tomorrow.* She consulted the dash clock. *Yep, it's too late on the east coast to call today.* She did some mental math and decided that Elsie should have landed within the past hour. *If she didn't get stuck circling Atlanta. I hope she keeps her promise and calls me, but if she doesn't, I'll call her.*

Back home in her studio, Saralynn realized for the first time in almost a week, that she was alone. Everyone had gone back to their normal routines and life went on. *And I'm a part of it.*

With several hours left to her, she tackled the latest commission piece and while she worked later than she had planned, it was with a great deal of satisfaction that she closed her studio door feeling that she had accomplished a good amount. *After what Christina said, I dare not disappoint her.*

There was still an abundance of food and she decided that she could eek out one more meal before it would be necessary to toss it all. *There was so much I never got a chance to sample.* On a whim, she pulled out everything and piled up a plate with first a bite of this, then another bite of that, until she had a dinner plate heaped high. *Call me a glutton!* But the shame didn't stop her from digging in, and when she was finished, Saralynn was satisfied.

She cleaned the kitchen, dumped many of the leftovers into the disposal, while others went into a large black garbage bag which she took out to the dumpster at the corner of the garage. Then she returned to the house, secured the doors, turned out the lights and made her way to the second floor.

"Mr. Walter, how are you tonight? Is this a bad time?"

She had sprawled across her bed, with a pillow under her head. There were two calls she needed to make. *And I need to do it while my resolve is up.*

"Saralynn, sugar. Is everything all right? Do you need us?"

"Everything's good, Mr. Walter. Is Miss Virginia where

she can get on an extension?"

She heard his voice in the distance. "Virginia. Pick up a phone. It's Saralynn."

"Hello, dear. I've thought about you several times today, but I didn't want to intrude."

"Well you should have called."

"I thought you might need some of your own space, at least for a little while. Did Miss Reid get off?"

Elsie! I forgot all about her and she hasn't called. "Yes Ma'am, we got her on that plane." *I'm not going to let them know I'm worried.* "I've got to call her before I go to bed to be sure she make it OK."

"So if nothing's wrong, what's up?"

"Walter!" Miss Virginia chided. "That's no way to talk to Saralynn. Nosy."

Saralynn laughed. *That felt so good.* "It's OK, you two. I just had something I wanted to share with you."

"Well share away."

"I'll need your help."

"You know that's a given. So what's up, my dear?"

Mr. Walter is so gallant. "I've made a decision." She hesitated, then plunged ahead. "You both have talked to me several times about inviting Jesus into my heart. Well, it's something that I want to do."

"Praise God," Mr. Walter cried.

"You have made us so happy, dear. And you have no idea what you've done for yourself."

"Thanks, Miss Virginia. I just wanted the both of you to know. And in the next few days, when those closest to me can get together, I want to formally ask Jesus to live with me. But I want those who mean so much to me to be a part of it."

"You know, Saralynn," Mr. Walter was saying, "the fact that you've shared with us tonight your intent to make Jesus a part of your daily life means that in truth, you already have. But we'll still gather your loved ones and make it official, because if there was ever anything that justified a celebration, eternal life is it."

Eternal life. That sounds so guaranteed and assuring.

They shared a quick prayer, then Saralynn dialed Elsie's number.

"Hello." The voice was low and lackluster.

"Elsie. You didn't call to let me know you made it home OK."

Her statement was met with silence. Then, finally, a pitiful voice said, "I meant to. It just didn't happen. But I'm here."

"Did you have any problems?"

"I don't guess. Changing planes in Atlanta was a chore, but I made it."

"I'm glad. I didn't want to call it a night without knowing you were home OK."

"I'm home, but I'm not OK. I keep wanting to call Alicia. I've picked up the phone three different times and her line just rings and then I..." she choked, "then I remember."

"I'm sorry, Elsie. I wish I could make that part of things better, but I can't. But we can keep in touch. You call any time you wish."

"Can't do that. You're busy and I'm so proud for you. But you don't need an old woman crying on your shoulder all day."

I don't, but I can't turn my back on her, either. "Nonsense! You're my surrogate grandmother now and don't you forget it."

"You're sweet to say that, but you'll soon get busy down there and forget about me."

"Now that's where you're wrong, Elsie."

"No," she said, "I don't think so. I saw you with those people. They love you and you love them. Looks like smothering to me, but you evidently thrive on it."

I've got one more call to make. "Look, Elsie. You're like me. You're tired. Let's both get a good night's sleep and I'll call you back tomorrow."

"OK. I'll probably be here."

I need to contact somebody with the condo association and see if they have social events that someone can invite Elsie to attend.

Even though it was late, Saralynn desperately wanted to share her decision with Katie, and she placed the call. "Hi," she said when the phone was answered, "I know it's late, but I had something I simply had to tell you."

"We're in bed, but we aren't asleep. Charlie's reading and I'm channel surfing. So what's up?"

"I've decided to ask Jesus to come live in my heart," she said quietly.

"Oh… oh, Saralynn. I am sooo happy for you."

She heard her friend talking to her husband. "Saralynn's accepting Jesus. Our prayers have been answered, Charlie."

"Oh, Saralynn, that's wonderful."

She shared with Katie her wish to have a gathering of her closest friends and to publicly acknowledge her decision.

"You just tell us when and where and we'll be there. I don't care what we might have to rearrange."

"OK," Saralynn said, suddenly feeling shy. "I'll talk to you tomorrow."

"Good night. And God love you."

As she was drifting off to sleep, thinking about calling the

Merry Heart

Boston attorney the next day, it made her think about Jon and MA.

I've got to call them, too. If they hadn't shown me the Good Shepherd window, I might never have done this.

She hit the alarm button, double-checking that the clock was set to waken her at six-thirty.

I've got things to do!

Chapter 18

Saralynn was awake before the alarm sounded, and swung her legs over the side of the bed as she knocked the button back into the off position. *I've gotten really spoiled not having to punch a clock, but I think I'm going to have to get serious with myself. I've got work to do, and it's not going to get done laying here in this bed.*

Despite the pristine day outside and weather that practically begged, "Come out and play," Saralynn entered her studio on the run and didn't slow her pace all day, except when she ran across to the kitchen to slap together a peanut butter sandwich, which she nibbled while she made phone calls.

Several times during the day, when she needed to change positions and give herself a chance to recoup, she made phone calls and wrote thank you notes for the many flowers and dishes of food her friends had provided for the funeral. *I simply cannot believe all the people I know here, people I care for greatly.*

"Oh, Saralynn," MA's voice echoed across the distance from northeast Mississippi. "Thank you for letting us know. Needless to say, I'm so pleased that you've decided to let Jesus into your heart, and I know Jon will be as well. He's in court or I'd call him right now."

"Please tell him how much I love you both. You showed me how Jesus works in your lives, even when I wanted to resist you."

"Listen, friend, when you have Jesus, you can't wait to tell everyone. The Bible commands us to do that, you know."

I've still got so much to learn. "I didn't realize that, but I'm so glad you didn't let my cold shoulder deter you."

"This is just so wonderful. I can't believe it."

Saralynn explained how she wanted to make her decision public before those friends and family closest to her. "I wish there were some way you and Jon could come. And there are others in Iuka that I've come to love as well."

"Well, Saralynn. With God all things are possible, so just keep us posted when you set a date and we'll see."

A second quick call went to Atlanta, to Christina Jacobs.

"Are you alright? I've worried about leaving you," her representative said after the pleasantries were out of the way. "So how are you making it?"

"By staying busy. I've been in the studio since daylight." She laughed. "I've accomplished a good bit, too." She glanced across the three fabric-layered panels she had completed and felt a sense of pride growing within her.

"Three more pieces finished today. I'm developing more productive techniques with each one. And they do look so good."

"You better believe they look good! I called Mr. Chambers

after I got back to the office this morning and told him that I'd seen several of the pieces."

"I hope he was pleased."

"He was, and I even bet him that it will be your artwork that sells those units." They're just unique enough in concept, and the fact that no two are exactly alike, is going to be the curiosity drawing card when he starts marketing them."

My work is going to sell those condos? "You're not serious?"

"My dear, I've never been more serious. I don't think you realize just how talented you are. It certainly was my lucky day when you allowed me to represent you."

"Oh, come on Christina. I'll admit, I'm good. But you're pushing the limit some."

"Tell you what, you just stand back and watch and see if what I'm telling you doesn't come to pass." Her voice took on a serious tone. "Now I know we need to schedule you for a gallery showing here shortly after the marketing for these condos begins."

Well…

"You wait and see. Saralynn Reilly's name is going to be on Atlanta's lips."

After thanking Christina for her enthusiasm, and for taking the time to travel to the funeral, Saralynn placed a third call to Lawrence McCollough in Boston. After waiting for several minutes, he finally picked up the phone.

"Lawrence," she said quickly, "I've caught you at a bad time, haven't I?"

"I was finishing something, but that's why I kept you holding. Now it's out of the way and we can visit."

"You're sure?"

"Trust me. So how are you? I thought about you over the

weekend. It must have been rough."

"It's not something I'd want to endure every day. But I'm OK. Really. I have periods when I get teary-eyed, but I'm OK."

"You've certainly had more than your share thrown at you in the last year or so. Don't want you getting sick from all this. You've got friends. Let them help you. Cry on their shoulders if you need."

"Thanks, Lawrence. I have been and I will continue to ask for help. When I need it."

"I'm assuming that aside from wanting to visit, you're curious as to what I've discovered."

"No sense beating around the bush, my friend. I'm not greedy, but I do have other commitments and I need some idea of how much time I'm going to have to allocate for estate work in Boston."

"The answer is, you can spend as little or as much time as you'd like."

"No safety deposit box, huh?"

"Not even any old records that would indicate she had one at some time in the past."

"So you think we're good to go forward with the will I found?"

"I can represent it without concern." She could hear him moving things around on his desk. "Like I told you, if you had siblings, or aunts and uncles, for example, there might be cause for worry. But as it is, as far as I'm concerned, you're good to go."

"Let me ask you something else that occurred to me last night."

"Shoot."

"When Mama left Mississippi the last time, she was in the

middle of settling her own mother's estate. My grandmother named her executor. But all of that is up in the air now. How do we handle that?"

"Naturally, being in Massachusetts, I'm not licensed to practice in Mississippi. But I feel comfortable telling you to see an attorney there who can petition the court, showing that Alicia died before completing her duties, that you are the next heir in line to your grandmother, and are in fact, the only heir. It should be cut and dried and then you can proceed."

I'll talk to Jon Walthall. He can help me.

"So what's my next move on the Boston end?"

"Six weeks after Alicia's death, I can probate her will and you can go forward on this end as well."

"Is there anything I need to do between now and then?" Unable to stay seated, Saralynn was buzzing around the studio cleaning and straightening as they talked. "What about things like the monthly condo assessment, Mama's utilities? What do I do about such things as that?"

"Normally I'd say pay them out of your pocket and then reimburse yourself after you get your authorization. But that won't be necessary. You were co-owner with your mother on all her investments and bank accounts."

I am? Since when? "I think you must be mistaken, Lawrence."

"That's why it was so easy at the bank to ask about a safe deposit box. Since your name is on everything there, they were only too happy to answer my questions."

"But Lawrence, wouldn't I have had to sign something?"

"Sure. And you did."

"When did I sign anything? I'm afraid the bank's made a

mistake."

"Nope. You're the one who's mistaken. Remember, your mother had done business with these folks for years. Alicia Bankston didn't move her money around. You signed the original signature cards when she opened the accounts."

Slowly the light bulb began to glow ever so dimly. *I do remember now. I was home on break from college and Mama insisted that I go to the bank and sign papers with her. "Just in case..." she said.*

"I don't imagine you ever wrote a single check in all these years, did you?"

"Sure didn't. That's why I didn't remember being on the account. I did what Mama asked because that was the easiest way to make Mama happy. And then I promptly put it out of my mind."

"Well it's your lucky day that Alicia insisted, because now that money is yours without being part of the estate."

A sudden thought began to form in her mind. "Lawrence... did they tell you how much was there? And is this the trust fund income or the investments?"

"I'm afraid I don't understand the distinction."

I don't want to air the dirty linen. But he needs to understand. "It's like this. My father's parents didn't consider Mama good enough, so they bought his freedom. They paid her a lump sum of money to give him the divorce and leave the state. According to correspondence I found at her house, she invested that money more than thirty-five years ago and never touched a penny of it."

"Man, she must have driven a hard bargain."

"You don't know the half of it." *I can't believe I'm telling this.* "She also made them establish a trust fund with the interest payable to her monthly and that's what she lived on."

"Whew! That's enough to make divorced men quake in

their shoes." Then his tone sobered. "So you think she was still getting monthly payments at the time she died?"

"I have every reason to believe that she was."

Evidently I've gotten his attention, because I can hear him moving around and papers shuffling.

"Do you know what happens to the principle in that trust fund upon her death?"

"No, I didn't even know the fund existed until Elsie and I were going through her papers looking for funeral instructions. Why? Is it important?"

"It could be. To answer your question, it would appear that the money derives from the monthly trust payments since there's just less than ten thousand in the account. We're going to need to notify the trustee that she has deceased."

'Has deceased' sounds so formal.

"So then it would stand to reason that the money she invested with… with…"

"I know, I can't think of the firm's name either, even though I read it on some papers in her bedroom."

"Anyway, that money I would guess was from the lump sum settlement she accepted in exchange for your dad's freedom."

That sounds so mercenary. "So what about the trust fund?"

"Simple. Once we notify the trustee, the payments stop."

"So what? Mama's dead." *I cannot call her 'deceased'.*

"Yeah, she is. But what happens to the money?"

"Knowing what I've learned about them in the past few days, I'd guess it reverts to them."

"Are they still alive?"

"I don't know. I didn't even have a clue who they were until last week. But I'd guess there's a fifty-fifty chance they're still alive."

"How about your dad? He still living?"

"Never met the man. Wouldn't know him if I saw him. So I don't have any idea."

"I need to look into this. If your grandparents are dead, we might petition the court to award the principle sum in that account to you."

"Well...!"

"Hey," he said and laughed, "stranger things have happened when law that doesn't always conform to common sense gets into the mix."

"Well you work on it and let me know. And I'll plan to see you in about six weeks."

"Take care, Saralynn. We will be talking before then, I promise."

"'Bye, Lawrence."

Saralynn went back to work, knowing she still had to return to Iuka and would have to be back in Boston as well. *And I still have all these commissions to finish. Plus, if Christina is serious about holding a gallery show, I'll need pieces for it as well.*

She was just closing the studio door behind her for the evening, when she heard the land line phone ringing. Saralynn turned back to answer it and noted by the Caller ID that it was Walter Kennedy's number.

"Hello?"

"Saralynn, how are you, dear?"

"I'm OK, Miss Virginia." She swiped a hand through her messy curls. "Tired, but OK."

"Oh, I hope you're not having problems sleeping. You need your rest."

"No, ma'am, it's not that. I've spent the entire day in the studio, since early this morning. I've accomplished a lot, but I'm also wiped out."

"Too tired to come to supper?"

Am I? "You know it would take a lot for me to turn down a chance to eat your cooking." She thought for a moment. *I need to get out of here for a little while anyway.*

"Tell you what. I'll come, if you promise not to go to any extra trouble, and if you won't be insulted if I don't stay too late."

"Just come. It'll all work out."

"That was absolutely delicious," Saralynn complimented the cook, when she had finished the last bite of pecan pie and ice cream. "But then the entire meal was delicious. I thought I asked you not to go to any extra trouble?"

"I didn't. It was just something I threw together this afternoon."

"I've lived here, remember? I know how you 'throw' things together."

"Well the main thing is we all enjoyed it. What does it matter?"

"I don't know about you two," her husband injected, "but I'm ready to adjourn to the recliners and let some of this good food settle."

Yeah. Settle around my waist where I'll never be rid of it! I weigh more right now than I ever have.

Once they were seated, Saralynn reached in her purse and pulled out the yellowed old envelope that had held the will and

Alicia's letter. "In searching for funeral instructions, I found this." She held the envelope out to Mr. Walter. "Thought you might find it as interesting as I did."

"Read it aloud, Walter," Miss Virginia urged.

"Well, let me get my reading eyes on." He swapped the glasses on his head for a pair out of a case on the table beside his chair, slipped the letter from the envelope, and began to read.

On three different occasions he stopped when something he read gave him cause for a second look, and glanced at Saralynn with wonder in his eyes. "There really are two sides to every story."

"This explains so much," Miss Virginia said softly. "Poor Alicia."

"This must have hit you pretty hard," Mr. Walter noted. "Has this changed anything in your mind?"

Saralynn thought for a few seconds before she answered, even though the decisions those answers represented had been formulated much earlier in the day. "If by changed, you mean have I decided to go back to Boston, the answer is 'definitely not'. Knowing that Mama stayed there because she felt imprisoned puts even more emotional distance between me and the city. Boston's a nice place, for someone who wants to live there. I don't."

Miss Virginia hugged her. "We're so glad to hear you say that."

"I don't want to be premature bringing this up, but what about Miss Sallie's house? It's yours now, you know."

"I know, and I've thought about it. But I haven't come to any decision, other than I want to hire someone as quickly as possible to get in there and cut the grass and clean it up outside."

The trio talked for a few more minutes before Saralynn insisted that she had to go. "It's been a long day, and it's going to be another killer tomorrow. But I'm so excited about what I'm accomplishing, the exhaustion is worth it." She had shared with them earlier about the Atlanta gallery owner's comments and the promise of a one-person show in the near future.

"We're both very thrilled for you about everything," Miss Virginia said as the two hugged good-bye. "You deserve every good thing that can happen to you and we're so proud to call you 'ours'."

After she was in bed and the lights were out, Saralynn recalled her conversation with Lawrence McCollough. *He never did tell me the balance in the investment account.*

"Saralynn!" Jon Walthall's cheery voice came across in fine form from the other end of the state. "To what do I owe the pleasure?" Say," he asked, suspicion evident in his voice, "you haven't already called MA and have me playing second fiddle?"

"No," she responded smartly, "you're number one on my list this morning. And as much of a pleasure as it is to talk with you, this call is strictly business."

"Let me turn on my cabbie's meter and you can fire away," he quipped.

"You can joke, but I already owe you something, and I certainly intend to pay for all the work you do."

"All in good time. All in good time. I've got my pen poised over my legal pad, so fire away."

Saralynn explained the legal situation existing with her grandmother's estate, the fact that it had been left solely to Alicia, who had not completed settling that estate before she died. "Now I have an estate in Boston, where I am executor. And I have an estate here in Mississippi, that is an unresolved asset of the estate in Boston, to which I have no clear legal claim. What do I do and can you handle the Mississippi end?"

"I'll answer your second question first. Yes, I'm licensed to practice anywhere in the state, but isn't there an attorney there you'd rather use?"

"I'm certain there is an attorney locally my friends would recommend, but you happen to be my choice, if you'll take the job."

"You know that goes without saying."

"There are just some aspects of Mama's business, as it relates to the estate here, that I'd just as soon be kept out of the public eye as much as possible."

"What are you getting at, Saralynn? We're not talking about something illegal, are we?"

"No. No. Nothing like that. Trust me."

"You know I do. I just didn't want you to be getting in over your head."

"You'll understand when I show you some of the documents I've found. I just want to try and protect Mama's privacy as much as I can."

"Gotch'a. Then get me the documents on the Mississippi end of the deal and let me get to work."

"I'll overnight them. They should be there by morning."

"So when are we going to see you again? I was hoping you'd say you were driving the papers up."

I knew that question was coming. "I'm not yet certain what my schedule will be." She fingered some notes on her desk, remembering another call she needed to make, and knowing that the morning was slipping away. *Got to get down to some productive* work. *And soon!*

"I'm not sure right now what my schedule will be for the next few weeks. I'm waiting for some definite word from my Boston attorney about when I'm going to need to be there. And I'm running very much behind on this commission for the Atlanta condo complex. So I need to stay here and work as much as I can."

"I understand."

"Besides, Jon. I'm tired. I'm so very weary. I just want to stay home for a while and sleep in my bed and not live out of a suitcase."

"I can appreciate that. Say, Saralynn… MA couldn't wait to tell me about your decision to become a Christian. I'm so glad to hear that and I'm so proud for you."

"Thanks, Jon. That's another reason I want to hang around here for a few days."

"Well, you just keep us posted."

Saralynn ended the call and sat, deep in thought in her office chair, before she reached for the phone book to look for a number.

"Saralynn. What a nice surprise. I had you on my prayer list to call today… those first few days after a death are usually a roller-coaster, and I try to check in periodically. But it's fine that you called first," the pastor at Rials Creek assured her.

I don't know Brother Tommy as well as I want to, but he's so warm and friendly. I feel like I can talk to him.

"This isn't a bad time for you, is it?"

"Not at all. I don't have anything to do right now except visit with you. So what's on your mind?"

Saralynn thanked him for all that he had done on short

notice and under somewhat of a handicap. "It meant so much to me to be able to bring Mama home to bury her, especially when I discovered that was what she wanted." She felt a sob rising in her throat and fought to keep it down. "Then I'd had my husband and son's ashes for over a year and didn't know what to do with them, and it just suddenly seemed appropriate that all three be buried together."

"If that was what you wanted, then it was definitely the appropriate thing to do," he reassured her. "And I was glad to do what I could. You know, there are a lot of people in this community who think very highly of you."

Saralynn felt herself blush and gave silent thanks that the pastor couldn't see her. "There are many very wonderful people here." *People who tend, out of kindness, to overlook some awfully big flaws. But then I guess that's why I love them so much.*

"I hope you'll pardon me for being so direct, but I get the feeling there's something else besides the funeral on your mind. The 'unsaid' is shouting at me."

"You're pretty perceptive, because there is something else." *Really it's the main reason for my call.* "There's something I want to share with you; a decision I've made that I'm so very pleased about."

I never thought I'd see the day I wanted to call friends to share this news!

"It sounds important."

"It is to me. I've decided to accept Jesus as my Saviour and ask Him to live in my heart. And I want to make my decision public."

"That is wonderful!" was his immediate response. "May I ask you to share with me how you reached that decision?"

Now I feel sort of awkward saying this. But here goes. "I've felt an emptiness in my life for years, but never understood what it was until I moved here and began to become friends with people who had something I didn't quite understand. But I knew I wanted whatever it was."

"You're talking about Miss Virginia and Mr. Walter."

"Most definitely, but many others as well. In fact, there are people right there in the church who probably don't know how I envied whatever it was that made them able to be positive, even when things weren't always good."

"It was the Holy Spirit at work in their lives."

"I understand that now. But I didn't in the beginning. I just knew they had something I wanted. And I didn't know how to get it."

There was no response from the other end and Saralynn realized the pastor was letting her talk. "As I began to ask one, and then another, they would tell me how Jesus lived in their hearts. They'd talk about God like He was a member of their household."

"How did you take that?" the pastor asked quietly.

"At first, I thought they were nuts. Except I knew them as reasonable, intelligent people, so how could they be crazy?"

"You're saying they showed you how to be a Christian as opposed to telling you how to do it."

"They did both, but if that hadn't shown me first, I doubt I would have ever believed their explanations."

"But the important thing is that I know now what it is that made them different from me, and I want to be a Christian. I want what they have."

"Why don't I drive over and we can talk more about this."

I guess I thought it would be asking too much to expect him to come to me, but that's what I really wanted. "Certainly. If you're sure it's not an imposition." For a moment she felt like she might be inconveniencing him. "I'm sure you already had some sort of an agenda for today."

"True. But nothing on my list is as important as rejoicing with one of my congregation when they've made a decision as important as this."

He called me 'one of my congregation'. Sounds like he included me, whether I included myself or not.

Unwilling to involve herself in one of the commission pieces, Saralynn stayed busy with clerical tasks while she waited for the pastor to arrive. Some thirty minutes later, they were seated at one of the cutting tables while she explained how her journey had brought her not just from Boston to Magee, but from that of a totally uninformed non-believer, to a believer who understood that the real journey was just beginning.

"I want to publicly make my decision known to the church during the service this coming Sunday, because it truly has been the church as a whole that has shown me what it means to live with Jesus in my heart."

"Then by all means, you shall," the pastor agreed. "At the conclusion of the service, I'll ask you to come forward and share with the congregation just what you've told me today." His face took on a most earnest expression. "You know, Saralynn, I doubt that many of them can truly appreciate how our actions speak so much louder than words."

Am I going to come across looking like a goody-two-shoes?

"I don't want anyone to get the idea that I think I'm better than they are."

"Not to worry. That won't be the case, although I believe

some will be forced to re-examine how their smallest actions can be viewed by others."

"OK. I just don't want to offend anyone. I love them too much."

The pastor had risen to wander about the studio, examining one, then another of the finished commission pieces that were sealed in plastic to protect them from dust and grime. "These are absolutely breathtaking," he said, as the two continued to talk.

"Thank you. I've never loved work more in my life than I do right now."

"And it shows, too. Say, have you given any thought to when you want to hold your baptism?"

This is one of the things I'm uncertain about. That's why I've been on the Internet researching the subject.

"May I ask you a question?"

"Of course…"

"From what little I know about baptism, some churches baptize babies and others only after people are older. And some of them do it by splashing water on the baby's head and others dunk you completely under the water. I don't understand."

"Don't feel intimidated by that. In the United Methodist Church, as do several other denominations, we do sprinkle water on the heads of infants that are presented to us by their parents. Then, when that child is older, he or she attends a confirmation class where we teach them what it means to be a Christian, to invite Jesus into their hearts."

"So then I can't be baptized in the Rials Creek church since I wasn't splash… er, sprinkled as a baby?"

"No, no. Not at all. We also baptize adults who, like yourself, were never presented for the sacrament as a baby. And," he said, "it would be my distinct pleasure to baptize you. Because you see, Saralynn, I've understood for the first time today the marvelous way that God has been at work in your life. As His servant, nothing would make me happier than to baptize you in His name."

The two discussed dates and then Saralynn found the courage to ask another question that troubled her. "Are you the only one who can baptize me, or can another pastor do it?"

"Oh, you mean there's someone else you'd rather have perform the sacrament. Well, of course, any minister of the gospel can officiate." He looked rather chagrined. "I'm sorry. I didn't mean to indicate that I had to be the minister. I certainly understand if there's another pastor you'd prefer."

I've explained it badly and maybe hurt his feelings.

"I didn't phrase that very well. I had assumed that you would be the minister. But there's another minister who has touched my heart, and I wondered if there was some way he could participate as well."

"And who might this pastor be? Do I know the person?"

Saralynn smiled as she thought about the young pastor in Iuka who had reached out to her. *I know now that I'm going to have some sort of life in Iuka and that will be my church home there. I really want him to baptize me too.*

She explained the situation and her wishes, and why. "So you see, it's not a popularity contest, but since it was there that I truly began to understand all that I'd learned at Rials Creek, I'd like for him to be involved."

"Oh, I certainly have no problem with sharing the honors. It's done all the time. The only problem I see is that we normally hold baptism on Sunday morning, and that means he would have to be out of his pulpit."

I hadn't thought about that. That would be asking way too much.

"But that doesn't mean it couldn't be done," he continued. "We have two choices. We could hold the service on Sunday evening, and he could drive down as soon as he finishes his morning service and have plenty of time to get here." He thought for a moment. "Of course, then he'd have to spend the night. Or we could hold a special service at a time he could be here."

Of course he'd have to spend the night. Why wasn't I thinking? That would be asking too much, although I could offer to pay for his gasoline and he could stay here.

"Tell you what," the pastor proposed, "I need to let you get back to work. Why don't you talk with your pastor in Iuka and see what works for him and let me know."

He is so willing to accommodate my wishes. He doesn't appear to feel threatened at all.

"I'll do that," she agreed. "I'll talk to him this week and we'll go from there. But regardless of when we schedule my baptism, I want to go ahead and share my decision at church this coming Sunday." The two were walking toward the door as they talked.

"Then that's what we'll do. Now, would you mind if we had a word of prayer before I leave?"

Saralynn placed her hands in his, as they stood just inside the garage, and listened as the pastor prayed.

Oh wonderful, loving Lord. My heart is bursting with happiness right at this moment to learn of the way You have been dealing with Saralynn and that she has freely and willingly asked Your Son Jesus to live forever in her heart, so that she might someday live with You for eternity. We thank you, Lord, for the care You've taken of Saralynn over the past year and a half, even as You have used ordinary human beings to answer the prayer she didn't even realize she was praying. And we thank You for Your Son, who is the truth, the light, and the way. Thank You for loving us when we are so unlovable, for not giving up on us when we've already given up on ourselves, for holding us safely in the palm of Your hand when we feel most vulnerable. In Jesus' holy name I pray. Amen.

"Amen," she whispered, so overcome with emotion she feared trying to speak the word aloud.

After the pastor left, she returned to her studio where she tackled the next three pieces on the list, and put in a long afternoon, stopping only long enough to make a peanut butter sandwich and pour herself a glass of the traditional southern sweet tea that she had come to love.

The last days of the week flew by in similar fashion. While Katie and Donna and Bess, along with Miss Virginia, and a number of others in the church and community called to check on her, they were respectful when she assured them that she was coping and was also deeply immersed in her work.

The only conversations of any length were with Jon Walthall regarding her petition to the court asking to be named substitute executor of Miss Sallie's will and with the pastor at the Iuka United Methodist Church.

"The papers are ready, Saralynn. They just need to be filed. I can do it by mail... or, if you've decided when you're going to be baptized, MA and I might just drive down and I could file them personally before we head back home."

I thought it was too much to hope that MA and Jon could be here, but this sounds too good to be true.

"That sounds wonderful, Jon. It would mean a lot to have you here. I've got to call Reverend Kirk and see if he can participate. Let me do that and I'll get back to you in a day or so. Meanwhile, just sit tight on those papers."

Her call to the pastor, whom she had talked with several times following Alicia's death, was comfortable and enjoyable.

"I'm pleased that you would want me to participate. But are you certain your pastor there won't feel like I'm intruding?"

"Trust me, that won't be a problem. His only concern was how it might work into your schedule."

"When does he want to do it?"

"He's open. He said it doesn't have to be a Sunday morning, he'd be glad to do it on Sunday night, or even at a special time during the week."

"Hang on a second and let me look at the calendar." Saralynn could hear him flipping pages. "This might just work out," she heard him say more to himself. Then he was back on the phone. "If your pastor could make it work, I could be down there a week from this coming Sunday."

"You can do it that quickly?"

"Believe it or not, yes I can. "You see, I've taken that weekend as vacation time. My wife and I are driving to the coast on Friday to attend a very special reunion of my seminary classmates on Saturday. We had planned to stay over until Monday morning and be back in Iuka Monday night. But we can amend those plans."

"But your wife. Won't she object?" *I used to hate it when Peter would obligate me for something without at least mentioning it beforehand.*

"Tell you what; you're probably keeping me out of the

doghouse. Let me call her and I'll get back to you in the next few minutes. In the meantime, call your pastor and see if the morning service a week from Sunday works for him."

This is all just coming together.

A quick phone call to her pastor revealed that the date in question would be perfect and, when the pastor from Iuka returned the call a few minutes later, everything was quickly set.

"My wife was thrilled to hear about your decision, and that you wanted me to participate. She said to tell you that you saved her from a boring weekend of being sociable with all those spouses she barely knows."

"Then you'll plan to stay here at my house. Will you be coming in Saturday night or Sunday morning?"

"Can we leave that decision open for the time being? I can let you know early next week."

"If I don't know until you ring my door bell, that's fine. Your room will be ready and waiting whenever you get here."

She decided not to wait, and dialed Jon Walthall's office again. This time it was MA who picked up after the receptionist asked Saralynn to hold. "Hey, friend. Jon's tied up with a client right this minute, so I thought I'd talk to you instead."

"It's great to hear your voice. You must have just gotten there in the last few minutes, because Jon said he hadn't seen you when we talked earlier this morning. Did Jon tell you about our conversation?"

"He did, and I assume you have news."

"I do. We're going to hold my baptism a week from this coming Sunday morning, and Reverend Kirk is going to be able to participate."

"Wonderful. I'll tell Jon we'll plan to drive down Saturday

afternoon. Then he can go to the courthouse on Monday and we'll leave for home."

When they came for Mama's funeral, they stayed at a motel. But not this time. I've got two guest rooms.

"Don't make any motel reservations, because you're staying here with me."

"Are you sure that won't be too much trouble?"

"MA, you saw the size of this house. And I'm just one person rattling around in it most of the time. There's plenty of room and it's what I want. So that settles that." *At least as far as I'm concerned.*

Then it was back to work with a vengeance, at the same time she began to plan what would be necessary to get her house in order for guests. *At least I've got an entire week.* But just to be certain she was ready in every sense of the word, Saralynn put in a rare Saturday work day in the studio, pausing only to call Elsie, whose depressed demeanor continued to trouble her.

I'm making myself a note right now to call the condo association president on Monday. I need to talk with him anyway about Mama's unit. I wonder if by any chance they have a waiting list of people wanting to buy in that complex, or am I going to be stuck with a condo I don't need or even want.

At church on Sunday morning, one after another came to Saralynn to hug her, or shake her hand, and comment on Alicia's passing. *Everyone seems so happy. Like winning an Academy Award or something.*

At the conclusion of the morning service, the pastor asked

Merry Heart

Saralynn to come forward to join him in front of the altar rail.

"This is a very joyous day for me," he told the congregation. *Everyone is smiling.* And, as she looked from face to face, feeling not the least bit uncomfortable about being in the spotlight, she realized how blessed she was. *Almost every face I see here is one I can call friend or at least good acquaintance. There are very few here who didn't come either to the funeral home beforehand or to the service itself.*

"Saralynn Reilly, who made herself one of us long ago, has now decided she wants to make herself one of God's children also, and she's here this morning to tell us about her decision."

"As I look out on the congregation this morning, I see so many of you who have befriended me and loved me and not given up on me. It has meant more to me than you will ever know."

She continued with her story, explaining how their actions – actions that were representative of the kind of people they were – had shown her what being a Christian really meant. She recounted her recognition that they had something she didn't, and how she wanted that. And she recognized that many of them had expressed their concern that she too, needed to make Christ a part of her life.

"I'm convinced that God uses people, who often don't even realize it, to do His miracles. Whether you knew it or not, He was using each of you. Over and over." She felt the tears close to the surface, and hurried to finish. "Thank you for allowing Him to use you, because I have decided that I want to ask Jesus to live in my heart and in my life. I'm here this morning to make that decision public."

The pastor hugged her. "We thank you for being willing to stand and declare your intent this morning." He informed the church that Saralynn's baptism would occur the next Sunday. "With a special guest of Saralynn's who will assist me." Then he pronounced the benediction and the congregation stood to dismiss.

"You know," he said quietly, leaning over to whisper in her ear, "There are several people in our congregation right now who need to make the same decision you have. Don't you have to wonder how God may have used your testimony this morning to speak to their hearts?"

God used me?

Chapter 19

The next week flew by, as Saralynn spent her days closeted in her studio, concentrating solely on production. It was an emotionally satisfying time, although she dragged herself across the garage each evening, too tired to do anything but make a sandwich and go to bed.

I haven't watched TV or even read a book in what seems like weeks. Maybe I need to hire an assistant, at least someone who can handle all the clerical chores.

Saralynn had been gratified, and a little bit overwhelmed, at the number of inquiries she was getting by mail and the internet from designers and decorators wanting more details on her work. *So far I've not taken the time to even acknowledge those notes. I'll ask Katie if she knows anyone who might be interested in working a few hours a week.*

Her days were carbon copies of each other for the most

part, although she did take time to visit Emma one day when she simply had to look at something besides the four walls of the studio, and late in the week, she created a menu plan and laid in a supply of groceries in preparation for her weekend guests.

I think I'll invite everyone over here after church Sunday night. Just light finger foods.

She also made good on her promise to call the president of the condo association in Boston, where she learned two promising pieces of news.

"Yes, Ms. Reilly, we do have a complete slate of activities and parties for our residents and everything is publicized in the monthly newsletter that goes to our members."

"I understand that, Mr. Samuels. Unfortunately, Miss Reid has been out of the loop, by her own choice, of course, for so long, I doubt she has the courage to venture out on her own."

"So you were wondering if someone in the complex might befriend her and encourage her to become involved?"

"You read my mind," she told him. "And it may take two or three different people contacting her before she decides to try. I'm just concerned about her state of mind. Every time I call, it's always the same. She and my mother were like sisters for more than thirty-five years and I know she misses Mama. But that situation isn't going to change. Elsie is the only one who can change."

"We'll see what we can do," he promised.

The president also told her of two individuals within the complex who were interested in down-sizing but didn't want to leave the area. "Mrs. Bankston's unit would be perfect for either of them and they could stay right where they are. Give me your number and I'll mention to them that you're interested in selling."

Yes, I am very interested in selling. Thank you, Lord, for helping me to see the path I should take. Boston is a wonderful city and I'll never regret having lived there. After all, it's where I met Peter and from that, I had Marc. But it's a case of been there, done that, have the T-shirt and don't want to do it again.

The decision about her future had solidified itself in the days following Alicia's funeral. In a moment of despair, she realized in the middle of one of the commissioned pieces that, in one way or another, she was in possession of multiple homes.

Good grief! There's my house in Boston, and now Mama's condo. Then there's the Jackson house in Iuka, Miss Sallie's house here, and I'm leasing yet a fifth house. That's quite a change from a year or so back, when I didn't have anywhere to live. Now I've got too many choices.

Saralynn had evaluated her options and knew without hesitation that she did not want to return to Boston to live. *I did toy with the idea of keeping Mama's condo, but it's just something else to maintain and pay bills on. I won't be in Boston enough in the future to make it financially feasible to keep the place. Better to sell and just stay in a hotel.*

The decision to make a hotel her future home in Boston was also indicative of the decision she had made to follow through at the end of the two year lease, which was only a few months away, with the tenant's purchase option on the house she and Peter had so lovingly restored.

That's another part of the past that needs to be put to rest. I'm at home here in Mississippi now. My work is here, my chosen family is here, and this is where I need to stay.

The only decisions that had not solidified were the questions she had surrounding Miss Sallie's house. *At one time I thought it would be the end of the world if I didn't get that house. Now that I have it, it's not that I don't want it, but I don't feel like I'll be incomplete if I don't live there.*

She also wrestled with the issue of the Jackson house and finally acknowledged that she was pretty well stuck with it as long as Emma was alive, or at least as long as she was physically able to make periodic trips home to Fishtrap Hollow.

And I'm not sure I'd sell it today if I could. I kind of like the idea of having a place there where I can go when I need a change of pace.

On Friday at lunch, Saralynn put away her tools and materials and prepared to close the studio for the weekend. Her ten and twelve hour days had paid dividends, however, because the stack of wrapped pieces ready to ship to Atlanta was growing as her fear of not finishing them all on time began to diminish.

It feels good to see progress. And to be happy doing what I'm doing. It was interesting to hear Elsie's take on all this when we talked last night.

The evening before, exhausted as she was, Saralynn had made it a point, after she'd gotten ready for bed, to place a call to Boston. *I've GOT to check on Elsie.* The woman had answered her phone with little enthusiasm, causing Saralynn's heart to momentarily fall. *I guess I was expecting a complete transformation.*

"I'm glad you called," Elsie had informed her. "You'll never believe what has happened."

"I'm sure I won't. So why don't you tell me?"

"I've been invited to go to a party here in the complex tomorrow night."

Thank you, Mr. Samuels! So who invited you? Is it a birthday party?

"Not a birthday party. There's a group here in the complex who are single. Either widowed or divorced, and a couple are like me, they never married."

"Sounds like you'd have a lot in common."

"They call themselves "The Stag-Arounds" and they get together twice a month on Friday night for a party."

"So are you going?"

"At first I wasn't. But would you believe I've had four different people call me? One of them was a man. So I finally told them I'd come, but I didn't promise to join their group or anything."

"That's probably wise that you don't obligate yourself, especially if you don't like it. But hey, it'll give you a night out. So I say go and enjoy."

"That's what I thought, too. I wonder why I never heard of this group before?"

"Who knows?" *It's because you and Mama were your own Stag-Around group of two and you were totally oblivious to everything going on around you. Something tells me Mama made Elsie a hermit and she never saw it happening.*

"You have fun tomorrow night and I'll call you in a few days so you can tell me all about it."

"Before we go, tell me how you are," Elsie urged.

"Busy. Very busy. And very tired. But I'm happy. Each day that I can finish another piece of that Atlanta commission, I become a little more satisfied. It's amazing how much I don't miss my design business there in Boston."

"That's because your mother wanted you to be a designer and you did whatever she wanted. Now you're doing what you want to do, and you're happier."

I wonder if you've just come to this conclusion, Elsie, or if you always knew that Mama manipulated me? But I'm not going to ask because it will accomplish nothing and change even less. That was in the past.

"You might be right," she agreed. "At any rate, I'm really happy now."

"You deserve it."

"And Elsie? There's something else I want to share with you that is making me very happy."

"You're dating again!"

"No, no, nothing like that."

"Oh." The disappointment was evident in her voice and Saralynn could just see her friend deflating like a punctured balloon.

"I've accepted Jesus as my Saviour. I did it in church last Sunday and this coming Sunday, I'm going to be baptized. I wanted you to know, because I think this is as much a part of my happiness as anything."

"That's good, honey, if that's what makes you happy. You know I don't put much stock in religion. I can't see what it's ever done for me, good or bad. But I don't think less of anyone who thinks it helps. It's your decision and I'm glad you're happy. You deserve some happiness after what you've gone through."

Elsie's take on religion could have been me a couple of years ago. It was OK for those who want it, but it meant nothing to me.

"It does make me happy, Elsie. And I wanted to share the news with you."

After she had finished the call and put out the light, Saralynn lay in the darkened bedroom, looking at the moonlight flooding through the large window opposite the bed, and thought again about Elsie and the comparison between the two. *I would never have seen myself as Elsie, but I do now, in more ways than one. Mama dominated her time and Elsie never made a life for herself after* that. And that's what she did to me, as well. Poor Mama. I've got to continue to work on Elsie. She needs a life, but more than that, she needs to know God like I've come to know Him.

Her guests – both couples — arrived on Saturday evening and the five of them had feasted on a cold cuts platter and the salads she had prepared, followed by an evening visiting and talking, before everyone adjourned upstairs for some rest.

"Tomorrow's going to be a big day and a busy one," Jon had counseled. "We'd all better take our weary bones off to bed."

"I couldn't agree more," said the pastor, who added, "But let's join hands for a word of prayer before we go our separate ways for the night."

Dear Father, We thank you for the fellowship of believers that You have provided for us and the fellowship of friends that we have enjoyed here tonight. We thank You especially, Father, for Saralynn and for the decision she has made for You. Touch her Father in a special way tomorrow and walk with her, beside her, and carry her when necessary through the remainder of her journey with You. In Your Son's name. Amen.

Saralynn had feared she wouldn't be able to sleep, but had it not been for the alarm, she would have snoozed right on the next morning. She was in and out of the shower in record time, for her, and had breakfast almost ready when her guests trooped downstairs a little later.

Then it was time to dress and get to church in time for Sunday School and then the worship service that would follow. Once they arrived at Rials Creek, it was almost impossible to make their way through the sanctuary to the Sunday School classroom for all the people who wanted to stop and talk to her guests.

In the class itself, the teacher recognized Saralynn and asked her to introduce the two couples, which she did. Then the lesson began and before she knew it, they were all filing into the sanctuary for the service.

At the appropriate time,, the pastor asked Saralynn and Reverend Kirk to come forward to the baptismal font. As they stood in a semi-circle facing the congregation, and the pastor began to read the Service of Baptism, Saralynn could feel her heart swelling up as if it could burst. When the congregation pledged to support her in her Christian journey, she realized that being a part of the family of God meant that you were no longer a loner, but a team player with responsibilities.

That's why people have done so many nice things for me, even from the beginning, because they are God's workers. Now I'm one as well.

"I baptize thee in the name of the Father, and of the Son, and of the Holy Spirit. Amen."

While the pastor was repeating those words, he was anointing Saralynn's head with water. Then, the pastor from Iuka who had been assisting, offered a prayer that Saralynn thought she'd never forget.

I simply can't believe how emotionally-changed I feel after just a symbolic ritual. I know the purpose of baptism is to represent being cleansed of your sins, but I never expected to feel truly clean. My heart feels almost light and… merry.

While Saralynn and her Iuka pastor returned to their seats in the sanctuary, the congregation sang a hymn whose words spoke to Saralynn in a way they never had before.

"*Have thine own way, Lord. Have thine own way. Whiter than* snow, Lord, Wash me just now, As in Thy presence, humbly I bow." These words have so much more meaning than they once did.

Following the service practically everyone in the congregation had to line up to speak to Saralynn and, in many cases, to once again offer a word of welcome to her guests. *If we don't soon get out of here, we might as well just hang around for the evening service.* But she wasn't ruffled. These people were her friends, her adopted family, and they were simply extending southern hospitality along with the right hand of Christian fellowship.

Let's face it. I'd be very hurt if all my friends didn't visit with my company. Thankfully, I knew all along this is the way it would be.

"Lunch is on me," Jon Walthall announced when they were finally able to break away. And I've invited your pastor and his wife to join us."

"But, Jon. I can't let you do this."

"Guess what, Saralynn. I'm a big boy and I don't need your consent."

"Pay him no mind, Saralynn. I've been his wife long enough to know when he takes that tone, it's a done deal."

They took two vehicles and met at one of the local restaurants that featured a good Sunday buffet and, before Saralynn knew it, almost two hours had passed. "Good grief, look at the time. It's after two-thirty."

"Whoa," Brother Tommy exclaimed, "I've got to get back to the church. I'm still not ready for tonight's service."

"And I've got to get home and get my goodies fixed for tonight. You are coming, aren't you?" she asked her pastor.

"Susan and I will be there," he promised. "Count us in."

Back at home, Saralynn quickly changed from her good clothes into jeans and a T-shirt. Once in the kitchen, she began preparing the food she would serve after the evening service. In addition, she had mentioned to Katie Brooks that morning that she and Charlie were expected as well.

I couldn't believe Katie left her own church to come be there for my baptism. Charlie couldn't come because he directs their choir, but Katie was there. She had tears in her eyes when it was over. How she can believe so strongly in God, knowing that she's going to have to give up that precious little boy, used to trouble me. But now I think I understand.

MA and Molly Kirk insisted on helping, and with three pair of hands, the food for the party was quickly prepared and stored away. Then they pulled out the plates and napkins and set up the serving table, so that only last minute tasks would occupy them when they returned from church.

"It's a school night and tomorrow's a work day, so people won't linger long. I want to be able to get this food on the table pretty quickly so my guests aren't inconvenienced."

"You know, Saralynn, I've been in many churches in my role as a pastor's wife, but I have to say, Rials Creek is one of the most welcoming congregations I've ever encountered. Outside of Iuka, of course."

"Iuka IS very loving and warm. After having experienced Rials Creek for a year, if your church hadn't measured up, I'd have turned and run the other way."

"Just goes to show you what having God as a member of your congregation does for your members." It was MA who offered this observation, and Saralynn turned and looked at her in amazement.

"But God is a member, as you put it, of all congregations. Isn't He?"

"MA is being factious," Molly explained. "There are, sadly,

some congregations who behave more like social clubs and less like churches. That's what MA means."

"Oh…"

"It's sad, but true," Jon volunteered. He had entered the kitchen without them hearing. "For some churches it's all about the money and who you are. I'm so glad our church isn't that way."

The five of them continued to visit and talk until it was time to leave for church. They had fixed a quick sandwich to tide them over, and headed out. If the meeting and greeting during the morning service hadn't been enough, the Rials Creek members were all over the Iuka visitors. And, it being the evening service, everything was more informal.

Once the service ended and everyone headed for their cars, Saralynn felt a tap on her shoulder. Startled, she looked around to find a young woman she assumed was about her age. *Her first name is Deborah, but I can't remember her last name. She's one of the few members that I don't know that well. Is she the one who's the single, out-of-work mom we prayed for in Sunday School?*

"Hi, it's Deborah, right?"

"That's right, Ms. Reilly. Deborah Henderson."

"It's good to meet you. And, please, call me Saralynn. Was there something you wanted?"

The woman, dressed in shabby but clean clothing, dropped her head momentarily, before shyly raising her face again. "I just wanted to say, 'thank you'."

For what? I haven't done anything. "I'm afraid I don't understand."

"I wanted to thank you for being baptized this morning. God spoke to me during the service and gave me some guidance on a hard decision I have to make."

Saralynn was stunned and found herself momentarily speechless. "Well, I'm glad you found the direction that you needed. I'm not sure that I can claim any credit."

"Yes, you can. You see, God told me that I could look to you as a role model."

Oh, do I ever feel unworthy of that title. "Me? A role model?"

"Yes, you see I know that you lost your husband and son and came here and started over. That's what I'm going to have to do, too. Only I don't want to."

This is getting more and more confusing, and the others are waiting on me. But I can't walk away from this woman.

"Excuse me a minute, but let me ask you something. Are you doing anything for the next hour or so?"

"Just going to my mother's to pick up the baby. He disrupts the service too much so I don't bring him right now."

"Can your mother keep him a little longer? I'm having some guests over to the house for a casual get-together and I'd love to have you come, too."

"Oh, you don't want me. You barely know me. Besides," she looked down at her clothes, "I'm not dressed for a party."

"I'm going in and change into jeans and a T-shirt, so you'll be fine. Won't you please come?"

I need to talk with this woman, but I don't really know why. Is this God leading me?

After another moment of hesitation, the woman nodded. "I'll come. Thank you. But you'll have to give me directions."

Inspiration hit. "Tell you what. Let me go tell my friends what we're doing. Then I'll ride with you. If that's OK?"

"Well, sure. That would be great. Where are you parked?"

Saralynn pointed in the direction where she knew her

friends were waiting. *Probably impatiently.*

"I'm over there," Deborah explained, indicating the opposite direction. "Why don't you go find your friends and I'll pull my car over there and pick you up?"

"We were getting worried," MA exclaimed when she glimpsed her friend. "Is something wrong? People are going to be at your house and no one is home to let them in."

Oops. I forgot that.

"Look, don't ask questions. Here's my key. All of you head out to the house and get the party started. I've invited another guest who doesn't know the way and I'm going to ride with her." As she spoke the last words, an older model Ford Taurus came around the corner. It was Deborah, and like its owner, the car was clean, but from the look and sound of things, it definitely had more miles on the odometer than was prudent."

She watched as the tail-light of Jon's car disappeared into the darkness. When her ride pulled alongside, she opened the passenger door and slid in.

"I'm sorry the car is such a mess. With an eighteen-month-old, it's hard to keep things clean."

"How well I remember," Saralynn agreed. She indicated the route her driver should follow.

Should I be nosy enough to ask what her big decision is? Does she want to confide in me or did she let her guard down and that slipped out?

"You said you had a difficult decision to make." She smiled at her new friend. "I don't mean to pry, but if you'd like to talk about it, I've got an ear that isn't busy. And I can probably find a vacant shoulder, as well."

The sound of Deborah's laugh was so unexpected that Saralynn gasped.

"Am I that transparent?"

"I'm not sure I know what you mean."

"God did tell me during the service this morning that I needed to talk to you. I wanted to ask how you found the courage to completely pull up stakes and start over where you were a total stranger."

Oh. "Well, for starters, Deborah. You give me too much credit. I'm far from brave and, in fact, when I first came here, my mother brought me kicking and screaming. I did not want to visit a third-world country where I knew no one."

"So why did you stay?"

"Because after I got here, I began to meet people who befriended me. Genuine, honest people doing what God told them to do to help me. Only I didn't realize all this at the time."

"I just assumed you made up your mind you were going to leave where you were, and this was where you chose to be."

"It is now, but it certainly wasn't then. This place grows on you."

"And that's a big reason why I don't want to leave."

"OK, I'm just going to be nosy. Why do you think you have to leave?"

Her new friend gripped the steering wheel so hard Saralynn feared it would break into pieces. "In one word… finances." Or rather the lack of…"

"I don't understand."

"I quit my job when the baby was born because my husband wanted me to be a stay-at-home mom." The look she gave Saralynn was imploring. "You can understand that, can't you?"

"Sure. When Marc was born, I was working for myself, so I just cut back on my client list until he was almost two years old.

I'm so glad I did."

"I loved it, too, even though the money was tight. But about five months ago, my husband left me. Ran off with another woman. They worked together."

"Oh, Deborah. I'm so sorry."

"It was a shock, alright. But an even bigger shock was that he took all our money."

"He took your money? And left you with nothing."

"That's about the size of things."

"How have you been living?"

"I had a little money stuck back; I made good in the job I quit." she sighed. "My husband was never really keen to work, so I had to support us, and my parents have been more generous than their finances really allow. But I can't keep taking from them."

"Can't you get another job?"

"I've looked and looked. The full-time jobs that I've found don't pay enough to allow me to hire a baby-sitter and still have enough money left over to really make a difference. It would have almost cost me money to take those jobs."

"What about a part-time job?"

"Those jobs have irregular hours, only pay minimum wage or slightly above, and, again, a baby-sitter would be a problem."

"So why have you decided that you have to leave here?"

Deborah negotiated the final turn onto Wilson Floyd Road and Saralynn knew they weren't far from home. Time was short.

Then the young woman began to speak. "My house is being repossessed, so I'm going to be out on the street. And my friend, Louise, is working at one of the casinos up in the Delta. They're hiring and they pay really good wages. She says if I'll come up there, I can share her apartment and the rent, and we can get work schedules that will let her look after Daniel while I work."

This poor woman doesn't see any other way out.

"Are you and your husband divorced?"

Deborah turned the car into the driveway that Saralynn indicated and pulled up beside almost two dozen other vehicles parked around the house. "We will be in another thirty days. That's one of the reasons the house is going back. I couldn't make the payments and pay my lawyer, too."

"Did you get the house in some kind of an agreement?"

"There's been no agreement? My husband doesn't even have a job now. He's letting that woman he's living with support him."

"Surely you're getting some kind of child support?"

"I've not seen a penny from him."

"That is unforgivable."

"I agree, but it's like as soon as he realized he was going to have to pay, he got fired. And he hasn't tried to work since."

"Is there any way you can negotiate with the mortgage company to buy a little more time?"

"That's the biggest insult. The house is financed in his name alone, even though I've been making the payments since he left, so that Daniel and I would have a roof over our heads. But when I couldn't make the payments, my husband refused. Says he doesn't need the house any more and he doesn't care if the bank takes it."

Talk about scum of the earth!

"So he's going to allow his wife and child to be turned out in the street?"

"That's about the size of it. I tried to talk to the bank, but because my name wasn't on the loan, they wouldn't even listen to anything I had to say."

I've got guests in the house and I need to be in there. But Deborah needs me as well.

"Come on," she said, her mind made up. "Let's get inside to the party."

"Oh, I'm sorry," Deborah wailed. "I've kept you from your guests. I am so sorry."

"You haven't kept me from anything, but I have a friend in there who is an attorney and I want you to talk with him. Some fresh eyes might have another option no one else has thought about."

"I can't afford another lawyer. I'm still making payments to the one I have."

"This lawyer bill is on me. I want to know if there isn't some other solution for you."

Once in the house Saralynn made it a point to hook Deborah up with Jon before she began to mingle with her other guests. *I'm not even going to take time to change clothes, since I'm already late.*

By nine o'clock guests were making their good-byes and drifting toward the door, conscious that Monday morning would be knocking before they were ready.

"We had a great time," Bess Martin assured Saralynn. "Too bad you almost missed your own party."

"Well, it couldn't be helped." *I'm not going to share all that Deborah has told me, because I don't know how much of it is common knowledge.*

"Deborah is in quite a predicament, you know. She shared some of the mess with me when I kept Daniel a few times while she job hunted." She looked around, then lowered her voice. "In my opinion, some of these places where she applied turned her down because she's a single mother and they figure she'll be out a lot because of childcare problems."

"That's outrageous!"

"But that's also how it is out in the real world. When I was pregnant with my first one, I worked for a man in a small family-owned business. Every month when I had to go for my check-up, he moaned and groaned for a week about how much I was costing him."

"He didn't!"

"Oh, he did. But when his wife, who also worked there, became pregnant shortly after I returned from leave, he insisted that she take the entire day away from her job when she had her appointments. He didn't want her to be rushed."

"I never knew the work world was like that."

"Not all employers are that way, but too many are. Women get a raw deal in general, and with stuff like pregnancy and sick children, they really take the abuse. I think that's exactly what's happening with Deborah."

"We've got to do something."

She looked around, then glanced at her watch. "Look. Got to run. Kids need to be in bed and Doug is probably wound into a knot wondering what's taking me so long."

The two hugged. "Goodnight," Saralynn called to her as she crossed the yard. "Thank you for coming."

As the house emptied, Deborah and Jon came back from the living room where they had gone for privacy. Deborah reached to hug Saralynn. "Thank you, new friend. Thank you for caring. I'll talk to you before I leave. I promise."

Does that mean Jon couldn't help her?

"Please do," was all she could manage, because she felt

sick to her stomach. *This is so unfair.*

As soon as Deborah was gone, Saralynn turned to Jon. "Is there nothing that can be done?"

He shook his head. "As long as her husband refuses to work, there's no legal way to force him to get a job. His child support will accrue, but if he's not concerned about it now, he won't be concerned down the road."

"What about her house?"

"She's out in the street, unless she can manage to buy it from him. And fat chance of that with no income on her part. It's in his name and if he chooses to let it go back, she's helpless to do anything about it."

"What did you advise her?"

"To start making plans to move, because the bank won't care that she's going to be homeless."

I can't believe situations like this exist.

While she tried to be a gracious hostess to her guests, there was a part of her mind, and her heart, that would not let go of the travesty she believed Deborah's situation to be. Finally, she voiced as much to her friends. To her surprise, they all volunteered other situations where the law and regulations has penalized women, particularly single mothers and their children.

"Well, I'm going to do something," she vowed. "I just don't know what it's going to be. Yet."

"One of the biggest ways that women like Deborah are penalized in the work world is that they are forced to take jobs paying far less than they're worth, because those jobs are all they can get," MA said. "There really is a double standard."

"It is a shame that someone with Deborah's credentials can't get something besides a third shift burger flipping job," the pastor agreed.

Deborah's credentials. I don't even know what type work she's qualified to do.

"What are her credentials?"

"Didn't she tell you?" Jon asked. "She worked for nine years as the administrative assistant to the president of a large company in Jackson. That's the job she left when her baby was born."

"And now, all she can get is a job asking 'Do you want fries with that?'?"

"That's about how it shakes out," Jon agreed. "Some employer somewhere is missing out on one fantastic opportunity."

The hour was late and both couples agreed that the next day would be upon them before they were ready. The pastor and his wife planned to leave immediately after breakfast, headed north. Jon and MA would stay long enough for Jon to file the petition to the court in the Simpson County Courthouse in Mendenhall, then they also would be northbound.

Saralynn tumbled into bed feeling as if her baptism had given her a new lease on life but at the same time, she could not put Deborah out of her mind. *There has to be something someone can do.*

The alarm had to drag her out of bed, and had she not had houseguests, Saralynn guessed the alarm would have lost that round. But she knew her duties as a hostess and rousted herself out of the comfortable bed and into the shower. She was soon in the kitchen pulling together the components of breakfast when MA appeared in the doorway.

"You sleep well?" Saralynn asked her friend.

"Like a log. Didn't want to get up either. I dread that drive north." She fiddled with a curl that had escaped her head band.

"It just seems to take forever."

"I know what you mean. When I came back the last time, alone, it seemed like it took ten hours." She turned the bacon frying on the griddle built in to the electric range. "Where's Jon?"

"In the shower. I got in and got out ahead of him. I had something I wanted to talk to you about."

Something she doesn't want Jon to know?

"It's about Deborah."

"You, too? I thought about her off and on all night."

"But did you think that you might be the solution to her problem and she might be your solution?"

"I don't follow…"

"You were telling us you need to hire someone to help you in the studio, so you can concentrate on creating."

"And…?"

"Deborah worked nine years for the president of a large company. She ought to be able to do anything you'd need done."

"MA! That's a great idea… Except…"

"Except what?"

"Except she was probably dragging down a lot more than I can afford to pay, especially for what will be a part-time job at best."

"But does it have to be part-time? Couldn't it be almost full-time?"

"Now, look. It's either part-time or full-time. What's with this almost full-time?"

Her friend fixed her with a stern look. "Your career is about to take off. You need someone now to handle simple clerical chores. But in a matter of a few months, you're going to have to have someone who can meet the public, whether it's in person or on the phone. And your marketing is going to become even more critical. Deborah can probably do all of that." She looked hard at Saralynn again. "Think about it."

Gosh, she makes me sound so successful it's almost frightening. But what if she's right?

"There's still the money. It doesn't matter how qualified she is; there's only so much at this point that I can pay. What do we do about that?"

"That is what you and Deborah need to talk about. Preferably later today, before she has a chance to put any wheels under her idea to go work at the casino."

She's right. I owe it to the both of us to investigate this further.

Their conversation was interrupted when the other three guests joined them in the kitchen where a blessing by Jon was followed by eggs and sausage and grits, the southern delicacy Saralynn had learned to love and then cook. Toast and coffee completed the meal.

"I apologize for the toast," she explained. "I still haven't learned how to make biscuits. You know it's toast in the north."

"Oh, honey, Molly Kirk exclaimed, "I know how and I don't make biscuits from scratch anymore. You can buy them frozen in the grocery store. Just plop them down on the baking sheet and stick 'em in the oven. Nobody will know the difference unless you get a case of the guilts and confess!"

All at the table hooted with laughter and Saralynn decided she really liked this woman.

Once breakfast was finished, Saralynn refused all offers of assistance to clean the kitchen, insisting instead that her guests complete their packing and get underway. "All of you have a long trip ahead."

She has barely finished loading the dishwasher and wiping down the counters when the four trooped back through, luggage in hand. A round of neck hugs followed, then both couples began to load their cars. The last she saw was both vehicles making their way down the winding drive, until they disappeared among the trees that shielded the house from the road.

"I'll call after I leave the courthouse," Jon had promised.

"Make that call we talked about," MA ordered.

"What call?" Jon asked.

"Girl talk. Just drive."

Saralynn walked over to the car where the Iuka pastor and his wife were about to leave behind Jon and MA. "Thank you so much for all the trouble you've gone to. It really meant a lot."

"Listen," said the pastor. "In my business, that's ultimately what it's all about. I wouldn't have missed it."

"See you next time you're in Iuka," his wife added. "Do you know when that will be?"

"Right now, I don't. For now, I've got this commission to finish, which is on a strict deadline. Plus, I've got to go back to Boston at some point to deal with Mama's estate. Then, as soon as Jon files those papers, I'll have to look forward to a court date here as well."

"Sounds like you're going to be busy. Just don't forget where we are. Those are really nice folks at Rials Creek, but we're gonna give 'em a run for their money."

Saralynn laughed. "Please. I can't stand to be a pull-toy. Let's just say you've both got me, whenever I'm 'in residence' and end the contest."

"Deal," he said, and grinned. "See you in Iuka." With that his car was gone as well and Saralynn was left standing, alone, in the driveway.

The coach has turned back into a pumpkin...

She headed back to the house but detoured instead into the studio, where she settled into her office area and powered up the computer. "Forty-seven e-mails since Friday," she groaned. "And MA thinks it's going to get worse?"

From studying the subject lines, it was obvious that a few were spam, a couple were obviously supplier advertisements, but at least two-thirds of them were requests for information.

Right now I'm snowed under with this Atlanta job. But it won't last forever and I'll be needing more business. Only I don't have time to deal with potential customers and finish the job I'm on. Maybe MA was right...

She reached for the phone book and looked under Henderson. There were more than a dozen, but none under Deborah. *It's probably listed under her husband's name but I don't remember what it was. And I don't have a clue what her address is. So how do I call her?*

Struck with inspiration, she looked instead for Doug Martin's number and dialed it. *Bess said she babysat for Deborah while she job hunted. Surely she has the number.*

Bess did and provided it gladly. "I hope someone can help her."

"I do too," she replied, unwilling to divulge the idea that lay behind her call.

She and Bess visited for a few minutes, then ended their conversation. Before she could dial Deborah's number, her cell phone rang. *Jon!*

"Hey, there. MA and I are headed out of town. Your papers are filed and we should be able to go before the court in about two weeks."

"Do you think there's going to be any problem?"

"Nah. Piece of cake. There's no reason for the court not to grant your request."

"You sound awfully certain."

"Maybe I wouldn't be, except someone named Walter Kennedy had greased the skids. Say, didn't I meet him this weekend?"

"You did. More than once." She was puzzled. "But what do you mean he greased the skids?"

"Evidently, from what I could gather, he had already spoken to the judge and let him know that this was about to happen."

Well!

"Anyway, it didn't hurt. So that's done and we're on our way. Thank you again for a great weekend.

"It's I who should be thanking you. Uh, Jon. I've got another question."

"OK?"

"Once I have the authority to sell Miss Sallie's house, can I keep it for myself?"

"Sure. As executor of your grandmother's estate, you'll have to deed it to the Estate of Alicia Bankston. Then, as executor of your mother's estate, you can deed it to yourself."

"Sounds complicated."

"Not really. Between me and your Boston attorney, all you'll have to do is sign your name a few times as executor. We'll handle all the rest."

"If you say so."

"Why you planning to keep it? Gonna restore it and move in?"

"I'm not sure just what I'm going to do. Not right now. I just wanted to know if that was even an option."

They hung up and she dialed Deborah's number. *If I don't get off the phone, I'm never going to make production today.*

"Hello?"

Deborah's phone was answered by a timid, frightened voice.

"Deborah? This is Saralynn Reilly. Is this Deb…?"

"Oh, Saralynn. I didn't recognize your voice at first. This has been a bad morning with creditors calling. They don't seem to understand when I tell them my husband is the one who owes them, and that he isn't interested in paying them or me."

I can just imagine.

"Deborah. The reason I called… well, really there were two reasons."

"I was going to call you as well to apologize for dumping on you last night when you has guests. I was just so desperate for some reassurance."

"I'm afraid you were disappointed then, because I don't felt like I supplied any of that."

"Oh, no. It felt so good to have someone besides my mom to talk to. You know," she confided, "I think she gets tired of hearing me complain."

I don't even know her mother, so how can I tactfully answer?

Instead, she decided to skip it entirely. "Here's why I called. I wanted to thank you for coming to the party last night, especially on short notice. But also, I wondered if I might come over and talk with you? I just might have a proposal that would interest you."

"Well… uh… sure, I guess. When did you want to come?"

Saralynn could picture the house. Between Deborah's depression and a toddler tooling around, she imagined it was not in the shape Deborah would want a stranger to see.

"I've got some things I need to deal with this morning. Why don't we say three o'clock this afternoon?"

"Three? Three o'clock would be great. Daniel should be down for a nap." Saralynn heard undisguised relief in her voice as she provided directions. "I'll see you at three o'clock."

After they talked, Saralynn the clerical employee and human resources officer took off her administrative hat and donned her artistic one. What followed was an intense four hours of cutting, stitching and mounting, as Saralynn created yet another of the thirty pieces of art that everyone thought would catapult her to the big time.

In business less than a year and people are already talking about the "big time."

The prospects frightened her somewhat, but she knew she had no choice but to push on.

After a late lunch made from the last of the cold cuts tray, Saralynn showered and dressed in nicer clothes than she had worn in the studio and, with directions in hand, set out to interview Deborah Henderson. *I'll have to remember to call MA tonight and let her know how this all played out.*

About fifteen minutes later she pulled her Honda into the drive behind Deborah's old navy blue Taurus. *I thought it was black last night. But it doesn't matter, as long as it gets her where she needs to go.*

Deborah met her at the door. "You're going to have to forgive the looks of the place. I really am a better housekeeper than what you see."

What Saralynn saw was a house that, like its occupant, had once seen better days. It was as if the depth of the problem was so severe, even the physical structure had taken on the psychological worries of its tenant. True, children's toys were evident, and the furniture was well-worn, but everything was neat, the floors were vacuumed, the furniture had been dusted, and Deborah had put on some makeup, had styled her hair, and her dress, while far from new, was ironed perfectly.

All this tells me more about this woman that I like.

"Please," Deborah said. "Excuse my manners. Come on in and have a seat."

"Listen, Deborah," Saralynn began as soon as they were seated, "I'm not going to beat around the bush here. I'm just going to say what's on my mind and you can give me your honest impression. Don't worry about hurting my feelings."

"Go ahead."

Saralynn outlined an employment situation she visualized with Deborah working for her. She explained the different facets of the job, from establishing and maintaining contact with clients, at times possibly representing Saralynn in meetings, and keeping up with the burgeoning correspondence and the marketing.

"I need to be able to devote one hundred percent of my efforts to creating the product. I'm not a secretary or an administrative assistant, but I surely do need one. I thought with your background you'd be perfect."

"How did you know about my background?"

"Jon Walthall told me after your conversation with him last night. You should know, he was very impressed with you."

"He was a nice guy. Seemed genuinely sorry he couldn't help me."

"I'm not so sure he hasn't, if we can make this work."

"But what about the baby? What am I supposed to do with Daniel?"

"That's the beauty of this. I really don't want someone in the studio with me while I'm working, distracting me." She saw the other woman's face fall. "Don't take that personally. I always have worked better alone."

"So where would I work?"

"Here. From home. At least most of the time, which would satisfy most of your baby-sitting problems."

Tears came into the other woman's eyes. "That sounds like a job made in heaven. But you forget, I'm being evicted." She ran her hands though her hair, marring what had been a perfect style. "I need a job and I need another place to live, because I'm about to have this house pulled out from under me."

"I haven't forgotten about the foreclosure. How long before that happens? How long before they force you to move?"

"It will be about a month before the sale on the courthouse steps. I don't know how much time I'll have after that, or if I'll have any extra time. I guess part of that depends on who buys it."

Saralynn looked around the house which was, to her thinking, sparsely furnished. "How much do you have to move? Do you have a lot already in boxes, or what?"

"Nothing's packed. I just can't get motivated to pack, although when my friend Louise invited me to come live with her, I did go and find some boxes. But they're back there," she motioned toward the back of the house, "in the laundry room where I brought them in."

"What about your furniture?"

Saralynn saw tears begin to course Deborah's cheeks. "There's not much left. I've sold a lot to get the money for my lawyer, and just to buy diapers and groceries."

And I thought I had it bad.

"OK. Here's the deal I'm prepared to make you. Let's talk business here."

Over the next few minutes, Deborah shared with Saralynn the salary she had made at her last job, a figure that made Saralynn recoil. *Not that I don't think she was worth it, but will I insult her if I offer what I can pay?*

"I can't pay you that much now, and I don't know if I ever can. Not that I don't think you're worth it, because I'm convinced that you are. And I don't want to insult you." Saralynn named the salary that she was prepared to offer initially and watched for a reaction on Deborah's face. There was a reaction, but Saralynn couldn't interpret its meaning.

Deborah said nothing initially, then she volunteered, "I'm not insulted. Honest, I'm not, although it is tremendously less than I feel like I'm worth. I'm just trying to calculate how that would translate into paying my bills. If only I knew what I'm going to have to pay for rent somewhere, I could feel better about asking, 'When do I start?'."

"So if housing weren't an issue, you'd take the job?"

"You bet. I don't want to move away. I'm not brave enough to go somewhere and start all over."

"I think you're one of the bravest people I know, and I'm not just saying that," Saralynn affirmed. "But if we can keep you here, you'll be happy and I'll have some help that I desperately need. My business is simply growing faster than I ever imagined."

"But how am I going to help you if I don't have a place to

live?"

"Let's put it like this. You're going to work for me and you're going to stay here as long as the law allows, or until we find something else for you, whichever comes first."

"You said 'we'."

"That's right. I'm not going to let you be homeless. And you and I are going to pray that God will direct us to the home He has picked out for you."

"You really believe that He will show us that, don't you?"

"I certainly do. That's how I got that beautiful house where I'm living, and I had nothing at the time. Now, back to business. Do you own a computer?"

"It was going to be the next thing I sold, but yes, I have one."

"Good. Don't sell it. Because here's what we're going to do…"

Before she left that day, Saralynn wrote Deborah a check to allow her to catch up personal bills, buy some groceries, and to put some money in her pocket. "Let's just call it a signing bonus."

The two made arrangements to meet at the studio the next morning, where Saralynn would begin to show Deborah the work she would ultimately do from home. "Can you get a baby sitter for tomorrow? I'll pay them. I'm not anti-child, but my studio is no place for an active eighteen-month-old. Plus, we won't get any work done if we're constantly having to watch him."

Deborah agreed and hugged Saralynn with tears in her eyes. "When God told me to talk to you, I never dreamed this would be the outcome. I thought you were going to give me courage to move up to the Delta."

"And I never dreamed when you spoke to me last night at

church that this was God's way of answering my need for an assistant that I prayed for just last week. Someone who could make my life easier and increase my productivity."

"I guess God knew better than both of us, didn't He?"

On the way home, Saralynn thought about what she had done. *If it hadn't been for people here who helped me, when they didn't have to, I never would have been able to make it. It's only right that I pass it on when I get the opportunity.* She also considered the possibility of inviting Deborah and Daniel to live with her, at least temporarily, but quickly decided against it. *I'm getting my house for less than market value rent because I'm the only one living there, and they knew I wouldn't abuse the place. It wouldn't be right to bring someone else into the picture, especially someone with a small child.*

As she pulled into the twisting driveway and caught sight of the house she was currently calling home, Saralynn felt that life was good. *God, I know You have a house already picked out for Deborah; one she'll love as much as I love this one.*

Chapter 20

The rest of Saralynn's week was busy but uneventful, if you didn't count all the additional production she accomplished after Deborah took over the office.

"I can't believe what a quick study she is," Saralynn told Katie later that week. "I explain it once and she's off and running. The only bad part is, I feel guilty because I'm definitely not paying her what she's worth."

"Don't beat yourself up," Katie advised. "You're not deliberately trying to cheat her. And when you can pay more, you'll do the right thing. But look at it from her perspective. She doesn't have to move to the Delta and she has income from a job that doesn't require her to pay it all out in childcare. There are other ways besides money to compensate."

With nothing to do but create, it was a new world for Saralynn who made the most of the time and more and more pieces went into the stack for Atlanta. *I've gotten to the place where I can create one piece a day, as long as I use one day and do all my cutting and assembling of materials. This is working out well.*

Deborah would check in with her by phone first thing each morning, give Saralynn an update on any important e-mails received, and would provide a progress report on the marketing campaign Saralynn had begun on her own, but had to abandon when her time and energies ran short.

Plus, she had many useful suggestions on how Saralynn might more effectively get her name out in the public. "In my other job, I had to write news releases and place them with the appropriate media. Would you have a problem with me putting a release together about you and sending it out by e-mail?"

Saralynn gave her a free hand with the marketing and dived back into her work, determined to finish the last of the commission pieces within two weeks. She had made it through the first week right on schedule, when a phone call late one afternoon shattered that schedule.

"Jon," Saralynn greeted her caller when she answered the phone. "Long time no hear."

"Sorry, friend. But this isn't a pleasure call. At least not the way you mean it."

"What's wrong? Has the court turned me down to substitute for Mama?"

"Nothing's wrong legally. It's the Jackson house."

"The Jackson house? What…?"

"It's got a tree across one end of it. Or at least what's left of one end."

Immediately a visual image materialized in Saralynn's mind. "That big oak on the far end?"

"Bingo. We had a bad storm here this afternoon and it went down. The kitchen and the dining room are pretty much toothpicks."

This is unbelievable.

"Saralynn? Are you still with me?"

"Yeah. I'm here. I'm just trying to picture what you're describing." She mentally kicked herself. "You know, I almost had that tree taken down before I left there the last time, but it makes, er… made the kitchen so cool in summer, I hesitated to remove it."

"You can't foretell the future. If I'd been in your shoes I'd have left it as well."

"So what's my next move?"

It's so heart-breaking to think of that house partially destroyed. I don't want Emma to know. At least not yet.

"Jon. Can the house be salvaged or is it all gone?"

"That's what I'm telling you. One of the neighbors saw the tree go down and called several other men out there. They went over with tarps and secured things as best they could. It was almost a done deal before someone thought to call me."

Bless those men. I'll have to do something for them.

"But you need to be here to get the house stabilized for the short term. Which means meeting with an insurance adjuster."

"Just when I think I've gotten everything headed in the right direction, something else rears its ugly head."

"It's called 'life', Saralynn. Welcome to the real world."

"I know that. What do you take me for?"

"Lower your flags," he begged. "Lower your flags. You must be kin to MA."

"OK, Jon. I'll leave here in the morning and be there by

mid-afternoon. Do you think we'll be safe until then?"

"Should be. Your neighbors did a pretty thorough job. The part of the house with the tree on it isn't fit for anything but to push up in a pile. It's the rest of the house we want to protect."

"I understand. I've got a couple of things I need to deal with here before I can leave, but I'll get on the road tomorrow as quickly as I can."

This is one of the down sides to having multiple homes. Something always happens at the one where you aren't!

"Oh, before I forget, you won't be able to stay at the house, because the utilities are off."

"Then I'll get a motel room."

"Oh, no you won't. MA has given orders that you will stay with us. Just come by the office when you get here and you and I will run out to Fishtrap Hollow. Then I'll lead you to our house."

"Have you talked to the insurance company?"

"I called them before I called you. They'll have an adjuster out there Wednesday morning."

"You made the appointment before you knew when I would be there?"

"Yep. I knew you'd come."

"You know, Jon. I'm going to sic MA on you and I hope she shows you no mercy."

He laughed. "If I know MA, she won't."

Saralynn's imagination was no match for the reality she found once she reached the destruction. As she and Jon stood looking at what had once been a charming old farmhouse, Saralynn felt sick to her stomach. The culprit, a huge oak that looked even more immense in pieces on the ground, had literally crashed right through the kitchen and dining room.

"Flattened," she said for the third time. "It's like some giant took the heel of his boot and stomped this end of the house."

"Like I told you. There's nothing here to salvage. You'll just have to get a dozer to push it up into a pile. But before you do that, we need to get carpenters out here to secure the part of the house you'll be able to save. I assume you're going to rebuild?"

Gosh, how dense can I be? I hadn't even given any thought to replacing what's gone. But I'll have to.

"Now that you mention it," she confessed, "I don't guess I have any choice if I'm going to honor Mrs. Jackson's request that I keep the house for Emma."

This is going to be fun... trying to rebuild a house from long distance.

Saralynn put her arm around Jon's shoulder. "How am I going to manage? This isn't something that can be done in a weekend or even a week. Where do I begin?"

"You and I meet with the adjuster tomorrow and see what he has to say."

"And he writes us a check and we go hire a carpenter?"

"Whoa... not so fast. We don't want to accept the adjuster's offer unless we know that it's a fair one."

"And how do we know that?"

"We get a contractor to look at what's here and tell us what it will cost to replace it and stabilize the entire house."

This sounds like a vicious circle. "Like I said, 'How am I going to manage?'."

"You'll manage. I promise. Let's get to the house and I'll

try to reach a contractor I know who owes me a couple of favors. It would help to short-cut matters if he could be with us when we meet the adjuster tomorrow."

Saralynn followed the attorney back through Iuka and north out of town, to a lakeside development she hadn't seen before.

"Be it ever so humble…" he had said when he helped her with her luggage.

"It doesn't look too humble to me. Lawyering must pay well in Tishomingo County."

"One does what one can," he replied.

"Saralynn!" The voice belonged to MA who had come racing out of the house and into the driveway. "Welcome to our home. Which is going to be your home as long as you need it."

"Have you seen the damage?"

"No. Jon told me about it, but I haven't been out there. Is it that bad?"

"Let me put it this way. If this is to be my Iuka home as long as I need it, they'll be delivering my Social Security check here."

"Long live Social Security," MA crowed.

That evening, over steaks and baked potatoes and salad, the three discussed the best way to replace the damaged portions of the house. Jon had been able to talk with the contractor who promised to be there at seven o'clock the next morning.

"Even if he can't stay around to talk with the adjuster, he'll give us a written estimate of what it will cost to replace those two rooms and make everything look like it has always been there."

"Ms. Reilly, you're looking at no less than thirty-five thousand dollars to remove what's here and rebuild on the same footprint. I've been here for almost two hours going over everything and making measurements."

Saralynn looked at Jon, her eyes questioning, "Are you sure?" *I'm used to dealing with Boston prices, so I really have no basis for comparison.*

"Look, Wyatt," Jon said to the man with the sliver clipboard, "that seems a little low to me. Aren't you going to have to tear into the existing house somewhat to make a sound connection. And I'm not sure we haven't sustained some damage to the roof structure , or at least what remains."

"And does this include stabilizing the rest of the house so that weather can't do any more damage until we get all of this fixed?"

The contractor looked at them both. "Nope, this doesn't include boarding up what's left. And you didn't ask me to check the roof. But I'll do that right now."

As he was coming back around the end of the house, Saralynn saw a red SUV she didn't recognize coming their way. "Could that be the adjuster?"

Jon checked his watch. "Nine-thirty. If it is, he's right on time."

"OK, you were right. We're gonna have to do some work in that attic as well." He made some marks on his paper, stuck the end of his thick carpenter's pencil in his mouth, then wrote some more. "I see your adjuster is here, so I'll make this quick. On top of my original quote, ten thousand more to secure that roof structure and another five or six thousand to stabilize what's here. And that needs to be done ASAP."

"So fifty thousand dollars?" Saralynn asked.

"That's about the size of it. And it could be more, depending on how you finish things inside. I can't tell from looking at this pile of rubble just how fancy it was. I'm kind of going on what I see in the rest of the house. And don't forget… you had furniture and appliances in there, too."

I didn't even think about that! Guess I'm in shock.

"It wasn't fancy, but it was good stuff in those two rooms. I'm sure Saralynn will want to preserve the integrity of the house."

"That would be my suggestion. You go in and put granite countertops in this house, you'd never get your money back in a resale."

He's exactly right.

"I'd want to try and make it look like this never happened."

"So, most important, are you available to take this job?" Jon asked. "Do you have a crew you could put on it today, at least to get the house dried in before we have more rain?"

"Not today," he said at last. "But tomorrow? Tomorrow I can spare some guys to get us weather-tight. Then it may be a couple of weeks before I can get back to actually start the rebuild."

"How long do you think it will take for the rebuild?"

I thought I was through supervising renovation projects. Guess I was wrong.

The contractor, who estimated six weeks of construction, and the adjuster passed each other in the yard.

"Was that Wyatt Harkins?" the adjuster asked.

"It was," Jon replied. "And this is the home's owner, Saralynn Reilly. I'm Jon Walthall, her attorney."

"Frank Thornton, your adjuster," he said, and reached into his breast pocket and withdrew business cards, which he offered to each of them.

The adjuster was a short, balding man, with an ample girth and a dark black mustache. Saralynn thought he resembled some television character, but she couldn't think who.

"Now Ms. Reilly. There was really no need to bring in an attorney. I'm sure we can come to a fair settlement."

"Ms. Reilly just felt better having an attorney here. As well as a contractor."

"Did Mr. Harkins give you a quote?"

"He did."

"May I see it?"

Saralynn, who was holding the folded document looked at Jon, then said, "I think I'd like to see your numbers first, Mr. Thornton. Then we can compare and see if we're going to be able to do business."

"You're good," Jon commented. "I'm impressed; I may also be out of a job."

"Don't bet on it."

The adjuster spent more than an hour with his camera and tape measure and his laptop computer, before finally coming back to where Saralynn and Jon stood near the front porch.

"That tree really did a number."

Neither of them offered any comeback.

Seeing that he wasn't going to engage them in useless banter, the adjuster cleared his throat. "After looking at this carefully, I'm prepared to offer you a check this morning for twenty-seven thousand, four hundred and nine dollars."

That's almost half of what Mr. Harkins said it would cost.

Before Saralynn could respond, Jon interjected, "Does that figure include stabilizing what's left of the house to keep it safe from the weather, and have you calculated the damage to the roof structure over the rest of the house."

"Why do you ask?"

"Because I've been up in the attic. Much of that existing roof is going to have to come off, so the joists can be repaired. Then new decking will have to go down and the entire house will have to have a new roof."

"What's your point?"

"My point," Jon said, with an obvious effort to control his anger, "is that you would stand here and try to undercut this lady who, you might be interested to know, is the guardian for the true owner of this house."

"What do you mean she's a guardian? Is she the owner or not?"

"The woman this house belongs to is mentally-challenged and lives in a group home several hours away. This is the only home she has ever known and it's important to her welfare that when she does come to visit, things must be as close to original as possible. Otherwise it's upsetting to her."

The adjuster was shuffling his feet.

"Now Ms. Reilly is her legal representative and she's the one you're going to deal with. But just remember, when you low-ball this job, you're really doing it to a woman who can't help herself."

"Now Mr. Lawyer, don't you go accusing me of trying to take advantage of the situation."

"You said that, Mr. Thornton. I didn't. But it does appear that you are deliberately under-pricing this job."

"How much do you think it will cost?"

"Double your number, Mr. Thornton, and you might be

close enough that we begin negotiating," Saralynn declared while Jon was still opening his mouth. "And don't forget there were antiques and appliances in there as well."

"Double!" the adjuster howled. "That's a hold-up."

"Doesn't feel very good to be held up, does it Mr. Thornton?"

"Little lady, you are something else."

"First of all, Mr. Thorton, I am not a 'little lady'. And second, I've worked in structural design for a number of years. I know all the tricks of the trade, the ethical ones and the unethical ones – the ones that smell."

The adjuster was backing up, his hands held up in mock surrender. "I'm sorry. I didn't mean to make anybody mad. But I can't go fifty-five thousand plus, which is what you're asking."

Saralynn could see Jon's eyes boring into her. "Go get him," they seemed to be saying.

"Then how much would you go, Mr. Thornton? Make it your best and if it's not, I'll have Mr. Walthall here filing suit before the sun goes down today. You see, I have a fiduciary responsibility to my ward, and I take that responsibility very seriously."

"OK. OK. Sheesh, you win. But I still can't go fifty-five thousand. My bosses will kill me."

"Then give us your best number and let's get on with the day. We have things to do whether you do or not."

The man's fingers ran over the keys on his laptop until finally he said, "The absolute best I can do… and I'm going out on a limb here… is… forty-eight thousand, six hundred."

Saralynn and Jon merely glared at him.

"Look, folks. I can't do any better than that. I just can't. I don't even know how I'll justify this much to my supervisor."

The other two said nothing.

"Look, this ain't my money, you know. I have a responsibility. I can't just…"

"Your best number, Mr. Thornton," Saralynn demanded. "Now."

He was silent and appeared to be studying them both. "Fifty-thousand even, that's my best and final offer. Take it or leave it folks. That's as good as it's gonna get."

"We'll talk about it," Saralynn informed him.

She and Jon withdrew several feet away and put their heads together.

"You are awesome," Jon commended her. "I need you in court with me."

"I've had to deal with his kind before, and thought I was through. Guess you might say some of my venom is anger at having to revisit this type of situation."

"You gonna tell him you'll take it?"

"More or less. You've got work to do and the sooner we get rid of him, the sooner you can get back to town."

They walked back to where the adjuster stood, fidgeting.

"It's going to take fifty thousand, five hundred, Mr. Thompson, and I'm going to stand my ground, because I owe it to my ward to get a crew in here to safeguard what's left."

With somewhat poor graces, the adjuster nodded his head. "You got it."

He pulled out paperwork and began to write.

"And that figure doesn't include contents. Make a note on your files, because I'm going to compile an inventory. Then we'll talk some more."

Without saying another word, the adjuster filled out his

paperwork and handed Saralynn a draft, got into his vehicle and left.

"Well," she said, "I guess that's that."

Jon was grabbing for his cell phone. "Let me call Wyatt so he can be prepared to get his crew in here tomorrow."

That call complete, the two left in Jon's car, headed back into Iuka. "You'll need to deposit that draft today. It can take as long as ten days for it to be honored. I told Wyatt to put tomorrow's work on the tab and we'd write him one big check at the end."

After she had handled the bank deposit, Saralynn headed back out to her hosts, where MA had promised she would have lunch waiting. Jon, it seemed, had an afternoon meeting out of town and would be leaving before noon.

"It'll just be us," MA had promised. "And we can talk."

True to her word, her friend served up a plate of homemade chicken salad nestled in Phyllo dough bowls, along with a side of steamed vegetables and peach tea to drink. Between bites of flavorful chicken chunks, Saralynn shared the events of the morning.

"Jon likes to see a woman stand up for her rights," MA said, "but I think sometimes he reconsiders that position when it comes to me." She laughed. "He must have been very impressed."

"You know, I thought dealing with vendors and workmen in my design business in Boston was rough. That was a piece of cake compared to all I've had to deal with since May a year ago." She took another sip of tea. "You have to give me the recipe for this tea. It's great. But you know," she said, changing the subject, "I never dreamed I could be as strong as I have been. That's been the most amazing thing to me."

"God meets us wherever we are, and He compensates

where we're weak."

"I guess you're right." Saralynn grinned. "So the strongest thing we can do when we feel inadequate is to lean on God. I like that."

The girl-talk conversation continued throughout the afternoon, concluding when Jon arrived home. That was also when Saralynn shared with her hosts the plan she had formulated.

"I'm going back home tomorrow. At least for a week or so, until Wyatt is ready to begin the actual reconstruction."

"Now you know you're welcome to stay with us as long as you need," MA interrupted.

"I know, but this has nothing to do with where I'll stay while I'm here. I've got those last few commission pieces to finish and get shipped to Atlanta. I want that job out of my hair before the rebuild starts, so I can concentrate on it. And I still have Mama's estate to settle, don't forget. Not to mention Miss Sallie's business. I think I should just go into estate settlement business."

"How many pieces have you finished?"

"The commission was for thirty and I have twenty-one wrapped, and ready to ship."

"However are you going to ship thirty of those items?" Jon asked. "The freight alone will be obscene, not to mention what it's going to cost to crate them safely."

"That's another reason I need to go back tomorrow. The same questions have been bothering me, and I've decided I should just rent a small van and drive them to Atlanta myself." She giggled. "In truth, 'mama' here isn't comfortable trusting her babies to strange hands."

"Hey," MA affirmed, "I'm with you. Those are too beautiful, too valuable to take a chance."

"So you see, I need to get the last nine finished. Get all of them crated in some form, and then allow two days, maybe three to drive to Atlanta, make the delivery, and get back home."

"I'll keep you posted on when Wyatt plans to get on the job," Jon assured her. "And don't be surprised if it's more like three weeks."

"You forget, Jon, I've dealt with workmen for years. They almost always estimate too optimistically."

"And we'll see you when you get back," MA added. "Your room will be waiting, but don't expect the bed to be turned down with a mint on your pillow. We're going to treat you like family."

Chapter 21

As Saralynn left Iuka the next morning, she detoured to Fishtrap Hollow to assure herself that work was indeed underway on stabilizing the remaining portion of the house. As she came back through town and crossed the railroad tracks that ran parallel to Front Street, she paused to look right and left.

This railroad track goes in both directions and in either case, you only see just so far. Beyond that, you have to trust that the tracks continue. And regardless of whether you go east or west, you can get to somewhere else from here. It was a lot like life. *That's heavy. But if you don't know what lies around the curve, how do you know which way to go?*

She giggled self-consciously, glad that no one was with her to overhear her sudden detour in philosophical thought.

How many times have I crossed these tracks since the first time I came to Iuka? Why did I get so deep in my thinking this morning?

She pointed the nose of her car south and began what she

knew would be a long and tiring trip. It would have been a lonely journey as well, she reflected later, if she hadn't had a head full of thoughts to occupy her mind and help to pass the time.

When she reached an area where she knew she could depend on the cell phone signal, she dialed Deborah. *I'm not used to having anyone I have to check with. Surely she would have called me if there had been a need.*

"Good morning, Deborah. It's Saralynn," she said when the woman on the other end answered. "How is everything there?"

"Things are good on this end. We're getting new inquiries about you and your work in every day's e-mail. And I'm responding and sending out our literature."

She said "we." I like that. Deborah has already taken ownership which was what I wanted.

"Listen, Deborah. I'm on my way home." She consulted the dash clock. "I should be there between three and four o'clock. Can you come over sometime before bedtime so we can compare notes? I've got several things to share with you."

"Sure. What time works best for you?"

Inspiration hit. "Tell you what. Get a baby-sitter. I'll pay. You meet me at the house at six o'clock and we'll go out to eat. I'm going to be too tired to cook."

Deborah agreed and Saralynn turned her attention to other matters. There was a lot to accomplish in a short period of time.

I've got to finish this Atlanta job and get it delivered. Then there's the possibility of the Atlanta show, which is another reason I want to deliver these pieces. I'd like to sit down with Christina.

When at last she glimpsed the gap in the pine trees that was the entrance to her driveway, Saralynn breathed a prayer of thanksgiving for safe travel and for the fact that her journey was at an end.

She made quick order of checking into the studio and re-assuring herself that the finished pieces were still safely stacked in the corner. *I don't know how I think something could have happened to them, but I worry nevertheless.* With the car unloaded, she dumped dirty clothes into the laundry hamper and went to get a shower. The hot water was a therapeutic rejuvenation. *I needed this.*

Deborah arrived almost exactly at six o'clock, and Saralynn informed her, "I thought we'd go to Jackson to eat. If we go anywhere locally, we're going to run in to people we know and they'll have to stop and visit."

Her dinner companion agreed.

When they had been seated at an Italian restaurant that both women particularly liked, Saralynn began to explain what was about to happen.

"So you see. The next two weeks are going to be very hectic, because I've got to finish the last nine pieces and get them delivered to Christina. Then I've got to go back to Iuka for who knows how long.

"So how does this affect me?"

"Simple. I'm going to need you more than I ever did."

"I'm here for whatever. Just tell me what to do."

Saralynn explained the need for her assistant to stay on top of matters on a daily basis. "Don't hesitate to call me if you need me. I promise it won't be a bother." Then she re-thought that last statement. "At least it won't be a problem *after* I get back from Atlanta. Between now and then, however, I need you to run interference big time."

"You've got to concentrate all your attention on the Atlanta commission."

"Right. And it's going to take early days and long nights to make it happen."

Deborah was obviously deep in thought. "Then I guess I better contact those women in Pachuta and reschedule their visit."

"What is a Pachuta and what women are you talking about?"

"That's what I was about to tell you."

"You've definitely got my curiosity aroused."

"You know the fabric piece you made for Boswell?"

Saralynn did. It was a small piece that she had created early on out of affection for the part Boswell had played in her life. It hung in the waiting area outside the administrator's office.

"Well, Pachuta is a small town almost on the eastern state line. It seems that some author wrote a book about Boswell, and he made an author's appearance at the library in Pachuta. A group of ladies who read his book decided to make a visit to Boswell to see the place for themselves. While they were there, they saw your piece and asked who made it.

"So? I'm still not understanding."

"They called. They want to hire you to create a piece for their library, and they want to meet you and tour your studio."

"Well that's a first!"

"I told them I'd try to schedule them, but I think I'd better put them off for a while."

"Do that. Don't discourage them, but just explain that I'm going to be very involved in production and that we don't schedule studio visits when I'm working on a commission."

Gosh, that sounds really uppity. But I don't have a minute to spare.

As Saralynn drove east in her rented van, the back loaded with thirty plastic wrapped fabric sculptures, each one wrapped in a blanket as additional insurance, she looked back on the past two weeks and all she saw was a blur. Her days had begun by daylight and ended long after dark.

Bless Deborah's heart. She made sure that I ate. And she totally protected me from interruption. How thoughtful of her to call all my closest friends and ask them to respect my need for uninterrupted work time. Then she even put together a blog she sent to them each day, giving them a progress update.

The only calls Saralynn took were from Jon Walthall, who phoned only when it was necessary. The only calls she made were to Lawrence McCollough in Boston regarding the progress on entering Alicia's will into probate, and to Elsie who, Saralynn was glad to hear, was beginning to sound more upbeat.

"Can't talk long," she had advised Saralynn during one call. "I'm going out to eat with friends and I've still got to shower and dress."

Elsie's starting to make a new life for herself. I'm relieved.

Almost before she was prepared, the Atlanta skyline came into view and Saralynn pulled over to the shoulder of the road to consult the instructions Christina had given her.

"I've never been any closer to Atlanta than the airport to change planes, so you'll need to give me some good directions."

Christina had obliged. "I'm thrilled you're bringing them personally. I want you to meet the builder, and see where your masterpieces will hang."

"Masterpieces? Please, Christina. Isn't that being a little

over the top? Masterpieces? I don't think so."

"You sell yourself short, Saralynn. In fact, I have something I want to talk with you about while you're here. I'd planned to fly back to Mississippi so we could discuss it, but you saved me the trouble."

Try as she might, Saralynn couldn't get the gallery owner to divulge further details, and as she navigated her way around a city she found more confusing than Boston, she kept hearing the echo of Christina's words: *"I'd planned to fly back to Mississippi so we could discuss it."* It must be something big.

After getting lost a couple of times, and wondering if she would ever find the gallery, Saralynn turned up a street she'd already passed three times and found herself staring at the sign for her destination. *So close and yet so far away.* She was glad to see a small parking area next to the building. *I'll bet something like that is as rare in Atlanta as it is in Boston.*

She had called once she got into the city, and before she could get the van pulled to a stop in a parking space labeled for gallery parking only, the side door opened and Christina was at the van door to welcome her. Walking a few steps behind was a man Saralynn didn't know.

"Darlin', it's soooo good to see you." She hugged Saralynn so tightly the young artist thought she would explode.

"Glad to be here, for more reasons than one," Saralynn assured her. "I'll be glad to get these pieces unloaded and into someone else's custody."

"Speaking of that," Christina, said, "meet your client, Robert Chambers. He's building the condos where your work is going to sell every unit as soon as buyers see them."

"It's good to meet you, finally," Saralynn assured the

builder. "Thank you for all your confidence in my work."

After visiting in the parking lot for a few minutes, the three agreed that it was time to unpack the van.

"The condos aren't quite ready for these yet," Christina told her, "but I've agreed to store them here until time to hang them." She called for help and two young men appeared with a large flat-bed hand truck. They carefully and gingerly unloaded the van and stacked the contents on the four-wheeled vehicle. Two trips later, all thirty pieces were stacked in the gallery storage room.

They're obviously accustomed to handling valuable pieces of art. "Masterpieces" Christina called them. I've got to make her tell me what her great idea is. The suspense is killing me.

"I can't wait," Christina announced. "I've got to see at least two or three of these." She looked at the builder. "May I?"

He grinned and looked at Saralynn. "I have to admit, I'm anxious to see them myself. Do you mind?"

"They're yours now, not mine."

"Or they will be his as soon as he writes that final check," Christina interrupted. "Not that we're money-hungry or anything."

For the next few minutes the three cautiously unwrapped a few pieces. "Breathtaking," the builder would say after each one. "I can't decide which I like best."

"You've definitely got a winner here, Saralynn," Christina assured her. "Now, I know you've got to head back tomorrow, so Robert and I would like to take you out to see the condos. To see where these masterpieces are going to hang."

While Saralynn was about to burst to know what "deal" Christina had for her, she was also curious to see where her creativity was going to be at home. In the end she tamped down her curiosity and got into the builder's crew cab pickup truck for a trip across town. Having never been in Atlanta before, she was mesmerized by what she saw. And somewhat horrified when the truck pulled to a stop in front of one of the most disreputable looking buildings she had ever seen.

This is where my work is going? It looks like skid row!

As if he could read her mind, the builder said, "Don't judge the book by its cover, Ms. Reilly. We're concentrating all our efforts inside right now to rehab this building into thirty highly-sought-after condos. Work will begin soon on the exterior and I promise, you'll never recognize this place when you see it next time."

True to his word, the difference between outside and inside was more pronounced, Saralynn thought, than night and day. She was taken with the innovative floor plans that buyers would be forced to choose from, and saw immediately that her hard work would be the first thing they and their guests would see upon entering each unit.

"Do you know how many artists would actually pay big money to have their work front and center like this?" Christina asked. "These thirty pieces are going to launch you, my friend."

I feel like I should pinch myself.

The builder dropped them back by the gallery, where Saralynn got into her van to follow Christina to her own condo several miles away.

"You will stay with me," the gallery owner had insisted, when Saralynn called to tell her she was delivering the pieces personally. "I have three bedrooms and I live alone, if you don't count my cat."

She's someone else with more house than they need, sounds like.

Once she had unloaded her overnight case in the spacious

bedroom that her hostess indicated, and had freshened up, the two women met back in the living room. The condo was in a high rise overlooking the city, and the corner living room boasted two walls of glass that made the Atlanta cityscape look like a giant wall mural. The other two walls were filled with pieces of art, each one exquisite in its own right, Saralynn decided. But one could only look at the view for so long, while curiosity was burning a hole in her imagination, Saralynn decided.

"OK, Christina. I'll bite. I'm consumed with curiosity about this deal you spoke of on the phone. It must be something pretty important if you were going to fly out to talk to me." She poked her finger at her friend. "So tell all. Inquiring minds demand to know."

Christina laughed. "You win. I was going to save it until after dinner. You should see where we're going!" At the look on Saralynn's face, she continued, "But I won't keep you in suspense any longer. Besides, this way we can discuss all the details while we eat."

Tell me, puleeze!

"You're moving here, to Atlanta. I've got more work lined up than you can ever hope to complete. We need to set up a small facility with some carefully-chosen artists to help you execute your designs."

Saralynn went cold all over. "You want me to move where?"

"Here. To Atlanta. You have no idea how big this is going to be. We need to be in the same city to make it easier." She was going on and on. "Besides, you'll love it here. How you've managed to exist and create in that backwater where you live now is beyond me. Now you don't have to exist under those primitive conditions any longer."

"But I like where I live," she protested. "Really."

"Maybe you think you do now, but I guarantee, after a month here in Atlanta, you'll never go back. You don't know what you're missing."

But I don't want to move to Atlanta? I don't want to leave Magee and my friends. What was it Donna asked me when I was trying to make a decision about Iuka? "Have you asked God where He wants you to be?" Now that I'm a Christian, I guess I need to do that. Only what if He wants me to move here?

"This is so sudden, Christina. I truly appreciate all you're doing to promote me, but I'm going to have to think about it."

"What's to think about, my dear? This is a chance of a life time." She sounded somewhat miffed that Saralynn wasn't eagerly embracing the opportunity.

What's to think about? So many things… do I want to leave Magee? Do I want to move here? What about Iuka? Most of all, God, what do You want me to do?

About the Author

John Shivers began his writing career at age 14, stringing for his hometown newspaper. During those same formative teen years, he wrestled with a call to ministry, finally choosing to pursue a writing career instead. A freelance writer, editor and storyteller, John's byline has appeared in over 40 Christian and secular publications, winning him sixteen professional awards.

Hear My Cry, his first book, was published in 2005, and paths converged; his goal of becoming a published novelist was realized and with it, came the realization that writing could be a ministry. John explains that once his definition of ministry would have been defined and confined by structural and denominational walls. His writing allows him to minister to readers of all faiths and stations.

Broken Spirit is the first volume in the Renew A Right Spirit trilogy and he is at work on the second volume entitled *Merry Heart*. Coming next in 2007 is *Paths of Judgment*, the second volume of the Create My Soul Anew trilogy, the continuation of the story begun in *Hear My Cry*.

John, his wife, Elizabeth, and their Cocker Spaniel, "Miss Maddie," live on the family farm in Calhoun, Georgia where the wooded hills supply him with nourishment for his soul and his creativity.

www.johnshivers.com